EPIC ZERO

Books 1-3

Epic Zero: Tales of a Not-So-Super 6th Grader

Epic Zero 2: Tales of a Pathetic Power Failure

Epic Zero 3: Tales of a Super Lame Last Hope

By

R.L. Ullman

But That's Another Story... Press

For Lynn, Matthew, and Olivia,
my superhero family

GET MORE EPIC FREE!

Don't miss any of the Epic action!

PRAISE FOR EPIC ZERO
Readers' Favorite Gold Medal Winner

"What a fun read! I knew this was a great children's/young adult book when my 11-year-old kept trying to read it over my shoulder. This is a delightful read for children and tweens, even for children who don't always enjoy reading. I loved the main character, I loved the message, I loved the illustrations; I just plain loved this book." **Rating: 5.0 stars by Tracy A. Fischer for Readers' Favorite.**

"An awesome and inspirational coming of age story filled with superheroes, arch-villains, and lots of action. Most highly recommended." **Rating: 5.0 stars by Jack Magnus for Readers' Favorite.**

"With Epic Zero, Ullman reminds me of why I used to love superheroes." **Rating 5.0 stars by Jessyca Garcia for Readers' Favorite.**

"As if a good read wasn't enough, Ullman goes that extra mile by adding illustrations and statistics, as well as a Meta glossary of terms and superpowers. These added features will appeal to those boys and girls who enjoy the science in science fiction." **Rating: 5.0 stars by Francine Zane for Readers' Favorite.**

TABLE OF CONTENTS

Epic Zero: Tales of a Not-So-Super 6th Grader

ONE

I HATE MY BIRTHDAY AND HERE'S WHY

The alarm clock wails like a banshee, but I've been awake for hours. Without lifting my head from the pillow, I silence it with a well-practiced karate chop. I've stalled long enough. Just like on every other birthday I can remember, it's time to see if I've gained any Meta powers overnight. I take a deep breath. Then, I launch into my standard testing routine.

I close my eyes tightly and then open them as wide as I can. No heat vision or pulsar beams come shooting out. *Not an energy manipulator.*

I flex my fingers and toes but don't sense any

mystical forces coursing through my veins. *Not magical.*

I try to remember last week's pre-algebra homework. Can't remember—which is doubly depressing since I got a C the first time around. *Not super-intelligent.*

I carefully feel around my head, body, and limbs. No evidence of sprouting horns, tail, or extra appendages. *Not a Meta-morph.*

I sit up, grab three tennis balls from a can next to my bed, and start juggling. After keeping the balls in the air for a whopping three seconds, they all hit the ground and bounce limply away. No improvement to pre-existing poor hand-eye coordination. *Not a super-speedster.*

I stand up, walk over to my dresser, and reach underneath. It's packed with clothes and probably weighs over 500 pounds. I count to three and lift with all my might. Dresser doesn't budge. Possibly broke my back. *Not super-strong.*

I jump on my bed, put my hands out like Superman, and hurl myself across the room. I hit the floor hard, belly-flop style, knocking the wind out of me. Note to self, next year try the other way around—jump from floor onto bed. *Not a flyer.*

One more to go.

I close my eyes and concentrate on reading the mind of someone close by. I hear a loud knocking and then—

"Elliott Harkness, get out of bed you loser! You'll be late for school!" My sister, Grace, is at my door. No minds read. *Not a psychic.*

That makes me 0 for 8 on Meta powers. Another year, another epic failure.

I drag myself off the floor, pull on some clothes, and trudge into the bathroom. In the mirror, I find my unremarkable self staring right back at me—short and scrawny with a nest of brown hair and eyes the color of shoe leather. I look too young to be twelve, too plain to be popular and too ordinary to ever be a Meta.

You see, I live in a family of superheroes. We're part of a super-team known as the Freedom Force, the greatest heroes ever assembled. In our lingo, a "Meta" stands for Meta-being, which is what we call a person, animal, or vegetable—don't laugh, it's happened—that possesses powers and abilities beyond what's considered normal. There are eight Meta types: Energy Manipulation, Flight, Magic, Meta-morphing, Psychic, Super-Intelligence, Super-Speed, and Super-Strength.

On top of that, there are three power levels: a Meta 1 has limited power, a Meta 2 has considerable power, and a Meta 3 has extreme power. If you don't have any powers at all, then you're known as a Meta 0. We call them "Zeroes" for short, which also stands for ordinary.

Just like me.

I turn out the lights and head for the Galley. I have fifteen minutes to scarf down some breakfast before school. When I get there, I find my super-family at their usual stations.

Mom is leaning against the fridge, arms crossed and

brow furrowed, "packing" sandwiches into our lunch bags without using her hands. You see, Mom's a Meta 3 psychic who goes by the superhero handle Ms. Understood. Her powers include telekinesis, which allows her to move stuff around using only her mind, and also telepathy, so she can read other people's minds.

As you can imagine, having a mind-reading mom presents some serious challenges! She claims to use her powers only in the line of duty but based on how often I get in trouble, I suspect she isn't telling the whole truth on that one.

Like most mornings, she's already in full uniform, just waiting to see what evil the day brings. She wears a black bodysuit and mask to blend into the shadows, where she can put her deadly powers to work undetected. Plus, her superhero insignia looks like a giant eye, which not only intimidates the bad guys but also makes you think twice about drinking milk straight from the carton!

Dad is ironing his cape by the breakfast nook. He takes law and order to a whole new level. On the law side, he's the leader of the Freedom Force and goes by the name Captain Justice. He's got Meta 3 super-strength with muscles so dense he's pretty darn invulnerable. And look out when the bullets start bouncing off of him!

On the order side, let's just say that he likes things tidy. His red, white, and blue uniform must be crisply pressed, and there can be absolutely no dirt or smudges on his pristine, chest insignia of the golden scales of justice. He's so obsessive, he even lifts my furniture to hunt for dust bunnies! Like, someone please create a criminal distraction!

Grace, my fourteen-year-old sister, is perched on a stool, worshipping herself in a compact mirror. She's a Meta 2 flyer, but my parents expect her powers will eventually reach Meta 3 levels. She's still learning to be a hero but lately seems much more interested in becoming an international celebrity. When she started out I suggested the name Self-Centered Lass, but she ignored me and chose Glory Girl. Glory Girl? Really? Please, get over yourself!

"Good morning, Elliott," Mom says.

"Morning," I say, waiting for some cursory acknowledgment that it's my special day. But there's nothing.

See, I know my life probably sounds glamorous and all, but trust me, it's not. Living with a bunch of do-gooders comes with some major drawbacks. At the top of the list is the fact that while superheroes are really great at the big things—like thwarting the forces of evil—they really stink at the little things.

Like, for example, remembering their kid's birthday.

I grab a cereal bar out of the pantry.

"Not hungry?" Mom asks.

"Nope," I say. "Not anymore."

"Well, Grace," Dad says. "Looks like you made the morning paper."

"I did?" Grace squeals with delight.

"You sure did," Dad says. "Look at this headline."

Grace snatches the paper and starts reading. "America's newest Meta-star does it again!' Wow! I look amazing!" She turns the paper to reveal the front page, featuring her in her Glory Girl outfit standing over an unconscious supervillain known as Catastro-flea. "Doesn't my costume totally pop?"

Truthfully, she did look kind of awesome in her crimson bodysuit featuring white shooting stars across her top and legs—her cape billowing perfectly in the wind. But I wasn't going to tell her that.

"Looks like people are starting to take notice of your super-skills," Dad says.

"Maybe Captain Justice should hang up his tights," Mom jokes.

"You might be right, dear," Dad says. "Maybe I'll ride out my golden years in a Fortress of Solitude."

"Sure you will, Dad," Grace says, rolling her eyes. "I'll call Meta Meadows Retirement Home and see if they've got a spot for you. Hope you like tapioca."

"I haven't had tapioca since the Ghoulish Gourmet tried poisoning my dessert at the Mask of the Year Awards," Dad says. "On second thought, I've probably got a few more years of caped crusading in me."

"I figured you'd say that," Grace says. "Speaking of capes, I've been thinking about shaking up the whole hero thing. Maybe getting some brand sponsors and putting their logos on my costume. You know, like sports stars do. Do you think I need an agent for that?"

"Grace, you know we don't work for money," Dad says.

"Oh, come on!" Grace says. "Aren't we allowed some perks with the job? I mean, we're on call, like, all the time."

Just then my phone vibrates in my pocket. It's a text message from TechnocRat:

<TechnocRat: Dog-Gone barfing in Mission Room. Can u clean up now?>

Dog-Gone is the name of our German Shepherd who has the power to turn invisible. One second he's sitting there, staring you down with his pitiful big-eyed begging act, the next he's gone. Conveniently, his powers seem to activate whenever food goes missing. I'm guessing he hijacked someone's breakfast when they weren't looking.

Cleaning up after Dog-Gone is bad enough but doing it on my birthday just seems like cruel and unusual punishment. I should've gotten a super fish.

I exit the Galley to the West Wing stairwell, my sneakers echo down the fifty-five steps and five stair landings. Oh, I should probably mention that my house is kind of unusual. You see, we live in a satellite parked deep in outer space called the Waystation. The Waystation serves as the Freedom Force's headquarters, as well as the home away from home for most of the team.

You may be wondering why we're up here. Well, let's just say we do our jobs really well and there are plenty of creeps out there who'd love nothing more than to show up on our doorstep and try to settle the score. In fact, that's exactly what happened a few years back when the Slaughter Squad busted through the gates of our old headquarters on Earth. They almost had us, but that's why we moved to the Waystation—because up here we're *way* out of reach.

I stop at the utility closet to grab a mop, a bucket, and some disinfectant because Dad's such a germaphobe. Knowing Dog-Gone, I'll probably have to wait around for all the invisible chunks to turn visible to be sure I don't miss anything. It takes me a while to collect the cleaning stuff because it's all shoved in the back, like someone wanted to hide it or something.

Finally, armed with everything I need to tackle the job, I make my way to the Mission Room and open the door.

"HAPPY BIRTHDAY!"

The cleaning supplies clang to the floor.

To my surprise, standing before me are all of the members of the Freedom Force: my parents, Grace, Shadow Hawk, TechnocRat, Blue Bolt, and Master Mime.

"Happy birthday, Elliott," Mom says.

"H-How?" I stammer.

"Tricked you, didn't I?" TechnocRat says, sitting on my dad's shoulder and stroking his whiskers with a smug look on his white, pointy little face.

"What about Dog-Gone?" I ask.

"He's fine," Dad says. Dog-Gone appears from beneath the round conference table, his tail wagging a hundred miles per second. I swear he's smiling.

"You didn't think we'd forget your birthday, did you?" Mom asks.

I shrug. "Well..."

"Can we just get this over with?" Grace mutters.

"Grace, please," Dad says. "It's your brother's day."

Then, Master Mime uses his magic to conjure up a giant purple finger that flicks out the lights. Mom brings over a huge cake with twelve lit candles and everyone starts singing Happy Birthday, except for Master Mime and Dog-Gone, who obviously can't talk.

"Now make your wish," Mom says.

I close my eyes and take a deep breath when...

"Alert! Alert! Alert!" The alarm from the Meta Monitor blares through the Waystation. "Meta 2 disturbance. Power signature identified as Reptvillian. Alert! Alert! Alert!"

Before the lights even come back on, the Freedom Force springs into action. Blue Bolt and Master Mime are already gone. I just catch the flames from TechnocRat's jetpack and the silhouette of Shadow Hawk's cape as they disappear from the room. Dad and Grace leave without saying a word. I'm all alone with Mom who's still holding my cake.

"Elliott," she says. "I'm so sorry." Her eyes look sad, but her body's leaning towards the door. I can tell she wants to split.

"It's okay," I say. "Go ahead, somebody needs you."

She brushes my cheek. "My baby is so grown up."

I take the cake from her. "Oh," I say, "don't forget that Reptvillian is a Meta 2 on super-strength, but also a Meta 1 psychic, although he hasn't shown any evidence of telekinesis."

"Thanks for the tip," Mom says. "Don't be late for school." Then, she winks and leaves.

I look down at the candles still burning on my cake. I never did make my wish. Not that it matters anyway.

I'm still a Zero.

Meta Profile

Name: Captain Justice
Role: Hero   Status: Active

VITALS:

Race: Human
Real Name: Tom Harkness
Height: 6'3"
Weight: 220 lbs
Eye Color: Blue
Hair Color: Blonde

META POWERS:

Class: Super-Strength
Power Level: ■■■■
- Extreme Strength
- Invulnerability
- Enhanced Jumping
- Shockwave-Clap

CHARACTERISTICS:

Combat	95	
Durability	96	
Leadership	100	
Strategy	94	
Willpower	91	

TWO

I SEEM TO BE QUITE THE TROUBLE MAGNET

I can't decide what's worse, being abandoned on my birthday, or watching Grace take off to save the day while I have to go to school. Yet, here I am, standing in the Transporter like a good little soldier, trying to make it to class before the attendance bell goes off. The Transporter is a teleportation system between the Waystation and Earth. It scans your body down to the subatomic level, scattering everything at point A and reassembling it at point B—all in a matter of seconds.

The Transporter, like the Waystation and every other gadget the Freedom Force uses, was designed by TechnocRat. It's amazing to think he was once just an ordinary rat in a secret government laboratory, but after being injected with an experimental brain tissue growth serum he became the smartest creature on the planet. He sometimes gets edgy with less intelligent people—also known as everyone else, and he hoards camembert cheese by the barrelful—the snobby, expensive kind, but the ideas that come out of his little noggin are astounding.

Moments later, I feel the pins-and-needles sensation of my atoms pushing back together. I watch the overhead console change from green to red and then the Transporter door slides open. Suddenly, I'm no longer standing in the Waystation, but in a spacious suburban living room.

It has a large white sofa, two navy blue sitting chairs, a wooden coffee table, and a flat-screen TV. Against the far wall are bookcases filled with the classics and framed pictures of Grace and me as little kids. Every room in the house, from the kitchen to the bedrooms, is fully furnished. We even have spare clothes in the closets and shelf-stable food in the pantry... It's like we actually live here, but the beauty of it is, we don't. It's the Prop House.

We call it the Prop House because that's exactly what it is—a prop—designed to make people think it's our home. Our parents wanted us to attend a regular school and try to be "normal." So, in order to be eligible for public school, we had to have a proper mailing address. That's where the Prop House comes in. No one knows it's just a front that houses the Transporter up to our real home on the Waystation.

To prevent anyone from discovering our true identities, my parents make routine appearances as suburbanites in the neighborhood, picking up the morning paper or mowing the lawn. On the rare occasion that someone rings the doorbell, deafening alarms blast through the Waystation. One of us—typically me being the only one around—then has to race to the Transporter and make it down to answer the Prop House door as if nothing's out of the ordinary. Usually, it's not a problem, but it can be awkward if you're in the middle of a shower, or worse, stuck on the can.

Note to self: I really need to talk to TechnocRat about installing an intercom system from the Waystation to the Prop House. Then, I could talk to people and ask them to hang on a minute or, in the case of those annoying vacuum cleaner salesmen, just tell them to "get lost!"

I step into the living room and wrap my hand around a miniature Statue of Liberty model sitting on an end table. When I pull sideways the figurine makes a clicking noise and a gigantic mirror slides down from the ceiling, concealing the Transporter. Then, I walk out the front door and lock it behind me.

It takes me five minutes to reach Keystone Middle School. It's week six of a forty-week school year and I diligently check off each and every day on my wall calendar. The middle school pools three local elementary schools, which means there are three times the number of sixth graders I try to avoid. Don't get me wrong, I can make friends if I want. But why bother? It's not like I can ever bring anyone back to my house to hang out.

Just then my phone buzzes. It's a text from Mom:

<Mom: Sorry about bday! Have a gr8 day! Luv u!>

It's not unusual for Mom to check up on me after a total parenting disaster like this morning. Believe me, I appreciate it, but I'm never quite sure if it's for my benefit or hers. I'm in the middle of texting her back when I run smack into what I think is a brick wall. Turns out it's another student.

"Sorry," I say.

"You got a problem?" rumbles a deep voice from high above.

"No," I answer, my neck craning so far back to see the kid's face I think my head's going to fall off. Angry eyes bear down from beneath a bushy unibrow that looks like it may flutter off and attack me. "I didn't mean to crash into your... gigantic-ness."

"You making fun of me?" says kid giant.

"Well, no, I..."

Then, I notice students circling around us. They're coming in waves, like sharks drawn to chum. I don't like where this is heading.

"You're annoying," kid giant says.

"You must be pen pals with my sister," I say. "Now how about we walk away and pretend this whole thing never happened?"

Then, the kids start closing in, chanting "Fight! Fight! Fight!"

Great, now I'm the morning's entertainment. I want nothing more than to lift into the air like Grace and fly out of here. But, of course, I can't. I'm a freaking Zero.

Kid giant grabs my shirt collar.

"Hey, c'mon!" I plead. "You don't want to do time for hurtin' little old me?"

Then I see his massive fist go back. And that's when everything goes dark.

***

Well, I may be the first kid in history to be hospitalized for fainting during a fight. The nurse told me I crumpled to the ground right before the big lug swung at me and was rescued by the Cafeteria Lady who happened to be in the parking lot pushing a cart of strawberry milk.

It's just so embarrassing on so many levels.

And to top it off, my mom had to leave the Freedom Force to meet me at the hospital while they ensured I didn't have a concussion. After taking me home to the Waystation and confining me to bed rest, she left me alone with my neurotic thoughts. Now all I can do is sit and wonder what creative nicknames my classmates are going to bestow upon me tomorrow.

Elliott the Unconscious? Harkness the Horizontal?

The Narcoleptic Kid? The possibilities seem endless. And, oh, the fun Grace is going to have with this one.

After several hours of reliving my nightmare over and over again against the backdrop of mindless cartoons, I'm antsy to get out of here. I need to do something to take my mind off it all and I know just the thing!

I yank off the covers when Dog-Gone, who's curled up at my feet, gives a low growl.

"Oh, knock it off," I say. "I don't care what Mom told you. I'm getting out of bed."

Dog-Gone turns invisible. The dude who said dogs are man's best friend clearly never met mine.

"Hang on," I say. "I'll give you a treat if you don't tell her."

Dog-Gone reappears with a cocked ear. But then he disappears again. That dog really knows how to work a bribe.

"Two treats," I say quickly. But he doesn't show. Not that I expect him to anyway because I know what he's really after. "I'm not giving you the whole bag," I say. "You'll get sick. Three treats or nothing and that's my final offer."

After a few seconds, the mercenary reappears, his tail wagging in victory.

"Okay, deal. Follow me. And be quiet about it."

Trust me, sneaking around when there's a Meta 3 psychic on the premises is no easy task. I can only hope Mom is caught up in some complicated forensics analysis or something and won't bother mind-linking with me.

We make it safely down to the Galley where I pay off my debt of three doggie treats. I tell Dog-Gone to make himself invisible, and then tiptoe my way up to the Monitor Room. This will definitely take my mind off of things.

You see, the Monitor Room houses the Meta Monitor, which is our one-of-a-kind computer system that operates like a burglar alarm on steroids for detecting superpowers. The Meta Monitor constantly searches for disturbances in the Earth's molecular structure. Like the uniqueness of fingerprints, every superpower leaves a distinct and detailed signature. The Meta Monitor reads this signature and then matches it with its extensive database of Metas to determine who, or what, may have caused it.

Currently, there are four hundred and thirty-two villains in the database. Two hundred and seventy-one are under lock and key. Ninety-nine are considered inactive—in other words, they either got out of the game, were wheeled off to an old age home, or vanished off the face of the Earth. That leaves sixty-two bona fide nut jobs out there who are completely unaccounted for and just waiting to stir up trouble.

How do I know all this? Well, I guess you can call Meta-mining my hobby. I've spent countless hours digging through the database, studying up on every villain I could, memorizing their origins, aliases, powers, weaknesses, fighting tendencies, and so on. I figure if I'm going into the family business, then I should probably have this stuff down cold. Plus, it beats the pants off of doing homework.

The Meta Monitor has state-of-the-art telescopes that can pick up visuals of any point on the Earth's surface. I key in a few commands and the screen begins rotating through several famous landmarks. The White House; The U.S. Capitol; The Hoover Dam; Mount Rushmore. Everything looks peachy. Nothing suspicious. Maybe if I fish where the fish are?

I punch in some more commands and up pops an image of a gigantic prison. It's known as Lockdown, or more formally, Lockdown Meta-Maximum Federal Penitentiary. It's the only super-maximum security prison specifically designed to contain the world's most dangerous Metas. Dad told me that Lockdown almost didn't happen. The skeptics didn't believe that one place could safely hold so many super-powered criminals. After all, the potential for something to go horribly wrong increases dramatically when only a few feet of concrete separate the evilest beings on the planet.

Over time, however, Lockdown has more than proven its worth. One reason for this is TechnocRat, who designs each cell to neutralize the special abilities of its occupant. For example, if a villain has Meta 3 super strength, then his or her cell is outfitted with super-malleable walls designed to absorb the energy of a power punch and send it back with twice the force. TechnocRat can devise a way to contain any criminal. And fortunately, it's worked every time.

The other reason is my dad. His day job as warden of Lockdown allows him to keep close tabs on the inmates. Of course, his Meta identity is a secret so none of the villains know that he's the one who put them there in the first place.

It's also a well-guarded secret that the only set of blueprints for Lockdown and the way out of each cell is stored in a special vault right here on the Waystation. That's another reason our headquarters is in space. It keeps the prisoners on Earth and their escape plans in orbit.

Well, it seems like nothing is doing at the prison either. Perhaps—

"Elliott Harkness!"

I jump a foot off my chair.

Busted.

I turn around to find Mom standing with her hands on her hips, also known as full anger pose. Dog-Gone is by her side. I should've given that mutt four treats.

"Just what do you think you're doing?" Mom asks. "You're supposed to be in bed."

"I'm bored," I answer.

"And since when does boredom give you permission to ignore the doctor's orders?" she asks.

"Um, when I'm really bored?" I answer. "Besides, I

thought you might have sent a telepathic hint to my mind suggesting it would be okay. So, whose fault is this really?" I smile. She doesn't. Never, *ever*, try reverse psychology on a psychic.

"Okay, okay." I set the Meta Monitor on autopilot and slide off the chair. "Nothing ever happens on my watch any—"

"Alert! Alert! Alert!" the Meta Monitor blares. "Meta 3 disturbance. Repeat: Meta 3 disturbance. Power signature identified as Meta-Taker. Alert! Alert! Alert! Meta 3 disturbance. Power signature identified as Meta-Taker."

"Really?" I say. "Like that couldn't have happened a minute ago?"

"Elliott, not now," Mom says, racing to the console. It looks like she's seen a ghost.

She hits a few buttons and a visual of the villain called Meta-Taker appears. The first thing I notice is the outfit. He's wearing a dark hooded cloak, like some sort of monk. But when he moves, you can see massive muscles rippling beneath his robes. Then, the camera pulls in closer and I do a double take.

His skin and hair are pale white, like bone—and a strange orange energy that seems to have a life of its own blazes around his eyes. For his tremendous size, he's surprisingly graceful, yet there's something robotic about him. And he's standing near a gigantic hole in the ground which makes the whole scene look like the Grim Reaper surfacing from the underworld itself.

Dog-Gone growls.

"Um, Mom. What's up with that guy?"

"His name is Meta-Taker," she practically whispers. "He's the most powerful enemy we've ever faced. We thought he was dead ... buried alive ... it's been over twenty years."

"Well, I can assure you, he ain't dead," I offer.

"No, he's not," she says, her voice quickening. "I'm activating the distress signal."

As soon as she says that, I know it's serious. Each member of the Freedom Force wears a special nano-communicator housed inside an everyday object—like a watch or a necklace—which produces vibrational patterns signaling different things. The distress signal is reserved for the most urgent of issues and directs the team to head immediately to the Waystation—do not pass go—do not collect 200 dollars.

"I need to get ready," Mom says.

"I'll help," I say.

"No," she says forcefully. "This isn't a game. This is a job for the Freedom Force."

I look down. Her words sting.

"Elliott," she says, grabbing my hands. "Trust me. You need to stay here, where it's safe, and rest up. Keep an eye on Dog-Gone."

"I understand," I say reluctantly. "Be careful."

"I will," she answers, squeezing my hands before

leaving.

I take a deep breath. Dog-Gone and I stare at the image of Meta-Taker.

I heard what she said, but I'm getting awfully tired of sitting on the sidelines.

Then, a light bulb goes off.

"You know what, old boy," I say. "You're not the only one here that's good at hiding."

Meta Profile

Name: Ms. Understood
Role: Hero   Status: Active

VITALS:

Race: Human
Real Name: Kate Harkness
Height: 5'6"
Weight: 130 lbs
Eye Color: Brown
Hair Color: Brown

META POWERS:

Class: Psychic
Power Level: ▉ ▉ ▉
- **Extreme Telepathy**
- **Extreme Telekinesis**
- **Group Mind-Linking**
- **Long-Range Capability**

CHARACTERISTICS:

Combat	80	
Durability	42	
Leadership	88	
Strategy	85	
Willpower	95	

THREE

I DO SOMETHING ASTRONOMICALLY DUMB

While the team assembles for a briefing in the Mission Room, I buy Dog-Gone's silence—this time with five doggie treats—and stow away on the Freedom Flyer. The Freedom Flyer is the rocket-powered shuttle we sometimes use to get from the Waystation to Earth and back again. It's spacious enough to hold the entire team and is outfitted with weapons and deflector shields in case of attack. It can also really motor, reaching the upper limits of supersonic speed at Mach 5.0.

This shuttle is actually the Freedom Flyer II. Freedom Flyer I is grounded in the Hangar due to some steering column damage that happened when Master Mime used it as a battering ram against the Brutal

Birdmen. After that episode, TechnocRat revoked Master Mime's pilot's license.

The Freedom Flyer II is designed to be more durable than the original, but more importantly, it has a larger supply compartment big enough to fit yours truly.

Now I just have to wait for the team to show up.

Since I've got the time, I download Meta-Taker's profile to my mobile. I realized that I'd never come across his record before because it wasn't logged in the active database at all, but instead was in the file of deceased Metas. After a few seconds, the profile appears. It reads:

Name: Meta-Taker

Real Name: Unknown

Height: 8'0"

Weight: 1,200 lbs

Eye Color: Orange

Hair Color: White

Meta Class: Meta-morph

Known Powers: Can duplicate the power of any Meta in his immediate vicinity. Can duplicate the powers of multiple Metas at once which may result in a cumulative power build if Metas are of a similar power type. This may result in Meta 4 power levels.

I stop and read that section again:

This may result in Meta 4 power levels.

What??

I've never even heard of Meta 4. I didn't even know it was possible. If Meta 3 is classified as extreme power then what is Meta 4? God-like? No wonder Mom turned as white as a ghost. I keep reading:

Known Weaknesses: None

Origin: Unknown

Background: A being of unparalleled power, Meta-Taker emerged with the sole purpose of ruling Earth by eliminating its Meta hero population. With powers too strong for any one hero to stop, a group of heroes banded together with the united goal of ending his rampage. They called themselves the Freedom Force. Despite heavy casualties, the Freedom Force eventually subdued the villain, burying him alive thousands of feet below the Earth's surface.

Known Crimes: Responsible for the deaths of original Freedom Force members Dynamo Joe, Madame Meteorite, Robot X-treme, Rolling Thunder, and Sunbolt.

Status: Assumed deceased

I swallow hard. It dawns on me that I've never asked my parents how the Freedom Force came together in the first place. Ever since I can remember they've always been there. They're the good guys. The idea that heroes can die never even crossed my mind.

Right now, hanging with Dog-Gone is beginning to sound better and better. I decide to split, but when I move to pop open the compartment door, the team boards the Freedom Flyer.

I'm trapped!

Just. Freaking. Wonderful.

If Mom finds me, I'm dead meat. And, Grace will have an absolute field day at my expense. Better to stay quiet and sneak out once the mission is over and we're back safe and sound at the Waystation. Just then, I hear the hatch door close so I brace myself for take-off.

My thoughts wander back to Meta-Taker. If he was buried thousands of feet below ground then how did he get out? Had he been clawing his way to the surface for the last twenty years? Didn't he need to eat and breathe?

Before I can figure it out, we've landed. I hear muffled voices from the team, including Grace's over-confident platitudes, and then the hatch opens. I get bounced around as they file out of the Freedom Flyer.

After a few minutes, I open the compartment door and confirm the cockpit is empty. I move to the front and duck behind the pilot's chair so I can safely look out the front windshield without being seen.

We've touched down at some sort of construction site. To the side, I can see the hole Meta-Taker emerged from. It looks much bigger in person, like it was made by some kind of giant mole or something. But as fascinating as that is, I'm here for the main event, which is unfolding about a hundred yards away.

The Freedom Force is circled around Meta-Taker, giving him a wide berth. Meta-Taker stands calmly in the center, that freakish orange energy crackling wildly from his eyes. But even more freakishly, despite the threat of all the heroes around him, his face is expressionless.

Dad is calling out. He's ordering Meta-Taker to surrender, but the brute isn't responding. Dad lifts a nearby pickup truck and throws it at Meta-Taker, who reaches out casually and catches it like a Frisbee. Then, he tears it in half like paper.

That's when the other heroes jump in.

Nearly faster than my eye can track, Blue Bolt launches at Meta-Taker. She's the fastest Meta alive and wears a lightning bolt on her costume because she strikes at super-charged speed. I once clocked her circling the globe in ten seconds flat, which is ten times longer than it takes her to eat a double cheeseburger.

Meta-Taker, however, isn't impressed. He duplicates Blue Bolt's power and swings at her like he's playing baseball without a bat. There's a massive popping sound and then all I see is a blue streak flying through the sky. It looks like she'll land hundreds of miles away.

Then, Master Mime steps into the fray. His parents died when he was a teenager, and he took up street miming to survive. One day, he found a strange purple amulet in his tip jar. With the amulet, Master Mime discovered he could conjure hard-light energy constructs in any form he could imagine. And with all his years of miming, he's a must-have partner on the Waystation for charades.

I watch Master Mime forge a javelin of purple energy and hurl it at Meta-Taker. But the villain has already duplicated Master Mime's powers, forming a shield of purple energy that easily blocks the javelin, shattering it in half. Then, Meta-Taker creates an energy lasso and hog-ties Master Mime, sending him crashing into Shadow

Hawk.

With those heroes out of the way, Meta-Taker uses Master Mime's powers to form a massive energy hammer and tries pounding the remaining good guys. My parents and TechnocRat dive for cover, barely avoiding being flattened. This isn't going well.

And then I realize I haven't seen Grace.

She wasn't standing in the original circle and isn't in the fight. I look high above but can't spot her in the air. My heart starts beating fast. Where is she? Is she hurt? Or dead? I need to find her!

I punch the hatch release, jump out of the shuttle, and land on top of something I'm not expecting to be there. The impact of my hand hitting skull dislodges my phone from my grasp. I tumble onto my backside.

Sitting up, I'm suddenly staring at a short, bug-eyed, bald man with crooked teeth and a more crooked nose. He's wearing a reddish-brown costume covered in some kind of goopy slime. Although I've never seen him before, he seems oddly familiar. Then, my mind clicks to his Meta profile.

It's the Worm.

The Worm is a small-time criminal, a Meta 1 meta-morph with the unusual ability to secrete mucous from his pores, allowing him to tunnel through the ground like an earthworm. He's mostly wanted for street muggings and the occasional bank job. What's he doing here?

Then, I realize there's something even stranger

hanging around his neck. At first, it looks like a Christmas ornament on a chain. But then I realize it's some sort of orb. It's smooth and white and pulsating. My eyes are drawn to it. I can't turn away. It's absolutely mesmerizing.

"Who are you?" the Worm says, snapping me back to reality.

"Stay away!" I yell, scrambling to my feet.

"You scared of me?" the Worm says, flashing an ear-to-ear grin.

"Back off!" I shout, looking for somewhere to run. "I'm a Meta!"

"A Meta, huh?" says the Worm, clutching the orb. "You look like a lost little boy to me." Then he lurches forward. "Boo!"

I take off.

I'm not looking where I'm going. I'm just trying to get as much distance between me and the Worm as possible. And that's when I feel a meaty hand grab me by the back of the collar and lift me high into the air.

The next thing I know, I'm gazing into the wild eyes of Meta-Taker.

"Let me go!" I scream, trying to kick free.

But Meta-Taker doesn't respond. He just stares at me, and I'm helpless to do anything but stare right back. To my horror, he's even more frightening up close. His teeth are like knives, each one sharpened to a skin-piercing point. His breath is foul, like he's swallowed a barge of rotten fish. And his eyes—his eyes are like doorways to the gates of Hell.

"Elliott!" I can hear Mom's surprised scream.

"Release him!" Dad commands.

But Meta-Taker isn't interested in what he has to say.

"Please," I plead. "Let me go. I don't have powers. I'm just a Zero."

I look over at my parents. They're frozen.

"Drop the boy and take me," Dad says, inching closer with his hands in the air. "He has nothing for you, Meta-Taker."

Meta-Taker's eyes narrow. It's as if he's sensing me—studying me. Then, his orange flames crackle slowly towards me. I push hard against his massive body, but I can't break free. The flames dance across my skin and then seep inside my mouth. I feel a warm sensation flush through me. My body feels paralyzed!

But, suddenly, the brute stops cold and looks at me strangely.

And then his flames snuff out.

Meta-Taker registers a look of surprise. And then he clutches his head and screams in agony, dropping me hard to the ground.

"I'm inside!" Mom shouts. "I don't know how, but I'm in! Now! Do it now!"

"Glory Girl!" Dad calls into the open air.

Right then, out of nowhere, a crimson streak falls from the sky and catches Meta-Taker off-guard, pushing him back towards the very hole he came out of. Meta-

Taker teeters at the edge, and then stumbles over backward, disappearing into the abyss.

"Quick," Dad says. "Bury him!"

The heroes combine their powers to fill in the hole with as much dirt and debris as they can find. The immediate threat is neutralized.

"TechnocRat," Dad says. "We need a cell to contain him. And fast."

"Working on it, Captain," the little rat says, flipping open a computer mounted on his jetpack.

"Great job, Glory Girl," Dad says. "Holding you in reserve kept your powers hidden from Meta-Taker and added the element of surprise we needed."

Grace beams. She's the hero.

And I'm the goat.

Mom runs over to me. "Elliott, are you okay? What in the world are you doing here?"

"I don't know, Mom," I answer. "I really don't know."

Just then, a large fly buzzes around my head a few times and drops on my knee. It stares at me with its big, green eyes before I shoo it away. Strangely, it doesn't leave. It hovers for a few seconds, probably feeling sorry for me, and then it looks at me, looks at my mom, looks at me again, and takes off.

It's been that kind of a day.

Mom kneels and hugs me. "Thank goodness you're okay."

"Elliott, you're grounded," Dad says. "That was irresponsible. You could have gotten yourself or someone else killed."

"That's fine," I mutter, accepting my punishment. I deserve whatever book they're going to throw at me.

"I don't know what happened," Mom says with a shudder. "I couldn't get inside his head for the longest time, and then all of a sudden, I could. The anger inside of him was so intense."

Then, I remember the Worm and that weird orb.

"Hey," I say. "You wouldn't believe who else was here. The Worm! We've got to catch him!"

"The Worm?" Dad says, looking around. "That lowlife? He must have been passing through. This fight was way out of his league. I'm guessing he slithered away happy not to be mixed up in all of this."

For some reason, I'm not so sure, but after all of the trouble I've caused I decide to keep my mouth shut.

"Why don't the three of you head back to the Waystation," Dad says. "We'll find Blue Bolt and wrap it up from here."

Mom, Grace, and I head up the Freedom Flyer ramp. Right before we take off I remember I had dropped something. My phone!

I lower the hatch, and after a few minutes of frantic searching, find it tucked beneath a rock. It looks a little more beaten up then I remember, but then again, so am I.

Meta Profile

Name: Meta-Taker
Role: Villain   Status: Deceased

VITALS:

Race: Unknown
Real Name: Unknown
Height: 8'0"
Weight: 1,200 lbs
Eye Color: Orange
Hair Color: White

META POWERS:

Class: Meta-morph

Power Level: ▮▮▮▮▮

- Extreme Power Duplication (Physical + Molecular Morphing)

- WARNING: Duplication of several Meta powers at once may result in Meta 4 Power Levels

CHARACTERISTICS:

Combat	100	▬▬▬▬
Durability	100	▬▬▬▬
Leadership	28	▬
Strategy	73	▬▬▬
Willpower	85	▬▬▬

FOUR

I PUT MY NEW "POWERS" ON SPEED DIAL

After tossing and turning, hopelessly trying to erase the day's events from my mind, I finally manage to doze off. But then I'm woken moments later by my phone vibrating on the nightstand like a rabid woodpecker. Half asleep, I lift my head, fresh drool running down my chin, wondering what all the ruckus is about.

Only the Freedom Force has my number and they returned hours ago after depositing Meta-Taker in his cozy new prison accommodations at Lockdown.

So, I'm clueless about who's texting me.

Clawing for my mobile, I palm it and pull it close. The light from the display panel temporarily blinds me, but my eyes adjust quickly to find ten text messages and more coming in by the second:

>Taser: Big score 2nite. Anyone in? ☺<

>Brawler: Pizza? Where? Time?<

>Taser: No idiot! Bank job. Keystone Savings. 11 PM.<

>Makeshift: Tx for invite. What about Freedom Force?<

>Brawler: U not bringing pizza? :(<

>Taser: Not concerned about FF. Small job.<

>Taser: And no pizza!!!<

>Makeshift: What's the split?<

>Taser: 33% each.<

>Makeshift: I want 60%. U clearly need help.<

>Taser: 40% max.<

>Makeshift: 55%.<

>Brawler: How about doughnuts?<

>Taser: 45%.<

>Makeshift: Forget it. Need 2 wash parrot 2nite.<

>Taser: Fine. 50%?<

>Makeshift: See u at 11! ☺<

At first, I have no clue what's happening. And then it hits me like a ton of bricks. This isn't my phone. It's the Worm's phone! They must have been the same color and the same brand. We must have mixed them up when we collided!

The only sound I hear is my heart thumping against my chest. I throw off the covers, jump out of bed, and start pacing. As if this whole mess couldn't possibly get any worse, Mom and Dad are literally going to kill me if they find out a villain has my phone! They'll have me drawn and quartered, and then they'll take my quarters and draw and quarter them again.

Another text comes across. I tap the button to read it when I realize something is wrong. Where's the security code screen? There's no security code screen?

Wait, there's no security code screen! My phone has a security code screen! And then I remember I'd set it to wipe the device after three failed security code attempts.

Yes! Yes! Yes! I may get to live!

I flop down on the bed, relief washing over me. But I still need to tell my parents. They have a right to know that an official piece of Freedom Force property has fallen into the hands of a known criminal. That would be the right thing to do. But then again...

The Worm isn't really a threat, is he? I mean, c'mon, it's the Worm. A Meta 1. I'm sure he messed up the security code by now and erased all the data. So, do I really need to tell my parents? I can just say my phone got obliterated in the battle by some rogue laser beam and now I need a new one. Then, they can still get in touch with me, and I can hold on to this one! I look down at The Worm's phone. More texts:

>Brawler: Never heard back on the doughnuts?<
>Taser: NO DOUGHNUTS U IDIOT!!!!!!!!!<
>Brawler: Ok. U don't have 2 yell! :(<

I stay up all night flipping through the Worm's

contact list and trolling through his texts. Most of it's in shorthand, but I manage to identify his ordinary contacts like his mom, his dry cleaner, his favorite Mexican restaurant, his barber—don't know why a bald man needs a barber—from his Meta contacts.

By the end of it, I'm pretty sure that Taser is the Meta 1 energy manipulator that can shoot electric currents from his hands. And Brawler is the Meta 1 strongman that gets his strength from radioactive beer. But I can't find any reference to whoever "Makeshift" is. However, it's clear from the group texts that they've been talking about pulling off a job for a while but have never gotten it together. They also use a lot of freaking profanity.

But despite all of my searching, I'm not able to find anything linking the Worm to Meta-Taker. Maybe Dad's right. Maybe the Worm was just in the wrong place at the wrong time. But there's something strange about that orb. What is it and what's the Worm doing with it? I can't shake the feeling that there's something more to this story.

Something I'm missing.

At this point, I'm completely bleary-eyed when my alarm goes off. Somehow, morning snuck up on me which means it's time to get ready for school. Oh. Joy. I wait a few minutes and my second alarm comes right on schedule.

There's a knock at my door.

"Hey, *Powerless Boy*," Grace says mockingly. "Get up or you're gonna be late!"

I look down at the Worm's phone.

Powerless Boy, huh? Maybe. But then again, maybe not...

I dress quickly and head down to the Galley for breakfast. After my screw up the day before, I know this isn't going to be pleasant.

"Good morning, Elliott," Mom says. "How are you feeling?"

"Um, kind of tired," I answer. "And sore."

"Remember, Elliott," Dad says sternly. "You're grounded. I expect you home right after school."

"I know," I say. Truthfully, being grounded didn't mean much. I'm always home right after school anyway.

"And no monitor duty," he adds.

"Got it," I say. Well, that part sucks.

"Look for me on the five o'clock news," Grace says smugly. "They want to interview me about how I saved the world from Meta-Taker."

"Oh, I'll be sure to tune in for that," I say with dripping sarcasm as I grab a cereal bar and stuff it into my backpack. I sit down at the table and take a deep breath. Here goes nothing. "Oh, I almost forgot. I need a new phone. Mine was vaporized by one of Master Mime's energy sprockets."

"Okay, just get one from TechnocRat," Dad says.

"Cool." Whew! That was easy. Now for part two. "I

also had the weirdest dream last night."

"Really," Dad says, not lowering his paper. "What kind of dream?"

"Well," I say. "I had this dream that Keystone Savings Bank was going to get robbed. I had this really clear image that three Metas were involved."

Dad lowers his paper a little. "That *is* weird."

"Yeah," I say. "There were three guys. All Meta 1's. An energy manipulator, a really strong brutish guy, and one I couldn't make out too clearly but seemed kind of harmless."

Dad and Mom look at each other.

"I feel like it might happen tonight. Around eleven."

"At eleven?" Mom says with a surprised look. "Well, that's certainly specific. Okay, I guess we'll keep our eyes and ears open."

There, the seed is planted.

"Hogwash!" Grace says. "Your brain must've bounced when Meta-Taker dropped you on it." She scoops up her backpack and races for the Transporter. "Later peeps, I've gotta split!"

I grab my bag and chase her down, managing to make it right before the door shuts. We travel in silence and re-atomize at the Prop House.

"Are you such a loser that you have to make up stories for attention?" Grace asks. "It must really suck being you."

She walks outside and looks both ways to make sure

no one's around, and then takes off into the air, leaving me alone on the front stoop. I lock the door and head off to school.

All of a sudden, my phone starts going nuts again. More texts:

>Taser: Anyone got smoke bomb?<

>Makeshift: Nope.<

>Brawler: Yes. Why?<

>Taser: Need for job.<

>Brawler: 4 2nite?<

>Taser: No 4 gopher in my garden. YES 2NITE!<

>Brawler: Still yelling! :(<

That actually makes me chuckle.

Then, my cell is yanked right out of my hands.

"Well, look who came back," kid giant says, tossing my phone from one over-sized mitt to the other. "It's the wimpy kid. I got a week's detention because of you. And the Cafeteria Lady's been giving me the stink eye."

I stay calm despite my inner sense of panic. I need that phone back! Without it, I can't keep pretending I have powers. "Listen," I say. "I'm sure I can avoid injury and you can avoid incarceration if you simply give me the phone and we go our separate ways."

Another crowd starts forming. Here we go again.

"Uh-uh," he says, dangling the phone in front of me, "If you want it, come and get it."

I reach out and he steps backward. The other kids laugh. He holds it out and I try again. Same result. He's baiting me. Toying with me.

"C'mon," I say. "We're going to be late for class."

"This is much more fun than class," he snorts.

Just then, a girl I've never seen before strides forward. She's a little taller than me and is dressed kind of preppy with a white oxford shirt and slim, dark-washed jeans. She's really pretty, with long dark hair falling in ringlets to her shoulders. I have no idea what she's doing.

She looks at me with her bright, green eyes and says, "You heard him. If you want your phone, take it from him."

But I don't move. I'm so shocked she's talking to me that I'm glued to the spot.

Suddenly, the girl steps forward, punches kid giant in the gut, and says, "If you tell on me, I'll do it again. But harder next time."

Kid giant topples over, struggling to catch his breath.

"Never show weakness," she says. And then she hands me my phone and walks away.

Meta Profile

Name: Glory Girl
Role: Hero   Status: Active

VITALS:

Race: Human
Real Name: Grace Harkness
Height: 5'3"
Weight: 101 lbs
Eye Color: Blue
Hair Color: Blonde

META POWERS:

Class: Flight
Power Level:

- **Considerable Flight**
- **Limited Super-Speed in combination with Earth's gravitational force.**

CHARACTERISTICS:

Combat	29	
Durability	26	
Leadership	40	
Strategy	28	
Willpower	57	

FIVE

I BITE OFF MORE PAIN THAN I CAN CHEW

The texts keep rolling in all day. There are threads about bank vault designs, security camera locations, getaway routes, and contingency plans should a good guy show up. Everything finally settles down at four o'clock. Their plan is set.

And I'm home alone. Grounded.

Well, I guess Dog-Gone is around, but he disappeared after eating my cereal when I went to the bathroom. The school day was a total blur. Aside from keeping up with the flurry of text messages, I found myself thinking a lot about that girl from this morning.

She ended up being in my Social Studies class. That's where I learned her name was Cammie and she'd just moved to town. She seems really smart and raised her hand a lot to answer questions. She didn't look my way once.

I keep thinking about what she said. *Never show weakness.* Does she think I'm weak? Deep down, I know the answer. I never stand up for myself. Not to Grace. Not to that bully. Not to anyone. Maybe it's time I started.

Being grounded was infinitely more boring than just being home on a regular day, and I was getting tired of sitting around twiddling my thumbs. Dad said I can't do monitor duty, but he didn't say anything about the Combat Room.

The Combat Room is on the lowest level of the Waystation. It's where the Freedom Force hones their powers and practices their fighting skills. The Combat Room was designed by TechnocRat and uses advanced holographic technology reinforced with force fields to project hard images that look and feel real. The Combat Room can create any situation imaginable, from a run-of-the-mill street mugging to an all-out Meta villain assault. While I've watched countless hours of Combat Room training from the safety of playback video, I was never allowed to participate in an actual combat scenario.

But that's about to change.

I enter the Combat Room and take a deep breath. The room is massive, equivalent to a large aircraft hangar. The entire space is stark white with no windows or doors—except for the one I came in from. It's also eerily silent.

Until you make GISMO aware of your presence.

"GISMO," I call, my voice echoing through the vast chamber.

There's a low hum followed by a series of beeps.

"GISMO online," comes a warm, mechanical voice. "Good afternoon, Elliott Harkness."

GISMO is short for Global Intelligence Simulation Model Operator. GISMO was designed to run the Combat Room. It's GISMO's job to track the progress of participants through the simulation. If things are going well, GISMO can make the challenge more difficult. If things are going poorly, GISMO can end the simulation with a simple voice command.

Now, all I need to do is pick a training module. The words "never show weakness" stick in my mind.

"GISMO," I say. "Please load training module SS12."

There's a pause.

"Simulation warning," GISMO states. "Training module SS12 is an intermediate module for Meta's possessing super strength."

"Yes, GISMO," I answer. "I understand. Please load training module SS12."

Another pause.

"GISMO is not authorized to load training module SS12 for Elliott Harkness. Elliott Harkness does not possess Meta level super str—"

"Override sequence B321ZFINAL," I command.

"Module loading," GISMO replies.

You pick up all sorts of tricks hanging out with TechnocRat.

The barren room instantly transforms into a dark, smoky saloon filled with large, tough-looking men covered in tattoos. Some are drinking beer while others are playing pool. One of them is even wearing an eye-patch. I'm lost in the power of the simulation. The flickering neon lights. The music blaring in the background. The smack of pool balls colliding.

I check out the bar and notice all the seats are taken except for one way down at the end where a strange woman is standing. Her face seems young, but her hair is long and silver. She's dressed in a dark business suit with white, vertical pinstripes. She looks totally out of place, which probably means that she's somehow important to this simulation module. So, I mosey on down and take the seat beside her.

"What'll it be, buddy?" asks the bartender, a beefy man missing several important teeth.

I've never ordered a drink from a bar before. I look over at the woman. She's watching so I can't blow it.

"I'll have a Shirley Temple, please," I say. "Shaken, not stirred."

"Right," the Bartender says, rolling his eyes.

"Hang on," I say, turning to my companion. "Let me

see what the lady would like."

"Oh, I am no drinker like you," she says with a strange accent I can't place.

I nod and the bartender goes to fix my beverage.

After a few seconds, the woman speaks. "Tell me. Are you the one?"

"What one?" I ask. I don't know what she's talking about.

The bartender brings my drink. I take a sip.

"Do not be funny, boy," she says. "Are you the one sent by the Emperor? Are you the Meta who will help me find the orb?"

I do a spit take.

Did she just say *orb*?

"I knew it," she says angrily. "I knew it as soon as I saw you. You are too puny. Too small."

"Now hang on, Lady," I say. "I'm a member of the Freedom Force."

"I knew the Emperor would betray me," she continues. "He will pay eventually. But you must pay now. Comrades, kill him!"

Well, that doesn't sound good. All of a sudden, I have a flashback of Dad warning me to stay out of the Combat Room because it's possible to be knocked out, or even killed, during the simulation!

I leap off my chair just as all the goons in the bar surround me. My heart is pounding so hard I think it's going to burst out of my chest and fly straight out of the saloon. There's no time to think. The man with the eye patch is standing in front of me, waving a pool cue over his head.

Then, he swings at me.

I duck and the cue shatters against the bar. A piece ricochets and hits me hard in the jaw. That hurt! This is for real! This guy's actually trying to kill me!

"Get him, fools!" the woman commands.

Another guy lunges at me, but I somersault between his legs and kick him from behind, sending him headfirst into a chair. "Take that!" I yell, sort of impressed with myself. But, there's no time to pat myself on the back. I'm well outnumbered. I look for an opening, but there's none to be found.

"You are no Meta," the woman says. "You are just a boy. Soon to be a very *dead* boy."

I have to get out of here. But how? And then I notice the eye-patched man. If I can charge his blind side then maybe, just maybe...

"I may not be a Meta," I say. "But I'm certainly no weakling."

I go for it, darting towards the one-eyed man, but I'm quickly caught up in a tangled mass of arms and legs.

"Let me go!" I scream. But no matter how hard I push, I can't break free.

They've got me.

The woman laughs. She grabs a bottle and smashes it against the bar, leaving a sharp, jagged edge. "You shall be a warning to all of the heroes of the Freedom Force."

Then, I remember that I can stop this if I want to. All I have to do is call out GISMO's name and this nightmare will be over. But the eye-patched man grabs my head and pulls it back, exposing my neck. I try to say the words, but I can't. I can barely breathe.

The woman approaches slowly, savoring every moment. She stands in front of me and pushes the edge of the broken glass against my neck. I can feel it cutting into my skin!

I'm going to die. I'm going to die in this room for being a Zero. A stupid, freaking Zero.

"Goodbye, boy," the woman says.

I close my eyes and wait for the end.

But instead, I feel a strange tickle by my ear.

Opening one eye, I see the familiar shape of a Hawk-a-rang wrapped neatly around the bottle. Then, it snatches the glass clear from the woman's hand.

Could it be?

As if on cue, Shadow Hawk appears, floating down from the rafters with his long, black cape trailing behind him. He lands softly, uncurling his Hawk-a-rang. His eyes are like narrow, white slits set inside his black cowl. His lips are curled into a menacing sneer. He stares at the broken bottle and says, "Didn't your mother teach you it's not polite to hit a kid with glasses?"

"Who are you?" says the woman.

"Me?" he answers. "I'd say I'm your new problem."

Shadow Hawk flexes his arm and strikes the eye-patched man with his Hawk-whip. The man cries out in pain, dumping me unceremoniously to the floor.

I land on my back and look up to see the thug holding his head. And then, something weird happens. His face starts to flicker. And for a moment, I'm staring at something not quite human at all.

His skin turns pale yellow. His one good eye molts from brown to neon green. His ears curl upwards, stopping in points beside his temples. Then, he shakes his head and reassumes his human appearance.

"Get him!" the woman screams.

I look back at Shadow Hawk as the men approach, but the hero stands his ground. "GISMO," he calls. "End program."

"Training module ended, Shadow Hawk," GISMO says.

Instantly, the saloon, along with the woman and all her henchman, disappears. Shadow Hawk and I are all that remain in the plain, white room.

"Aren't you supposed to be grounded?" Shadow Hawk asks, helping me to my feet.

I nod, still trying to catch my breath.

"You realize that was an advanced combat module," Shadow Hawk says. "You should never let a simulation get so out of hand that you could be seriously hurt."

"No kidding," I say, rubbing my sore neck. "I guess I got in over my head. Sorry I was such a goober."

"A goober?" Shadow Hawk laughs. "That's not what I saw. What I saw was inexperience. Someone who doesn't yet understand his limits. But with practice, you can make progress. And with progress, you can get better every single day. Take it from me."

For the first time, I see Shadow Hawk in a different light. Standing before me is a member of the greatest super-team ever assembled who has absolutely no Meta powers. He's a Zero, just like me, but he's pushed his mind and body to the limits of human potential. And because of that, he's probably one of the most dangerous members of the Freedom Force.

"Come on, kid," Shadow Hawk says. "Let's grab a soda pop from the Galley. Maybe I'll teach you a few things."

"Really?" I say. "You'd do that?"

"Sure," he says. "You're part of the team, aren't you?"

"Yeah," I say. "I guess so."

We walk a few steps and then I stop. "Shadow Hawk, can I ask you something?"

"Shoot, kid," he says.

"Those guys in the simulation, they weren't human, were they?"

Shadow Hawk smiles. "I was wondering if you caught that. No, they're not human. They're known as the Skelton, an alien race of shapeshifters obsessed with conquering neighboring galaxies—including ours."

We walk a few more steps.

"So, wait? You mean they're real?" I ask. "They've tried to conquer Earth?"

"Oh, they've tried," Shadow Hawk says. "Several times. But don't worry, we're the good guys. The Freedom Force has always been there to stop them."

My mind starts spinning. So, if the Skelton are real, then is that orb the woman was yammering about the same as the one the Worm had around his neck? And, if so, what did she want it for? I was about to ask Shadow Hawk but then thought better of it. What if he thinks I'm being ridiculous? After all, he just told me not to worry about it. Besides, I have a more pressing issue to attend to.

"Shadow Hawk, can I ask one more thing?"

"Sure, kid."

"You're not going to tell my dad I was in the Combat Room, are you?"

"Nah," Shadow Hawk says. "I think you've had enough punishment for one day."

We laugh and head for the Galley.

Meta Profile

Name: Shadow Hawk
Role: Hero   Status: Active

VITALS:

Race: Human
Real Name: Unknown
Height: 6'2"
Weight: 215 lbs
Eye Color: Unknown
Hair Color: Unknown

META POWERS:

Class: None
Powers Level:
- Meta 0
- Master detective, expert marksman, and highly-skilled martial artist.

CHARACTERISTICS:

Combat	92	
Durability	56	
Leadership	93	
Strategy	100	
Willpower	100	

SIX

I BREAK THE LAW INTO A GAZILLION PIECES

It's 10:57 p.m. and I can't stop pacing.

I'm three minutes from either getting away with my pretend new powers or going down in a massive ball of flames. My parents haven't mentioned the bank heist once since I shared my "dream" with them earlier this morning. In fact, I think they've forgotten all about it.

I glance at the Worm's mobile again. There aren't any meaningful texts since this afternoon, except for one ridiculous exchange where Brawler lost his costume. Forty-five texts later, he realized it was in the backseat of his minivan the whole time.

Freaking. Genius.

10:58 p.m.

I run my hands through my hair. This is crazy. Here I am, relying on a bunch of Meta 1 losers to rob a bank precisely at eleven o'clock so I can con my parents into believing I have Meta powers. What am I doing?

10:59 p.m.

Oh, god. What if they don't hit the bank? I'll look like a fool again. Grace will say this is just another ploy to get attention. She'll say I'm jealous of her. She'll call me pathetic. She'll recommend my parents abandon me on a deserted island and pretend I never happened. Then, she'll break through our shared wall and use my bedroom as her personal dressing room. I can see it now—the mirrors, the costumes, the hundreds of Glory Girl posters lining the walls. Boy, would she love that.

They have to hit that bank.

I peek at the phone again. Still no texts. I look back up.

11:00 p.m.

I raise my eyebrows, waiting for the Meta Monitor to sing its song. I stand silently for thirty seconds. Sixty seconds. Two minutes. But, there's nothing. Those idiots! Where are they? They were supposed to rob the bank at 11:00 p.m.!

I stare at the phone. Still no texts. What the heck are they doing? I scream in frustration and collapse on my bed. How could I ever have trusted those crooks? Grace is right. I am pathetic. Just look at me. I close my eyes and let out a deep breath. It's over. I'll never be a Meta.

Not even a sham.

"Alert! Alert! Alert!" the Meta Monitor sounds.

I spring from my bed and glance at the clock.

11:04 p.m.

"Meta 1 disturbance. Repeat: Meta 1 disturbance. Multiple signatures. Power signature one identified as Taser. Power signature two identified as Brawler. Alert! Alert! Alert!"

YEEEEEEESSSSSSSSSSSSSSSSSSS!!! They hit the bank! They hit the bank! Those idiots hit the bank!

I stop dancing and regain my composure. I run up the twenty-three steps to the Monitor Room to claim my big "I-told-you-so" moment. Luckily, Dad is on duty tonight.

"Elliott," Dad says. "I was just about to call you. Did you hear the alarm?"

"The alarm?" I say, feigning surprise. "Yes, I may have. Whatever was it for?"

"Well, Keystone Savings Bank is currently being robbed. Wasn't that your dream last night?"

"Oh, that's right," I say nonchalantly. "I had completely forgotten all about it. It was supposed to happen at eleven. Gee whiz, I forgot to look at the time. Is it eleven already?"

"You said there were three Metas, correct?" Dad asks. "The monitor is only showing two."

"Two?" I say, confused. "Did you say two? Oh, well, perhaps I was mistaken. These dreams are so hard to decipher sometimes." Where the heck is that third idiot? Now, Dad will see right through me.

"Alert! Alert! Alert! Meta 1 signature registering. Identity unknown."

"Oh, there we go," I say. "There's your third crook." Whew!

"If there's an unknown Meta, we'd better summon the whole team," Dad says. "I don't know what we're dealing with here. Did your dreams tell you anything about the third Meta?"

I can tell him the third Meta had the text handle "Makeshift," but that would just raise a lot of questions I didn't really want to answer. Better to say nothing.

"Um, no," I say. "But maybe I should come along. You know, since it was my dream and all."

Dad looks at me and smiles. "Sorry, Elliott. After the last incident, we can't risk it. But you really got me thinking. I realized that out of all of us, you're the one I admire the most."

"Me?" I say. "Why me?"

"Well, we all have responsibilities around here. Whether it's stopping a bad guy or ejecting the trash. But you have the greatest responsibility of all."

"I do?"

"*I* think so," Dad says. "Who knows more about the Freedom Force than you? Who knows all of our secret identities, the location of our secret headquarters, all of our powers and weaknesses? You do. And you keep it locked up tight. That's a pretty big responsibility."

"Yeah, I guess," I say, kind of shell-shocked.

"Well, I want you to know that you're a big part of our family, whether you have powers or not. Remember, just having Meta powers doesn't make you a good person. Look at all of those supervillains out there. In the end, it's what's in your heart that counts, and I think you may have the biggest heart of all."

"Gee," I say. "Thanks."

"Just believe in yourself, son. You'll be amazed at what can happen when you do."

"So, does that mean I can come?" I ask.

"Well, no," Dad says. "We still don't have a full understanding of your powers yet. And besides, you're grounded, remember?"

"Yes, sir," I answer. "I remember." Wait, did Dad just say I had powers?

"Why don't you go back to bed and see what else you can dream about. We'll be back later. And remember, no monitor duty." He pats my head and takes off.

I'm way too wired to go back to bed. Instead, I head down to the Galley for a late-night celebratory snack.

When I arrive, I hear snoring from beneath the dining table. It sounds like Dog-Gone has snagged someone's leftovers and is invisibly sleeping it off. I open the pantry and grab the nearest non-nutritious snack I can find. I'm so pumped by what I just pulled off that I can't sit still. I decide to take my candy bar for a stroll.

Today is a massive victory. Dad is convinced I have powers. Now I just need those knuckleheads to pull off another job. Another job means another dream. And another dream means I can continue to convince the Freedom Force that I'm a Meta. Then, I can get my own costume and go on adventures with them.

There's just one catch. I need those idiots to not get caught. I stuff the candy into my mouth, pull out the Worm's phone and type into the bank job thread:

>Worm: Hey, FF coming! Run!<

Beads of sweat drip down my forehead. Now I've sunk so low I'm actually helping the bad guys get away. Does that make me a criminal too? I'm pretty sure I know the answer to that one. But, I need them. Plus, no one's really getting hurt, are they? Now, if they'll just respond. My phone buzzes. A text from Taser:

>Taser: WHAT? Really?<

They got it! I type again:

>Worm: YES! GO! NOW!<

>Taser: Tx bro!<

Great, I'm officially a criminal.

I'm pretty sure Dad wouldn't be so proud of me now.

I look up to see where I've wandered to and as if by some cruel twist of fate, I'm standing in front of The Vault. The Vault is the fortified chamber that stores the secret blueprints for Lockdown—the super-maximum Meta prison. The Vault is designed to be impenetrable.

The door is 21-inches thick, weighs over 20 tons, and is made of pure tungsten—the strongest metal on Earth. The only way in is to know the entry code, and only two people in the world know that—my dad and TechnocRat.

I study the keypad where you enter the passcode. There are nine individual spaces with only letters available, no numbers. I start working through some options in my mind.

J-U-S-T-I-C-E. Seven letters. Not enough.

L-O-C-K-D-O-W-N. Eight letters. Still short.

C-R-I-M-I-N-A-L-S. Nine letters. Maybe?

I punch it in and a red light flashes on the console with a warning. It reads:

ERROR. *TWO ATTEMPTS REMAINING.*

I keep thinking.

V-I-L-L-A-I-N-S. Eight letters.

P-R-I-S-O-N-E-R-S. Nine. Could be?

I type it in and up comes another warning. It reads:

ERROR. *ONE ATTEMPT REMAINING.*

Okay. Time to stop. Who knows what will happen if I get the last one wrong? I back away and turn around. I need to find something else to do before I get myself in even more trouble. I just need to put the passcode out of my mind. Yep, just think about something else. Something else entirely.

Well, that's not working!

The passcode has to be something less obvious. Think! Okay, The Vault was designed by TechnocRat. If I were TechnocRat, it would need to be something meaningful to me that I wouldn't forget. Now, what would I remember if I were a super brilliant, yet incredibly irritable rat?

Cats? No way. Secret laboratories? Definitely not. What are genius rats into these days? Super-conductors? Motherboards? Cheese? Cheese!

C-H-E-E-S-E. Six letters. Even if I added an 'S' it's only seven...

Not it.

Then, it hits me. That crazy rat. Could it be?

I cross my fingers. If this doesn't work I'll either trigger an alarm that runs straight to my dad's brain or set off a booby trap that will catapult me into outer space. Out of the two, I'd definitely prefer the latter. Here goes nothing. I exhale and punch into the keypad.

C-A-M-E-M-B-E-R-T.

Nothing.

Okay, I'm officially a dead kid walking.

Suddenly, a loud BING echoes down the corridor, and the console turns green. I hear several mechanical locks rotate and unhinge from the inside. And, to my sheer and utter delight, the door swings wide open.

I did it! I cracked The Vault!

I breathe a sigh of relief and step inside. The interior is much larger than it looks from the outside. There are dozens of filing cabinets all neatly organized in rows. Each cabinet has a number and name beneath it. I quickly deduce that the number must represent the corresponding prison cell number at Lockdown and the name must be the prisoner held captive inside. I move through the rows, recognizing many of the names listed as dangerous Meta 3 criminals with unbelievable powers:

Bone Crusher. Lady Killer. Gargantuan.

All locked away under one roof.

My destination, however, is the last filing cabinet. The top drawer reads:

Cell# M27 -- Meta-Taker.

I reach up and pull it open. Inside is a long tube. I take it out, twist off the cap, and unroll the blueprints onto a nearby desk.

They're the plans for Meta-Taker's cell.

There are lots of technical specifications outlining the dimensions of the cell, the thickness of the walls, the location of the air ventilation system, and so on. What I'm most interested in, however, is located in the bottom right corner. It's the containment plan. I read it closely:

The prisoner is to be kept in a continuous state of suspended animation (otherwise known as hibernation). The temperature of the room is to be kept at 20°F (-7°C) at all times. This will keep the prisoner in a state of hypothermia. The lower body temperature will stop all cellular activity, decreasing the body's need for oxygen while keeping the cells alive. The prisoner will not have any need for food or water in this state. This containment plan replicates the hibernation pattern of animals. Room temperature is to be monitored 24 hours a day, 7 days a week.

Okay, that rat is amazing. But, I sure hope his containment plan works because I can't think of anything worse than a ticked-off Meta-Taker waking up inside a facility loaded with hundreds of Meta prisoners.

Meta Profile

Name: TechnocRat
Role: Hero   Status: Active

VITALS:

Race: Rat
Real Name: Lab Rat 2324B
Height: 7 inches
Weight: 0.75 lbs
Eye Color: Pink
Hair Color: White

META POWERS:

Class: Super-Intelligence
Power Level:

- **Extreme Analytical Skills**
- **Extreme Information Synthesizing**
- **Extreme Learning Capacity**

CHARACTERISTICS:

Combat	10	
Durability	14	
Leadership	85	
Strategy	100	
Willpower	96	

SEVEN

I NOW WISH TO BE CALLED AWESOME BOY

So, here we are, Grace and I, two kids with Meta powers heading to school via a sub-atomic teleportation device. We land at the Prop House when Grace finally blows a gasket.

"You got lucky," she says. "That's all."

"Oh, I wouldn't exactly call it luck," I say, buffing my fingernails. "Sounds like someone's upset she's no longer the only Meta kid around."

Grace turns a deep shade of purple and huffs, "It's dumb luck until you do it again."

Let's just say the ride to the Prop House was a chilly one. Grace is miffed because, apparently, everything in my "dream" came true last night. The Freedom Force arrived seconds after Taser, Brawler, and the mysterious Makeshift escaped from the scene of the crime.

Then, Mom and Dad spent the entire morning asking me all sorts of questions about my dreams. When did they start? Could I see people clearly in them? How did I know when they would happen in real life?

Oh, they did stop for a minute to ask Grace how she wanted her eggs. And then they turned right back to me.

Me. Me. Me.

It's shaping up to be a beautiful day.

We exit the prop house to find a surprise sitting on our front steps.

It's a girl.

"Who the heck are you?" Grace asks.

"I'm Cammie," the girl says, her bright, green eyes sparkling. "Elliott's friend."

Wait, she knows my name? And did she just say she's my friend?

"Elliott's friend?" Grace says. "Elliott doesn't have friends."

"Shut up, Grace," I snap. "I guess you should be *walking* to school now." Grace hated to walk anywhere when she could fly. Now, because of Cammie, she's stuck.

"We'll continue this later," Grace says, her eyes throwing daggers at me. She pulls her backpack over her shoulder and storms off.

As I lock the door, it hits me that I've never really

talked to a girl alone other than my sister.

We look at each other awkwardly and start walking.

"Well, she seems lovely," Cammie says.

"You have no idea," I say. "So, um, what are you doing here?"

"I pass by your house on the way to school, so I thought I'd walk with you," she says. "You know, in case you need protection or something."

I look over to see if she's serious. Her smile tells me she's not.

"Thanks," I say. "But that bully hasn't come within five-hundred miles of me since you clobbered him."

"Yeah, sorry about that," she says. "I didn't mean to step in, but..."

"No, it's okay," I say. "You did the right thing. I never did get to say thanks. So, thanks."

"No problem," she says. "I actually wasn't even sure you were home. Your lights were off the whole time. It's, like, totally dark in there."

"Oh, are they?" I say, looking back at the house. Yep, she's right, it's pitch black inside. I have to think fast. "Um, yeah, Dad gets a little crazy trying to save money on the electric bill. We're all so used to it we operate on radar now. You know, like bats." Note to self: have TechnocRat fix that asap.

Time to change the subject.

"So, you're new, huh?"

"Yeah," she says. "My dad, he... moves around a lot.

I guess you could say he doesn't stay in one place for very long."

"Wow, that sounds rough," I say.

"Yeah. I don't have many friends because of it," she says. I can tell by her slumped shoulders that this makes her sad.

Is that why she was waiting for me? Maybe she knows I don't have friends either.

"You sure seem to know a lot about the Civil War," I say. "Maybe even more than Mrs. Gittes." Mrs. Gittes is our Social Studies teacher. She kind of looks like a frog, especially when she wears that green turtleneck.

"Oh, yeah," Cammie says. "I guess I like studying things like that. My dad always says it's good to learn about history so you don't end up repeating the mistakes of the past."

"Makes sense," I say. I can tell there's something more she wants to say about her father, but she doesn't. And given my own family dynamics, I don't want to press her.

We walk in silence for a bit.

"So, what do you think about Glory Girl?" she asks.

Well, that was unexpected. I want to say: *Actually, you just met the old sourpuss a few minutes ago after we teleported to earth.* But I think better of it. All I manage to say is, "Um..."

"I think she's an egomaniac," Cammie says.

"You do?" I reply, my voice rising a full octave

higher. I clear my throat. "I mean, you do?" I say, regulating my voice.

"Oh, please," she says. "Didn't you see her on the news last night? She made it all about her. Give me a break! I don't understand why she's all the rage. I think she should call herself Ego Girl."

"Now, that's a good one!" I snort. We just may get along after all. "So, if you're not a fan of hers, then who's your favorite hero?"

"In comic books or real life?" she asks.

"You read comic books?"

"Of course I do," she says. "They're not just for boys, you know."

"I didn't mean it like that," I clarify. "I've just never met a girl that liked comic books before. I read them all the time."

"Well, so do I," Cammie says. "And, to answer your question, my favorite comic book hero is Saturn Girl. She's pretty deadly."

"And in real life?" I ask.

"That's easy," she says. "It's Ms. Understood."

"Really?"

"Really," Cammie says. "She just seems so—down to earth. You know what I mean?"

"Oh yeah," I say. "I know."

"How about you?" Cammie asks. "Who are your favorites?"

"That's easy," I say. "In comics, it's definitely

Batman. And in real life—"

"Wait," Cammie interrupts, "let me guess. Shadow Hawk?"

"Hey, how'd you know that?" I ask.

"Well, it's only logical. Isn't Shadow Hawk the real-life version of Batman? He's just the smartest and most athletic man on the planet."

"Yeah," I say. "I never thought about it like that. I guess they are similar."

"And like you, they're both a bit mysterious," she adds.

I feel my cheeks flush. "You think *I'm* mysterious?"

"I think there's more to you than meets the eye, Elliott Harkness."

I'm pretty sure I'm redder than a tomato by now. Fortunately, we reach the school entrance.

"Well, it was great walking and talking with you," she says.

"Yeah, thanks for protecting me," I say. "You're like the Secret Service for sixth graders."

She laughs. "No problem. See you in Social Studies."

Then, she smiles and walks away.

***

School was pretty much background noise for the rest of the day. Cammie and I talked a bit in class, and she asked me if I wanted to grab a milkshake after school, but I was still grounded. I breathed a sigh of relief when she didn't ask me why.

My luck continued after school as I also received a new stream of texts from Idiots Incorporated:

>Taser: New job. Who's in?<

>Makeshift: I'll play!<

>Demento: In.<

>Brawler: ☺ What is it?<

>Taser: Gold. Truck.<

>Brawler: They make gold trucks?<

>Taser: No u dufus! Gold arriving by truck!<

>Brawler: My bad.<

>Demento: Time?<

>Taser: Midnight.<

Flipping back through the Worm's contact list, I confirm that Demento isn't a breath mint, but rather a villain named Dr. Demento, a Meta 1 psychic. Then, I see this, and my heart drops to my toes.

>Taser: U in Worm?<

>Brawler: Plus, I still have your crowbar.<

Great. Now the floodgates have opened.

I don't know what to tell them. Sorry guys, thanks for inviting me to hit the truck, but I'm actually not the Worm at all, but just a twelve-year-old kid that picked up his phone by mistake while my super-hero family was putting away some Meta creep.

I breathe in deeply and exhale.

Just relax and cut it off quickly.

>Worm: Sorry. Prior obligation. U keep crowbar.<

Did it work? Please, please work.

>Taser: OK no prob.<

>Brawler: I can? TX! ☺☺☺<

Whew! I'm off the hook, and the Worm is short one crowbar.

After the criminals go through another exhaustive sequence of planning their crime, I have all the pertinent information. Now it's time to prove my "dreams" are more than just "dumb luck."

I wait until after dinner and find Mom and Blue Bolt hanging out in the Galley. Here goes nothing.

"Mom, I had another dream."

"You did?" she says. "Tell me about it?"

"There were four villains," I say, "All after one truck transporting gold. Same three from the night before plus a fourth with psychic ability. It's going down at midnight."

Blue Bolt rounds up the others in a flash, and I brief them as well. The look on Grace's face is priceless.

Now, all I have to do is wait.

Dog-Gone and I play the longest game of fetch known to man.

When eleven o'clock rolls around, the heroes throw me a curveball I'm not expecting. Since the villains got away last time, the Freedom Force decide to leave early to lay a trap. My flirtation with powers is about to end prematurely.

I can't let that happen.

So, as soon as they split, I hit the texts.

>Worm: WARNING! FF setting trap!<

>Taser: WHAT? How u know?<

>Worm: Trust me.<

I wait for the inevitable text telling me the job is off. Instead, I get this:

>Taser: No worries.<

Wait, what? No worries? What the heck does that mean? He must not have understood me.

>Worm: YO! I SAYS FREEDOM FORCE!!!!!<

>Taser: Yep. I SAYS NO WORRIES. ☺<

Something isn't right.

How are those morons going to stop the Freedom Force?

I start to panic. If these guys think they can take out the most powerful heroes in the universe, then they have something up their sleeves. I need to warn the Freedom Force. And pronto!

Dog-Gone and I run up to the Meta Monitor and pull up the communication system.

"Waystation to Freedom Flyer II," I call.

There's no response, only static.

"Waystation to Freedom Flyer II," I call again.

More static.

This isn't good at all. Not only do I have to help the criminals escape, but I also have to prevent the Freedom Force from being ambushed.

I just need a way to get there.

I can't use the Transporter because there's no nearby connection. I have to find some other way. But how?

Then, it hits me.

I flip to the hangar bay camera.

And there it sits, waiting for the joyride of its life.

Freedom Flyer I.

Meta Profile

Name: Blue Bolt
Role: Hero   Status: Active

VITALS:

Race: Human
Real Name: Maya Williams
Height: 5'8"
Weight: 135 lbs
Eye Color: Brown
Hair Color: Black

META POWERS:

Class: Super-Speed
Power Level: ■■■
- Extreme Speed
- Enhanced Endurance
- Phasing through objects
- Super-Fast Reflexes

CHARACTERISTICS:

Combat	86	
Durability	60	
Leadership	76	
Strategy	79	
Willpower	90	

EIGHT

I FEEL LIKE I NEED TO DIE NOW

Of all the stupid things I've done, this is probably the one most likely to get me killed. My plan was simple enough. Hijack the Freedom Flyer I, set it on autopilot and swoop in to save the Freedom Force. Unfortunately, my plans usually have a way of backfiring on me.

After the infamous Master Mime-Brutal Birdmen scuffle, I knew that steering the Freedom Flyer I was going to be a challenge, but I had no idea the autopilot had been junked as well. So, here I am, flying a supersonic shuttle at 5,000 feet above the ground with a broken steering column, a damaged autopilot, and no clue as to how I'm going to land this thing.

Getting the Freedom Flyer off the Waystation was no big deal. I'd played around in the computer flight simulator for so many years that I knew how to start it up and get it going. Bringing it back down, however, is another matter altogether. I never practiced landing. Flying was always the fun part.

I try several more times to get in touch with the Freedom Flyer II, but all I hear is static. There are no new texts on either my new mobile or the Worm's phone. I have an empty feeling in my stomach that something is wrong.

I just don't know what.

But that will have to wait because the problem with the steering column is even worse than I thought. The air is so choppy it's constantly throwing the shuttle off course. When I pull back for more altitude the shuttle lurches to the right. I correct this by pulling the steering column down, which straightens the shuttle sometimes, but other times throws it to the left. I'm working really hard to just keep a consistent cruising speed and stay flying in one direction.

The only thing that is working is the navigation system. It's automatically synched to the Meta Monitor, which tracks any signs of Meta powers and provides the exact coordinates of their location. So, I have a pretty good read on where the action is happening. I just need to get there without overshooting it by hundreds of miles in the blink of an eye.

But, I've totally got this!

I hope.

There is one other small issue to sort out. I have no idea what I'm going to do when I actually get there. I need to help the bad guys escape so I can continue my charade, while simultaneously ensuring that none of the good guys get hurt. Plus, my parents are absolutely going to flip out when they see me. I'm actually not sure who will kill me first.

I'm lost in thought when the Freedom Flyer chimes in, "Visual confirmation at 0300."

I zone in on the area the Freedom Flyer is signaling. There are dozens of trees felled in the same direction as if some giant steamroller plowed them over at the roots. My eyes follow the path of destruction, stopping at a very large fire where giant plumes of black smoke billow up to the clouds. At the center of it all is a familiar object that looks like it's shattered into a million pieces.

It's the Freedom Flyer II.

Two thoughts cross my mind. One, it took something awfully powerful to do that to a Freedom Flyer. And two, I'm flying a much weaker version.

I have to locate my family and get out of there fast.

It doesn't take me long to find them.

Several miles ahead it looks like a Fourth of July celebration gone wrong. There are massive explosions everywhere accompanied by blinding flashes of light. I'm still too high to identify specific people, but I can see them all down there, scampering around like ants.

I can't shake the horrible feeling that this whole thing

is my fault. I have to help, but my first job is to figure out
how to safely land this thing without getting myself killed.

Apparently, someone else has other ideas.

I notice the purple energy rocket about two seconds
before impact. There's no time to pull up the deflector
shields. I brace myself for what is sure to be an epic
collision.

I'm not disappointed.

The explosion is deafening. My head slams into the
console, which can only happen if the pilot's seat I'm
strapped into has completely detached from the cockpit
floor. I feel woozy like I'm floating outside my own body,
but somehow stay conscious. It takes a few seconds to
reorient, then I realize I'm not exactly floating, but rather
free falling through the air, debris from the Freedom
Flyer plunging all around me.

The good news is that I'm not dead.

The bad news is that I have seconds to act before I
become the world's largest pancake.

My right hand fumbles to open the armrest and
access the remote pilot touchpad. After some careful
manipulation, I activate the propulsion jets mounted to
the bottom of the pilot's chair. They engage and the
upward thrust of the jets slows my descent. I'm safe for
now, but I know there's only enough fuel to bring me to
the ground. I have to find a safe place to touch down
before another rocket knocks me clear out of the sky.

As I get lower, the explosions seem to be getting

louder, which means I'm getting closer to the action. I try to turn, but the steering difficulties from the shuttle seem to have carried over to the chair as well. I manage to strong-arm my way to an area I think is a good distance from the fighting.

All the while, there's one detail that keeps playing over and over again in my mind.

That energy rocket was purple.

The only Meta I know that can create purple energy constructs is Master Mime.

But I don't have time to solve that one either because things are about to get much, much worse.

"Well, well, well," comes a familiar voice. "Look who decided to drop in."

My chair lands smack in front of the Worm and some other masked moron.

"And how considerate of him to bring his own front-row seat," the Worm adds. He's standing with his puny arms folded across his chest and a smug look on his face. The orb is still hanging around his neck, pulsating more rapidly than the last time I saw it.

The other guy isn't anyone I've seen before. Based on Meta profiles, I can tell he's not Taser or Brawler or Dr. Demento. He's small. Probably smaller than me. He's wearing an orange costume with a strange black and white concentric circle design. His mask covers his eyes and he has a dark mohawk and goatee. Is this Makeshift?

I try standing up but I'm held down by the seatbelt

of my chair. I'm still buckled in!

"Please, don't get up on our account," the Worm says, reaching into my pocket to remove his mobile phone. "I certainly hope you enjoyed being me. I'm still not sure why you wanted to be me, but I'm grateful, nonetheless. You see, once I realized who you were, it was child's play getting you to set up your family."

"You won't stop the Freedom Force!" I declare.

The villains laugh.

"Oh, we're not planning on stopping anybody," the Worm sneers. "We thought it would be much more entertaining to watch them stop each other."

The Worm spins my chair and what I see is so unexpected it takes my breath away.

Because the Freedom Force is in full-on combat—with one another!

Master Mime is trying to pin down Blue Bolt with a pair of giant purple pincers. TechnocRat is chasing Shadow Hawk and Grace with a futuristic ray gun. And Mom has Dad on his knees with her mind control powers.

"Stop it!" I yell. "Make them stop!"

"What's the problem?" the Worm asks. "You've never seen your parents fight before?"

"H-How are you doing this?" I stammer.

"Now there's an interesting story," the Worm says, dropping to one knee. "Would you like to hear it?"

I nod.

"Well, you see, one night, really late, I was sitting outside my trailer, drinking a beer and feeling sorry for the pitiful state of my life, when the most incredible thing happened. Something really big fell out of the sky. Now, I could tell this 'thing' was in serious trouble. It was covered in flames and there was a long trail of smoke. I watched the darn thing fall. It fell all the way down until it crashed into the mountains creating a huge explosion. I knew right away it wasn't a plane or a helicopter or anything... human."

The Worm wipes his mouth. "So, I finished my beer and went into the mountains. The crash was so massive it didn't take me long to find it. There was a trail of destruction that went for miles. Anyway, I followed it until I came upon the cockpit. It was split completely in half—broken right down the middle like a cracked egg. And you'll never guess what I found inside. Go on, guess."

"I have no idea," I say annoyed. "Enlighten me."

"The pilot. Can you believe it? The sucker was still alive, lying flat on his back. His skin was puke yellow and he had these bright green eyes and these pointy ears. He was wheezing and coughing up all this blackish-colored blood. It was disgusting. It didn't take a doctor to know he was in bad shape. Well, he looked me up and down and I could just tell I wasn't the guy he was hoping for. But you know what they say, 'the early Worm gets the bird.' Anyway, he was holding a box, protecting it like it was some kind of baby. He told me that it was all up to me. That I should take the box, but not open it. Take it and hide it somewhere where 'the others' wouldn't find it. He said the survival of the universe depended on it. You know what happened next?"

I shake my head.

"He died. I never found out who these 'others' were and frankly, I didn't care. You ever been given a present you weren't allowed to open? So, of course, I opened it, and inside was this little beauty." The Worm grabs the orb and starts rubbing his thumb over its smooth surface.

"I figured I could probably pawn it off. You know, get some cash and maybe retire down in Florida. But then something weird happened. The orb started talking to me. Not out loud or anything, but inside my head. I thought I was crazy at first but... it kept telling me that I was now the most powerful being on the planet. It kept saying it over and over and over again. I couldn't shut it up. Can you believe it? Me, a Meta 1, the most powerful being on the planet? At first, I didn't believe it either. But then, it showed me what we could do."

The Worm stares over my shoulder to where the heroes are fighting. "And then I started to believe it."

I look at the orb. Somehow it's responsible for all of this madness. The Worm is using it to control the Freedom Force! Then, things start to click. The Worm had the orb when Meta-Taker appeared. The giant hole! The Worm must have tunneled down and freed Meta-

Taker so he could use the orb to control him!

And that alien ship must have been a Skelton ship!

I need to get that orb. I need to take it away from him.

"Without that orb," I taunt, "you're still just a loser."

The Worm slaps me hard across the face.

"Correction," The Worm says, circling. "I *was* a loser. But aren't all Meta 1's losers by definition? Aren't we the laughingstocks of the Meta community? The misfits. The clowns. Just look at us. Gifted with all of these wonderful, but *useless* powers. So, I started thinking *what if?* What if the tables were turned?" He looks over at the heroes battling. "You want me to stop the fighting, don't you?"

I nod.

"Watch this!" And then, the Worm calls out, "Stop!"

The heroes freeze in their tracks.

"Come here!" he orders.

They turn and walk towards us like robots.

"Here are the greatest heroes in the world," the Worm says. "All at my beck and call. If I say 'run,' they'll run. If I say 'attack,' they'll attack. I suppose I could keep them around. Perhaps I can use them as a Meta army of sorts? But, heroes always find a way to save the day, don't they? Nah, I think it's best if we get rid of them."

"Wait," I say. "What do you mean?"

"I mean get rid of them. Have you met my associate? He goes by Makeshift."

The little man steps forward. I knew it!

"He looks so unassuming doesn't he?" The Worm says. "Just another worthless Meta 1. Another *loser* just like me. Don't you think things would be different if there weren't so many Meta 2's and Meta 3's walking around? Shouldn't Meta 1's have a chance to be the most powerful beings on the planet?"

"Wait. What are you going to do?" I ask.

"Makeshift," the Worm says. "Get rid of 'em."

The little man steps forward and puts out his hands. "I've never done so many at once before."

"Wait!" I cry out. "Hold on!"

Suddenly, a giant yellow circle spews out from his hands and surrounds the Freedom Force. It starts to expand and contract around them, picking up more and more speed with each rotation. And then, with a giant WHOOSH, it collapses on itself, taking the Freedom Force with it!

"No!" I scream.

There's nothing left where they stood. Just patches of dirt and grass. That's it. Just dirt and grass. And it's all my fault. I made them come here. I led them to their deaths.

The Worm comes towards me. "Now, we weren't expecting you here, but it certainly helps tie up any loose ends."

He pulls a knife from behind his back.

I can try to run, but what's the point? There's

nothing left. I feel tired. Woozy. Like my eyelids are tied to anchors. I feel myself giving up. Slipping into darkness. I just wanted to be part of the team.

But instead of the sharp cut of a knife, I feel a different kind of sensation, like I'm lifting into the air.

"Hey!" the Worm yells.

I look down and notice the Worm getting smaller and smaller.

I have no clue what's happening.

Then, I glance up.

For a moment, I think I see a tiny fly with bright, green eyes carrying me off into the sky.

And then, I'm out.

Meta Profile

Name: The Worm
Role: Villain   Status: Active

VITALS:

Race: Human
Real Name: Harold Stent
Height: 5'7"
Weight: 135 lbs
Eye Color: Brown
Hair Color: Bald

META POWERS:

Class: Meta-morph
Power Level: ▮

- Limited Tunneling
- Slippery Exterior
- Night Vision

CHARACTERISTICS:

Combat   24 ▬
Durability 30 ▬
Leadership 15 ▪
Strategy   20 ▬
Willpower   40 ▬▬

NINE·

I GET THE SHOCK OF MY LIFE

"Elliott!"

I hear a faint noise in the distance.

"Elliott!"

Repeating itself. Getting louder. Strangely familiar.

"Elliott!"

Then, I feel a sharp smack across my cheek.

"Elliott!"

Slobber rolls down my chin.

I open my eyes. Everything is fuzzy. Blurry. But I can just barely make out the silhouette of a person standing in front of me. By the shape, I can tell it's a girl. Ever so slowly, she comes into focus. She's staring at me. Staring with these bright, green eyes. I know those eyes.

"C-Cammie? Where am I?"

I rub my cheek, which is still smarting like crazy. Did she just slap me?

I take in my surroundings. It's morning and we're in front of the Prop House. At first, I think I'm dreaming, but then I realize I'm still strapped into the pilot's chair from the Freedom Flyer I. No such luck.

"What are you doing here?" I ask.

"Don't you remember?" Cammie says. "I rescued you."

"You did what?" I say. "Rescued me from what?" I struggle to replay everything I can remember. Then it all comes flooding back: the Worm, the orb, Makeshift, my family. The fly with the bright, green... green...

My eyes lock onto Cammie's.

And then, I synthesize a million pieces of information at once.

"Y-You're the fly?" I stammer. "You were that weird fly that landed on me after the Meta-Taker fight?" I unclick myself from the pilot's seat and scramble to my feet. I feel unsteady. "Who are you? What do you want from me?"

"Oh, relax," Cammie says, rolling her eyes. "Don't you think that if I wanted to kill you I would have done it by now? Or let the Worm do it for me?"

I hesitate. "Maybe. Or, maybe you wanted to kill my family too. Just like the Worm did."

"Elliott," Cammie says. "I'm truly sorry about your family. I didn't see that coming or believe me, I would have helped. But I also know what it's like to lose someone you love. You see, the Worm confirmed my deepest fears. My father is dead."

Her father? What is she talking about?

And then, I realize what she means. That alien that crash-landed on Earth with the orb. It feels like someone dumped a bucket of ice down my shirt.

"Your father was a Skelton!" I blurt out. "So, that means..." Instinctively, I move behind the pilot's chair.

She smiles. "Guilty as charged." And then, before my eyes, she transforms from the girl I know as Cammie to an alien version of herself. Her eyes brighten from emerald to neon green. Her skin takes on a pale, yellow hue. Her ears climb upwards, stretching to her temples. Her clothes transform from preppy to... regal. Her white top and skirt are adorned with gold trim, and thick, gold jewelry surrounds her neck and wrists. "My birth name is K'ami Sollarr," she says, her tone turning much more formal. "I am the daughter of the Chief Scientist of the Skelton Empire. Or, at least, I was."

All of the horrible things Shadow Hawk told me about the Skelton pop into my brain. "You're evil. You're here to take over Earth."

"No, Elliott," she says. "I'm not here to take over Earth. I'm here to save it."

"Yeah, right," I say, mapping out escape routes.

"Tell me," she says. "Are all humans the same? Do you share the same beliefs as the Worm?"

"No," I answer. "That's ridiculous."

"It is, isn't it?" K'ami says. "Yet, you stand here accusing me of the same thing. You must understand that just as all humans are not the same, neither are all Skelton. Most exist only to conquer, but there is a brave minority of us that believe there is another path. My father was one of those. That is why he stole the Orb of Oblivion."

"The orb of what?"

"The Orb of Oblivion," K'ami says, "It is a cosmic parasite of sorts, a sentient object of dark matter that seeks out unfulfilled desires and feeds off of them to make itself stronger. Its powers are as expansive as the imagination of its host."

"So, you're saying that this orb is feeding off the Worm?"

"Yes," she says. "And it is getting stronger by the day."

"So, how do you know so much about this... Orb of Oblivion? How do I know you're not making this whole thing up?"

K'ami lowers her head. "As you have alluded to, my people are conquerors—destroyers—always looking for more influential ways to expand our Empire. We have spent centuries looking for the Orb of Oblivion. Some thought it was only a legend—a fantasy told to small children. But the Emperor believed it was real. He demanded that every inch of the universe be searched and cataloged in his quest to find it. Many thought it was a fool's quest. Until one day, it wasn't.'"

K'ami looks up to the sky. "A strange signal was picked up on the far side of a desolate galaxy. It was determined that the signal had come from the implosion of a large star. Our calculations had not predicted its demise, and our scientists could offer no justification. It was determined that something unnatural had happened. So, a squadron was deployed to investigate. After many cycles, they had all but given up identifying a cause when a final reconnaissance drone made a remarkable discovery. It was an orb. It was lying on the surface of an unnamed moon orbiting a barren planet. No one knew how it had gotten there. Yet, there it was."

She pauses. I notice her voice has lowered and she's clenching her fists.

"It was brought back to Skelton. Naturally, as Chief Scientist, my father had the task of confirming that the orb was legitimate. He was a good man of extraordinary intellect and integrity. One night, he came to my room. It seemed as if the weight of the universe was on his shoulders. He sat for a long time in silence. And then he told me that the orb was talking to him. That every time he touched it, it would tell him to do dangerous things. When I asked what he meant, he would not say."

"We sat in silence for a while longer. And then he told me that the orb did not find itself on that little moon by accident. Somebody had put it there—far, far away where no one would ever find it. Then, he said something even more remarkable. He told me that the Orb of Oblivion had orchestrated its own freedom. That somehow, the orb had convinced that star to explode so it would emit a light so bright it would shine across the galaxy. So it could be found. My father wondered aloud that if an object of such power could convince a star to explode, then what would it be capable of doing in the hands of a Skelton Emperor? We both knew what he had to do. He made me promise that I would be strong—that I would never show weakness. That is the last time I saw him."

"So, he stole the orb and brought it to Earth?" I ask. "Thanks a lot."

"My father was a man of peace," K'ami says. "His landing on Earth was not his fault. It was mine."

"What?"

"You see, on our world, bloodlines share a powerful bond. A direct psychic link of sorts. My father had arranged to hide me with friends he had trusted, but after he left they betrayed him. I was turned over to the Emperor. I was... tortured. They exploited my psychic connection to track my father down. Somewhere deep in space, they caught up with him. After a terrible battle, he prevailed, but his ship was badly damaged. Earth was the closest planet to land and try to recuperate. It was then that he disconnected from me. I had betrayed him. I waited for him to reach out to me again, but he never did.

I feared he was dead, but I had to know for sure. Now I do."

Tears well up in her eyes.

"I'm sorry," I say.

"After that, I expected they would kill me," K'ami says. "It was their mistake that they did not. I conserved my strength and waited for the right moment. When that moment arose, I struck. I stole a supply ship and followed my father's path to Earth. I swore that I would finish what he started. I had just enough fuel to make the journey. As soon as I landed on your planet, I could sense the immense power of the orb. It was palpable, as if it was calling out to me. I followed it to its source. And that's when I discovered you."

"Me?" I say. "What do I have to do with all of this?"

"You, Elliott Harkness, are the savior of the universe."

"What?" I say. "Are you nuts? If you knew anything about me you'd know that I pass out in the face of danger." I start inching towards the Prop House. "Look, I'm really sorry about your dad, but right now I just want to go to my room, curl into a little ball, and never come out."

Then, something unusual catches my eye.

The door to the Prop House is ajar.

We never leave the door unlocked, let alone open.

Never. Ever. Ever.

"What is wrong?" K'ami asks.

I push the front door. It swings open with a creepy screech. Although it's dark inside, I can tell immediately that something isn't right. I turn on the lights.

At first, it looks like the house has been robbed. Tables and chairs are turned over, bookshelves are emptied, the television is smashed, pictures shattered. Then I realize, this is no burglary. Everything is still here, although now completely destroyed.

Whoever did this wasn't looking to steal anything.

They were looking for something.

My eyes immediately zoom to the end table. The miniature model of the Statue of Liberty is lying on its side, the giant mirror nearby is cracked from top to bottom. I feel short of breath. Someone has found the Transporter.

Then, I remember Dog-Gone.

"I've got to go!" I say, rushing inside.

"I will go with you," K'ami says, quickly following behind.

I pull the statue and the giant mirror slides up into the ceiling. Behind it is the Transporter. If it's damaged in the slightest, my atoms could be transferred to Pluto! It looks fine, but then again, I don't know the first thing about teleportation tube maintenance. There's no doubt this could backfire in a big way.

"What is this primitive device?" K'ami asks, looking inside.

"It's a teleporter," I answer. "It transmits to our

secret headquarters in space. Look, I appreciate you saving me and all, but I can't guarantee this thing still works. So, if you want to back out now, I'll completely understand."

"Elliott Harkness," K'ami says with a look of utter disbelief. "Do you really think that after being captured, tortured, and escaping from the clutches of the Skelton Empire I'm going to let a potential sub-atomic mix-up scare me away?"

"Um, right," I shrug. "Okay then, let's go."

We enter the chamber and the door closes behind us. We watch the overhead console move from red to green. Although my stomach starts to get that funny feeling as the Transporter does its thing, my mind is racing trying to figure out who ransacked the Prop House and, more importantly, what's waiting for us on the other side.

In a few seconds, we're going to find out, ready or not. The console moves back to green and the doors pop open. K'ami and I jump out prepared for the fight of our lives.

Except, there's nothing.

The room is empty. It's eerily silent. I had hoped Dog-Gone would be here to greet us, but he's not. Unless he's here already, but invisible.

"Dog-Gone," I whisper.

But there's no response. I start walking around the room, feeling underneath the tables to ensure he isn't hiding. Or sleeping. Or worse.

"What are you doing?" K'ami whispers back.

I realize that K'ami doesn't know about Dog-Gone, and because of that, I probably look like a crazy person. I decide that I'll keep him as my little secret for now. Just in case she turns on me.

"Um, nothing," I answer. "Just looking for a blaster or something. C'mon, let's go." Not finding Dog-Gone makes me very, very nervous.

We exit the Transporter and head for the Meta Monitor. I can just sense that someone's up here.

"Welcome home," comes a voice dripping with malintent.

Sitting on the bottom stair is a skinny, masked man. He's wearing a green costume with two white lightning bolts that start at each shoulder and meet in the middle of his chest. His hair is white and spikey like he just stuck a knife in a toaster. I know immediately that it's Taser!

I turn to escape, only to find an enormous brute filling the entranceway behind us. His head seems way too small for his massive frame. He's wearing a burglar mask and a costume with giant spikes on his shoulders. It's Brawler!

"The Worm thought you might try to go home," Taser says. "Nice digs you got here. It's a little out of the way for pizza delivery, but I could get used to it."

"What are you doing here?" I ask.

"We need to get into Lockdown," Brawler says.

"Shut up, you big lug," Taser barks. "It's none of

your business, kid."

"Sorry," Brawler says, looking like he dropped his ice cream cone in the dirt.

"Why do you need to get into Lockdown?" I ask. There are only two reasons I can think of as to why a criminal would want to be within a mile of the place. And that's either to kill someone inside or break someone out.

"Well, now that the cat's out of the bag, word on the street is that you've got all the blueprints up here," Taser says. "Pretty clever, but now that we're all together I suggest you make this easy and tell us where they're stashed. Otherwise, things may get a little rough for you and your weirdo girlfriend."

"K'ami," I whisper, "Turn into a fly. Save yourself."

"No Elliott. I am staying with you."

"Now, what say we make this easy?" Taser says.

"What say you shove it!" I shoot back.

"So that's how it's going to be, huh?" Taser says. "You heard him then, fellas. Waste 'em."

Fellas? Other than Taser, I only see Brawler.

But as the two villains start to close in, there's nowhere for us to go.

We're trapped!

Meta Profile

Name: Taser
Role: Villain   Status: Active

VITALS:

Race: Human
Real Name: Calvin Sharpe
Height: 5'11"
Weight: 170 lbs
Eye Color: Blue
Hair Color: White

META POWERS:

Class: Energy Manipulation
Power Level: ▉

- **Limited Generation of Electric Volts**
- **Immune to Electricity**

CHARACTERISTICS:

Combat	51	
Durability	32	
Leadership	24	
Strategy	31	
Willpower	40	

TEN

I LIED, NOW I GET THE SHOCK OF MY LIFE

"**E**lliott Harkness, use your powers!" K'ami yells, pressing back to back with me.

I'm now staring down Brawler, who's filling the doorway behind us with his ginormous muscles, while she faces Taser, who's blocking the stairs and gearing up to unleash an up-close-and-personal display of pyrotechnics.

"What are you talking about?" I say. "I don't have powers."

"Use them," K'ami orders. "Now!"

"I don't know what you're talking about!" I scream back.

Then, I hear a crackling noise. I peer over my shoulder and see electric volts leaving Taser's fingers.

They're white and stringy and heading straight for K'ami.

I expect her to get out of the way, but she doesn't move. Without thinking, I pull her by the elbow and wheel around in front of her. I feel an intense, burning sensation on my chest, and then the currents arc over my head and strike Brawler square in the face, stopping the big man in his tracks.

"Ouch!" Brawler yelps. "That hurt!" He's clearly dazed but tries to take another step. Then, his massive muscles start contracting violently. "W-W-W-Why d-d-did you hurt m..." His eyes roll back in his head, and he comes toppling down with a tremendous thud. His body convulses on the floor for several more seconds before stopping.

He doesn't move again.

I look down at my chest. My shirt is singed black, but it's like the volts never even touched me. I look up to find everyone staring at me with their jaws hanging open. Everyone that is, except for one.

"Well done, Elliott Harkness," K'ami says. "Now it is my turn." Then, she morphs into a fly and makes a beeline for Taser, hitting him with such force that he smacks his head against a stair tread and lands in a crumpled heap. But before he can rise, K'ami is on him like a winged whirlwind, landing blow after blow until Taser's eyes go white and he's down for the count.

It's over.

"Impressive," comes a nasally voice. "But you're still

going to die."

I spin to find a small man stepping out of the shadows. He's got an egg-shaped head, dark glasses, and wears a doctor's coat over his green, surgical scrubs.

It's Dr. Demento!

This must be the other 'fella' Taser was referring to! He's a Meta 1 psychic, which means that he's about to throw a royal mind-bender our way! There's no time to react!

I brace myself, when suddenly, Dr. Demento is slammed from behind with incredible force. He flies forward, hitting his head against the underside of the stairwell and falling to the ground unconscious.

Just then, Dog-Gone appears in front of me, his tail wagging.

I wrap my arms around him. "Good boy! I'm so happy to see you." He licks my face over and over. I feel tears sliding down my cheeks because I realize this fleabag is all the family I have left.

As K'ami glides over, Dog-Gone begins to growl.

"Can this creature be trusted?" she asks, returning to her natural appearance.

"I think he's wondering the same thing," I answer, shielding my face as I wipe the tears away. "Why did you just stand there when Taser attacked? You could have been killed."

"But you did not let that happen," she replies. "Did you?"

"Well, no," I say. "I wasn't going to sit back and let you fry."

"Just as I had hoped," she says. "If you are going to save the universe, you must show no weakness."

"Universe, shmooniverse," I say, feeling my chest. I look down my shirt to see if I'm injured, but there are no marks on my skin. "Why didn't I turn into toast back there?"

"I was hoping you would tell me," K'ami says. "After all, it was you who did it."

"That's the thing," I say. "I don't know what I did or how I did it. The volts hit my shirt, but then they just sort of bounced right over me. They never even touched my body. What kind of power is that anyway?"

"All I can offer is an account of what I have witnessed," K'ami says. "When I came upon you during the Meta-Taker battle you were in a dire situation. Naturally, I thought the beast was going to destroy you. But, to my surprise, he did not. When he tried to explore your powers there was something deep inside of you that neutralized his, if only for a moment. Of course, at the time you did not realize that Meta-Taker was being controlled by the Worm, or that, in turn, the Worm was being controlled by The Orb of Oblivion. So, when Meta-Taker sensed your powers, I heard something I never imagined I would hear in a million lifetimes."

"And what was that?" I ask.

"I heard the Orb scream," she says.

"Um, you heard it do what?" I say.

"I know it may seem strange," she continues. "But I realized upon landing on Earth, that I had a psychic connection with the Orb. And although the connection was weak, it was true. Somehow, I could sense its presence. At first, this surprised me. I could not understand how it could be so. But then I came to make sense of it. You see, the Orb had a direct psychic bond with my father, and my father had a direct psychic bond with me. So, by this association, the Orb and I are connected. I would not say the bond we share is strong, but it is there. It is through this connection that I was able to track down the Orb and find you. And that is how I learned a most surprising thing."

"Oh, joy," I say. "I can't wait to hear this one."

"Elliott Harkness, the Orb of Oblivion is afraid of you."

"What?" I laugh. "It's afraid of me? You're freaking nuts."

"You are the only one capable of capturing it."

"Riiight," I say. "Well, you'll have to tell the Orb to get in the back of the line, because the only thing I'm interested in capturing right now is the jerk who offed my family."

"Alert! Alert! Alert!" the Meta Monitor blares. "Meta 1 disturbance. Power signature identified as the Worm. Alert! Alert! Alert!"

"Speak of the devil," I say, starting for the Meta

Monitor. But then, I realize we can't just leave these losers lying around. I run to the Equipment Room and grab some industrial-strength cable. In no time, we tie them up.

"Dog-Gone," I say, "Can you drag these guys into the utility closet and lock them inside?"

He looks at the massive size of Brawler and then back at me. He cocks an ear.

"Dog-Gone," I start, "Don't even think about—"

Then, he turns invisible.

Yep, you can't teach an old dog new tricks. But, I don't have time to negotiate.

"Look," I say firmly, "if you get all these guys locked up, I'll give you the entire darned bag of doggie treats. Deal?" I can only imagine the mess that's going to be waiting for me if I survive this thing.

Dog-Gone becomes visible, his tail wagging.

"Good," I say. "And, be quick about it. If any of them wake up before you get them inside, the deal's off."

Dog-Gone licks his lips and starts dragging Brawler by the foot.

I turn to K'ami. "Follow me."

I lead her up the stairwell and into the Monitor Room. The screens are flashing on Meta 1 alert. I hop into the command chair and take control of the keyboard. After a few commands, I pinpoint the location of the Worm.

He's at Lockdown, just as Taser said he'd be. But

what did he want the escape plans for? Every horrible villain on the planet is residing there. Who's he trying to free? Could it be Gargantuan? Or Black Cloud? Then, I flashback to something he said about the Freedom Force: *Perhaps I could use them as a Meta army of sorts.*

That's when a strange thought crosses my mind.

What if he wants to free *all* the villains?

O... M... G...!

"K'ami," I say, "how powerful did you say the Orb was again?"

"As I had mentioned," she says. "The power of the Orb is limited only by the imagination of its host."

"Yep, that's what you said." I realize that the Worm may be far more imaginative than I hoped. It appears that stopping the Orb has now jumped to job number one. And lucky me, apparently I'm the only person in the entire freaking universe who can do it.

I turn to K'ami. "Okay, so how am I supposed to capture the Orb exactly? Is there some instruction manual or something you're keeping from me? Or, do I just yank it off the Worm's scraggly little neck?"

"Unfortunately, it will not be that easy," K'ami says. "If you touch the Orb directly it will try to take control of your mind. We cannot risk this. Instead, we must find the Shield Box."

"What's a Shield Box?" I ask.

"Before my father left Skelton, he told me that he had built a special containment box to house the Orb. He called it a Shield Box. I do not know what it was made of, but I do know that it was effective in keeping the Orb from direct skin contact while also shielding my father from its psychic control. If we can locate the Shield Box, we have a chance at capturing the Orb of Oblivion."

Then I remember something the Worm said. About how the alien had given him a box and the Worm had opened it and...

"I know where the box is!" I say.

I start punching into the keyboard.

The Worm's profile pops up on the screen.

"The Worm told me he saw your father's spaceship crash to Earth from outside his trailer. So, he lives in a trailer park. And he said the ship crashed in the mountains. So, his trailer park must border a mountain range." I triangulate the Worm's last four weeks of Meta 1 signatures with the locations of all the trailer parks in the country and their proximity to any mountain ranges. Then, I let the Meta Monitor do its work. One minute later a set of coordinates appears.

Bingo! Grant City Trailer Park. Sixty-three miles west of the Prop House.

"That is his home?" K'ami asks.

"Yes," I say. "But both of the Freedom Flyer shuttles are trashed. We can take the Transporter down to Earth, but after that I don't have a way for us to get there. Maybe we can hitchhike or something?"

K'ami shakes her head disappointingly. "Elliott

Harkness, did you forget already?" she says, transforming into a fly. "I have already carried you over one-hundred miles to get us here. What is sixty-three more?"

Meta Profile

Name: Brawler
Role: Villain   Status: Active

VITALS:

Race: Human
Real Name: Duncan Meeks
Height: 6'5"
Weight: 350 lbs
Eye Color: Brown
Hair Color: Black

META POWERS:

Class: Super-Strength
Power Level:

- **Limited Strength**
- **Limited Invulnerability**
- **Limited Earthquake-Stomp**

CHARACTERISTICS:

Combat	68	
Durability	65	
Leadership	5	
Strategy	8	
Willpower	27	

ELEVEN

I ATTEND AN ALIEN FUNERAL

We leave Dog-Gone to his job, with an advance payment of ten doggie treats—just to be safe. Then, we return to Earth via the Transporter.

I strap myself back into the pilot's seat and then K'ami hauls me sixty-three miles over land and sea without taking a single break. Talk about super fly! Although we cruise along at a good clip, I'm able to get K'ami to answer a few questions that are "bugging" me, so to speak.

First, I learn that all Skelton are shapeshifters. Their genetic makeup is so close to human biology that it's easy for them to morph into human form. However, transforming into a species with a totally different genetic profile is far more difficult. Most Skelton can only morph into one or two of these other species. Occasionally, a Skelton is born with the rare ability to transform into an unlimited number of forms, but they're taken from their families at birth to be trained as part of an elite killing force. According to K'ami, the name of this death squadron translates roughly into English as "Blood Bringers." That sure doesn't sound like a glee club.

Next, I learn that K'ami's particular shape, the fly, is a more well-traveled pest than I imagined. Flies first made their way to Skelton thousands of years ago as stowaways on scout ships that had visited Earth. Given K'ami's incredible strength while in fly form, they've clearly undergone some improvements since then. But otherwise, their contributions to Skelton society remained similar to their earthen cousins. On both planets, they typically end up beneath someone's shoe.

Finally, I dig in a little deeper about this Skelton Emperor. After all, if this guy had been searching for years to find the Orb of Oblivion I have a sinking feeling he's not just going to fold up the shop and give up on it. And surprise, surprise, the Emperor is not a very nice fellow. As Skelton history goes, he was originally eighteenth in line to ascend the throne, but he murdered his parents and siblings to claim the crown. Then, he proceeded to dispose of anyone he thought would oppose him, starting with their heads and working downwards. He rules his world with an iron fist and believes there can be only one master of the universe which, of course, he thinks ought to be him.

So, the two-part plan is simple.

First, we need to get the Orb of Oblivion. And second, we have to get it the heck off of Earth as quickly as possible. But I'll have to figure out *how* we'll actually be doing this later because we finally find her father's ship.

Or should I say, what's left of it.

For the last several miles we've been tracking debris from the crash, we saw bits and pieces here and there, but as we continued to follow the trail the debris was in much larger chunks. When we finally reach the heart of the scene, I feel K'ami shudder. I can't blame her. The magnitude of the destruction is unreal.

It appears that upon impact the ship burrowed itself deep into the face of the mountain, like some massive gravy divot in a heap of mashed potatoes. And just as the Worm described, the cockpit is chopped completely in half. You couldn't have split it more evenly if you had used a chainsaw.

We descend smoothly to the ground, landing smack in the middle of the compartment halves. As I unbuckle myself from the chair, K'ami changes back to her natural form. I see tears in her eyes, but she wipes them away quickly and regains her composure.

"We must find the Shield Box," she says.

I nod in agreement, but I'm not sure the worst is over. From what the Worm told me there's a body around here somewhere. Her father's body.

K'ami heads for one half of the cabin. I search the other.

I enter my side of the cockpit, and what I find astounds me. Every inch of the interior is lined with buttons, switches, and monitors of all different shapes and sizes. There are alien markings all over the place that I can't begin to understand. Towards the front of the ship's nose are a pilot's seat and some sort of helmet that's connected to the roof by a thin cable. I climb inside and take a seat in the chair. I can only imagine what TechnoRat would have thought about all this advanced technology. He'd probably memorize every detail and have it replicated within the hour. Boy, I miss that rat.

Without thinking it through, I reach up, grab the helmet suspended above me, and pull it onto my head.

There's a loud whirring noise and then all the monitors flick on. Red lights begin flashing all over the place. I have a sneaking suspicion I've done something incredibly stupid.

"Stop!" K'ami says, charging in and ripping the helmet off my head.

"Ouch," I say, rubbing my noggin. That'll leave a mark. "Sorry. I didn't know that was going to happen."

"Skelton warships operate by sentient control," she says. "Unless you are intending to send a personal invitation for the Emperor to join us, then I suggest you refrain from touching anything you do not fully understand. Is that clear?"

"Crystal," I answer, sliding off the chair. "Did you ... find anything?"

K'ami pauses for a moment and then looks down. "Yes."

I feel terrible for her. Although my family is gone, I didn't face the harsh reality of seeing them dead. In some strange way, I feel lucky. "Then we should give him a proper burial."

She nods.

I touch her shoulder and exit the cockpit. Immediately upon entering the other side, I find his body on the floor. He's lying face up, his eyes wide open and his arm propped up against the console like he's hoping someone will help him stand up. His clothes are covered in dried, black blood. It looks like he suffered a slow, agonizing death.

It's strange seeing the body of a man—an alien man—that I've never met before but know so much about. I step outside and find a piece of wreckage I can use as a shovel and begin digging a large hole. K'ami sits nearby, facing the mountains. I work slowly, giving her time with her thoughts. It takes a while to get the hole deep enough, but when I'm ready, we lift her father's body and place it inside.

K'ami bows her head and begins the ceremony. "It is tradition to return a noble Skelton man to the soil from which he came. Though we are far from home, my father, R'and Sollarr, gave proof that his was a soul that could not be confined to the soil of just one world. By his brave actions, this world, and all worlds known and unknown, owe him an eternal debt of gratitude. Father, I pledge that I will finish what you have started. Strength be with you on your eternal journey. Never show weakness."

As day turns to night, we bury him and mark his grave with a large rock.

When we're done, we rest under the starry sky.

"Those villains back at your headquarters mentioned they were looking for blueprints for a place called Lockdown," she says. "What is this Lockdown?"

"Oh, yeah," I say. I debate holding the secret back from her, but I have nothing to lose. At this point, it's us against the world. "I guess I should connect the dots for you. Lockdown is a super-maximum jail that holds our most dangerous Meta-powered criminals. We keep the designs for their containment cells on the Waystation."

"And how do you keep these prisoners confined?" she asks. "Won't they just break out? Like the Meta-Taker, how do you keep someone like him confined?"

So, I explain all the details of Lockdown and how Meta-Taker's cell works. She tells me there was once a prison moon orbiting Skelton where they sent all of their criminals. One day it was taken over by the prisoners, and all the guards were taken hostage. But instead of negotiating with the criminals to free the captives, the Emperor simply blew up the entire moon, loyal subjects and all. If that's a preview of things to come I'm far from comforted.

We sit in silence for a while.

Then, she says, "I thank you, Elliott Harkness. I thank you for everything. What do you say on your planet? Now we are BFs?"

"No, K'ami," I smile back. "It's called BFFs. And yes, I feel the same."

She brushes a strand of hair from her face. It's hard to tell from her alien complexion, but I think she's blushing.

"I guess we should try to find the Shield Box?" I say, quickly changing the subject. "The Worm says he didn't take it with him, so it must be around here somewhere."

"But where?" K'ami says.

"I don't know," I mutter. "Where would you be hiding if you were a Shield Box?"

"What did you say?" K'ami says, snapping to attention.

"Me?" I say. "Nothing. It's just an expression. You know, like, if you were a Shield Box, where would you be?"

"That's it!" K'ami says.

"That's what?"

"The Shield Box," she says. "It must not be *just* a box! It's alive!"

"What is it with you aliens and everything being alive?" I ask.

"You do not understand. On the red moon orbiting

Skelton lives a rare creature with remarkably dense skin. Every cycle, each of these creatures produces a gem that is highly valued on our planet. They bury themselves in the ground until they are ready to hatch. When they climb to the surface, they are harvested for their bounty. Then, they dig back underground and do it all over again."

"You mean, like an oyster?" I ask.

"Somewhat," she says, standing up. "They are large, simple organisms, impervious to any form of stimulation: electricity, fire, water... and, apparently, mind control. On our world, they are known as Sheelds."

I'm still confused.

"On your world," K'ami says, "they would be spelled S-H-E-E-L-D-S."

"Wait a minute," I say. "So, this S-H-I-E-L-D box we've been looking for is really a S-H-E-E-L-D box? Made of one of these alien thingies?"

"Yes," she says. "I am certain of it. It is here, but it has probably buried itself somewhere." K'ami drops to her hands and knees. "Help me look."

I join her and together we comb through every inch of rock surface surrounding the wreck but can't turn up anything. When we finish, we're completely spent. There's no sign of it anywhere on the mountain. It seems hopeless.

Then, my eyes drift back to the cockpit, and I have a flash of inspiration.

"Can these things dig through stuff harder than

rock?" I ask.

"I suppose so," K'ami says. "They operate purely on instinct. If they are frightened they would burrow through anything to reach safety."

"Right," I say. "The Worm told me he opened the box right when he got his grubby little hands on it."

"What are you thinking?" K'ami asks.

"Follow me." And I lead her back into the cockpit where we found her father.

We look down and, sure enough, there it is. A round hole cut straight through the metal of the ship and into the underlying rock. Right beneath the area her father was lying. We missed it.

K'ami kneels and starts scooping out metal shards and loose dirt. After a few minutes, she reaches in elbow-deep and pulls out a strange looking object that's slightly bigger than her palm. It's square and brown with a thick, rippled hide. If you weren't paying attention, you could easily mistake it for a leather box.

"That's a Sheeld?" I ask.

"Yes," she says. "This is a Sheeld."

"And it's alive?" I say.

K'ami tickles its underside and it opens up, revealing its fleshy, red interior. "Yes," she says. "Thankfully."

Then, I notice something strange stuck to the roof of its mouth. It looks like a small, blue disc.

It's pulsating.

"What's that?" I ask.

K'ami peers inside and her expression turns dark. She grabs the disc and crushes it in her hand.

"What is it?" I ask.

"A Skelton tracking device," K'ami says. "The Blood Bringers are coming."

Meta Profile

Name: K'ami Sollarr
Role: Hero   Status: Active

VITALS:

Race: Skelton
Real Name: K'ami Sollarr
Height: 5'0"
Weight: 100 lbs
Eye Color: Green
Hair Color: Black

META POWERS:

Class: Meta-morph
Power Level:

- **Considerable Shape-Shifting**
- **Considerable Flight, Strength and Speed in Fly form.**

CHARACTERISTICS:

Combat	75	
Durability	45	
Leadership	36	
Strategy	73	
Willpower	75	

TWELVE

I GO STRAIGHT TO THE SLAMMER

So, here's the situation. On one hand, we have a Meta 1 villain armed with the most powerful weapon in the universe trying to take over the world. On the other, we have a group of psycho extra-terrestrials speeding to Earth to destroy it. And somehow, stuck in the middle of it all, with the fate of the entire galaxy hanging in the balance, is an alien fly-girl and yours truly.

It certainly doesn't inspire confidence.

After much heated debate, K'ami and I finally agree that we can only deal with one twisted reality at a time. And since the Blood Bringers haven't even shown up yet, that leaves us with one viable option. So, we hightail it to Lockdown to take out the Worm.

The place looks exactly as I remember it.

By day, it's the most impressive prison facility in the world. By night, it's the keeper of nightmares.

As we approach, it's hard not to feel like ants marching towards a giant picnic basket. First, we're greeted by a fifty-foot perimeter wall that's smothered in razor wire and motion sensors. We follow the wall until we reach the front gates—massive structures forged from impenetrable tungsten steel. Guard towers are stationed every twenty feet outfitted with spotlights and ground-to-air machine guns. Inside the perimeter, the main building rises like a steel octopus, soaring hundreds of feet high with eight separate wings sprouting out like tentacles.

I'd visited Lockdown once before to drop off Dad's lunch after he accidentally left it at home. I was so freaked out I didn't go any farther than the front gates. This time I won't be so lucky.

Well before we even reach the gates, I notice a few things that set my spine tingling. First, there's no one around. Normally, the place is swarming with guards, maintenance workers, and hundreds of other people. But at the moment, the prison looks like a ghost town. And as disconcerting as that is, unfortunately, it's not the most disturbing thing. That distinction goes to the front gates themselves, which are currently sitting wide open. Typically, you'd need a Meta 4 assault to get inside the place. But today, the prison seems to be inviting us inside. And I'm pretty sure neither of us thinks that's a good thing.

I turn to K'ami, her face a picture of determination.

"What do you think?" I ask.

"The Orb is here," she says. "I sense it."

"Then it's up to us," I say. "Never show weakness."

"Never show weakness," she agrees.

We step through the gates and head for the main building. We move warily, our eyes darting about the compound for signs of life, but there's nothing.

A few minutes later we reach the main building. The doors are closed. A sign on the building reads:

Stop! Extreme Danger! Official Access Only.

I turn the door handle and push. The door swings open. It all seems way too easy.

It seems like a trap.

I can tell K'ami's thinking the same thing. But, what other choice do we have? She nods and we go inside.

The hallway is dark and narrow. Small sconces line the walls, providing enough light to see only a few feet in front of us before we are swallowed into the darkness. The hum from the air conditioning system provides a steady stream of white noise, accompanied by freezing cold air. K'ami shivers and crosses her arms.

"What now?" I ask.

"Now," she says, "we go forward."

On our left, we pass a doorway to the main control room. Through a skinny window we see several computer stations and monitoring kiosks. All of them are unmanned.

The hallway veers left before presenting another set of doors. A sign above reads:

Meta Wing M: Meta-morphs. Official Access Only.

A half-smashed security interface is dangling from the wall, and when I push on the doors, they open without triggering an alarm.

We step inside.

The light is somewhat brighter here, but it's still kind of dim. It's clear we've entered another long and narrow corridor, only this one is flanked by dozens of cells. Some of the cell doors have windows and others don't. Cell numbers are displayed prominently above each door and a small sign hangs to the right of each doorway.

We move down the hall.

The cells seem to be grouped by Meta class, starting with the Meta 1's. All the cells are closed, and I can see through the doors with windows that their respective residents are still locked up inside.

I read the signs as we move past. It's like a "Who's Who" of the evil and notorious:

Cell# M3: Pliable Pete – Meta 1. Can contort body into various shapes. Beware: may disguise self as food tray or utensil to procure exit.

Cell# M5: Amphibia – Meta 1. Can transform into water form. Beware: may float upside down to fake own death.

Cell# M7: Double Trouble – Meta 1. Can split into two identical beings. Beware: may instigate a fight with self to cause false distraction.

We then hit the Meta 2 section. The precaution language gets more serious.

Cell# M11: Pois-Anne – Meta 2. Poison kiss can paralyze. Warning: may fake need for mouth to mouth resuscitation.

Cell# M13: Mud Monster – Meta 2: Body is made of chemically altered mud. Warning: may try to sneak parts of body out as mud stains on clothing or bottom of shoes.

Cell# M17: The Phantom Raider – Meta 2: Can turn invisible. Warning: may appear not to be in cell but trust us—he's in there.

It's too quiet. I can sense that something is just waiting to trip us up. Then we reach the Meta 3 section, and my heart skips a beat.

Every cell door is busted open.

Every. Freaking. One.

I quickly skim the signs:

Cell# M21: Flameout – Meta 3: Can transform into a being of pure fire. Danger: do not enter under any circumstances! No smoking allowed!

Cell# M23: Black Cloud – Meta 3: Can transform into gaseous clouds emitting toxic fumes. Danger: do not enter under any circumstances! Do not break door seal!

Cell# M25: Berserker – Meta 3: Can transform into a giant beast of inhuman strength. Danger: do not enter under any circumstances! Beware of pet dander!

When we reach cell M27 all the hairs on my neck stand on end.

Cell #M27: Meta-Taker – Meta 3: Can duplicate the

powers of any Meta. Danger: do not enter under any circumstances! Do not leave unmonitored!

I'm instantly transported back to my face-to-face encounter with Meta-Taker. I can see his chalky white skin. Smell his hot, rotten breath.

I can't believe it. The Worm did it! He actually freed the most dangerous Metas on the planet. And then I realize, we're only in the Meta-morph wing. What about all the Meta 3 Psychics? Or the Meta 3 Energy Manipulators? Or...

I grab K'ami's arm. "We can't win this! We've got to get out of here!"

K'ami slaps me hard across the face. Boy, does she love doing that.

"Elliott Harkness," she says. "You are the savior of the universe and your planet's only hope. Pull yourself together."

I feel ashamed. She's right. I have to pull myself together. My whole life I've been dreaming of being a Meta. Now, without my family here, it's all up to me. I can't let them down. Even if I die, I'm going to make them proud. I start running her words through my mind over and over again. *Never show weakness. Never show weakness. Never show weakness.*

K'ami points to the end of the hallway at yet another set of double doors. "The Orb of Oblivion is through there."

We approach slowly. Both of us know that

whatever's standing behind these doors may be the last thing we ever see.

I look at K'ami and she nods. I take a deep breath.

Never show weakness.

Then, I push the doors open.

Meta Profile

Name: Dog-Gone
Role: Hero   Status: Active

VITALS:

Breed: German Shepherd
Real Name: Dog-Gone
Height: 2'1" (at shoulder)
Weight: 85 lbs
Eye Color: Dark Brown
Hair Color: Brown/Black

META POWERS:

Class: Meta-morph
Power Level: ■■ ■

- **Considerable Invisibility**
- **Can turn all or part of body invisible**

CHARACTERISTICS:

Combat	45
Durability	16
Leadership	10
Strategy	12
Willpower	56

THIRTEEN

I BATTLE A SLIMY WORM TO THE DEATH

"**C**ome on out," the Worm squeals. "Welcome to your funeral."

The doors let out to a massive courtyard that's roughly the size of two football fields and open to the night sky. It has an uneven octagonal shape formed by the walls of the eight building wings. Fittingly, it feels like we're stepping into the Roman Colosseum.

The Worm stands proudly in the center, surrounded by the greatest army of Meta 3 villains ever assembled.

"Oh, man," I whisper to K'ami. "This is exactly what I was afraid of. They're all here."

"Who are they?" she whispers back.

"Only the most dangerous supervillains on the

planet," I whisper. "Strongmen, Speedsters, Psychics, Magicians, Flyers, Energy Manipulators, Intellects, and last, but not least, Meta-morphs. There must be over fifty of them."

With all of their various sizes, shapes, and colors, it's like staring into a kaleidoscope of terror. I quickly pinpoint Meta-Taker, who is standing to the Worm's left.

My whole body is trembling. Beads of sweat trickle down my temples. I take a deep breath and then K'ami and I enter the arena, stopping twenty yards from the Worm.

I scan the villains. "Look at their faces, they're all blank. The Worm and the Orb are controlling them."

Out of the corner of my eye, I catch a flash of movement in the back of the motionless crowd. It's Makeshift. He's rocking back and forth like he's nervous.

Before we left the Meta-morph wing, I stuffed the Sheeld into my front pants pocket. It's bulging slightly so I try to cover it with my hand as naturally as possible.

This is really it. The final showdown. I have no clue how this is going to go down. I don't know if we should try to negotiate or just attack.

But apparently, K'ami has her own ideas.

"The power of the Orb is wasted on you," she says and spits in the Worm's general direction.

The Worm sneers. "Oh, I've been waiting for you, K'ami Sollarr," he says, gripping the Orb of Oblivion. "It appears we have a lot in common, don't we? Probably more than you care to admit. Tell me, did you clue in your little friend about our conversations?"

"What?" I say, turning to K'ami. "What conversations?"

"Do not listen to him," she says. But she won't look at me.

"I see you have not," the Worm says. "Well, your partner and I have become quite close over the past few days. Both of us trying to use the Orb to overpower one another. But as they say on our world, possession is nine-tenths of the law. My claim is much, much stronger. However, our little mind chats helped me learn that you had defeated the morons I sent to the Waystation. I'd given them the simple task of retrieving the blueprints so I could free my friends here, but I never really expected them to succeed. Turns out, I didn't need them anyway." Then he looks directly at K'ami, "Thanks to you."

"Be silent," K'ami whispers.

"Don't you think the boy deserves to know the truth?" the Worm asks.

"What's he talking about?" I demand. "What's going on?"

"What's going on," the Worm says, "is that your friend here told me how to free this guy." The Worm puts his hand on Meta-Taker's shoulder. "Once she gave me all the details about his cell, I was able to take him out of suspended animation. All I needed to do was get in through the air vent. It took me about fifteen minutes. Of course, it took him a little longer to regain consciousness. And boy was he peeved when he woke up! But all I needed," he says petting the Orb, "was a little mind control magic to get him back in line."

"You told him about Meta-Taker's cell?" I yell at K'ami.

"No!" she says defiantly. "He controlled me. He made me ask you, and then he stole it from my mind."

"And once I had Meta-Taker," the Worm continues, "he was like a Swiss Army Knife to help free the Intellects. Then, I used *their* brainpower to bust out the rest."

My mind races back to everything K'ami and I have gone through. What other secrets did she reveal? My weird powers? The Sheeld? I feel more confused than ever. Can I still trust her? Now I don't know what to do.

"You do not understand the scope of the power you possess," K'ami says. "The Orb will destroy you."

"Oh, trust me," the Worm laughs. "There's nothing overly complex here. It's quite simple actually. You see, whatever I want, I get. Like your death for instance."

The Worm clutches the Orb with both hands.

"Wait!" I yell, stepping in front of K'ami. "If you're going to kill her, first you've got to go through me."

"Elliott, no!" K'ami orders.

"Is this a joke?" the Worm says, laughing out loud. "So, what are you saying?"

"I'm saying that I challenge you to a battle to the

death. You think you were ignored? You think you were nothing? Imagine growing up powerless in a family of superheroes. Do you think anyone really pays attention to you? Do you think anyone really cares what your grades are, or if you have friends, or... if it's your freaking birthday?"

The Worm just stares at me.

"Well, I can tell you they don't. They tell you you're part of the family—part of the team. But you know in your heart of hearts that they're just humoring you—that they're trying not to hurt your feelings because your pitiful life isn't where all the glory is. So, I know *exactly* how you feel. And, you know what? I'm tired of it. That's not how I'm going to go down!"

"Fine," the Worm says. "Do you want me to kill you with Black Cloud or someone else?"

"No," I say. "I want *you* to do it. You may be the master of a Meta 3 army, but behind those blank stares, I bet none of them have an ounce of respect for you. I mean, who can respect a Meta 1 that can't even kill a twelve-year-old Zero?"

The Worm turns to his army. They stand motionless, but then Makeshift leans out and shrugs his shoulders.

"Very well," the Worm says. "As you wish. Makeshift, keep an eye on the girl."

"No Orb," I say. "You do it on your own."

"I won't need the Orb, boy," he says, confidently.

We square off. I quickly recall everything I can about

his Meta profile. Based on his fighting tendencies, his favorite move is to burrow underground and re-emerge behind his victim for a sneak attack. And he'll do it again and again until he wins. I feel pretty confident I've got his number.

His problem is that he doesn't have mine.

I crouch into the low frontal karate stance Shadow Hawk taught me, maintaining my balance to easily shift from defense to offense without losing energy.

I wait for him to strike first.

"What are you standing around for?" I say. "Are you afraid of me?"

"Hardly," he sneers.

Then, as expected, he dives to go underground. Unfortunately, his head smashes hard on the surface and his body topples over.

"Take that!" I say and deliver a blow to his solar plexus. Then, just as Shadow Hawk taught me, I get out.

The Worm scrambles to his feet, shaken and wheezing. "Lucky," he says. "Must be special soil here." His face is bright red. He turns to see if his army is still watching. They are. "Now you've made me angry!" This time he tries the same move, but to his left. He slams into the ground again and flips onto his back. I move in and kick him in the ribs.

He coughs violently and pulls himself up on one knee. He's dizzy. Disoriented. He staggers to his feet. "My powers? What are you doing to me?"

"Oh," I say, "I'm simply doing the same thing to your powers that you did to my family. I'm getting rid of them!" Then, I sock him square in the jaw. The Worm falls backward as several of his teeth go flying.

I bend over in pain. My hand is on fire. It feels like it's broken.

"Elliott!" K'ami yells.

I spin to find the Worm lying flat on his back, both of his hands on the Orb.

"You tricked me somehow! But now your little game is over," the Worm says, holding the Orb up into the air.

Suddenly, my head starts throbbing. It feels like my brain is being squeezed to a pulp. I hear his voice trying to enter my mind.

I try to resist it, to push it back out, but the force is overwhelming. One thought starts to build up inside of me—one word that will release all of the pressure. I build it up and build it up. And then, I release it like a raging volcano.

OUT!

The Worm screams. It's a terrible, high-pitched scream. Then his eyes go white, and he flops over like a limp noodle.

I look over at K'ami. She's also holding her head. Somehow, probably through her psychic link with the Orb, my thoughts impacted her also.

"W-What did you do to him?" Makeshift asks.

"Stay back!" I warn. "Or I'll do the same to you!"

Then, I look at the Worm's body. K'ami is huddled over him.

"K'ami, wait! What are you doing? I have the Sheeld."

"I'm sorry, Elliott," she says. And then she turns towards me, the Orb of Oblivion in her bare hands.

KABOOM!

There's a thundering pop from above, and I cover my ears to dull the sound. Then, it gets dark, like some giant planet is blocking the moonlight.

Looking up, I see an enormous spaceship hovering overhead and I realize things just went from bad to worse.

The Blood Bringers have arrived.

Meta Profile

Name: Makeshift
Role: Villain   Status: Active

VITALS:

Race: Human
Real Name: Irwin Cooper
Height: 5'2"
Weight: 170 lbs
Eye Color: Green
Hair Color: Black

META POWERS:

Class: Energy Manipulator
Power Level:
- Limited Space Manipulation
- Can teleport individuals and larger groups

CHARACTERISTICS:

Combat	15	
Durability	19	
Leadership	15	
Strategy	17	
Willpower	20	

FOURTEEN

I TAKE CONTROL OF ABSOLUTELY EVERYTHING

So much is happening it's impossible to keep track. K'ami is holding the Orb of Oblivion, a spaceship chockfull of blood-thirsty aliens is floating over our heads, the Worm is an unconscious vegetable, and all the Meta 3 villains are slowly regaining their wits.

And, oh yeah, apparently I'm the only sane person in the entire zip code.

I don't even know where to begin.

"W-What is that thing?" Makeshift asks, looking up.

"Oh, that?" I say. "That's some really, really bad news."

It's time to focus. The one thing all this craziness has in common is the Orb. I have to get it out of K'ami's hands and safely into the Sheeld. Then, we've got to get out of here before the Blood Bringers get their paws on it. I pull out the Sheeld and rub its underside. It opens up like a Hungry Hungry Hippo.

"Quick, K'ami!" I yell. Drop the Orb into the clammy thing!"

But she doesn't respond. It's like she's frozen in a block of ice. Her eyes are closed. Her head tilted towards the sky. "Such power," she mutters in a kind of daze. "I never imagined such power."

"K'ami! Can you hear me? Let! Go! Of! The! Orb!"

She turns and opens her eyes. Her pupils are dancing like flames. "No, Elliott Harkness," she says. "This is our only chance."

"Our only chance?" I say. "For what?"

"For survival," she says. "That is a Blood Bringer warship. No one ever escapes the Blood Bringers alive."

Just then, all sorts of noises erupt from high above. I look up to see a giant hole opening on the side of the warship. The next thing I know, dozens of smaller ships come pouring out and start flying towards us. There's no time to lose. Things are about to go freaking nuts.

"K'ami!" I order. "Put the Orb in the Sheeld!"

But it's too late. Within seconds, the smaller ships hit the ground, dumping waves of Blood Bringer soldiers into the courtyard. The aliens form a giant circle around us, including the Meta villains, many of whom have now fully recovered from the Worm's mind control and are completely confused by what's happening.

I take in our new situation. As far as my limited knowledge of alien warrior species goes, The Blood Bringers are an impressive group. Each of them is Sumo-sized and covered head-to-toe in some sort of leathery brown armor, the texture of which seems strangely familiar. They are carrying long, spear-like weapons with huge blades fixed to the ends. It seems like there are hundreds of them. I try to take a quick count but can't keep up. And it doesn't really matter anyway. We're totally outnumbered.

Makeshift drops into the fetal position and starts whimpering.

Suddenly, a group of Blood Bringers part and the biggest, baddest one I've seen yet steps forward. He's also outfitted in head-to-toe armor, but wears a long, gold cape and carries the largest weapon of the bunch. He stops about thirty yards from us, his piercing green eyes scanning us from beneath his helmet. Could this be the Emperor?

"Welcome to Earth, G'rarr Mongrell, High Commander of the Blood Bringers," K'ami says with a respectful nod. "I see our esteemed Emperor did not wish to get his hands dirty."

"K'ami Sollarr," the High Commander says, "Does your insolence know no bounds? Traitors are not permitted to use the name of the Emperor, the Lord of the Universe, in vain. Besides, you know all too well that killing is the birthright of the Blood Bringer army."

"I do know this," she says. "Just as you know that I am in possession of the Orb of Oblivion, the very object I am certain you are here to retrieve. Fortunately, I am feeling generous. I will give you one chance to call off your hounds and I shall consider sparing your life. If you choose otherwise, I regret to inform you that you, and all of your beasts, will die a painful, honorless death."

The High Commander delivers a deep, hearty laugh that rattles my bones. "Little girl," he says. "Do you forget to whom you are speaking? I am the High Commander of the Blood Bringers. I am the Destroyer of Worlds. I am the Harbinger of Death. Hand over the Orb immediately and I promise your ending will be a swift one. I cannot, however, promise the same for your lowly, earth-dwelling allies."

I hear growling and other bodily noises behind me. The Meta villains are getting restless.

But K'ami doesn't move. Instead, she gives a wry smile. "I know exactly to whom I speak, High Commander. Your offer is quite fair, but I fear you have chosen unwisely. Prepare to die."

The Orb begins to pulsate.

But nothing happens.

K'ami looks at the Orb, and then back to the High Commander. But he's just standing there, watching her. What's going on? Why didn't the Orb do its thing?

Then the giant takes a step forward. "Foolish girl,"

he says. "Did you not think we would prepare properly for a battle with the Orb of Oblivion? Your father was a traitor, but his research for the Emperor was quite thorough. That is why our armor is made entirely from Sheelds."

K'ami gives a look of surprise.

And before I can move, the High Commander points his weapon and fires a laser blast right through her.

K'ami falls backward.

I catch her before she hits the ground.

"Kill them!" the High Commander orders. "Kill them all!"

Suddenly, there's a loud roar and a white blur appears, delivering a powerful right hook to the High Commander's face. It's Meta-Taker!

There is a moment of stunned silence. And then a massive brawl erupts between the Meta villains and Blood Bringers.

I cradle K'ami in my arms. She's been shot clean through the chest. She's struggling to breathe, her whole body is shaking. Blackish blood is flowing everywhere.

"K'ami," I plead. "K'ami? Can you hear me?"

"E-Elliott," she says, coughing several times. "I-I am sorry. I-I thought with the Orb I could... save us. B-but I failed."

Tears stream down my cheeks. "K'ami, hang on. You're not going to die. You can't die."

She smiles feebly and squeezes my hand. "No, it is

too late... for me."

"No, we'll find a way out of this," I cry. "I promise. We always do."

"No, Elliott," she says. "P-Please, take the Orb in the Sheeld and finish what my father started. W-We will see each other again... someday. Thanks for being my good friend. M-My... B... FF... N-Never... show...weak ..."

And then, her green eyes roll back in her head.

She's gone.

I sit for a moment, holding her lifeless body in my arms.

And then, I yell.

I yell with grief.

I yell in anger.

I look up. A massive battle rages around us, but everything seems like it's moving in slow motion. The fighting has mushroomed from the courtyard to inside the buildings and even up to the sky. The Meta 3 villains are fighting for their lives. I spot the High Commander who is now mired in combat with Meta-Taker and several other villains at once.

It feels like I'm in a strange dream. A dream I can't escape from. And then, I hear someone calling me. It's faint at first, but then grows stronger and stronger.

Has everyone forgotten about it?

It's the one behind all of this death. All of this destruction. I look down at K'ami's body and there it sits, resting innocently in her hands.

The Orb of Oblivion.

I know I should put it in the Sheeld. Just lock it in the Sheeld and make a run for it. Run to safety, and then figure out what to do next.

But I'm tired of running.

I'm tired of playing it safe. I'm tired of being a victim.

I want to take control.

I know what I need to do.

I reach down and grab the Orb.

And everything shifts.

I feel a sudden, immense surge of power flowing through me. My body feels electric. I feel lighter. Like every molecule of my being is floating on air. It feels like I can do anything.

"And now you can," a strange voice says. *"Now you can be the greatest Meta that ever walked the planet. Isn't that what you always wanted?"*

Where is that voice coming from? It sounds so familiar. It sounds like... me?

"That's because it is you, Elliott," it says. *"You have always had the power inside of you. You just never knew how to access it."*

"Who are you?" I say.

"I'm you," it says. *"I'm a better version of you. I'm the person you have always wanted to be. Popular. Powerful. Proud. And now, you can have everything you've always wanted. Now it's all within your reach. Fame. Friends. Fans."*

"No," I say. "You're not me. I know who you are. I

know what you are."

"*Elliott,*" it says quickly. "*Don't be hasty. I understand it may take a while to adjust to your newfound powers. But if you'll just trust—*"

"No," I say. "I won't let you leech off me. I'm going to be in control."

"*Elliott,*" it says, its voice sounding more desperate. "*Just give me a chance. Give us a—*"

"I! SAID! NO!"

I push back with all of my will. I push back with all of my soul. I push back like my life depends on it.

And then, I feel the Orb flinch. Bend. Scream.

I surround it with my will. I overpower it.

I feel it succumb.

And then, I master it.

The Orb of Oblivion is now under my control.

I open my eyes.

The battle is still going strong. It's clear the Blood Bringers are well trained and far more organized than I imagined. They've pressed the Meta villains into a corner. The Metas are fighting individual battles. The Metas are losing.

I realize what I need to do. Then, I feel a tap on my shoulder. Makeshift is standing behind me. I make a fist.

"Wait!" Makeshift says quickly. "I think I can help you. See, your family isn't really dead."

"What?" I say. "What are you talking about?"

"Well," the little man continues, "See, my powers are

kind of strange. I call myself Makeshift because I can 'make' things 'shift.' Get it? You know, like teleport. So, things don't die when I send them away. I only shift them into a pocket dimension. I call it 'Exile.' It's an alternate universe that's like Earth, but it's not. Anyway, I can try to bring them back. If you want me to?"

I grab him by the shoulders. "Yes!" I say. "Yes! Do it now!"

"Well, okay," Makeshift says. I watch as he stretches out his hands, and a familiar yellow circle appears. It expands like a giant rubber band, moving faster and faster, and then, with a loud WHOOSH, it disappears. In its place, stand seven surprised figures.

My family!

They're all there: Mom, Dad, Grace, Shadow Hawk, Master Mime, Blue Bolt, and TechnocRat. The Freedom Force is back!

I run into Mom's arms.

"Elliott," Mom says. "Where have you been?"

But I'm so overwhelmed, I can't answer. It feels so great to have them back.

"Um, forget about him," Grace says. "What the heck's going on out there?"

They turn towards the war, and their eyes pop out of their sockets.

"Holy guacamole," TechnocRat whispers.

"There's no time for details," I say. "We need to help the bad guys beat the aliens. All of you know how to lead a team into battle. Mom, you take the Psychics. Dad, you've got the Strongmen. Grace, take the Flyers. Shadow Hawk, the Energy Manipulators. TechnocRat's got the Intellects, Master Mime the Magicians, and Blue Bolt the Speedsters. I'll take the Meta-morphs. Now let's go!"

I start into the fray, but the Freedom Force is glued to their spots.

"I said, let's go!"

"But, Elliott," Dad says, "these guys are dangerous. What makes you think they'll listen to us?"

"You're right," I say, flashing the Orb. "They won't listen to you. But I know they'll listen to me."

I focus on the Orb and it starts to pulsate. I use the Orb's power to access my knowledge of each and every Meta profile and then push this knowledge out, planting this information into the minds of each villain. Then, I command them to stop fighting independently and to reorganize into their respective Meta power classifications. Suddenly, the villains start to re-form, fighting no longer as individuals, but as teams.

"There, now they're ready for you." I turn to the Freedom Force, but they're just standing there with their jaws hanging open.

"Oh, and see that big one over there?" I say, pointing to the High Commander.

They nod.

"He's mine. Got it?"

They nod again.

"Okay then," I say. "Let's go!"

"Well, you heard the man," Dad says. "Freedom Force—it's Fight Time!"

I lead the way, and for the first time in my life, they follow *me* into battle.

Meta Profile

Name: High Commander
Role: Villain   Status: Active

VITALS:

Race: Skelton
Real Name: G'rarr Mongrell
Height: 6'9"
Weight: 320 lbs
Eye Color: Green
Hair Color: Bald

META POWERS:

Class: Meta-morph
Power Level: ▮▮▮

- **Extreme Shape-Shifting—can assume endless forms**
- **Extreme Flight, Strength, and Speed depending upon form taken**

CHARACTERISTICS:

Combat	100	▬▬▬
Durability	100	▬▬▬
Leadership	100	▬▬▬
Strategy	100	▬▬▬
Willpower	100	▬▬▬

FIFTEEN

I DOOM THE ENTIRE FREAKING UNIVERSE

With the help of the Freedom Force, the tide turns quickly.

Dad and Blue Bolt join the Strongmen and Speedsters together and strike at the heart of the Blood Bringer army. Mom and Shadow Hawk spread out the Psychics and Energy Manipulators and start picking off victims one by one. Grace takes her Flyers airborne to stop the flow of incoming spaceships while Master Mime and his Magicians provide ground cover. TechnocRat collects his Intellects and disappears inside the prison for reasons I can't begin to fathom.

It's an amazing battle. But I don't have time to sit around gawking.

I have to save the world.

My Meta-morphs are fighting on the far side of the courtyard, and I'm struggling to make my way over without getting dismembered, or worse, losing hold of all the Meta villains under my control. I dodge the metal leg of Retractable Man, vault over Tumbler, and use Ripcord as a slingshot. After avoiding a barrage of crossfire, I finally make it.

The Meta-morphs are more than holding their own. Flameout has a group of Blood Bringers pinned behind a giant wall of fire. Black Cloud is storming over packs of victims. The Berserker is doing his best impression of King Kong, swatting any ships that manage to break through the blockade that Grace and the Flyers have setup. But the Meta-morph I need is engaged in an epic battle with the High Commander.

Meta-Taker.

To my surprise, the High Commander is matching him blow for blow. Clearly, the High Commander is no ordinary Skelton. And if he can hang with a powerhouse like Meta-Taker, then just how strong is this guy?

I decide to find out.

I tap into the Orb and send a command into Meta-Taker's brain. *Power up! Power up until you can't power up anymore!*

Meta-Taker stops and then stretches out his arms. I feel a strange sensation radiating from his mind. Then, the orange energy from his eyes spills out in every direction. It's as if his whole being is unlocking—like every cell in his body is opening up—drawing in all of the Meta powers around him. Through his mind, I can feel the energy building up in his veins. It feels incredible. It feels like he's on a completely different level.

It feels like he's at Meta 4!

Now, let's see what this bad boy can do.

I send the command to attack and Meta-Taker charges the High Commander at ridiculous speed, plowing the alien into the building behind him with such force the entire structure collapses on top of them. Then Meta-Taker emerges from the rubble and bombards the High Commander with a flurry of pulsar beams, concussion blasts, and lightning strikes, resulting in a gigantic explosion that sends debris flying everywhere.

I order Meta-Taker to pull back. The air is so thick with smoke it's impossible to see anything. For any normal foe, that probably would be the end of the story, but I know the High Commander isn't any normal foe.

That's when I feel the ground trembling beneath my feet. And then, as the smoke starts to clear, I see humungous chunks of concrete being tossed aside like throw pillows. The next thing I know, something very large shoots up into the air and lands with an earth-shattering thud. But, to my surprise, that "something" isn't the High Commander at all.

The creature stands over two stories tall. At first, it appears almost ape-like, but with deep, red eyes and matted green fur covering every inch of its immense, muscled body. It pounds its chest and lets out a deafening roar from between razor-sharp teeth. And then, out of nowhere, it unfolds a giant pair of bat-like wings and makes an unbelievable fifty-foot leap straight into the chest of Meta-Taker. Meta-Taker crashes through a wall.

Now I can see why the Blood Bringers are an unstoppable killing force. And from what K'ami told me, I'm guessing this is just one of the horrific forms the High Commander can adopt. Even at Meta 4, I can't imagine how Meta-Taker will possibly win this fight.

But Meta-Taker brushes himself off and squares up to his enemy. Then, the villain activates his orange flames again, reaching out to draw in even more Meta power. What is he doing? Is he trying to reach Meta 5?

The creature doesn't wait to find out. Instead, it extends its giant wings and takes to the air again.

Before Meta-Taker can strike, his body starts to swell, his muscles inflating to grotesque proportions. It looks like he may have drawn in too much power. More power than he can possibly contain.

I frantically try to reverse my instructions. *Power down! Power down!* But it's too late. Meta-Taker is frozen in place. He looks like a giant balloon.

Then, the creature drops in front of Meta-Taker, opens its jaws, and snaps down.

The explosion is massive.

I'm instantly blown off my feet. All I can think about

is holding on to the Orb. My body smashes into something hard and unforgiving, knocking the wind out of me.

I find myself lying on the ground, covered in rubble. I'm still alive, except, in addition to a broken hand, I now have incredibly sore ribs. I draw the Orb close to my chest. Somehow, I managed to hang on to it.

The explosion was so blinding it takes a few seconds for my eyes to readjust. But when they do, I can't believe what I'm seeing. Everything within a twenty-yard radius of Meta-Taker has been completely vaporized. Flameout. Black Cloud. The Berserker. Everything and everyone is gone. Except for—

"No more games, earthling," the High Commander says. "Give me the Orb and I will let the girl live." The High Commander stands no more than ten feet away. Somehow he survived the blast and is now back to his original form. I notice immediately that most of his armor is shredded. And more importantly, he's missing his helmet. He must have ditched it when he turned into that monster. That means I can use the Orb on him! But then I realize what he said, and who he's holding.

Grace is hanging face-up beneath one of his massive arms. His other hand is wrapped firmly around her neck. Meta-Taker's blast must have been so powerful that it knocked Grace right out of the sky. And the High Commander is gripping her so tightly she's struggling to breathe. The terror in her eyes says all I need to know. I can't risk using the Orb on him when simply closing his hand would instantly crush her throat.

But I just can't turn over the Orb either.

"If I give you the Orb, you'll kill us all," I say.

"Perhaps," he says. "But I was not sent to your world to destroy it. My mission was to achieve two objectives. I have accomplished the first, and I will not leave until I complete the second."

My blood starts boiling. "So, I take it murdering a girl was one of your objectives."

"K'ami Sollarr was a traitor," he says. "She killed five guards during her escape. She was a dangerous criminal."

"She was my friend!" I shout. "My best friend! Better than you, or your stinking Emperor, or your whole freaking planet!"

He smiles. It's strange to see his face so clearly. He looks just like K'ami's father, but with a squarer jaw and a large diagonal scar that runs from his forehead, across his left eye, and down his cheek. "My hand is getting tired," he says. "So, I suggest we discuss my original bargain. Give me the Orb and I will give you the girl."

By now, I realize all the fighting has stopped. Everyone is watching us, waiting for my response. The fate of the whole universe is hanging on my reply.

Out of the corner of my eye, I catch the worried looks of my parents. I need more time to think, but I don't have it. I need to stall.

"What assurances will you offer me?" I ask.

"I offer you my word," The High Commander says. "On my world, our word is our currency. I give you my word that if you give me the Orb of Oblivion, I will leave you in peace."

If I've learned anything in this mess it's two things. One, my track record trusting Skelton is not a good one. Two, if I don't give him the Orb then Grace is a goner. I don't have time to think this through. But then, I realize I'm not alone in this either.

I reach out in my mind.

"Orb?" I say. "Who is your one true master?"

"You, Elliott Harkness," the Orb answers. "You are my one true master."

"I'm glad to hear that," I say. "Once, a very good friend told me a story about how you convinced a star to explode. Was that story true?"

"Yes," the Orb says. "I was weak—waning and insignificant. I convinced the star to give up its life for me so that I could become significant again."

"Yes," I say. "And you did become significant again. Very significant. That was selfless of the star, wasn't it? Sacrificing its life for such a great cause."

"Yes," the Orb says. "Yes, it was."

"What have you decided, earthling?" the High Commander demands.

I look at Grace's terrified face. "Order your men back to your warship. All of them. Now."

"Very well," the High Commander says, raising an

eyebrow. "Pull back! All of you!"

We watch as the Blood Bringers follow his orders, filing back into their spaceships and heading up to the larger warship in the sky. Only the High Commander and one ship remain.

"Well?" the High Commander asks. "Will you complete the bargain and grant me safe passage to my ship?"

"First," I say, "release the girl."

The High Commander laughs. "Do you take me for a fool? As soon as I give you the girl you will attack me with the Orb. Instead, we will do the exchange simultaneously. And then, you will allow me to go back to my ship unharmed. Agreed?"

I hesitate for a moment. What choice do I have?

"I'll give you safe passage to your ship. When you reach your ship, you'll turn around immediately and head back to your planet. You'll leave mine unharmed. Deal?"

"Agreed," he says.

"On the count of three then. One... two... three..."

He throws Grace to me, and I flip him the Orb.

Grace crumples in my arms. "Thank you," she says crying. "Thank you, Elliott."

The High Commander catches the Orb in his bare hands. "The Orb of Oblivion," he whispers.

"Now, go!" I command. "And never return!"

The High Commander looks up like he's startled. Like he forgot I'm even here. "Yes, I gave you my word."

"As did I," I respond. I throw him the Sheeld Box.

He catches it and hesitates before putting the Orb inside. Then, he snaps it shut.

The High Commander nods and then returns to his spaceship. We watch it lift off and then reconnect with the warship above.

Makeshift peers around a corner, "Um, did you just doom all of humanity?"

"Possibly," I say. "But I don't think so."

Just then, TechnocRat comes scampering out of Lockdown. "Elliott, the Intellects and I fixed all the Meta 3 cells. I thought I should put that brainpower to good use. Now we need to get these villains locked up again. I already secured my bunch."

So that's where he went! Man, I love that rat.

I look up at the sky. The warship starts turning away from Earth. I still don't trust that some giant laser beam isn't going to come firing down on us, blasting us all to smithereens.

"Dad," I say. "Can you and the Freedom Force make sure you get all these villains back in their cells? And I suggest you do it as quickly as possible."

"Sure, Elliott," Dad says. "Team, let's move!" Then, he stops and looks at Makeshift. "What about this guy?"

"He's okay. Leave him with me."

Makeshift and I stand for a while, watching the warship maneuver.

"Wait a minute," Makeshift says. "Are you still

controlling the Meta 3's?"

"Yep," I say.

"But you're not holding the Orb," Makeshift says.

"Nope. I realized I didn't have to."

Just then, the ship kicks on its jets and enters hyper-speed, disappearing into the night sky. The High Commander kept his word and so did I. I gave him safe passage back to his ship, but our bargain is over now.

I promised K'ami I would finish what her father started. Which means I can't let the Emperor get his hands on the Orb of Oblivion.

I close my eyes and reach out to the orb. I can still feel our connection.

"Orb," I say. "It's time."

"Yes," the Orb says. "I am ready."

"Thank you," I say. "You will shine as the brightest star in the universe for all eternity."

"Never show weakness," the Orb says.

"Yes," I say. "Never show weakness."

And then, somewhere in the distant galaxy, the Orb of Oblivion sacrifices its life and a Blood Bringer warship explodes into a brilliant flash of nothingness.

Meta Profile

Name: Master Mime
Role: Hero   Status: Active

VITALS:

Race: Human
Real Name: Daniel Kim
Height: 5'10"
Weight: 181 lbs
Eye Color: Brown
Hair Color: Black

META POWERS:

Class: Magic
Power Level:

- Extreme Energy Manipulation Powered by a Mystical Amulet
- Creates Hard Light Energy Constructs

CHARACTERISTICS:

Combat	86	
Durability	81	
Leadership	71	
Strategy	77	
Willpower	82	

EPILOGUE

THREE VERY LONG MONTHS LATER...

I hop into the command chair and set the Meta Monitor on manual control. It's Friday night, the busiest night of the week, and I'm hoping to get lucky. It's been months since I could use my right hand, but now that my cast is off, I'm itching for some action.

I brought popcorn with me, so I set the cameras to cycle through The Waystation to spot any furry predators. Not that I can find Dog-Gone anyway—especially if he's in stealth mode. Note to self: get TechnocRat to install heat-seeking cameras.

Dad is in the lab, analyzing my powers. Ever since Lockdown, he and TechnocRat have run me through a whole battery of tests. Apparently, my powers are similar to only one other Meta they've seen before. Meta-Taker.

They realized in testing me that perhaps they misclassified him. Our powers are so unique, they don't fit within any of the eight standard Meta classifications. So, they created a new one.

They're calling it Meta Manipulation.

We're still trying to make sense of it, but while Meta-Taker could absorb and use the powers of others, I can manipulate and even nullify the Meta powers of others. I found this surprising at first, but then I thought back to all the stuff that's happened to me. Like when the Worm tried to kill me but couldn't use his powers. Or when Taser tried to fry me, but his electricity bounced off my chest. Or how I canceled Meta-Taker's powers when he was holding me by my shirt.

And, of course, how I was the only one who could control the Orb of Oblivion.

The strange thing is that my powers seem to be reactive in nature, so they could have been there all along. I was just never in a dangerous enough situation with Metas to bring them out. Which also makes me wonder if Mom could really read my mind in the first place?

It's funny how life can kick you in the teeth.

I keep cycling through the Waystation cameras.

Speaking of Mom, I find her in the Bulk Transporter Room, unloading boxes from the Prop House. We decided to put the Prop House up for sale. After those Meta 1 morons broke in, we just didn't feel safe using it anymore. I mean, who knows how many of their friends they talked to? So, we packed everything up. Of course, we removed the Transporter and all signs of our Meta existence. In the meantime, Grace and I are being homeschooled by the Freedom Force. Shadow Hawk is my favorite teacher, he likes to ditch the books and take us to the Combat Room for a real education.

And not surprisingly, it's in the Combat Room where I find him. He and Blue Bolt are working on a few new moves together. It looks like they pulled up a robot assault scenario and are competing on who can disable them faster. I know Blue Bolt's a Meta 3 Speedster, but I'd never bet against Shadow Hawk.

TechnocRat and Master Mime are in the Hangar. TechnocRat refuses to let Master Mime pilot anything until he completes at least 1,000 hours in the flight simulator. I can't blame him. He's just spent months building the Freedom Flyer III. He keeps saying this one is the best version ever. And he's right because it's made with Skelton technology.

After Lockdown, we took K'ami's body to the site of her father's crash-landing. I thought it's only fitting that they be buried together. The Freedom Force helped to clear the area and we gave her a hero's funeral. I think about her a lot. She made me realize it's important to stand up for what you believe in. And the most important thing is to always believe in yourself.

It's strange, but I keep expecting to hear something from the Emperor. Sometimes I find myself waking up in the middle of the night drenched in sweat. I know I've had a nightmare, but I can't seem to remember what it was about. Mom says not to worry. It's probably just my mind processing everything that's happened. Maybe she's right, but I get a weird feeling every time it happens.

Speaking of weird, let's talk about Grace. Ever since Lockdown, it's like she's had a brain transplant. Suddenly, she's my new best friend. We started hanging out, doing stuff, and laughing together. Now don't get me wrong, we still have our moments, but they're much less frequent. I tease her all the time about saving her life, but I also tell her I'm glad she's my big sister.

I finally find Dog-Gone in the Galley. It looks like my popcorn is safe because he's splitting an ice cream sundae with Makeshift. We realized Makeshift wasn't such a bad guy after all. He'd just gotten mixed up with the wrong crowd. So, we sort of adopted him. He's not a full-fledged member of the Freedom Force yet, but he's proving himself every day. It looks like his next challenge will be cleaning up the mess I'm sure Dog-Gone is going to deliver.

Yep, it's just another day on the Waystation.

If only something would happen.

"Meta 2 disturbance," blares the Meta Monitor. "Power signature identified as Dark Mauler. Alert! Alert! Alert!"

Yes! I'm finally going to see some action!

I leap out of my chair and sail down the stairs to the

Mission Room to meet the team. But, to my surprise, they're already there.

"Elliott," Dad says smiling. "Now that your cast is off, the team has something for you."

Grace stands up and hands me a box. "Here, Bro. The rat and I made this for you."

I open it up. It's a costume. My costume!

It's a navy-blue bodysuit and mask, with red gloves, boots, and cape. On the front is a large, white Zero with a backslash through it. There's also a gold belt with a large "E." I can't believe it. It looks freaking awesome!

"So, kid," Shadow Hawk says. "I guess you picked a name."

"Yep," I say smiling. "Now you can call me—Epic Zero."

"Epic Zero?" Dad says. "Why Epic Zero?"

"Well," I say. "The Zero is because I can turn other Metas into Zeros. And the Epic is because I've been a Zero my whole life, and, well, I can't even begin to tell you how *freaking epic* it is to finally be here!"

"Epic Zero," Mom says. "I like it."

"Alright, enough yapping," Grace says. "It's time for Epic Zero here to make his debut. Show us what you've got, but remember one thing, don't block my good side."

She hugs me and everyone cheers.

Then, I go on my first mission as an official member of the Freedom Force. And from that day forward, I know that wherever there's evil, I'll be there.

Meta Profile

Name: Epic Zero
Role: Hero   Status: Active

VITALS:

Race: Human
Real Name: Elliott Harkness
Height: 4'8"
Weight: 89 lbs
Eye Color: Brown
Hair Color: Brown

META POWERS:

Class: Meta Manipulation

Powers Level:

- **Extreme Power Negation and Manipulation**
- **Vulnerable to non-Meta attack**

CHARACTERISTICS:

Combat	25	
Durability	12	
Leadership	55	
Strategy	65	
Willpower	77	

Epic Zero 2: Tales of a Pathetic Power Failure

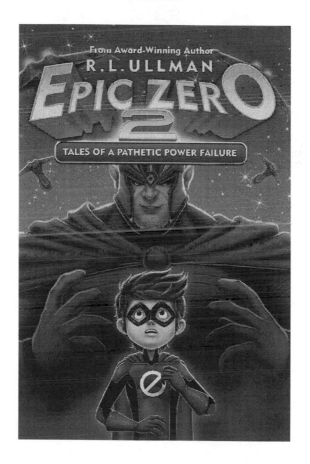

ONE

I MUST BE THE LAMEST SUPERHERO EVER

Truthfully, I should've been blasted to smithereens by now. But somehow, I'm still standing

I slide across the hood of a parked car, wrap my cape around my derriere, and duck beneath the window. I desperately need a few seconds to catch my breath. Here I am, supposedly the most powerful superhero in the universe, about to eat it big time.

I hear crunching in the distance. I stay as still as a mouse in a snake pit. The thought, "please fall into a manhole," auto loops in my brain.

But no such luck.

The crunching gets louder and louder, closer and closer, until suddenly, it stops.

I hold my breath, the silence drags on for an eternity.

Then, there's a whirring noise.

I bolt from the car just as I hear the FOOP of a missile launcher. The vehicle blows sky-high, the force of it propelling me into the air, over a spiked fence, and headfirst onto a schoolyard blacktop. I tuck my head into my knees and roll it out, but when I pop up my left shoulder is on fire with pain. It feels dislocated.

But hey, it's not all bad news. Fortunately, it's the middle of the night, so there aren't any kids around. That means the only life at stake is my own. And, at least for the moment, it saves me from more embarrassment.

Which is basically how my family sees me.

You see, I live in a family of superheroes—not just any yahoos in tights and capes—but members of the Freedom Force, the greatest team of Metas on the planet. A "Meta" is short for Meta-being—which is basically a person, animal, or vegetable (yeah, I know you've probably heard this before) with powers and abilities far beyond the scope of ordinary beings. There are nine Meta types, including Energy Manipulation, Flight, Magic, Meta-Morphing, Psychic, Super-Intelligence, Super-Speed, Super-Strength, and the newest one—Meta Manipulation.

Each power type can be further broken down into

power levels. A Meta 1 has limited power, a Meta 2 has considerable power, and a Meta 3 has extreme power. If you don't have any powers at all, then you're known as a Meta 0—or a "Zero" for short—which means you're powerless.

That used to be me, but not anymore.

Although sometimes I'm not so sure.

I'm a Meta Manipulator with the ability to negate the powers of others. So, my powers can turn any Meta 1, 2, or 3—into a 0. Other than Meta-Taker, the baddest of all bad guys who croaked in the battle at Lockdown, I'm the only Meta Manipulator around.

And as I demonstrated when I took control of the Orb of Oblivion—a cosmic entity of ridiculous power—and saved the world from the Skelton—a demented race of alien shapeshifters, I'm pretty powerful myself. The latest tests have me down as a Meta 3.

On the surface, everything seems hunky-dory. I've got superpowers, I'm on the Freedom Force, I get to call myself Epic Zero, wear long johns and fight bad guys. I'm living the dream!

So, what's the problem? Well, that's the funny thing.

My powers *are* my problem.

Let me give you an example. Two weeks ago, the Meta Monitor picked up a break-in at ArmaTech, a government-contracted weapons manufacturer. So, we loaded into the Freedom Flyer III and made it to the scene, only to find the Destruction Crew, a band of Meta

2 supervillains, shaking down the joint.

It had been a while since I went on a mission, so I thought I'd remind everybody of what I can do.

As soon as the Freedom Flyer skidded to a stop, I jumped into action. I figured if I could use my abilities to negate the Destruction Crew's powers, the fight would be over before it started. Yep, that was the plan.

And boy were those goons surprised when I marched out in front of them. Hey, I get it. I'm just a short, skinny 12-year-old kid. But Mom always says to never judge a book by its cover.

So, after they stopped laughing at me, I went to work. I concentrated like my life depended on it and pushed my Meta Manipulation energy all over them. But they just shrugged me off. That is, until they tried to use their powers.

You should have seen their faces when nothing happened! It was awesome! I thought this superhero thing was a cakewalk.

But then, Dad, who goes by the handle Captain Justice, couldn't use his Super-Strength.

And Mom, also known as Ms. Understood, couldn't use her Psychic abilities.

And it was the same story for the rest of the Freedom Force: including my sister Grace, who goes by Glory Girl, and TechnocRat, Master Mime, Blue Bolt and Makeshift.

I guess you could say my powers worked *too* well!

Once the Destruction Crew realized we were *all* powerless, well, that's when things got ugly.

Real ugly.

"Grab the kid!" one of the villains yelled.

They rushed me, took me hostage, and nearly escaped with me in our own Freedom Flyer! If it weren't for the street fighting skills of Shadow Hawk, the only one of us who didn't have Meta powers to begin with, I'd probably be six feet under right now.

I admit that was pretty bad.

But then it got worse.

"Sorry, Elliott," Dad said. "You're suspended."

"Suspended?" I said. "You mean, like, no longer on the team?"

"Yes," Dad said. "Exactly like that."

Dad told me I'm on the bench until I can better control my powers.

Are! You! Freaking! Kidding! Me!

So now I'm off the team. At least, until I can prove I deserve to be back in the starting rotation.

Which is why I find myself in my current predicament.

The guy hunting me down is named Buzzkill. He's a cyborg—part human, part robot with Meta 2 Super-Strength, and a generally nasty attitude. Neutralizing his Meta powers was easy enough. But now I'm a moving target for the ridiculous array of weapons he can conjure up from the mechanical side of his body.

Unfortunately, my Meta power has no effect on standard criminal tools-of-the-trade, including knives, throwing stars, guns, lasers, spitballs and, present case in point, heat-seeking missiles.

So, I'm in a wee bit of trouble.

I hustle off of school grounds and hang a right down the first alleyway I see. How am I going to deal with this guy before he obliterates me? I peer over my shoulder, but Buzzkill's nowhere in sight.

That's when I trip over a spilled garbage can and smash face-first into a brick wall.

Everything goes dark for a moment before I realize I'm flat on my back on a pile of trash bags. My nose is throbbing and there's a warm, wet drizzle on my upper lip. Instinctively, I wipe it. Yep, it's blood.

Marvelous.

I've literally run into a dead-end. What superhero does that?

I try standing up, but my body has other ideas. I'm still shaking out the cobwebs when I sense the area around me darkening. I look up, only to find Buzzkill standing over me, blocking out the moonlight.

"Hello, possum," he says with his deep, synthesized voice. His red, mechanical eye flickers in its socket like a metal-detector that's hit the jackpot.

"Can we talk about this?" I ask.

Buzzkill extends his left arm. His robotic fingers retract into his wrist socket, only to be replaced with a giant spinning buzz saw. "Certainly, Epic Zero," he says. "Shall we dissect your situation piece by piece?"

Well, this sucks.

Buzzkill amps up his buzz saw and swings at me.

I barely roll out of the way as he slices through a stack of bricks like a hot knife through butter. That was lucky! But he's not finished. Buzzkill wheels around for another shot. I spring to my feet, searching for a way out, but he's blocking the only exit!

I back up against the wall like a trapped animal. My shoulder is still throbbing, and my nose is spewing blood like a faucet.

The human-half of Buzzkill's face lights up in a menacing smile. "Game over," he says, revving his buzz saw to full throttle.

My heart is pounding. All I can think is *why*? *Why* can't I have super-strength like Dad and break this guy in two? *Why* can't I use telepathy like Mom and knock him to his knees? *Why* can't I fly out of here like Grace? *Why* am I so… lame?

Suddenly, Buzzkill steps forward and pins me against the wall by my neck!

He's gripping so tight I can't breathe! I want to end this, but I can't say the words…

His buzz saw is rotating so fast it's nearly invisible. Then, Buzzkill lurches back to deliver the deathblow.

I close my eyes.

This is gonna be messy.

"Drop the pizza cutter, Buzzkill!" comes a familiar voice. "The kid's all mine!"

I open my eyes to find a woman's dark, gloved hand wrapped around Buzzkill's mechanical wrist. And then, I watch Mom sock the villain square across the jaw, sending him flying.

"GISMO, end program!" Mom shouts, rubbing her knuckles.

"Training module ended, Ms. Understood," comes GISMO's warm, mechanical voice.

Instantly, Buzzkill and the alleyway disappear, leaving Mom and me all alone in the stark white confines of the Combat Room.

Based on Mom's expression, I suddenly wish Buzzkill finished the job.

"Elliott Harkness!" Mom lays into me, "What in the world are you doing here? You're supposed to be sleeping."

I try to avoid Mom's penetrating glare, but even if I avert that, I can't escape her superhero insignia of a giant eye which is staring me down, compelling me to tell her the truth—or maybe it's just a mom power. Unfortunately, I don't have a good get-out-of-jail-free card.

"I'm sorry," I say sheepishly. "I'm just trying to get some extra practice."

"I see," Mom says. "Well, next time set GISMO on an easier training module. If I hadn't tracked you down, who knows what could have happened down here."

GISMO is short for Global Intelligence Simulation Model Operator. GISMO runs the Combat Room where the Freedom Force hones their powers. The Combat Room can create any situation imaginable, including my near-death experience with Buzzkill.

"Good thinking, Mom," I say sarcastically. "Because you know real villains will let me off the hook if I just ask them to go easy on me. If I can't defeat them in a crummy training module, then what chance do I have on a real mission? I'll never be back on the team."

"Elliott," Mom says, putting her hand on my shoulder. "You've got to give yourself time to develop. You'll get there."

"Yeah," I say, "like when I'm eighty."

"Oh, Elliott," she sighs.

Just then, there's a loud crackle overhead. "Freedom Force to the Mission Room," comes TechnocRat's high-pitched voice over the intercom system. "Freedom Force to the Mission Room."

Mom and I hightail it out of the Combat Room and hit the East Wing stairwell. Oh, I should probably mention that we live in a satellite headquarters in outer space called the Waystation. The views of Earth are amazing, but it can get pretty lonely when you're left up here all by yourself.

Which I'm guessing is exactly what's about to happen to me.

We make it up to the Mission Room to find all of the heroes gathered: Dad, TechnocRat, Blue Bolt, Master Mime, Shadow Hawk, Makeshift, and my 14-year-old sister, Grace.

"Nice of you to finally join us," she says sourly, her arms folded across her chest.

"Sorry, we had an old tin can to dispose of," Mom says, winking at me. "What's going on?"

TechnocRat scampers onto the keypad and starts typing rapidly with his pink paws and tail. "Moments ago, we received a distress signal. A rather unusual distress signal. Take a look."

The giant screen powers on, and there's an image of a muscular, mustached man wearing a red mask and bodysuit with an insignia of a black atom on his chest. I know him immediately from his Meta profile. It's the Atomic Rage.

"Freedom Force," he says desperately. "You have to help us!"

The terror in his voice sets the hairs on my neck on end. The Atomic Rage is a major supervillain—a Meta 3 Energy Manipulator that can fire bolts of explosive, atomic energy. He's no chump change. So, why's he so freaked out?

"He's coming for us!" the Atomic Rage continues, his eyes bulging wide. "He's coming for us all! Help us! Please! Help—"

And then the video cuts out.

"Well, that was awkward," Grace says.

"What's that all about?" Blue Bolt asks, downing four power bars in a millisecond. "Besides, isn't he part of the Ominous Eight. Was he referring to them?"

TechnocRat's nose starts twitching. "Unfortunately, we're not sure. That's all of the transmission we received. The Meta Monitor pinpointed the location of the last power signature for the Atomic Rage. I also have readings for the rest of the Ominous Eight. I think we should investigate."

"Hold on," Grace says. "You want *us* to help those villains? What do we care if they eat each other? I mean, isn't that a good thing?"

"We're heroes," Dad says. "We're sworn to help all of those in need. Whether they're villains or not."

I glance over at Makeshift who smiles back.

"What if it's a trap?" Shadow Hawk asks.

"The thought crossed my mind as well," Dad says. "But I don't think the Atomic Rage is that good an actor. Nevertheless, whether it's a trap or if there really *is* someone powerful enough to take down the Atomic Rage and the Ominous Eight, we'd better bring the whole team."

"Great idea, Dad," I declare. "I call shotgun!"

Dad puts his hand on my shoulder. Here it comes.

"Sorry, Elliott," he says. "You're still suspended."

Of course I am.

"Freedom Force," Dad says. "It's Fight Time!"

The heroes pour out of the room.

Mom lingers behind. "And Elliott, no—"

"—Combat Room," I finish. "Yeah, I got it."

I watch her leave and then feel a soft nuzzle against my hand. Dog-Gone, our German Shepherd who can turn invisible, materializes beside me.

"Well, at least you didn't abandon me," I say, petting his head. "I guess we should grab a snack and go to bed. C'mon, let's see what's in the Galley."

Dog-Gone licks his lips.

We're halfway there when—

"Alert! Alert! Alert!" the Meta Monitor blares. "Meta 3 disturbance. Repeat: Meta 3 disturbance. Identity unknown. Alert! Alert! Alert! Meta 3 disturbance. Identity unknown."

Dog-Gone and I hustle to the Meta Monitor room.

The Meta Monitor is our computer system that detects Meta powers. The Meta Monitor can read disturbances in the Earth's molecular structure. Like fingerprints, every superpower leaves a distinct Meta signature. The Meta Monitor reads this signature and matches it with its database of Metas to determine who, or what, may have caused it.

I hop into the leather command chair, punch a few codes into the keyboard, and up pops an image of an abandoned warehouse. There's a red call-out that reads: *Identity Unknown.*

Whoever is causing the Meta Monitor to go bonkers

must be in there.

Somebody ought to check it out, but the Freedom Force is off saving the Ominous Eight. So that means there's nobody around but us.

I look down at Dog-Gone, who answers back with a low growl.

Scratch that.

It seems there's nobody around…

But me.

Meta Profile

The Freedom Force

Captain Justice

Class: Super-Strength
Meta: ▮▮ ▮▮ ▮▮

Ms. Understood

Class: Psychic
Meta: ▮▮ ▮▮▮ ▮▮

Glory Girl

Class: Flight
Meta: ▮▮▮ ▮▮

Shadow Hawk

Class: None
Meta:

Epic Zero

Class: Meta Manipulator
Meta: ▮▮ ▮▮ ▮▮▮

TechnocRat

Class: Super-Intelligence
Meta: ▮▮ ▮▮ ▮▮▮

Blue Bolt

Class: Super-Speed
Meta: ▮▮ ▮▮ ▮▮ ▮▮

Master Mime

Class: Magic
Meta: ▮▮ ▮▮▮ ▮

Makeshift

Class: Energy Manipulator
Meta: ▮▮

TWO

I SEE WHY CURIOSITY KILLED THE CAT

I know I shouldn't be doing this.

But I'm betting that hauling in a real villain will do more to convince my parents to put me back on the team than completing some training module. Of course, this could all be for naught if I get toasted.

So, here's hoping that doesn't happen.

I give Dog-Gone the slip by baiting him with doggie treats and locking him in the Galley. Boy, is he upset. I'm five levels down in the Hanger, and I can still hear him howling. I feel terrible, but thankfully dogs can't talk, so I know he won't be snitching on me anytime soon.

I hop into one of our brand-spanking-new Freedom Ferries and jet to Earth. The Freedom Ferry is

TechnocRat's latest invention. It's basically a slimmed-down version of the Freedom Flyer, designed to transport up to three people from the Waystation to Earth and back again. After having two Freedom Flyers demolished in less than a year, TechnocRat says he won't have to attend as many anger management classes when we inevitably wreck one of the Freedom Ferries.

But getting blown out of the sky isn't on the agenda.

I'm on a stealth mission.

It's early morning when I touch down, landing perfectly in a clearing in the middle of a forest, hundreds of yards from my destination. Admittedly, getting there is going to be a haul, but I don't want the noise of my rocket-powered shuttle giving me away.

I carefully pick my way through the underbrush, my costume catching on so many thorns I look like I've gone twelve rounds with a pack of angry porcupines. After a while, my skin starts itching all over, giving me the horrifying thought that I may be wading through poison ivy.

Freaking fabulous.

Then, through a small opening in the trees, I spot the warehouse.

It's a huge building that's clearly seen better days. Swaths of beige siding cling loosely to the exterior, the windows are all boarded up, and the lawn hasn't been mowed in years. The only sign of life comes from a chimney on the far side of the roof that's pumping out black smoke.

Which means someone's inside.

I don't see any security cameras or obvious booby traps, so I make a mad dash for the back door. When I get there, I press snugly against the rotting wall. The only sound I hear is my own beating heart—and goodness, isn't that deafeningly loud for a so-called superhero?

Now, I just need to get inside undetected.

I grab the door handle, roll my wrist, and pull. The door swings open with a screech so loud you'd think I let loose a colony of bats.

So much for the element of surprise.

Now I know why Shadow Hawk carries WD-40 in his utility belt.

I decide to lay low in case I've given myself away. I wait a good five minutes, trying to breathe as little as humanly possible. Since no one came to kill me, I consider the coast to be clear. count to three, and then slip inside.

It's dark—pitch dark.

I reach into my belt and pull out my flashlight, thankful I had the foresight to rummage through the Freedom Ferry's glove compartment before leaving the ship behind. I thought it might come in handy—Master Mime's extra ketchup packets, not so much.

I turn on the flashlight and shine it around.

The inside of the warehouse is cavernous. Wooden crates are stacked high on metal fixtures, a catwalk runs along the ceiling, and dust-covered forklifts are scattered all about, seemingly untouched for years.

There's a bunch of doors along the perimeter, all of them closed. Nothing seems particularly unusual, until my flashlight hits the last door on the right.

It's cracked open.

Bingo!

I slowly make my way over, careful not to knock over a crate, fall into a vat, or step onto some imaginary clown's horn my mind keeps placing in front of my feet. When I finally reach the door, I crane my neck, listening intently. All I hear is a low humming noise.

At this point, I have two options—enter the dark, scary room, or go home and face a really ticked off German Shepherd.

I came all this way, so logically I should probably see it through. So, why isn't my body moving?

Truthfully, I have no idea who, or what is behind this door. It could be mothballs and packing tape, or it could be the freakiest Meta villain in the history of caped crusading. Of course, if I were a real superhero I'd just step inside and deal with whatever came my way, but I'm not on the Freedom Force anymore, am I? So, I guess there's no obligation to go any further.

Then, I think about what Shadow Hawk would do.

And then I wonder why I had to think about that.

Well, here goes nothing.

I take a deep breath and enter the room.

A musty smell attacks my nostrils. I notice the room is windowless, which means it's somehow even darker than the main part of the warehouse. It's freezing in here, and my body starts shaking like a leaf. The temperature must be thirty degrees colder than the rest of the building. What gives?

I scan the interior with my flashlight. More crates. A stack of brown boxes. An empty storage rack. A broken conveyer belt. A mustached face. A pile of coffee cups. A... a...

I scream.

Flight mode kicks in, and I bolt from the room, my blood pumping in my ears. I've got to get out of here! I've got to get back to the Waystation! I've got to... to...

Wait a second!

I look behind me and realize I'm not being chased. Did I really see what I thought I saw? Or is my mind playing tricks on me?

I take a deep breath and re-enter the room, aiming my flashlight in the direction of the disturbing face. The light catches it full on. Yep, it's real—a pale, square-jawed face of a mustached, masked man. His eyes are closed, and he's wearing a red mask. But there's more than a face.

I scan down to his chest, his atom insignia flickering in the light.

It's the Atomic Rage!

I shine the flashlight all around. He's standing stock-still in some sort of a chamber. And he's not alone!

To his left are more chambers! Lots of them!

Fire Fiend... Airess... Die-Abolical... Think Tank... Back Breaker... Frightmare... Rundown....

It's the Ominous Eight!

They're all here! Unconscious!

I step closer to the Atomic Rage's chamber and touch the outside. It's smooth, and cold, and vibrating. That humming noise is coming from the chambers themselves! It's like the Ominous Eight are trapped in... refrigerators?

I shine my light on the Atomic Rage's face again and notice tiny icicles hanging from his eyelashes and mustache. Someone's put them on ice! They're trapped in some kind of frozen sleep—like suspended animation. It's like they're being preserved for something.

Then, I remember the Atomic Rage's distress message. Someone was coming for him. Someone was coming for all of the Ominous Eight!

And I must be standing in their secret lair!

I quickly deduce that I'm way out of my league.

I've got to get the Freedom Force!

I charge out of the storage room, but before I reach the exit, I notice something out of the corner of my eye.

Another door is open.

One that was closed before.

And the light is on.

My brain tells me to bolt. To get out of here as fast as I can, jump in the Freedom Ferry, and wait patiently for reinforcements.

But curiosity is pulling me towards the door.

I turn off my flashlight and grip it tight. It may be the only weapon I have. I know what I'm doing is incredibly stupid, but I can't stop my feet from advancing.

I peer into the doorway.

There's a large man in black leaning over a gigantic furnace. I follow the thick pipes as they run up the wall and out the ceiling. This must be where the smoke was coming from! The man nonchalantly tends the fire, placing logs inside to keep it going.

Even though his back is facing me, it's impossible not to notice his broad shoulders and massive muscles. My senses start tingling. It's time to start listening to my brain. I'm about to scram when—

He turns.

I'm frozen.

His face is way younger than his physique suggests— he looks like a teenager! His skin is pale, and his hair is light blond, bordering on white. There's something oddly familiar about him.

"Can I help you?" he asks, his face breaking into a disconcerting smile.

"Um, nope," I answer. "Just passing through. You wouldn't happen to know the fastest way out of here, would you?"

"As a matter of fact, I do," he says, his blue eyes erupting into smoldering embers of red. "Unfortunately, that exit is closed."

The door slams shut behind me.

How'd he do that?

Then, I see a wave of black atoms flashing around his fists.

I've got a bad feeling about this.

"You're a Meta," he says. "Show me what you've got."

How'd he know that? I don't know who this guy is, but he's dangerous, with a capital D.

So, I go with my first instinct and throw my flashlight at his head. As soon as it leaves my hand it stops in mid-air. Then, he twists his wrist, and it comes flying back at double the speed. I duck as it crashes straight through the wall behind me.

"Come on," he says, "You can do better than that. I can *feel* it."

Feel it, huh? Oh, he'll feel it alright.

I concentrate and blanket him with all of the negation energy I can muster.

Suddenly, the red embers crackling around his eyes go out, and the atoms encircling his fists disappear.

There, he's powerless.

"Yes," he says smiling, his head back, almost soaking it in. "Well played. You *are* powerful. Maybe I'll add you to my collection. You're Epic Zero, right?"

That's freaky. How does he know my name?

"Who are you?" I ask. My mind flips through every

Meta profile I've studied but comes up empty.

"Oh, you don't know me," he says. "But I know you. And if what I've heard and read about you is true, what you did at Lockdown against those aliens was impressive."

He takes a step towards me. This guy is huge. Even without powers, he could rip me to shreds.

"Let me solve the mystery for you," he says. "My name is Siphon, and I'm going to make every Meta on the planet my slave."

"Um, okay," I say, backing towards the door. "And why would you want to do that?"

"Let's just say I need them," he says.

Need them? For what? And then I remember the Ominous Eight in their chambers.

Siphon must have used Airess' energy manipulation powers to turn the flashlight back on me! And before that he used Think Tank's psychic powers to shut the door! And the atoms circling his fists must be from the Atomic Rage!

"Hang on," I say, "You said your name is Siphon. Like, you *siphon* the powers of others?"

"That's right," he says. "And I can't believe my luck that *you* wandered through that door."

"Um, and why is that?" I ask nervously.

"Because you're the one who took away the only family I've ever known," he says.

What? Now I'm really lost. What's he talking about?

Then, his eyes flare up again, the red energy swirling wildly around his face.

But... that's impossible! I made him powerless!

Suddenly, I realize where I've seen energy like that before. It couldn't be!

"Y-you're...," I stammer.

"Now you're getting it," Siphon says. "I'm Meta-Taker's son. Only I'm more powerful."

"Meta-Taker had a son?" I blurt out.

"Hard to believe, huh?" Siphon says. "But I'm not surprised you don't know about me. I've spent my entire life hidden away, just like he wanted. My father always said we were different than everyone else. We didn't look like other people, we didn't age like other people, we didn't fit in. We couldn't trust heroes or villains, it was the two of us against the world. And then, one day, he disappeared. Without a mother, I struggled to survive on my own. But I learned how to use my powers to get what I needed. I made it work."

His eyes look sad, like he's never told his story to anyone before. I couldn't imagine growing up so isolated—without a family. I know they get on my nerves, but not having them around...

"And when I heard he finally returned," Siphon continues. "I couldn't believe it. I was so excited to get back together. But then... you killed him. And I swore I wouldn't hide in the shadows anymore."

I watch as his neck veins pop out.

"Look, I'm really sorry," I say. "I had no idea. But I swear to you, I didn't do it. I didn't kill your dad. It was the Skelton. Those aliens at Lockdown—they killed your father."

"So now," he says, "I'm going to show all Metas what it's like to fight for survival. What it's like to beg— to grovel. Especially you."

"Was that the dinner bell I just heard?" I say. "Sorry, but I've got to go." I turn for the door when a giant demon materializes in front of me! I back up before realizing it's just an illusion—he's using Frightmare's magic! I grab the doorknob when it suddenly becomes hot to the touch! I pull my hand away. Now he's using Fire Fiend's power!

I turn to face Siphon. He raises his fists, the atoms from Atomic Rage's power swirling around them faster and faster. He's gonna vaporize me!

"Listen!" I yell, waving my arms in front of my face. "I didn't do it! I don't care how evil you are, no kid should suffer like you did!"

Siphon hesitates for a moment, staring at me.

And then, his whole body is encapsulated in a strange orange energy.

"Hey!" he screams.

The energy surrounds him. Engulfs him.

He starts lifting off the ground.

"What are you doing?" he yells. "Put me down! Let me go!"

But I'm not doing anything.
I don't know what's happening to him.
"Let! Me! G—"
And then he vanishes into thin air.

Meta Profile

Name: Siphon
Role: Villain   Status: Active

VITALS:

Race: Unknown
Real Name: Unknown
Height: 6'5"
Weight: 1,050 lbs
Eye Color: Blue
Hair Color: Blondish-White

META POWERS:

Class: Meta-morph
Power Level: ▮▮▮▮

- **Extreme Power Duplication (Physical + Molecular Morphing)**
- **WARNING: It is unknown if Siphon can reach Meta 4 power levels like his father, Meta-Taker.**

CHARACTERISTICS:

Combat	100	▮▮▮▮
Durability	100	▮▮▮▮
Leadership	40	▮▮
Strategy	80	▮▮▮
Willpower	90	▮▮▮

THREE

I DECIDE LIFE'S NOT FAIR

Sometimes there's no reward for doing the right thing.

I could have pretended the whole warehouse thing never happened. I could have returned the Freedom Ferry to its parking spot, refilled the tank with rocket fuel, and buffed it clean. I could have left the Ominous Eight in their freezers to become human popsicles. I could have said nothing about Siphon and his plans to rule over all Metas. I could have ignored the whole freaking thing.

But I couldn't do it.

I figured that if I want to *be* a superhero, then I need to *act* like a superhero. So, I called in the Freedom Force and told them everything.

And then my parents grounded me for a month.

Where's the justice in that?

Mom said I was impulsive, reckless, and obstinate.

Obstinate? Can you believe it?

I don't even know what that means!

Anyway, while I sat around fuming, the Freedom Force cleaned up the mess. Since the Ominous Eight were already on ice, TechnocRat simply transferred them in their cryo-chambers straight to Lockdown, the Meta maximum-security prison. TechnocRat said he'd build new cells for them once they got there.

So, I basically handed over eight Meta villains in one fell swoop. Did anyone say great job, Elliott? Nope. Did I get a pat on the back or a medal of honor? Nope.

Instead, I got punished.

And to top it off, Dog-Gone is furious with me. Since we returned to the Waystation, he's given me the cold nose treatment. I tried making peace with a game of fetch, but he wasn't interested. I didn't know how serious it was until he walked away from a doggie treat. He'll come around eventually.

I hope.

So, everyone's annoyed at me, and I'm equally annoyed at them. All I want to do is go to my room and shut the door, but it's Sunday dinner, and no one's allowed to sit that one out.

Joy.

If the team is not stopping some criminal mastermind, we get together every Sunday evening for a group dinner. Dad started the tradition before Grace and

I were even born. He calls it team building. From the hours of dish duty I'm stuck with, I call it a violation of child labor laws.

When dinner prep gets going, the Galley turns into a three-ring circus on steroids. Mom and Master Mime do all the cooking. Between Mom's telekinesis, and Master Mime's magic, there's always pots, pans, and food products flying all over the place. Blue Bolt sets the table, zipping back and forth in the blink of an eye. Makeshift creates desserts, porting in exotic ingredients from who knows where. Dad chases everyone around with a dustpan and broom, advocating kitchen safety. Grace and I pitch in where needed. But poor Shadow Hawk has the worst job of all. He has to keep TechnocRat's paws out of the kitchen until dinner is served.

With so much action, someone always ends up wearing part of the meal before it even starts. Tonight is my turn. So, after peeling a fistful of spaghetti off of my shirt, we're finally ready to sit down.

That's when Grace pokes the bear.

"Brother, dear," she says ever so sweetly. "Can you please pass the garlic bread? That is, if you're not too wiped out after your adventure."

I stare her down like a lion at an antelope convention. "Of course, dear sister," I answer, shoving the breadbasket into her hand. "It's no trouble at all."

"So, there's one thing I still don't understand," she says, chewing with her mouth open. "How did you manage to defeat this villain who was so powerful he captured the entire Ominous Eight all on your own?"

"I already told you," I say, digging into my spaghetti. "I didn't defeat him. Somehow he teleported away. Trust me, if that didn't happen he would've crushed me. After all, he *is* Meta-Taker's son."

Suddenly, I hear forks clanging on plates. I look up to see that everyone's stopped eating.

They're all looking at me.

"I did mention that, didn't I?"

"What do you mean, he's Meta-Taker's son?" Mom asks.

"Well," I say, "he told me Meta-Taker was his dad. I mean, he looked just like Meta-Taker. But a lot younger."

"Why didn't you mention this before?" Dad asks sternly.

Uh-oh.

"I... I thought I did," I say. "I mean, so much was happening when you got there. I thought I told somebody. I mean, I told one of you guys, right?"

But all I get back are blank stares.

Oh boy.

"Whoops," I say. "Sorry."

"*Whoops?*" Mom repeats. "*Sorry?* Not only were you impulsive, reckless, and obstinate..."

There's that word again.

"... but you also forgot to mention the most important part—that he's the son of the most powerful

Meta we've ever faced? Elliott, what's gotten into you?"

"I-I don't know," I say. "I guess it slipped my mind when you grounded me."

"Yeah," Grace says. "Along with your brain."

"Stuff it!" I snap.

"You stuff it!" Grace fires back.

"Enough," Mom says. "Both of you."

Shadow Hawk stands up. "I think we should head back down to that warehouse and look around some more. There may be some clues we missed."

The rest of the team rises in agreement. Grace shoots me a sly smile. I'm all alone at the table, except for Mom who hangs back for a minute.

She looks at me. "Elliott, why don't you clear the table and go to your room. We'll talk more when I get back."

"Awesome," I say. "I've been trying to go to my room for hours."

"And no shenanigans," she adds before leaving.

I throw my hands in the air. Yep, that's me, Captain Shenanigans. I put everything away, grab the basket of garlic bread, and head for my room.

I mean, c'mon! It was an innocent mistake.

You can't tell me they haven't made mistakes before. Granted, I've made a whole bunch of mistakes in a really short timeframe. But I'm a kid. I'm supposed to make mistakes!

I stop in the middle of the hallway, listening for the

pitter-patter of furry feet, but don't hear anything. I guess Dog-Gone isn't coming either. That's fine. I'd rather be alone anyway. Besides, he hogs the bed.

I slam the door behind me, flop down on my bed, and stare at the ceiling. If I'm stuck here for a month I'm going to go nuts. Maybe I can create a hologram or a paper mache version of myself. Then, I can go out and live in the real world while my doppelganger gets stuck in here serving out my punishment. Yeah, wouldn't that be grand?

Just wonderful.

BOOM!

Suddenly, the whole room tilts right, throwing me off my bed. Everything not nailed down to a surface crashes to the floor. Then, the room levels off again.

What the...?

"Waystation breached!" blares the Meta Monitor. "Repeat, Waystation breached! Automatic emergency response system activated! Repeat, automatic emergency response system activated!"

I spring from the floor. Um, did that just say 'breached?' That can only mean one thing—the Waystation has been invaded!

How is that even possible? I mean, we're hundreds of miles from Earth. Who could possibly board the Waystation?

I run to the porthole. From my window, I have a partial view of the Hanger. I look outside and do a double take. To my astonishment, attached to the end of the Hanger is some kind of a ship!

It's silver and sleek looking, with a long cylindrical body, and a narrow tower jutting up from its center. Thin fins run along its sides, and it's capped at the rear by large, powerful-looking jets.

How did it get through our sensors without being detected? That shouldn't be possible!

But now's not the time to worry about that.

Someone's on the Waystation!

I need to think. I can either stay here and wait to get whacked, or I can try to make it to a Freedom Ferry and get out of here.

Then, I remember Dog-Gone! He's alone out there!

I dig through my closet, grab a baseball bat, and head for the hallway.

Immediately, I've got problems.

The residential wing is cut off by a thick, steel barrier. This must be one of the emergency response actions the Meta Monitor executed. But all it's doing is trapping me like a sitting duck until whoever's here comes to find me. I can't let that happen.

Fortunately, I know a workaround.

"Override ZY78840C," I yell.

The barrier retracts into the ceiling. It's a good thing I proofread all of TechnocRat's manuals. I've got to find that mutt and get out of here.

Now, where would I be hiding if I were an invisible

dog? Of course!

I sprint up the West Wing staircase and hit the most logical place possible—the Galley.

I enter to find something I'm totally not expecting.

Sitting at the end of the table, eating our leftover spaghetti, is a monkey. He's black, furry, and absolutely stuffing his face.

Our eyes meet, but he keeps shoveling in as many noodles as possible. He doesn't even react to me.

Gross.

Whoever it is that's invaded the Waystation owns a pet that's more interested in raiding my refrigerator than Dog-Gone. I have no clue who this monkey belongs to, but that person must be here somewhere. I scan the room, but there's no one else around.

And speaking of Dog-Gone, I don't see him anywhere. I've got to find that fleabag before I take off. I just can't leave him here to be captured. Or worse...

I'm about to head out, when…

"Excuse me," comes a gravelly voice from behind.

I turn, baseball bat fully extended. My eyes dart back and forth, but there's no one here. It's just me and the monkey.

"I said, excuse me," comes the voice again.

"Who's there!" I yell. "Come on out!"

"Are you blind?" comes the voice again. Out of the corner of my eye, I see the monkey waving at me with his long, hairy arm.

No. Freaking. Way.

"Ah, yes, now you see me," the monkey says. "I was a bit worried for a moment." He stares at me with his large, brown eyes. As I look closer at his face and ears, I realize he's a chimpanzee.

"You did this?" I ask. "Who are you?"

The chimp picks up a long noodle and slurps it into his mouth. "Oh, this is so good. I haven't had food from our world in such a long, long time. You wouldn't happen to have Tabasco sauce, would you? I used to love Tabasco sauce."

"Um, no," I answer. "Look, I don't have time for this right now."

"No, you don't," the chimp says. "I suppose you've been invaded, haven't you?"

"I'll ask you one more time," I say, waving the bat. "Who are you?"

"Very well," the chimp says. "They call me Leo. Now, perhaps you can answer a question for me. Are you Elliott Harkness?"

The sound of my name coming from the mouth of a monkey takes me aback for a second. "Um, yeah," I answer.

"The Orb Master?" asks Leo.

Orb Master? What the heck does this monkey know about the Orb of Oblivion?

"I… I guess so," I answer.

"Excellent," Leo says.

Suddenly, I hear a THWIP and feel a sharp pain in my left leg. There's a small puff of smoke floating up from beneath Leo's table.

I look down to see a dart sticking out of my leg!

Then, I look back at Leo, who's busy slurping up another noodle.

And everything goes dark.

Meta Profile

The Ominous Eight

Die-Abolical

Class: Super-Intellect
Meta: ▪▪▪▪ ▪

Frightmare

Class: Magic
Meta: ▪▪▪▪ ▪

Think Tank

Class: Psychic
Meta: ▪▪▪ ▪

The Atomic Rage

Class: Energy Manipulator
Meta: ▪▪▪▪▪

Airess

Class: Energy Manipulator
Meta: ▪▪▪ ▪

Rundown

Class: Super-Speed
Meta: ▪▪▪ ▪

Back Breaker

Class: Super-Strength
Meta: ▪▪▪ ▪

Fire Fiend

Class: Meta-morph
Meta: ▪▪▪ ▪

FOUR

I THINK I'VE BEEN ABDUCTED BY ALIENS

"We should kill him," comes a girl's voice.

Well, that didn't sound neighborly, especially since I suspect whoever said it is talking about me! I only regained consciousness seconds ago, and I have no clue where I am, or what's happening around me.

Whatever that monkey hit me with was pretty potent, because my eyelids feel like they're stuck together with crazy glue. Fortunately, my ears are working just fine. So, for the moment, I figure my best bet is to play cadaver and collect intel.

Not that I could do anything about my situation even if I wanted to. I'm lying face-up on a cold table and my wrists and ankles are locked down tight. I hear loud shuffling to my right and then—

"Kill the Orb Master?" comes a raspy-voiced response. "Gemini, you're insane." I know that voice. It's that monkey who shot me—Leo.

"I'm not insane," Gemini replies. "I'm practical. Everyone in the universe is looking for him, which means everyone in the universe is now looking for us."

Um, what does she mean by *everyone in the universe?*

"We'll never survive an onslaught," comes a new voice—female, but deeper.

"We won't have to, Taurus," comes yet another voice, this time confident and male. "Don't forget, we're in the Ghost Ship. No one can track us."

"Right, Scorpio," Taurus says. "You be sure to tell them that when your molecules are scattered all over the galaxy. Besides, look at him—so puny and weak. I think we jacked the wrong human."

Ouch—now I'm captured *and* offended.

"We need answers," Scorpio says. "When is he going to wake up?"

"I'll stick him with a stimulant," Leo says. "That'll get him up."

Wait? What? "Hold your horses, Curious George!" I yell. "I'm up! Don't stick me with anything!"

With all of my might, I force my eyes open. Everything's blurry for a few seconds, and then my vision begins to clear. To my surprise, standing over me are a bunch of... teenagers?

Alien teenagers—about my age.

They're staring down at me warily like I could bust out of these shackles and steal their lunch money.

If they only knew...

I take in my captors.

In the front is a pretty girl with green skin, orange eyes, and two antenna stalks poking through her long, black hair. She's wearing a bodysuit that's color-split down the middle—half blue and the other half red. On her belt is a symbol that looks like a mathematical pi sign. Guessing by her irritated expression, she must be Gemini.

Standing behind her is the largest girl I've ever seen. She has a round face with strange blue markings all over it. Her hair is pulled up in a samurai-like bun. Her arms are ripped, and she's reaching down towards two long swords at her hips—her fingers twitching nervously. On her shoulder plates is a symbol of a creature with gigantic, violent-looking horns. I'm pegging her as Taurus.

On the other side is a red-skinned dude with cables running in and out of various parts of his body. He's staring me down through a pair of blue goggles. He looks wiry, but that's not the part that worries me. Behind his back I see a large tail waving menacingly back and forth. He's got to be Scorpio.

And finally, crouching in front of him is my old pal, Leo. He's brandishing a gigantic syringe with the business end pointed at my leg. There's a spaghetti noodle dangling from the fur beneath his chin. Nice.

"Well," I say, "this has been fun, but if you don't mind I'm kind of tired. So, how about we swing by my place and drop me off?"

"Sorry," Leo says. "But you're not going anywhere."

"Enough stalling," Scorpio says. "Tell us, where is the Orb of Oblivion?"

So, the chimp wasn't lying. This really *is* about the Orb.

Okay, so what the heck do I do now? If I tell them I blew up the Orb, along with a Skelton warship, they'll probably kill me on the spot. But if I make up some story about the Orb being hidden or lost or something, maybe they'll keep me around for a while—or maybe they'll kill me on the spot anyway. Decisions, decisions.

They're staring at me intently, hanging on whatever I'm about to say. Then, I realize I've got something they want. Maybe I'm actually in the power position here.

So, I get bold.

"Why should I tell you?"

Taurus grabs a metal bar, rips it off the wall, and snaps it in two.

"Hey!" Leo shouts. "Don't break my medi-wing!"

"Okay, I see your point," I say. "But I really can't think straight when I'm all pinned down like this. The blood is flowing away from my brain and I think my feet are asleep."

I watch their eyes drift to Scorpio.

Now I know who's in charge.

"Unshackle him," Scorpio says.

"What?" Gemini says. "Are you nuts?"

"Scorpio, please—," Taurus starts.

"I said, unshackle him," Scorpio repeats firmly.

Leo hops on the table and releases my arms and legs.

"Thanks," I say, rubbing my sore wrists. "Now we're getting somew—"

Suddenly, Scorpio's tail is inches from my face. It looks like a red battering ram perched on a slinky. Then, the tip turns bright orange and starts radiating heat. It feels like my skin is melting!

"Let's come to an understanding," he says. "We need something from you, the Orb of Oblivion. And you need something from us, your life. So, in order for you to get what you want, you're going to give us what we want. Is that clear?"

The temperature coming off his tail is so intense, sweat starts pouring down my face.

It's impressive. But I have powers too.

"I hear you," I say. "But I think it's only fair if we start from an even playing field." I concentrate and bathe him with my negation energy. I hope this works! Seconds later, his tail snuffs out.

Scorpio looks stunned.

"Scorpio!" Taurus says, moving forward.

"Wait, Taurus," Gemini says. "He has power."

Then it hits me. Scorpio? Taurus? Gemini?

"Hang on," I say. "Aren't your names, like, the signs

of the zodiac? But aren't there twelve signs?"

"We *were* twelve," Gemini says sadly.

Then, I realize there's only four of them. I look at Leo. "Hey, and isn't Leo supposed to be a lion? You know he's a monkey, right?"

Leo raises a fist.

"Leo, no!" Gemini orders.

"So, where are the rest of you?" I ask.

"Pisces and Sagittarius are piloting the vessel," Gemini answers. "Aries... disappeared. The rest are dead."

They all look down. It's quiet for a few seconds.

"Look, I'm sorry to hear that," I say. "And I'd love to help out in any way that doesn't involve my captivity. But I really have no idea what I'm doing here. Or what you want the Orb for."

Gemini looks at Scorpio who nods his approval.

"We're the Zodiac," she starts. "A band of survivors—vigilantes—bonded in a shared quest to destroy the one who annihilated our worlds."

"Annihilated?" The words shock me for a minute. "Y-you mean your world was... destroyed?"

"Not world, Orb Master," Gemini says. "Worlds. My planet was called Gallron. It was beautiful, with bright purple skies and rolling seas. At night, the moons would glow, illuminating the seven kingdoms filled with peaceful people. But now... now it's gone. If I wasn't sent into space on a scientific expedition moments before it happened, then I'd be gone as well."

"And it's the same for me," Taurus says. "I hail from Pollux, a planet covered with mountains and forests. The weather was harsh, but the people hardy. I was on orbital patrol that fateful day. There was going to be a celebration. But it never happened."

I look over at Scorpio, but he's silent. I can see his pain through his goggles.

"And what about you?" I ask Leo. "Didn't you say you were from Earth?"

"I did," Leo says, breathing out deeply. "This may be hard for you to believe, but…"

KABOOM!

Suddenly, the ship turns upside down, sending all of us crashing into the ceiling. Then, the ship rights itself, and we smash to the floor. Leo is lying on top of me, his tail planted squarely in my mouth.

I push him away, spitting out a mouthful of fur. "What was that?" I ask.

Suddenly, I hear clopping, like a giant horse is racing through the ship. Just then, a bearded figure appears in the doorway. At first, I think it's a man, but then I realize it's a muscular kid's upper body attached to the lower half of some kind of six-legged creature! He stares at me with his emerald eyes.

"Sagittarius!" Scorpio says. "What's going on?"

"We were hit with a concussion blast! That was only a warning shot," Sagittarius says. "It's a warship. They say if we don't land immediately, they'll destroy us."

"Impossible!" Scorpio exclaims. "The Ghost Ship can't be tracked!"

"Told you," Taurus says. "What are we going to do now?"

"Where's the closest landing point?" Scorpio asks.

"There's a small moon below us," Sagittarius says. "But we aren't faster than the warship."

"Whoa!" I say panicked. "Wait a minute. If the Skelton find out I'm on board, they'll kill me for what I've done!"

"Oh, they're not Skelton," Sagittarius says. "They're much, much worse."

Meta Profile

Name: Leo
Role: Vigilante   Status: Active

VITALS:

Race: Chimpanzee
Real Name: Alpha-1
Height: 3'6"
Weight: 105 lbs
Eye Color: Brown
Hair Color: Black

META POWERS:

Class: Energy Manipulator
Power Level:
- Considerable space manipulation
- Can teleport at rapid pace
- Exhibits strong natural agility

CHARACTERISTICS:

Combat	40	
Durability	24	
Leadership	70	
Strategy	84	
Willpower	77	

FIVE

I GET CAUGHT IN A TUG OF WAR

"**U**m, what do you mean by *worse* than the Skelton?"

Despite my overactive imagination, I simply can't fathom anything worse than the Skelton. From everything I've seen, the Skelton Emperor will do whatever it takes—and I mean *what-ever it takes*—to rule the universe. So, who could possibly be worse than that?

"That's a *Dhoom* warship," Gemini whispers, like it's obvious to anyone with half a brain.

We're now standing on the main bridge of the Ghost Ship, practically nose-to-nose with the most impressive spacecraft I've seen outside of a Star Wars movie. The ship is just enormous, fanning out from the center, its massive circular body dwarfing it's smaller, spherical cockpit. Two thin wings extend out from the sides, seemingly going on for miles, every square inch covered by some weapon that's pointed directly at us. The monolith drifts slowly forward, closing in for the kill.

I wait for Gemini to clue me in further, but apparently, the fact that it's a Dhoom warship seems to be explanation enough. "Sorry," I say, "I know I'm the new guy here, but who exactly are the Dhoom again?"

"Seriously?" Gemini says. "Don't they have schools on your planet? On Dhoom, there's no government, no laws, no justice—the only currency is strength. Their entire society is split into fiefdoms, each ruled by a crime lord looking to expand his empire by conquering worlds and enslaving whole civilizations. To rise to power on Dhoom, you don't ask, you take what you want."

I suddenly wonder if Dog-Gone is part Dhoom?

"Okay," I say. "I get that's bad, but how are they worse than the Skelton?"

Gemini looks me square in the eyes. "If you're captured by Skelton, they'll kill you. If you're captured by Dhoom, you'll beg them to kill you. Is that clear?"

"Crystal," I say.

"Scorpio!" calls a small girl wearing a red, scaled costume. She has black, spikey hair, and tiny, gill-like flaps on the sides of her neck that open and close. Based on the process of elimination, she must be Pisces. She pushes a few buttons at the controls and says, "We're being hailed on communications frequency X12. They want to talk."

"Open the channel," Scorpio says grimly.

Suddenly, the image of a man appears on the monitor. The first thing I notice is his blue skin. Then, there's his size. Even though he's projecting from the chest up, I can tell by his thick neck and broad shoulders that he's absolutely ginormous. And finally, there are his elliptical, yellow eyes with almost cat-like pupils—which only grow larger when they land on me.

His lips curl into a disturbing smile, exposing razor-sharp fangs. "What a pleasant surprise," he says. "I had thought you were just another smuggler ship violating interstellar trade laws. But it appears your cargo is far more valuable than I ever could have imagined."

"Who are you?" Scorpio asks.

"My true name will hold no meaning for you," the man says. "But you will know me best as the Overlord."

Gemini gasps. I catch the rest of the Zodiac shooting worried glances at one another.

Scorpio crosses his arms. "Yeah, we've heard of you. Now what do you want?"

"Originally, I wanted your ship. I haven't seen many custom builds like it," the Overlord says. "But now I will take something of far greater value—the Orb Master. Only I thought he would be more… impressive."

I sense this is going to be a theme.

"Transport him to my ship," the Overlord continues, "and I will consider letting the rest of you live. You have one minute to decide." Then, the communication cuts off and the screen goes blank.

Everyone turns my way.

Suddenly, I feel like the anchor on a hot air balloon.

"You're not going to give me to that guy," I say. "Are you?"

Gemini points at me. "Seize him!"

Before I can react, Taurus grabs my arms. I try pulling away, but she's way too strong.

"Wait!" Leo says. "We can't do it."

"Listen to the monkey," I plead. "He's got good ideas."

"You heard him," Gemini says, pointing back to the screen. "That's the Overlord! You know, the intergalactic crime boss of all crime bosses. The pirate that traffics illegal slaves across the universe. The torturer that experiments on beings for his own amusement. I say we dump this annoying kid now before it's too late."

"Annoying is a little harsh," I mutter. "Pesky, maybe, but annoying?"

"Listen," Leo says. "If the Overlord gets his mitts on the Orb of Oblivion we're as good as dead anyway. I know this isn't popular, but this kid knows where the Orb is. If we just turn him over, then the universe is lost."

"Leo's right," Scorpio says, stepping forward. "If we're going to avenge our worlds, then we need to stand and fight."

There's a long moment of silence. It's clearly tense.

Until, finally, Gemini relents. "Fine. We must fight for the lives we've lost."

Reluctantly, Taurus lets me go.

Gemini turns towards me. "You do know where the Orb is, right? We're counting on you."

I look at their hopeful faces staring at me—like a gang of ragamuffins begging for a free meal. I feel bad. I mean, despite the odds, they're actually willing to fight for me. Maybe even die for me. But the truth is, I don't have what they're looking for.

The Orb is gone. Destroyed. Kaput.

I can't let them risk their lives without knowing the truth. "So, here's the funny thing. I... kind of... well, you might say, I... um... I..."

"What?" Gemini says impatiently. "You what?"

"Blew up the Orb with a Skelton Blood Bringer ship somewhere in outer space," I finish quickly.

"What?" Taurus says.

"You idiot!" Gemini screams. "Do you know what you've done!"

"Well," I answer, "it sort of seemed like a good idea at the time. I mean, I didn't need the orb anymore, and I wanted to make sure those guys never returned to destroy Earth. So, I told the Orb to self-destruct."

Gemini shakes her fist at me. "I'm gonna make you self-destruct!"

"Hold it," Scorpio says. "You *told* the Orb of Oblivion to blow itself up?"

"Please, stop," Gemini says, her head in her hands. "I'm losing brain cells every time he speaks."

"The Overlord's calling back!" Pisces yells from the helm. "We need a decision!"

Gemini looks at Scorpio, who looks at Leo, who shoots back an expression I can't read.

"Patch him through," Scorpio says.

Just then, the Overlord reappears. "So, have you chosen to live, or to die?"

Scorpio takes a deep breath.

Well, it was an interesting life while it lasted.

"Our sincere apologies, Overlord," Scorpio says. "But we've decided to keep him."

What? Really?

The Overlord smiles. "I was hoping you would say that. Prepare for landing."

Suddenly, our ship jerks downward with incredible force. My feet leave the ground, and I slam hard into the ceiling. Instinctively, I curl into a ball, shielding myself from flying cabin equipment, flailing body parts, and a screeching chimpanzee.

It feels like we're on a permanent downhill rollercoaster ride—pinned to the ceiling by unrelenting antigravity. Stars zip past the windshield, but I know we're the ones moving at incredible speed. The Overlord must be forcing our ship down with some kind of propulsion beam! And when we land it's not going to be—

CRASH!

The collision is bone-rattling!

We're jolted from the ceiling back to the floor. My head bounces off something large and soft, which turns out to be Sagittarius' rump.

Miraculously, everyone seems okay. Badly bruised, but okay.

"Quick!" Scorpio commands. "Activate your stream suits!"

I watch the team push the Zodiac symbols on their uniforms. Suddenly, they're wrapped in a clear film that flexes in and out with their breathing.

Just then—with a loud POP—the Ghost Ship's exterior hatch opens. But I'm not wearing a stream suit! If I can't breathe in this atmosphere, I'll die!

Something slaps me hard on my chest. I look down to find Pisces standing there, a disc attached to my costume. She smiles and then pokes it.

Suddenly, I'm wrapped head-to-toe in a cellophane-like substance. I feel like a cucumber heading into the fridge, but at least I can breathe!

"Thanks," I say.

"Just don't die in it," she says. "It costs a fortune to clean."

Leo waves his dart gun at me, "Stay here and don't do anything stupid."

I follow orders as the Zodiac file out of the Ghost Ship and close the hatch behind them.

The next thing I know, it sounds like World War III out there. The way the Ghost Ship is positioned, I can't see any of the action, so I run through my options.

If the Overlord wins, I'll become his captive, and based on what I've learned that's not a good thing. If the Zodiac win, I'm still their captive, but now they know I don't have the Orb. So, that pretty much makes me expendable.

What to do?

Suddenly, I see a half-kid, half-horse fly past the windshield. I scramble over to the hatch, throw it open, and peek outside.

The scene is pure crazy town.

The Zodiac are standing back to back, trying to hold off hundreds of advancing Dhoom soldiers. I don't see how this could possibly end well.

But what happens next shocks me.

Scorpio uses his tail to generate a massive bolt of energy, blasting a clear path through the heart of the enemy. Taurus pounds the earth with her giant fists, causing an earthquake that topples a battalion of soldiers. Leo is teleporting all over the place, punching out Dhoom warriors one by one. Pisces is flying gracefully through space, creating tornado-like dust storms that lift dozens of soldiers and send them miles away.

And Gemini… well, let's just say I do a double take. To my right is a ten-foot-tall version of Gemini in red— and to my left is another ten-foot-tall Gemini, but in blue!

I can't believe it!

The Zodiac has Meta-powers!

But there are way too many Dhoom to hold back. I see Pisces get nailed with a boulder, Scorpio and Taurus are quickly over-run, and Leo looks like he's been captured. This is going south fast!

I should get out of here. I should figure out how to pilot the Ghost Ship and save myself. I don't owe these guys anything. I mean, they kidnapped me!

"Help!," Gemini cries.

The Overlord is standing over Blue Gemini while she's being pushed into the ground like there's an anvil on top of her! That's when I realize there was no propulsion beam forcing our ship down, it was the Overlord himself! He can manipulate gravity!

"Stop!" Red Gemini screams. But she's captured by Dhoom soldiers, helpless to save her twin.

Despite everything that's happened, I can't run away when someone's in trouble. I guess that's why I'm petitioning so hard to be a superhero.

I jump from the hatch and run towards the Overlord. "Release her!" I demand.

But the Overlord just stares at me with his electric eyes. "Ah," he says, "the Orb Master finally shows himself. I know several customers who will pay quite handsomely for your hide—dead or alive. So, let's end this, shall we?"

He raises his eyebrows, and Blue Gemini is pushed

deeper into the ground! He's going to bury her alive!

"No!" Red Gemini yells.

I haven't used my powers around this many Metas since I messed up the mission with the Destruction Crew. I don't want to accidentally negate the Zodiac's powers, but what other choice do I have? I focus deeply on the Overlord and let my powers fly.

Suddenly, Blue Gemini emerges from the ground, and the Gemini twins hurtle towards one another, merging into one with violent force. Fused back together, Gemini collapses to the ground. I must have negated her powers! Which means I saved her, but I still don't have control over my own powers.

The Overlord stares at his hands. "Impressive. You have eliminated my powers, but you have not eliminated me."

He takes a step towards me when he's suddenly engulfed in a strange orange energy.

No way. Not again.

"What is this?" he says. "Release me!"

The energy lifts him off the ground.

"What is happeni—"

And then, just like Siphon, he's gone!

I look around to find the Dhoom soldiers in shock.

I realize this is our chance. Maybe our only chance. I need to bluff like there's no tomorrow!

"Let go of my friends!" I command. "I… I am the Orb Master! Release them, or I'll do the same to you!"

Without their leader, the Dhoom look at one another, unsure if they should fight or run.

I raise my arms threateningly. "Now!"

They push their Zodiac captives into the center.

I spin, pointing at them all. "Now return to your ship. Go!"

The Dhoom retreat, scrambling over one another to get back to their warship.

Gemini is still on the ground, breathing hard. "Thank you, Orb Master. You saved my life."

"No problem," I say. "And you can call me Epic Zero. Or Elliott if you want. I'm really not feeling the Orb Master thing."

"Did you do that?" Gemini says, her eyes wide.

I could lie to her, but I'm not sure what that buys me. "No," I say. "That wasn't me. But I've seen it happen before. So, that's twice now."

"So have we," Scorpio says. "That's how we lost Aries our greatest fighter. He disappeared right before our eyes in that same strange energy."

"Great," I say, "so what the heck is going on?"

Scorpio scratches his head. "I don't know. But I may know someone who does."

Gemini glares at him "No, Scorpio. He's a madman."

"I know," Scorpio says. "Which is exactly why he may have the answer."

Meta Profile

Name: The Overlord
Role: Dictator   Status: Active

VITALS:

Race: Dhoom
Real Name: Unknown
Height: 6'9"
Weight: 546 lbs
Eye Color: Yellow
Hair Color: Bald

META POWERS:

Class: Energy Manipulator
Power Level: ▆▆▆▆
- Extreme gravity manipulation
- Can increase mass or density of objects or beings
- Can also negate gravity

CHARACTERISTICS:

Combat	95
Durability	66
Leadership	91
Strategy	100
Willpower	100

SIX

I HAVE QUITE A REPUTATION

You know it's been a strange day when you're hanging with a bunch of aliens, and *you* feel like the weird one.

After the Dhoom departed, Scorpio went right to work fixing the Ghost Ship. The good news is that despite our forced crash-landing on this nameless moon, the ship is salvageable. The bad news is that I still have no clue how to get back home.

I watch Scorpio detach cables from his body and plug them into different parts of the ship. It's like he's talking directly to the wiring itself! I bet TechnocRat wished he could do that.

I pick Scorpio's brain as he works. He explains how the Ghost Ship is invisible to conventional radar. It's designed to fly in 'pocket space,' which is a dimension of space that exists within traditional space but is hidden from view. The only way I can get my mind around it is to think about Dog-Gone when he's invisible, and there's no trail of crumbs to track him down.

"I just can't figure out how the Overlord found us," Scorpio says. "We should have been undetectable."

"Maybe it's Leo," I offer. "You guys ever bathe that chimp? I don't want to be rude, but he smells like—"

"Hey," Scorpio interjects. "It happened right after you used your powers on me. Maybe when you negated my powers, you negated the cloaking powers of the Ghost Ship?"

I look at him skeptically. "How's that possible? My powers only work on living things?"

"I don't know," Scorpio says. "But let me give it some thought. There has to be an answer."

Speaking of answers, there's one thing that's been bugging me. How did the Zodiac find me in the first place? I mean, there are billions of people on Earth. Finding me had to be like finding the proverbial needle in a haystack. I ask Scorpio the question, but he doesn't give me a straight answer. All he says is to ask Leo. Then, he tells me to get ready for lift-off.

Leo? Why Leo?

I climb inside the Ghost Ship. There's no sign of Leo anywhere, so I hook myself in. After a few minutes, we take off.

I try to make sense of what's happened. The Zodiac

want the Orb of Oblivion to take down whoever's responsible for destroying their worlds. But I don't know anything about this guy, or how they planned to use the Orb once they had it. I look for someone to talk to, but everyone's busy. Everyone, that is, except for Gemini.

She's sitting in the corner with her head resting on her knees. She's definitely had a rough time of it. But, if it wasn't for me, she'd have lost half her body. So, I figure she's my best bet. I unclick myself and make my way over.

"Hey," I say, sitting down next to her.

"Hey," she says. "Thanks again for saving me."

"No problem," I say. "I'm sure you would've done the same for me."

She looks at me, her eyebrows raised.

"Okay, maybe not. Look, I've got to be honest here. I have no clue what's going on. I don't know why you kidnapped me. I mean, I know you want the Orb of Oblivion, but why? What's this all about?"

Gemini looks at me like I have three heads. "What's this all about? Over 20 billion people lived on my world. They were artists, musicians, performers. All of them could split into two. Do you know what it's like to hear the screams of 40 billion souls? That's what this is all about."

"Sorry, I didn't mean it like that," I say. "What I'm trying to find out is who did this to you? To all of you?"

"Ravager," she says with disgust.

"Ravager? Who's Ravager?" I ask.

"Ravager is not a *who*, it's a *what*—a giant, nebulous cosmic entity that consumes the life force of entire planets to sustain itself. It's uncontrollable. Unstoppable. It travels across galaxies and wipes out solar systems. It destroyed my world, and one day it will destroy yours too. Unless, of course, you can stop it."

"*Me?*" I say, "How can *I* stop something that eats planets for breakfast?"

Gemini crosses her legs. "You're the mighty Orb Master, shouldn't you know?"

I rub my face. "Some mighty Orb Master I am. I don't even have an orb."

"So, we're basically screwed," she says.

"Yeah," I say. "That pretty much sums it up."

"Great," she says. "Glad you're on board."

So now this is my fault? Like I knew that I'm supposed to be the savior of the universe. Me, the guy who can't control his own powers. Me, the guy who gets sent to his room after dinner. Well, sorry, but that's utterly ridiculous.

We sit in silence for a few minutes.

"You said you've seen that orange energy before," she says. "The one that swallowed the Overlord."

"Yeah, it happened back on Earth," I say, happy to change the subject. "To this really powerful villain named Siphon. And you said it happened to your teammate?"

"Yeah, a few days ago," Gemini says. "His name is

Aries—also powerful. We were in the middle of a battle with a group of Baltian soldiers. The orange energy came, and then suddenly, he vanished. We haven't heard from him since."

My mind starts spinning. I mean, Siphon and the Overlord are major villains. If Aries is equally as strong, then whoever's doing this must be even stronger. But who could that be? I have no idea.

"So, who's this madman that has all the answers?"

"The Watcher," she says. "He's spent all of eternity observing the evolution of the universe."

Eternity? "So, he's like, millions of years old?"

"Billions," Gemini says. "Legends say that in exchange for his immortality, he swore not to interfere in the affairs of the universe."

"What kind of tooth fairy is out there handing out immortality?" I ask. "And where do I get in line?"

"Supposedly, it's a one-of-a-kind gift of the universe. But his gift is also his curse. While he's seen everything that's ever happened since the dawn of time, legends also say he's lost his mind."

"Wonderful," I say. "Can't wait to meet him."

"If he allows it," Gemini says. "No one's safely reached his world in centuries. We'll see him, but only if he wants to see us."

"Strap in!" Pisces orders from the helm. "Watcher World is approaching. Prepare for the descent."

I strap myself in, and lean over to look out the front

window, but all I see is a giant asteroid belt. There must be hundreds of rocks out there, in all shapes and sizes, smashed together to form an impenetrable wall.

Now I get what Gemini was saying. No one's reaching Watcher World unless the Watcher allows it.

We get closer, but the asteroids aren't budging.

"300 meters," Pisces says.

"Hold steady," Scorpio says coolly.

"200 meters," Pisces says.

Taurus looks at me nervously.

"Hold," Scorpio says, shifting in his chair.

"100 meters," Pisces says, her voice rising sharply.

Those rocks are huge!

"We should turn back," Sagittarius says.

"Hold course!" Scorpio commands.

"50 meters," Pisces says quickly. "Shouldn't we—"

"Hold steady!" Scorpio commands.

"Scorpio!" Gemini shouts. "Are you crazy!"

"10 meters!" Pisces shouts.

A giant asteroid—irregularly shaped and pock-marked—fills the entire windshield. It's not moving!

"Hold!" Scorpio yells.

We're gonna smash into it!

Gemini screams.

I shut my eyes and clutch the armrests.

But instead of being obliterated, nothing happens.

I open my eyes to find a ringed, red planet floating in space.

"W-What happened?" I stammer. "Why aren't we space-kill?"

"Because it was an illusion," Scorpio says. "Let's call it a test. We passed."

"Well, thank goodness for that," I say, sliding down in my chair. "But if there's a follow-up exam, I'm calling in sick."

Gemini shakes her head. "It's not that kind of a test. Scorpio, do you know where we'll find him? I mean, that's a whole planet down there."

"Yes," Scorpio says. "According to legend, he's west of the giant crater. I suggest we start there."

"Will do," Pisces says. "Prepare for landing."

We touch down minutes later. Despite the planet appearing red from outer space, the surface seems more purplish up close.

"Stream suits on," Scorpio advises. "As far as I know, no one has reached the surface for centuries. So, let's be ready for anything. And when we find the Watcher, let me do all the talking. Is that clear?" For some reason, he's looking at me.

Why do aliens think I cause all the problems?

We exit the Ghost Ship and hit the ground.

The sky is blood red and dotted with black clouds. Stringy, white lightning flashes overhead, occasionally striking the ground with violent results. The terrain is rough and challenging—ranging from tall, jagged rocks to deep, bottomless crevices. We carefully make our way, passing clusters of orange plant-like things swaying gently in the soft breeze.

After what seems like hours, Taurus has had it. She plops down on a rock, rubbing her feet. "We need to stop. I'm getting blisters."

I take a seat next to her, my own feet throbbing. It seems hopeless, like we've been walking in circles.

Suddenly, Sagittarius rears up on his hind legs and points towards the sky. "There," he says.

We look up to see a white object sitting high atop a mountain. Bingo! But how are we going to get way up there?

"Stand together," Pisces says. "And stay close."

From what I can tell, Pisces is an energy manipulator that can control the density of air molecules. We form a tight circle around her, joining hands. Pisces concentrates, creating a platform of air that lifts us off the ground and to the top of the mountain.

We step off onto the summit to find a large, white structure that looks like a Greek temple—square in shape with wide marble columns. At its center is a giant chair with a large, robed figure sitting in it.

The Watcher!

"Remember," Scorpio says. "I'll do the talking."

As we approach, I try calculating how old this guy is. Gemini said he's been around since the beginning of time, so if the known universe is something like ten or twelve billion years old, then this dude has had loads of birthdays. I mean, what do you get for a guy who's seen everything?

We climb the marble steps, Scorpio in the lead.

The Watcher's head is down like he's sleeping. In his right hand is a thin, golden staff. I study his bald head, expecting to see tons of liver spots or something, but it's totally smooth.

As we reach the top step, we look at one another, unsure of what to do next. We're here because Scorpio thinks the Watcher may have the answer to what's happening with these vanishing people, including Aries. I guess if you've seen everything you can solve lots of mysteries. Hopefully, this guy never misses a trick.

Scorpio clears his throat, about to speak, when—

"Bring me the Orb Master," comes a deep voice.

Oh, geez.

Suddenly, The Watcher lifts his head—revealing a surprisingly young-looking face.

But that's not what gets my attention.

His eyes are completely white!

The Watcher is… blind?

Meta Profile

Name: Gemini
Role: Vigilante   Status: Active

VITALS:

Race: Gallronian
Real Name: Steva Duon 12
Height: 4'6"
Weight: 103 lbs
Eye Color: Orange
Hair Color: Black

META POWERS:

Class: Meta-morph
Power Level:

- Can split into two identical bodies
- Each body can increase in size up to 10 feet
- Retains experiences each divided self obtains

CHARACTERISTICS:

Combat	45	
Durability	21	
Leadership	72	
Strategy	75	
Willpower	89	

SEVEN

I WANT TO HURL MYSELF OFF A CLIFF

"Bring forth the Orb Master!" the Watcher commands.

You ever have a weird dream where you're called to the Principal's office, but have no clue what for?

Well, that's exactly how I'm feeling—except magnified a gazillion times.

Even though he can't see me, the Watcher turns his head in my direction—like he senses me standing behind the Zodiac.

"Bring him to me," the Watcher demands.

The alien teens part nervously, giving me a clear path straight to the Watcher. So much for Scorpio doing all the talking! Other than jumping off the cliff to my death, I have no choice but to step to the front of the class.

It's not until I'm standing in front of the Watcher that I realize how enormous he is. Maybe it's because he's sitting down, but I'm guessing he's at least ten feet tall standing at full height. There's a faint, white glow radiating from his body, making him seem almost heavenly. I'm still shocked that for a dude who's billions of years old, there's not a single wrinkle anywhere on his face. If I could bottle that formula I'd be the richest guy on Earth.

I stand awkwardly for what seems like an eternity. I don't know if I should start talking or wait for him. And then—

"Why did you destroy the Orb of Oblivion?" he bellows.

I refrain from wetting myself.

Honestly, I'm not sure what to say. "I, um, thought it was the best idea at the time?" I squeak out.

"Then you are a fool," he responds. "You have destroyed the one agent capable of saving the universe."

Okay, I don't care who this guy is. I'm getting sick and tired of being called a fool over this Orb thing.

"Look, I may have been a bit rash," I say, "but the Orb didn't exactly come with a return address."

"You are flippant," the Watcher says. "I sense you have no remorse for what you have done. The Orb was a tool to be used for good, not a piece of trash to be so recklessly discarded."

Wait, what?

The Orb is a tool for good?

That doesn't jive with anything I know.

I mean, K'ami died to keep the Orb out of the hands of her own Skelton people.

I distinctly remember her describing the Orb as a parasite that preyed on its host's most selfish desires. She said it was a living entity of great power that would only be used for death and destruction. I mean, it was purposely placed on a remote planet at the far end of the galaxy so no one would ever find it. How can that possibly be a tool for good?

Something is not adding up.

I look into the Watcher's white eyes and wonder how much he really can see. I mean, Gemini did call him a madman. So, is he really this great observer of life, or is he just a big fraud?

I decide to test the waters.

"With all due respect, Mr. Watcher," I say. "But that's a complete load of crock."

I hear gasps from behind me.

"Elliott," Gemini whispers. "What are you doing?"

"Don't worry," I whisper back. "I've got this."

Her jaw goes slack.

"First of all," I say, "if you really *can* see everything, as my good friends here believe, then you'd know that before the Orb got into my hands, it was stolen by the Skelton Emperor who wanted to take over the entire universe. And second, if it weren't for me and my friends, we'd all be toast by now. So, for somebody named the Watcher, I'm a little surprised by your lack of clarity on this one."

The Watcher's face turns dark.

"Oh, no he didn't," Gemini whispers behind me.

I feel someone pulling my shoulder from behind.

But I press on. "In fact, I'm guessing you can't see more than a few feet in front of your face. Can you?"

Scorpio grabs my arm. "Time to go, hotshot!"

I shrug free and stand my ground.

The Watcher smiles.

"You have proven your foolishness once again, Orb Master," he says. "One does not need sight to have vision. Just as one does not need great insight to understand we are all pawns in a game in which we have no control."

Game? What nonsense is he talking about? "Sure, big guy," I say, turning to the Zodiac. "Let's get out of here. This guy *is* nuts."

"You may leave if you wish," the Watcher says. "But if you do, you will not gain the knowledge you so desperately seek. As I have been so painfully reminded, I am not to interfere in the affairs of the universe. But seeing how you have come such a long way, I will risk making an exception. You may ask me one question."

Scorpio raises a hand, stopping us. "Hold on." He turns to the Watcher. "What happened to Aries?"

The Watcher raises an eyebrow. "Is this the question

you most wish for me to answer? How about you, Orb Master? Is this *your* one burning question?"

I know the Zodiac want to find out what happened to Aries, but I have something else I need to know.

Something all of this 'Orb Master' talk is making me think about.

Something I've been suspecting for a long time.

I approach the Watcher and swallow hard. "Is the Orb of Oblivion still out there?" I ask. "Did it survive?"

The Watcher smirks. "As you have said yourself, the Orb of Oblivion is an entity—a cosmic entity, but an entity nonetheless."

Wait, I didn't say that out loud. I thought about it, but I didn't say it.

"And as all creatures are born with an innate biological tendency towards self-preservation, the Orb took whatever steps were necessary to ensure its own survival. Therefore, I am certain that if you are searching for the Orb of Oblivion, you will not have to travel far."

What does that mean? I won't have to travel—

And then it hits me.

The Orb of Oblivion is... inside of me!

Suddenly, I feel sick to my stomach.

I hear the Watcher's deep laughter echoing in my brain.

Then, everything gets blurry and my knees buckle. Suddenly, I'm floating. I look up to find Taurus standing over me, my arms and legs hanging down. Is she carrying me? Stars drift past overhead and then fade to darkness.

***

There's a low humming noise, and I'm being gently bounced around. I open my eyes and take in my surroundings. We're back on the Ghost Ship. Members of the Zodiac are walking back and forth, checking controls, and pushing buttons. I lean over and look out the window. We're deep in space. There's no sign of Watcher World.

I slide back in my chair, the realization of what the Watcher said still sinking in. This can't be happening. I thought I was done with the Orb. I mean, I watched the High Commander take it aboard his ship. I sensed it blowing up somewhere in the universe. But instead of being destroyed, the Orb somehow stuck to me.

It just doesn't make any sense.

I close my eyes and breathe deep. Then, I reach into my mind to connect with the Orb, to talk to it like I was able to do before, but there's nothing.

Nothing at all.

My mind drifts back to my family and I wonder what they're thinking. My parents are probably panicked. I can just see TechnocRat working all night in his lab figuring out a way to track me down. I've been gone so long I'm sure even Grace is missing me. And Dog-Gone—well, hopefully, that furball is okay. Boy, it'd be great to see him again.

But I'm stuck here. All on my own.

Some hero I am.

First, I'm kicked off the Freedom Force because I can't control my powers. Now, I'm stuck in outer space with no shot of getting home.

I feel a tear slide down my cheek and wipe it away quickly. *Never show weakness.*

I watch Leo swing over to Scorpio. Then, they both look my way and start whispering back and forth.

I'm sure they're talking about where to dump me.

Just then, Gemini slides into the seat next to me. "So, how are you feeling?"

"You mean, after learning I've got an alien parasite wedged in my body, or realizing I may never see my family again?"

Gemini's antennas droop, and she looks down. Ugh! I totally forgot about her situation. That was a really insensitive thing to say.

"Sorry," I say embarrassed. "I forgot your whole world is gone."

"It's okay," she says, rubbing her eyes. "I mean, I'm just getting used to the idea. Truthfully, I'm still in shock. But the Zodiac is my new family now. A dysfunctional family, but a family nonetheless."

"Yeah, they seem like a good group. Except for Leo. He gives me the creeps."

"He's a little strange, but he means well," she says. "I

have to say, you impressed me on Watcher World, I didn't expect you to take it to him like that." She flips a strand of hair off her face and smiles at me kind of funny.

"Thanks," I say, feeling myself turning red. "Honestly, neither did I. But he just got my goat. I mean, what's his deal anyway? I didn't expect him to be blind. I thought he was supposed to see everything?"

"I know," Gemini says. "The legends never said anything about that. And what did he mean when he said he was 'painfully reminded' about interfering in the affairs of the—"

"Scorpio!" Pisces yells from the helm. "We've got company!"

I lean over and look out the windshield. To my surprise, several large ships are surrounding us. Ships I've seen before. Skelton warships!

"But how did they find us?" Scorpio asks.

"We're being hailed!" Pisces says.

Suddenly, the image of a square-jawed, yellow-skinned man appears on the screen. He wiggles his pointy ears as he scans our faces with his neon-green eyes. Then, I realize he's wearing a crown on his head.

It's the freaking Skelton Emperor!

This is not good.

"I am not patient," he begins. "So, I will be direct. You are harboring a known intergalactic criminal and enemy of the Skelton Empire. This miscreant is responsible for aiding a known traitor in the unprovoked murder of a Blood Bringer platoon, as well as the destruction of an imperial Skelton warship. For your own freedom, I advise you to turn the offender over immediately or be implicated as an accomplice in his nefarious acts."

What? That's not what happened!

"Pardon me, just stating the obvious," Leo says to the team, "but that's the Skelton Emperor. We should really think this through."

What? I thought he was on my side?

But he's right, if the Zodiac has any chance of making it out alive, I'll need to give myself up. Otherwise, the Emperor will kill every last one of them. I look at Gemini. They've suffered too much. I can't let that happen.

Scorpio looks at me and then turns to the Emperor. "I'm sorry," he starts. "But—"

"Wait!" I say, stepping forward. "I appreciate what you're about to do, but I'll go."

"What?" Gemini says. "You can't—"

"No," I say. "It's okay. Let me go, and then you guys should get out of here as fast as you can."

"But he'll kill you," Taurus says, her fists clenched.

"And if I don't go, he'll kill *you*," I say. "All of you. Trust me, this is for the best." I stride to the center of the bridge and face the Emperor. "Take me. I'm ready."

The Skelton Emperor can barely conceal his glee. "Beam over the Orb Master," he commands. "Now."

Orb Master? This isn't about my so-called 'crimes' at all, is it? He wants me because of the Orb!

Suddenly, I feel a strange sensation.

I look down to see crackling orange energy around my arms. Suddenly, my feet leave the ground. I'm being lifted into the air!

This doesn't seem like any teleportation device.

"What is happening?" I hear the Emperor shout. "I ordered you morons to beam him across!"

Wait a minute! This is what happened to Siphon! And the Overlord!

"Elliott!" Gemini screams.

I see her racing towards me.

And then I'm gone.

Meta Profile

Name: Watcher
Role: Cosmic Entity   Status: Active

VITALS:

Race: Inapplicable
Real Name: Watcher
Height: 10'0"
Weight: Unknown
Eye Color: White
Hair Color: Bald

META POWERS:

Class: Inapplicable
Power Level: Incalculable

- Observes all events in the universe
- Cannot interfere in any way, or will suffer dire consequences

CHARACTERISTICS:

Combat	Inapplicable
Durability	Inapplicable
Leadership	Inapplicable
Strategy	Inapplicable
Willpower	Inapplicable

EIGHT

I ENTER A GAME OF NIGHTMARES

I'm in a bed.

But it's not my bed. The covers are stiff, and the pillow is too thin. I also don't feel the weight of Dog-Gone pressing against my body. Usually, he hogs the covers and pushes me to the edge. This time I'm all alone and I don't think that's a good thing.

I don't know where I am, or how I got here. Then, it all comes racing back to me and my stomach drops in dread. The last thing I remember is being swept up in that mysterious, orange energy that zapped Siphon and the Overlord. On the one hand, it saved me from being delivered to the Skelton Emperor's warship. But on the other, it may have killed me, so if I'm in heaven right now I'll be really, really annoyed.

I open my eyes, only to be blinded by bright lights glaring above. I shield my eyes and take in my surroundings. Well, if I'm not dead, I'm guessing it's the next best thing.

I'm in a small, white room roughly the size of a minivan. Other than the bed I'm lying in, which is sitting smack dab in the middle of the room, the only piece of furniture is a white bench to my right where my costume is sitting—neatly folded. So, wait a minute, does that mean...

I peek under the covers and realize I'm wearing white pajamas.

Whew!

That could have been embarrassing.

Hold on! I don't remember putting on pajamas!

Wonderful.

As my eyes adjust, I notice something else that's weird. There's no door. So, how in the world did I—

"Good morning," comes a voice.

I jump out of my skin.

To my right, sitting on the bench, is a tall, thin man who simply wasn't there a second ago. He has white, slicked-back hair and pale, purplish skin. He's wearing a crisp, black business suit with a white pocket square and tie. What's even more bizarre is that his eyes don't have pupils—instead, they're filled with stars.

"My apologies, I did not intend to alarm you," he says, pulling out a small, round tin from inside his jacket pocket. "Mint? After sleeping for so many days, I can only imagine how foul your mouth must taste."

"Who are *you*?" I ask. "And exactly how long did you say I've been sleeping?"

"Suit yourself," the man says, opening the tin and popping a small, white mint into his mouth. "To answer your first question, I am known as Order. And as for your second question, you have been slumbering for five days, four hours, twenty-three minutes, and thirteen seconds. Exactly."

"What?" I say. "Are you serious?"

"You will find that I am always serious," Order says.

"Okay," I say. "Can I, um, go home now?"

"Home?" Order says. "Oh, I am afraid not. You have been chosen to participate in a most important contest."

"Contest? What contest?"

Order smiles, his teeth are perfectly straight. "I see you are confused," he says. "Do not worry, everything will be made clear in time. But first, I think it would be best to show you what you are playing for."

Order snaps and an image of outer space appears on the wall. A black and pink planet hovers in the center, surrounded by three smaller moons.

"This is Protaraan," he says, cheerfully. "One of my favorite worlds. It has a truly marvelous landscape—with vast grasslands and deep, majestic seas. It is the home to some of the galaxy's most wondrous creatures. The

Protaraan people are industrious and peaceful, and the wildlife is plentiful and diverse. Did you know there are ten thousand four hundred and ninety-three sub-species of crustaceans alone?"

Suddenly, a tiny speck appears, like a firefly in the night, heading straight for Protaraan. As it advances, it leaves a bright trail behind it, like the tail of a comet.

The image pushes in closer, and I realize that firefly is actually a person. A man—made of fire!

"Who's that?" I ask.

"The Herald," Order sighs, "signaling the beginning of the end."

I have no clue what he means by that. I watch as this Herald dude starts looping Protaraan over and over, his trail getting brighter and brighter, until a shape emerges that resembles electrons circling the nucleus of an atom—which, in this case, is Protaraan. In my gut, I feel like something bad is about to happen, and I'm not sure I want to stick around to find out what.

"Well, what do you know?" I say, turning to Order. "That Herald certainly puts on quite a show. So, what's next? We go for milkshakes and call it a night?"

But Order doesn't respond. He's fixated on the events unfolding before us. Reluctantly, I turn back to the image and do a double take.

Creeping in from the bottom of the scene is a mysterious, green mist. At first, it's narrow and stringy, but as it approaches Protaraan it expands larger and larger until it covers the surface area of the entire planet itself! The Herald bolts from the scene, leaving a fiery trail behind him.

Now I can't even see Protaraan through the green haze. I'm about to ask Order what's going on when the green cloud suddenly solidifies—and then clamps down on the planet's surface!

That green thing is... alive?

The green mass pulsates, and then, without warning, it constricts, applying an incredible amount of pressure to the trapped world. There's a tremendous CRACKING sound.

"It's crushing it!"

"No," Order says. "It is consuming it."

KABOOM!

Suddenly, there's a deafening explosion accompanied by a blinding flash of light! I shield my eyes, but I'm not quick enough. For a few seconds, all I can see is white. My ears are ringing like crazy. When I'm finally able to blink my way back to vision, my jaw drops.

Protaraan is gone.

All that remains is a sea of pebbles floating aimlessly in space. At the top of the image I catch the tail of a green mist, moving slowly out of frame.

"I-It's gone!" I say astonished. "All of those people are... are..."

"Extinct," Order says. "Now you understand the magnitude of what you will be playing for—the fate of an entire planet."

"I-I don't understand?" I say.

And then it clicks.

That green mist that ate Protaraan is...

"Ravager!" I blurt out.

"Yes," Order says. "Ravager. The Annihilator of Worlds."

That freaky thing destroyed the homes of Gemini, Scorpio, and the rest of the Zodiac! That's the cosmic creature the Orb of Oblivion was supposed to destroy? How the heck am I supposed to stop that?

My mind is racing. I still have no clue what I'm doing here. Or, more importantly, how I'm going to get out of here. I breathe deeply and try to re-center myself. If I don't figure this out I've got no chance of getting home.

"Okay," I say. "Let's cut to the chase. How do I play this game you're talking about? And how am I gonna get back home?"

"It is quite simple," Order says, dabbing his eyes with his white handkerchief. "You have been selected as a galactic champion—my champion—to compete for the fate of a planet. If you win, the planet survives. But if you lose..."

"It's eaten by Ravager?" I finish his sentence.

"Yes," Order says, standing. He clasps his hands behind his back and begins pacing. "It has been this way through all of eternity. You see, my brother, Chaos, and I are tasked with keeping all things in proper balance. My job is to ensure structure, discipline, and boundaries. My brother's role is quite the opposite. His job is to promote stress, disorder, and randomness. We are constantly at odds. To be truthful, I find it all quite exhausting."

"So, you're like... Gods or something?" I ask.

"Oh, no," Order says. "We are more than Gods. Much more. You could say we are the very fabric of the universe."

"That does sound exhausting," I acknowledge.

"Indeed," he says. "Instead of constantly trying to undo all the other has done, we have agreed to a simple contest to be held after the birth of a new solar system. What I just shared with you was a replay of the outcome of our last contest. Unfortunately, my champions lost. That is where I hope you will come in."

"What do I need to do?" I ask.

"You, and three other champions I have selected, will compete to recover a hidden artifact. The team that recovers the artifact first will determine the fate of a planet. If my team wins, the planet will survive for another million years. If my brother's team wins, the planet will be sacrificed to Ravager, and his champions will be granted new worlds to rule."

He stares at me as I process what he said.

This isn't a game of tiddlywinks he's talking about here. I mean, I don't even have control over my powers. Doesn't he want to win? Maybe he should have picked Dad or Mom or anyone else on the Freedom Force. But not me!

"Hey, listen," I say. "I'm really flattered you want me on your team. I mean, I'm never picked first for anything, not even checkers. But this is serious stuff you're talking about. I think you've got the wrong guy."

Order smiles again. "I have observed millions of champions in my time. Sometimes I am right. Sometimes I am wrong. But you have been selected, and therefore, you must compete."

"And what if I refuse?"

"As our agreement stipulates, if any selected champion refuses to participate, then that team must automatically forfeit the match. And if that team is mine, an entire planet will be destroyed."

I breathe deeply. I think about Gemini and what's happened to her world. She's lost everything she's ever known. I could never willingly let that happen to anyone else. I couldn't imagine being responsible for the deaths of billions of people.

"You've got me there," I say. "Okay, I guess I'm in."

"As I knew you would be," Order says. "Now please, get some rest and eat." He snaps again, and a tray of food appears at the foot of the bed. There's pizza, and cucumbers, and tortilla chips, and root beer. All of my favorite things! It smells amazing!

I dive in. It feels like I haven't eaten for days.

"Tomorrow, you will meet your teammates," Order says. "But before I leave you, I will share with you what you will be playing for in *your* contest."

He snaps again, but I'm so famished all I can focus on is the food.

"When the door appears tomorrow morning," Order says, "make sure you exit wearing your costume."

At this point, I'm totally pigging out. I should probably ask what I'm supposed to do when I need to use the bathroom, but when I look up, Order is gone.

I glance over to see what it is I'll supposedly be playing for. And that's when I drop my pizza.

Because hovering before me is a familiar blue-green planet.

Earth.

Meta Profile

Name: Order
Role: Cosmic Entity Status: Active

VITALS:

Race: Inapplicable
Real Name: Order
Height: appears 7'0"
Weight: Unknown
Eye Color: Inapplicable
Hair Color: White

META POWERS:

Class: Inapplicable
Power Level: Incalculable

- Balances his brother, Chaos, to ensure structure, discipline, and boundaries throughout the universe

- Cannot harm other Cosmic Entities

CHARACTERISTICS:

Combat	Inapplicable
Durability	Inapplicable
Leadership	Inapplicable
Strategy	Inapplicable
Willpower	Inapplicable

NINE

I GET MISTAKEN FOR SOMEBODY ELSE

Needless to say, I didn't sleep a wink.

I mean, how could I after learning my actions will determine the fate of Earth! I tossed and turned all night long, thinking about all of those innocent people down there, and all those kids just going about their business worrying about pimples, homework, and social media cred. They have no clue what's going on up here. None of them are fighting for their lives to stop a globe-gobbling pile of glop!

Nope. Apparently, only I'm dumb enough to get signed up for that one.

And what the heck *am* I doing here anyway? Why would Order pick me? I mean, I'm just a kid, not some freaking galactic gladiator. Why didn't he choose Dad, or Mom, or even Grace? They're playing in the big leagues with full control of their powers. Me? I'm squarely in the minors with no clue how my powers work.

I look around the tiny room. There's no clock so I have no idea what time it is. Order said a door would magically appear when he's ready for me—whenever the heck that is.

To my surprise, a door did appear at one point. Thinking it was game-time, I got suited up, only to burst through the door and crash into a toilet. So, instead of answering the call of adventure, I answered the call of nature.

Yep, villains fear me.

It feels like I've spent hours in solitary confinement. To prevent myself from going stir crazy, I've done everything from jumping jacks to the Hokey Pokey. But mostly, I've done a lot of thinking.

Especially about the Orb of Oblivion.

What I don't get is if the Orb is somehow inside of me, then why isn't it working like it did before? The last time I had it, we were mind-linked, and it was talking to me like crazy. Now there's complete radio silence. I'm beginning to suspect it's mad at me for blowing it up, which is probably justified.

The Orb is a cosmic parasite. When it was a physical entity, outside my body, it mentally bonded to its host and fed off their deepest desires. So, what's it doing now that it's inside of me? The image of a radioactive tapeworm comes to mind.

I'm feeling restless, so I hop off the bed to top my astounding push-up record of five when I notice something unusual.

There's a door.

A gold door.

The last door that materialized was white. So, I'm guessing this has to be the one!

I rush over to put on my costume when, suddenly, I get the jitters. Is this really it? If so, what happens next could determine the fate of everyone on Earth— including my family.

And it's all up to me.

I pull on my mask and straighten my cape. The words of a brave friend echo in my mind: *Never show weakness.*

I take a deep breath and push through the door.

I step into a large, white chamber with walls that climb hundreds of feet high. There are gold doors all around the perimeter, just like the one I entered from. The chamber is windowless, so I still can't tell whether its day or night.

Order mentioned I'd be meeting my teammates, but there's nobody here but—

"Are you friend or foe?" comes a voice.

I spin around to find a stern-faced man standing behind me. Where'd he come from? His dark eyes study me from beneath a thick, leather headband adorned with the symbol of a black eagle. With his long, black hair, and tan costume he appears Native American, but his skin is blue! He folds his arms across his broad chest and repeats, "Friend or foe?"

"Friend," I say quickly. "I-I think we're supposed to be teammates."

The man studies me and then extends a hand. "I am called Wind Walker, Crosser of Realms."

I shake his hand. "And I'm Epic Zero, a member of the Freedom Force. Well, sometimes I'm a member of the Freedom Force. I mean, when I'm not grounded." I smile lamely.

I can tell by his arched eyebrows he's far from impressed. Way to go, Elliott.

Suddenly, another door opens, and a large figure emerges. At first, I think it's a man, but he looks young— like he's only a few years older than me. His muscles are huge, but that's not his most impressive feature. That belongs to the pair of long, curved horns protruding from his forehead. Could it be?

"Please," he says, squeezing his giant hands into fists, "tell me you're the bad guys, because I want to get this over with and get back to my friends."

"Whoa, big fella," I say. "You're Aries, aren't you?"

He looks at me funny, trying to place me. "How'd you know that? Who are you?"

"My name is Epic Zero," I say, trying to muster

more confidence this time around. "I'm a hero on my world, a member of the Freedom Force. For the last few days, I've been traveling with your team, the Zodiac."

There, that was better.

He looks me up and down. "You're Epic Zero? You're kidding me?"

Or not.

Suddenly, there's a SLAM.

"What's he doing here?" comes an angry, female voice.

I turn to find a girl standing in the doorway. She has long brown hair and wears a blue mask and bodysuit with white shooting stars across her top and legs. Wait, why do I know that costume? And how come her angry expression look so familiar?

Then, she points at me and commands. "Stand down, super-creep!"

Wait? What? Super-creep? Me? Her voice is so familiar.

"Who are you?" Aries asks.

"Who am I?" she says. "I'm Glory Girl. And I'm taking this goober out."

Glory Girl? Grace?

But Grace doesn't have brown hair?

The next thing I know, she charges me. But before she gets far, she's frozen in her tracks.

"Halt, heroes!"

I try turning, but I'm frozen too!

Just then, Order appears, hovering in the air above us. He lands without a sound and snaps his fingers. Suddenly, we can move again.

"I suggest you refrain from harming one another," Order says. "After all, you will soon be working together."

"Are you nuts?" Grace exclaims. "I'm not working with him! He took over my entire planet!"

"Grace, what are you talking about?" I ask, totally confused.

"Don't you dare call me by my first name, you tyrant!" she screams back.

"What?" I say. "What's wrong with you?"

"There is nothing wrong with her," Order says. "For, on her world, you *are* a tyrant."

"Her world? What are you talking about?" I say, more confused than ever.

"Perhaps I can explain," Wind Walker says. "For my powers allow me to walk between worlds—and between universes."

"Hold on there," I say. "Are you saying there's more than one universe?"

"Yes," Wind Walker says. "I am certain that you perceive your reality—the here and now—as the only form of reality—as a single, unfolding series of events. But the truth of reality is far more complex. For while we are standing here in our universe, other realities are co-existing with ours—mirror universes, in a sense—where events still unfold chronologically, but with drastically different outcomes."

"So, you're saying there are two of her?" I say, pointing to Grace. The very thought makes me shiver.

Wind Walker smiles. "Yes, just as there may be hundreds of mirror worlds, there may be hundreds of versions of her, just as there may be hundreds of versions of you."

"Hundreds of Graces," I say. "I think you just exploded my brain." If he's serious then that would explain why she has brown hair instead of blond. And why her costume is blue instead of crimson. That's not my sister! It's some freaky alternate universe version of my sister!

"So, hang on," I say. "You mean, on your world I'm like, the king?"

Grace folds her arms and spits. "I didn't say 'king.' I said 'tyrant.'"

"Cool!" I say.

"Enough," Order says. "There is little time, and you must learn the rules."

Grace shoots me a nasty look. I wouldn't trade my sister for this version any day of the week.

Order snaps, and a holographic map segmented by gridlines appears. "You will be battling on Arena World—a planet with varied terrain and extreme weather conditions. Do not underestimate these facts. How you deal with Arena World may ultimately contribute to your victory, or your defeat."

Well, that sounds ominous.

"As I have explained to each of you," Order continues, "you will be competing against the team of my brother, Chaos, to recover a hidden artifact. This is the artifact you seek." Order snaps and a silver cube with an orange glow materializes. "This is the Building Block. I must warn you, the Building Block is not just an object—it is a sentient being. Therefore, you may want to consider it as a player in its own right. And it can be deadly."

Great, now we've got to fetch a tissue box with attitude problems.

Order snaps again and the image of Arena World shifts to an image of Earth. "This is a battle with the ultimate stakes. If you are defeated, billions will lose their lives. Today, you will get to know one another and learn how to work together. You will practice as a team and become familiar with each other's powers."

I peer over at Grace, who's still giving me the evil eye.

"And tomorrow," Order continues, "you will fight for your lives. But before I depart, I think it is only fair to reveal who you will be facing in combat. Study my brother's team carefully and determine your course to victory."

He snaps again, and disappears, leaving behind four holographic images of our enemies.

There's some villain I don't know but is a dead ringer

for a Skelton Blood Bringer.
And then, there's Siphon!
The Overlord!
And... Mom?

Meta Profile

Name: Glory Girl (2)
Role: Hero   Status: Active

VITALS:

Race: Human
Real Name: Grace Harkness
Height: 5'3"
Weight: 101 lbs
Eye Color: Blue
Hair Color: Brown

META POWERS:

Class: Flight
Power Level:

- **Considerable Flight**
- **Limited Super-Speed in combination with Earth's gravitational force.**

CHARACTERISTICS:

Combat	29	
Durability	26	
Leadership	40	
Strategy	28	
Willpower	57	

TEN

I COMPLETELY HUMILIATE MYSELF

So much for working as a team.

After Order dropped the bomb about our competitors, he vanished without a trace. Then, instead of coming together as a team to strategize, the four of us wandered into separate corners. Truthfully, that's fine by me, because after what's transpired in the last five minutes, there's a heck of a lot I need to process.

First, I still need to wrap my head around this mirror universe thing. It's hard to imagine there's some duplicate of me out there doing things I couldn't even dream of—like, for example, conquering Earth. I mean, how'd something like that even happen? I can't believe it's even real.

But then again, it's impossible to write off when a

duplicate of my sister is pacing back and forth less than twenty feet away. To keep everything straight in my mind, I've labeled her Grace 2—and it's pretty clear she hates me. I really don't know how we're ever going to work together to save Earth.

And then there's the other doozy.

Apparently, we're going to be fighting Mom!

I mean, clearly, she's not my mom—my mom's a hero through and through. So, that means on some bizarre Earth, Mom is a villain! This is like, total insanity! I don't know if this version of Mom is from the same Earth as Grace 2 or not. I guess she could be Mom 2, Mom 3, or Mom 103 for all I know.

My head is pounding.

Before Order split, he left behind a buffet with all sorts of food on it. I see Wind Walker and Aries loading up their plates and talking. My stomach is rumbling, so I figure I'd better grab something now. After all, who knows how long it'll be until I can eat again.

As I approach, I catch the heroes in mid-conversation.

"—don't know if they can work together," Wind Walker says.

"Fabulous," Aries says. "Then we're as good as dead."

"How's it going, fellas?" I say, grabbing a chicken drumstick.

Aries looks at me with a serious expression. "If we're

going to have any chance at winning this thing, you're going to have to bury the hatchet with her."

"Me?" I say. "You saw what happened. She's got the problem, remember?"

We look over at Grace 2, who's now sitting with her back against the wall, her head resting on her knees.

"That may be true," Wind Walker says. "But it is up to you to solve it. The lives of billions depend on it."

"Why is it my job? She started it! I didn't do anything to offend her but breathe."

I glance back over to see her wiping away a tear.

Suddenly, my dad's words pop into my head. *"We're heroes,"* Dad said. *"We're sworn to help all of those in need."*

Sometimes it stinks being the good guy.

"Fine," I say, looking at Wind Walker and Aries. "I'll do it."

But how? Out of the corner of my eye, I spy a pile of jelly doughnuts on the table. Maybe…

I grab a napkin, wrap up a doughnut, and take a deep breath. Then I walk over to Grace 2 and slide down next to her.

"Jelly doughnut?" I offer. "They're my sister's favorite."

"Thanks," Grace 2 says, "mine, too." She reaches for the doughnut and takes a big bite. "Sorry for attacking you," she says, talking with her mouth full. "I lost my marbles when I thought you were someone else. But I guess you're you, and not the person I thought you were."

"No problem," I say. "You really caught me off guard. I mean, I didn't know about this whole mirror universe thing. It kind of blows my mind when I think about it."

"Yeah, me too," Grace 2 says. "It's weird."

I study her closely as she chews. Except for her brown hair, she's the spitting image of my sister, even down to the freckles on her nose.

Unbelievable.

"So," I say, "if you don't mind me asking. Was that your mom up there? I mean, mine's a hero on my world."

Grace 2 breathes out. "Yeah, that's my mom—Ms. Understood. I haven't seen her since she and my dad got divorced."

"Divorced?" I exclaim.

"Yeah," Grace 2 continues. "She used to be a superhero, but then turned into a villain. My dad was pretty bummed about it, so much so that he actually hung up his tights. Especially after—well, after you became supreme ruler and outlawed all superheroes."

"I did what?"

"Outlawed all heroes," Grace 2 repeats. "You offered a bounty to anyone that brought you a superhero. And once you got them, you canceled their powers—permanently. It then became a free-for-all for the villains, who pretty much did whatever they wanted. They started forming these Meta gangs, marking their turf. But there's still an underground group of heroes like me that work day and night to stop you. We call ourselves the Freedom Force. And one day, we're going to take you down and set the world right again."

I watch her get more and more agitated as she speaks.

"Hang on," I say. "Remember, it's not me who's doing this. It's your brother on *your* world."

"Sorry," she says, deflating. "You're right. This whole thing is so overwhelming. And then to see my mom up there…"

"Hey," I say, putting my hand on her shoulder. "I get it. But we're the heroes, right? We need to save the day when others won't."

She smiles at me, "You're right. I guess if we're going to work together, we should put this behind us, shouldn't we?"

She reaches out her hand, and we shake.

"By the way, Elliott," she adds, "you're blond in my universe."

"What?" I say. "You're kidding?"

As we stand up, we're joined by Wind Walker and Aries. Aries gives me a nod. "We good?" he asks.

"Yeah," I say. "We're good."

"Excellent," Wind Walker says. "Now we must learn about each other's powers and abilities."

"And that is precisely why I have returned," comes Order's voice from above, spooking the pants off of us.

"I'm getting tired of this guy," Grace 2 whispers.

"Prepare yourselves," Order says.

Suddenly, all of the gold doors around the chamber pop open.

"I don't have a good feeling about this," Aries says.

"This exercise will not be as difficult as the task you will face tomorrow," Order says. "Nonetheless, it should prove quite... educational." And with that, he disappears.

"Close ranks," Wind Walker says, and we all gather back-to-back in the center of the room, awaiting the arrival of whatever nightmare Order is about to throw at us.

We stand there for what feels like an eternity. I take a deep breath. These guys are counting on me to pull my weight, but I can't even control my powers. I need to make sure that when I use them, I don't accidentally cancel out theirs.

That is, as long as whatever it is we're about to face even has Meta powers. Because if it's anything else, then I'm essentially useless.

Just then, we hear beeping—lots of loud, high-pitched beeping. Like there's some big hullabaloo among a bunch of—

"Robots!" Grace 2 yells.

Robots. Of course, robots.

I'm about to inform my teammates that I'll be about as helpful as a pinecone when the mechanical monsters suddenly attack us. They're big and fast. I barely catch their features—menacing red eyes, pincer-like arms, and spiked, spinning wheels—as they head straight for us.

I dive out of the way in the nick of time, as a bot slides past me, leaving behind a giant skid mark.

This isn't good! My powers don't work on robots!

But they're no problem for my teammates.

Aries holds his ground, shattering robot after robot with his powerful fists! Wind Walker's opened some kind of mystical void around his body that's like a roach motel—robots check in, but they don't check out! And Grace 2 has taken to the air, picking up robots one by one and dropping them to their doom from terrifying heights!

We'd probably get out of this mess if it wasn't for the fact that the robots just keep coming—wave after automated wave.

I'm pretty much dead meat sitting here, so I pick myself up and bolt towards Wind Walker. Maybe he can protect both of us with that rift thing he's got going on. I make it halfway when I suddenly realize my feet aren't touching the ground anymore.

I'm floating! With a robot latched onto each arm!

I try to pull free, but their grip is too strong.

"Help!" I call, but the other heroes have their hands full.

We're cruising at a good clip when the robots suddenly change course. Before us is a giant column in the corner of the chamber—a thick, marble column.

"Put me down!" I yell.

But they don't listen. Instead, they make a beeline straight for it, which can only mean one thing.

They're going to smash me against it!

We pick up speed!

We're going so fast I can't even speak, my face is stretched back like I'm nose-diving in an airplane. The column is getting closer and closer. We're going to crash!

I close my eyes.

And one overriding thought takes over.

STOP!

Suddenly, there's a deafening SCREECH, and I'm jerked forward. The robots release their grip, and I go flying head over heels, landing inches away from the base of the column.

What happened?

I turn, to find the two robots standing stock-still behind me—stopped dead in their tracks.

I thought it...

...and they did it?

But that's not my power? My powers only work on Metas. I-I haven't been able to do that since... since...

O.

M.

G.

"Epic!" Grace 2 calls from above. "Are you okay? Sorry I couldn't get here faster."

"Yeah," I say, standing up. "I'm good."

"Nice work," she says, landing beside me. "Funny, your powers are exactly the same as my brother's."

"Really?" I say. For some reason, that gives me a weird feeling, but I can't put my finger on why. I'm just so confused right now.

Seconds later, we're joined by Aries and Wind Walker. There's a mountain of robot parts behind them.

"Everyone okay?" Aries asks.

"Yep," Grace 2 says. "We're fine. I guess we showed those tin-bots a thing or two."

"Indeed," Wind Walker says. "But we fought as individuals. If we are going to be victorious tomorrow, we will need to fight as a team."

"I agree," Aries says. "Otherwise, we'll have no chance. I'm pretty clear on your powers," he says looking at Wind Walker and Grace 2. "But what exactly do you do?" he says, looking at me.

"Me?" I say, stalling for time. "Great question." What do I tell him? My Meta Manipulation powers can cancel the powers of other Metas. But that doesn't explain what I just did to those robots who don't have powers.

"He's omnipotent," Grace 2 says. "Just like my brother on my world."

Omnipo-what?

"Omnipotent?" Aries says. "What's that mean?"

"It means all-powerful," Grace 2 says. "If he thinks it, it'll happen. Isn't that right, Epic?"

All-powerful? Wait a minute. Is that what the Orb of Oblivion is—omnipotent? And it's... inside of me.

"Epic?" Grace 2 repeats.

I look up to find them staring at me. "Yeah," I say. "That's right."

"Well, then," Aries says, breaking into a huge smile. "Now I see why Leo wanted you. I guess we don't have anything to worry about." He puts his big hand on my shoulder. "We've got Epic Zero."

"Right," I say, faking a smile. "I guess we do."

Meta Profile

Name: Aries
Role: Vigilante   Status: Active

VITALS:

Race: Ani-man
Real Name: Ramm V'kkar
Height: 6'5"
Weight: 325 lbs
Eye Color: Brown
Hair Color: Bald

META POWERS:

Class: Super-Strength
Power Level: ▉▉▉▉
- **Extreme strength**
- **Invulnerability**
- **Limited super-speed**
- **Power-Charge**

CHARACTERISTICS:

Combat	100	
Durability	100	
Leadership	62	
Strategy	65	
Willpower	95	

ELEVEN

I GO OUT OF MY MIND

Let's just say Order was less than impressed.

He muttered something about picking the wrong group of heroes and then sent us back to our rooms to rest up for tomorrow's battle to the death. That's okay with me because, honestly, I'm still not sure what happened out there.

It's no secret I was in serious danger with those robots. I mean, 1 thought I was going to croak! But instead, the Orb of Oblivion took over.

Believe me, I'm grateful to be alive. But I'm also freaking terrified.

Especially after hearing what Grace 2 had to say. Because if she thinks her brother's powers are like mine, then I'm going to have a bigger fight on my hands then finding the Building Block. After all, her brother is pure evil.

Of course, he and I aren't the same person. I mean, I suppose it's possible that I'm just a good guy and he's a natural psychopath. A good example of that is Mom— she's a hero on my world, but a villain on Grace 2's world. But there's also another possibility.

One that's less pleasant to think about.

Maybe he *was* good just like me but then *turned* evil. Not because he wanted to be a villain, but because he couldn't help it—because he was corrupted—by a second Orb of Oblivion.

The thought sends a chill down my spine.

Two Orbs of Oblivion?

It's staggering to even consider it. But the more I think about it, the more I realize it must be true.

How else could he have become a tyrant? I mean, my powers are strong, but not that strong! And how else could he permanently cancel a Meta's powers? Grace 2's words echo in my mind: *If he thinks it, it'll happen.*

Isn't that how the Orb works?

So, if that's also true for him…

I think back to what happened with those robots and remember the Watcher's words: *the Orb took whatever steps were necessary to ensure its own survival.* It's pretty clear. The Orb wouldn't let me die because it wanted to save itself!

And then I realize what's really happening. The Orb is using me—resting inside of me—gathering its strength.

And when it's ready, it's going to make its move.

Sweat drips down my forehead.

I mastered it before, but what if it's too strong this time? What if it turns me into a monster? What if it takes over my mind and I become a puppet—a shell of a person—existing only to do its bidding?

It's only a matter of time.

I feel like puking.

Suddenly, I'm absolutely exhausted. My eyes start drooping, and my limbs feel like lead—like I'm sinking into the bed. I know I need sleep, but I have way too much to figure out. I try to fight it, but I'm slipping— going down. What's happening? Is this one of Order's tricks?

I need to stay awake.

I… need… to…

✳✳✳

I'm sitting in a room under a blinding spotlight. I shield my eyes when I notice the outline of someone sitting across from me—deep in the shadows.

"Why are you fighting it," comes a boy's voice. It sounds somehow familiar.

"What?" I say. "Who are you?"

"Why fight it?" he repeats. *"You know you want to be just like him."*

"Like who?" I say. "What are you talking about?"

The boy laughs. *"C'mon,"* he says. *"Do I need to spell it out for you? Like Elliott 2—Elliott the king—the most powerful Meta on his planet."*

"I don't want to be like him," I say.

"Don't you?" the boy says. *"Isn't it what you've always dreamed of? No one would be more powerful than you. You can make up all the rules—do whatever you want. You could make the world peaceful, or even rule it if you wanted. Who'd stop you?"*

"Who are you?" I ask. But deep inside, I already know the answer.

"Let's not play games," he says. *"You need me. So, let me help you. I promise you won't regret it. You'll be thanking me later."*

"I don't want anything to do with you," I say. "I want you out. Tell me how to get you out."

"You know I can't do that," he says. *"I know you don't want to hear this, but you're the one. We're a team—a partnership to the end. Soon, you'll see. We're meant to be together."*

"Liar!" I yell, standing up from the chair.

The boy laughs. *"You'll see,"* he says. *"You'll see soon enough."*

"Get out!" I yell. "Get out of—"

***

"—me!"

I shoot up. I'm still in bed.

But I'm not alone.

"It is time," Order says, seated on the bench.

"I-It's morning already?" I ask. "I feel like I haven't slept at all."

"You slept," he says. "And dreamt."

I run my fingers through my hair. "I guess I did. I just don't know what it means."

"Do you know why I selected you?" Order asks.

"Because you want to see a world die?" I say.

"No, Elliott Harkness," he says, staring at me, the stars in his eyes twinkling brightly. "Because I want to win. Not just for today, not just for tomorrow, but for all of eternity."

"Um, okay?" I say. What's he getting at?

He stands up and folds his arms. "Can you imagine a universe where everything flourishes? Where there is no death, no destruction—where everything moves in perfectly predictable harmony, forevermore."

For a second, I'm not following him. And then a lightbulb goes off.

"Wait a minute," I say. "Are you saying you want to get rid of your brother? You want to get rid of Chaos? Like, lock him up or something."

"No," he says, looking down at me. "I want to destroy him."

What? Destroy Chaos? How do you destroy Chaos?

"B-But," I stammer, "wouldn't that throw everything, like, completely out of balance? Don't you need him to keep the universe stable? I mean, don't we all kind of need him?"

Order's eyebrows furrow. "Do we? Did you enjoy watching Protaraan being destroyed? Did you hear the screams of a trillion creatures meeting their end? Do you think you will be able to save your planet? And even if you do, will your descendants be able to do the same when their time inevitably comes?

There's logic to what he's saying. But something just doesn't seem right.

"I-I thought we were trying to stop Ravager?" I say. "I thought that's what this whole thing was about."

"That is what it has been about for millennia," he says. "But this time it will be different. Because I found you."

"Me? Why me?" I ask, although I'm pretty sure I'm not going to like the answer.

"While I possess great power," he says, "I am also constrained by it. I have limitations. For example, I am unable to harm another cosmic being. It is written in the stars."

"So?" I say. "What does that have to do with me?"

"You are the Orb Master," he says. "You are not a cosmic entity, yet you have a cosmic power growing inside of you. Thus, you are not constrained."

The words take a minute to sink in.

"Wait," I say, "so you're saying you want *me* to use the Orb of Oblivion to take down Chaos?"

Order smiles, his perfect teeth gleaming. "When the

appropriate moment arises, you will act."

"Are you kidding me?" I say. "I won't do it!"

"Oh, Orb Master, you will," he says. "You will because you will have no other choice."

I'm speechless. I… I don't even know what to say.

"Now rise, and prepare yourself for battle," he says. "Put on your costume and join your teammates in the main chamber. The contest will start momentarily."

And then he snaps, and he's gone.

I grab my stomach.

I need to get this stinking Orb out of my body.

Before it's too late.

Meta Profile

Name: Wind Walker
Role: Hero   Status: Active

VITALS:

Race: Capachee
Real Name: Wohali Staar
Height: 6'1"
Weight: 215 lbs
Eye Color: Green
Hair Color: Black

META POWERS:

Class: Energy Manipulator
Power Level:
- **Extreme Space Manipulation**
- **Can travel across worlds and universes**

CHARACTERISTICS:

Combat	90	
Durability	45	
Leadership	95	
Strategy	91	
Willpower	99	

TWELVE

I GET A BAD CASE OF DEJA VU

To say my head isn't in the game is an understatement.

Here we are, about to launch into the greatest battle in the history of mankind, and I can't stop thinking about what Order said: *"When the appropriate moment arises, you will act."*

What the heck does that mean?

Is he going to brainwash me into destroying Chaos? And how exactly does one destroy Chaos anyway? I have a sneaking suspicion I'm going to find out, like it or not.

I consider mentioning my secret mission to my teammates but decide against it. With so much at stake, I don't want anything distracting them from the task at hand. I mean, we have a whole planet to save! A planet with billions of people on it who are counting on us.

Including my family.

Looking at Grace 2, I can't help but think of them. The fact that I'll probably never see them again brings a tear to my eye, but I wipe it away. I need to be brave— that's what my parents would want. I suddenly have an overwhelming urge to wrap my arms around Dog-Gone and nuzzle into his furry face. But I'll never get that chance again either.

I wonder if there's a Dog-Gone 2?

We're standing in the main chamber, waiting for Order to magically appear. Aries is jumping up and down, psyching himself up. Wind Walker is meditating peacefully in the corner. Grace 2 and I are just standing around, waiting for this nightmare to begin.

"You ready to go?" Grace 2 asks.

"As ready as I'm gonna be," I answer.

"You know," Grace 2 says. "It didn't really occur to me before, but whose Earth are we trying to save anyway?"

That's a great question! It hadn't dawned on me that maybe the Earth we're fighting for isn't mine. Maybe it's hers, or some other version. "Yeah, I hadn't thought of that either."

Suddenly, I have a sliver of hope. Maybe my family will be spared after all! Then again, knowing my luck, what are the odds of that? But I guess I wouldn't try any less if it wasn't my Earth anyway. When lives are at stake, heroes don't mail it in.

"It doesn't matter," she says, "because we're gonna win anyway. Right?"

"Yeah," I say. "Right."

I'd love to be as optimistic as she is, but truthfully, I'm not so sure.

Our briefing on our opponents was like a "Who's Who" of the galaxy's most dangerous Meta 3 villains: there's the Overlord, an Energy Manipulator who can control gravity; Siphon, a Meta Manipulator who can absorb the powers of others; some Skelton Meta-Morph shapeshifter who I'm sure will be a load-and-a-half; and, maybe the scariest of them all, Mom 2—a Psychic.

So, this isn't going to be a walk in the park.

Not by a long shot.

Just then, Order appears with the artifact—the Building Block—in his hands.

"Champions," he begins. "The time has come. Once again, take note of the object you seek—the Building Block. It will be hidden somewhere on Arena World. As I have warned, some of you may not survive this ordeal, but I urge you to always remember what you are fighting for." He snaps, and a hologram of Earth appears next to him.

I study it closely. It sure looks like my Earth. All the continents are the same. The oceans look about right. I just can't tell.

"I will remind you of the rules one final time," Order says. "If you recover the artifact first, you will preserve the lives of this world for another million years. If my brother, Chaos' team wins, the planet will be destroyed, and his champions will each be given a new planet to rule. Aside from this, there are no other rules. Now it is time to go forth and compete." He looks me in the eyes. "And to win."

Order snaps again, and we are suddenly encased in that strange orange energy that brought us all here in the first place.

I catch Grace 2's face, her eyes are wide.

I turn back to Order, who's smiling at me.

And then, he's gone.

***

We materialize in a valley encircled by sweeping, ice-capped mountains. As we touch down, our feet sink ankle-deep into the snow-covered ground. It's bitterly cold, and a sharp wind is whipping snowflakes sideways like sheets of rain.

It's a blizzard. Great.

Order was right when he said the terrain will be a big factor. Within seconds, I feel like a popsicle. Grace wraps herself in her cape, shivering like crazy, Wind Walker grits his teeth, and Aries' horns start collecting icicles.

If we don't get out of here fast, I don't think we'll make it to find the cube. But which way should we go? We're surrounded by giant, craggy mountains.

As if reading my mind, Grace 2 chatters, "A-Allow m-me." Then she takes off into the air.

We watch her push upwards through the blustery sky, climbing higher and higher until we completely lose sight of her in the swirling wintery mix. She's gone for a long time. Soon, Wind Walker and Aries start looking as worried as I feel. I'm about to suggest we somehow go after her when she suddenly drops back in our midst.

"What took you so long?" I ask.

"You're not going to believe it," she says, "but that way," she points to the mountains in front of her, "is a city—like, a big honking city with buildings and streets and everything. And it's raining!" She turns the other direction, "and over there is a forest with trees, and vines, and it's bright and sunny."

Wow! This world *is* crazy.

"Well, I can't imagine the Building Block is buried here," Aries says, shuddering. "We'd die of hypothermia before we even found it. I say we hit those other areas."

"I agree," Wind Walker says. "And if we split up, we can cover more ground."

Grace 2 and I exchange looks. Even though we barely know each other, there's a familiarity between us that feels comforting. She nods.

"Glory Girl and I will team up," I say. "We'll take the city."

"Very well," Wind Walker says. "We will search the forest." He steps forward and shakes our hands. "Good hunting, my friends."

"Find that cube," Aries says, flashing a grin. "Don't let us find it first."

"You're on," I say.

Then, we watch the heroes run the other away.

Grace 2 reaches out her arms. "May I?"

"You may," I answer, turning around.

Grace 2 puts her arms beneath my armpits and locks her fingers across my chest. She gathers herself, and then we're off—flying through the harsh climate.

The change in weather is abrupt. One second, we're being battered by fierce winds and driving snow, the next we're being tickled by a warm, gentle mist. I've never seen anything like it. And it's not just the weather.

Over the mountains, just as Grace 2 said there would be, is a sprawling city—five times bigger than Keystone City and at least twice the size of Manhattan. Buildings of all shapes and sizes extend for miles, disappearing at the horizon. At first, it seems like your everyday run-of-the-mill city, but as we pull closer I pick up strange differences in architecture. Like, all the windows are circular instead of square, and the streets are curvy instead of straight.

There must be thousands of buildings, streets, and alleyways down there. And somewhere, possibly hidden in this vast urban jungle, is a silver cube smaller than a bread box.

Awesome.

We land in the middle of a large intersection when I realize something I failed to notice before—there aren't any cars. Or buses. Or... people.

Where are all the people?

"It's like a ghost town," Grace 2 says.

"Somehow, that's not reassuring," I say. "Now how the heck are we supposed to find the Building Block? We can't look in every single building. There's got to be a better way."

"I've got an idea," Grace 2 says, staring into space.

"Great, lay it on me," I say, relieved at least one of us is thinking clearly on how to start looking for this thing.

"Well," Grace 2 says, "maybe we ought to ask *him*?"

Him? I spin around to see who she's looking at.

In the distance, there's a large, green object hanging off the side of a building. At first, it looks like one of those creepy gargoyle statues, you know, the ones that serve as waterspouts or something. And I was pretty good with that explanation... until it unfurls a pair of gigantic bat-like wings.

And then I realize it isn't a statue at all.

We watch as the creature rises to full height, extending several stories taller than first appeared possible. It opens its red eyes, pounds its chest, and bellows something awful. Then, I realize I've had the misfortune of seeing this creature before.

And this time, I might not be so lucky.

"Run!" I yell as it leaps from its perch.

Grace 2 takes to the air, while I bolt through the front door of the nearest building I can reach. I cruise through the lobby, leap over a desk, and duck behind it, my heart pounding out of my chest.

That's no gargoyle!

That's a Skelton! And not just any Skelton! That's a Blood Bringer—the worst kind of Skelton!

Blood Bringers are an elite killing force that can change into any form imaginable. And I'm pretty sure this one knows I'm the guy that blew up an entire squadron of his buddies, along with the Orb of Oblivion.

Or, at least that's what I thought I did. Because, apparently, the Orb isn't so easy to get rid of.

Suddenly, a small insect buzzes over the desk, and lands by my foot.

What tripped me up last time was that the Blood Bringers were armored in Sheelds—those clam-like creatures whose skin is resistant to the Orb's powers.

The bug hops onto my foot and stares at me with its large, green eyes. Two thoughts cross my mind. One, this entire planet is empty, except for us. And two, I've got a long, long history with green-eyed bugs.

I stay as still as a log.

And then I swat down with all my might!

The bug darts safely out of harm's way, and then transforms into the largest Skelton I've ever seen—a seven-foot-tall specimen of pure ugly. He stares me down with his piercing neon-green eyes and says, "You will have to excuse me, but I find it hard to believe *you* are the one responsible for the death of my brothers."

Here we go again.

"Nevertheless, it is my duty to avenge them. Perhaps I should introduce myself. I am the Destroyer of Worlds, the Harbinger of Death. I am the High Commander of the Blood Bringers. The new High Commander."

Of course he is.

I quickly scan his body up and down and realize I'm pretty much doomed. Just as I feared, he's covered head-to-toe in leathery brown armor. I'd know that texture anywhere—it's Sheeld—probably standard issue for them now. So even if I wanted to use the Orb of Oblivion—which I don't—I couldn't.

But I still have *my* powers.

"Sorry to disappoint," I say, "but you won't be avenging anybody today." I concentrate hard and bathe him with my negation powers.

"Ridiculous child," he says, advancing towards me. "Prepare to—" Then, he stops and realizes something is wrong. He tries and tries but can't transform his body into anything. "What did you do?" he says.

I cross my arms and smile. "So, tell me, what do you think of me now?"

The High Commander lets out a deafening war cry and lunges towards me. I dive out of the way as he crashes into the desk behind me, shattering it to pieces.

Even though he's powerless, he's still capable of

crushing me. I need to get out of here and find Grace 2! I need her help!

As he rises, I hustle out of the building and back to the main street. Grace 2 spots me from up high and floats down to meet me.

"Where'd you go?" she says. "I've been looking all over for you!"

"Fly in my soup," I say. "Now let's get out of here!"

Suddenly, the entire façade of the building explodes outwards, blowing Grace 2 and me onto our backsides.

When the dust clears, the High Commander stands before us. "No more games, child," he says. "Now is the time for rev—Ahhhhhhh!"

Suddenly, the High Commander drops to his knees, grabbing his head.

"Get away from them!" comes a female voice.

We turn to find a woman in black standing behind us.

It's Mom!

"I brought them into this world," she says, "and I'll be the one to take them out."

Meta Profile

Name: High Commander
Role: Villain   Status: Active

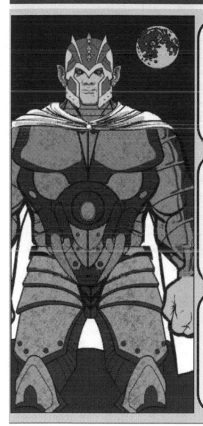

VITALS:

Race: Skelton
Real Name: Unknown
Height: 7'0"
Weight: 350 lbs
Eye Color: Green
Hair Color: Bald

META POWERS:

Class: Meta-morph
Power Level: ▮▮▮

- Extreme Shape-Shifting—can assume endless forms
- Extreme Flight, Strength, and Speed depending upon form taken

CHARACTERISTICS:

Combat	100	▬▬▬
Durability	100	▬▬▬
Leadership	100	▬▬▬
Strategy	100	▬▬▬
Willpower	100	▬▬▬

THIRTEEN

I SEEM TO BE A GLUTTON FOR PUNISHMENT

It's really great seeing Mom again.

There's just one problem, she's trying to kill me.

Mom 2 has already knocked the High Commander out of commission—and he's on her team! We need to act fast because she's a psychic, and psychics are known for—

"Aaahhh!" Grace 2 screams, dropping to the ground holding her head.

Too late! Mom 2's got her!

But why not me?

"Elliott," she says, "Why are you fighting with those heroes? And what happened to your hair?"

My hair? I'm confused for a second, and then I

realize she has no clue about mirror universes. She thinks I'm Elliott 2—her blond, villainous son from her world!

Maybe I can use it to my advantage?

Grace 2 is squirming, clearly in a world of pain.

"Just a big mix-up, Mom," I say, standing up.

"That's what I thought," she says. "So, do you want to finish her off, or should I?"

Finish her off? That's her own kid!

"I-I h-hate y-you!" Grace 2 sputters out.

"I'll do it," I say quickly before Mom 2 gets trigger happy. I need to make my move now before she realizes I'm not who she thinks I am. But how am I going to stop her without risking Grace 2's life? I can't act faster than Mom 2 can think! I mean, it takes me a few seconds to get my own powers going! By then, she may turn Grace 2 into a vegetable!

"Now's our chance," comes a voice in my head.

What? Oh no.

"It's our only chance to save her life," it says.

"What are you waiting for?" Mom 2 asks. "Do it!"

Grace 2 is writhing on the ground. She screams out again. Mom 2 must really be turning the screws.

"Don't ruin this for me, Elliott," Mom 2 says. "You're already the ruler of Earth. When we win, I get my own planet to rule."

Grace 2 stares at me, her eyes pleading.

I have no other choice.

"Use me," the Orb says.

"Who's that?" Mom 2 says, snapping her head my way. "Wait… you're not my son!"

"*Orb,*" I command. "*Knock her out. Now!*"

Suddenly, Mom 2 screams, and then falls to the ground like a limp noodle.

"No, Mom," I say. "I'm not."

"W-What happened?" Grace 2 asks groggily. "Did you do that?"

I slump to the ground, exhausted.

"*And now we're one,*" the Orb says. "*Now we're fully one.*"

Which is exactly what I was afraid of.

"Elliott, are you okay?" Grace 2 asks, sliding over and putting her hand on my shoulder.

"I'm not sure," I say. The last time the Orb and I were connected, I was able to use my willpower to completely master it. But this time, it feels different—like we're sharing space in my brain—like I'm not alone. "I just need a minute."

"I think she was really going to kill me this time," she says. "You saved my life."

"No problem," I say. "I didn't realize your mom was so evil. It was… shocking."

"Tell me about it," she says. "I've been dealing with it since I was little. Dad tried to protect me from her, but I guess you can't always shield the ones you love. But even I didn't realize how deep her madness ran. I guess I do now."

"I'm so sorry," I say.

"It's not your fault," Grace 2 says. "At least there's some comfort knowing she's a good person on your world."

"The best," I say. Suddenly, I feel an overwhelming wave of emotion. Images of my family flash through my mind. I don't think I've ever missed them more than I do right now.

"Hey," Grace 2 says, putting her arms around me. "We'll get through this."

I smile and wipe my eyes. Even though I don't have my family here, Grace 2 is the next best thing. "C'mon," I say. "Let's find that stupid cube. We've got a planet to save."

We lock hands and pull each other up. Mom 2 and the High Commander are still out, and I don't want to be hanging around when they wake up. We've got to find the Building Block, and even though I don't like it, I know what I need to do.

"Orb," I think. *"Can you locate the Building Block?"*

"The cube is a cosmic entity," it replies. *"I can sense its energy but can't pinpoint its exact location. We need to travel further north."*

Well, that's better than nothing, so I tell Grace 2 I've got a hunch. She wraps her arms around me and we take off again.

I feel guilty not telling her about the Orb, but I don't want to freak her out either. After all, I think it's the Orb that corrupted her brother. So, telling her may cloud her trust in me. Especially with the war being waged inside my head right now.

"Why don't we just end this silly game?" the Orb asks.

"Shut up," I reply.

"We can do that," it says, *"we don't need Order or Chaos. We can make our own destiny. Together."*

"Stay focused," I command. *"And please, stop talking."*

"You don't want to know where the cube is?" it asks.

"Of course I want to know where the stupid cube is," I say.

"Then I guess I'll keep talking."

And it's like this the rest of the way—the Orb yammers on and on about "destiny" and "ruling the universe." I try to ignore it, to treat it like background noise, but it's not easy when you can't turn it off.

We're in the air for a long time, and Grace 2 is noticeably tired from lugging me such a long distance. We pass through several more changes in scenery—islands, grasslands, swamps—and every time it's like crossing some abrupt, imaginary divide.

And then we enter a desert.

"The Building Block is hidden here," the Orb says.

White sands spread out beneath us for miles. It's hot—oppressively hot—with not even the hint of a breeze. Beads of sweat form on my forehead and trickle down the back of my neck. Strangely, you'd think the landscape is beautiful here if you weren't fighting for survival.

Grace 2's loft lowers noticeably, the harsh climate

sapping her strength. We'd better be close because I'm not sure she's going to make it much farther.

And then, up ahead, I see it, rising above the sea of whiteness into the burning sky—a giant pyramid. At first, it seems like a mirage—an optical illusion conjured up by my tired brain. But as we get closer I know it's real. I studied ancient Egypt and its pyramids in school, but I've never seen a real one before. It's truly an engineering marvel—triangular in shape and faced on all sides with polished limestone.

"The artifact is inside the pyramid," the Orb says.

"We've found it!" I yell to Grace 2. "It's in there!"

She whoops with delight.

But our celebration is short-lived because there are three small dots at the base of the pyramid, only one of which is moving. Someone is waiting for us next to a pair of bodies lying in the sand.

It's Siphon! And the bodies are Aries and Wind Walker!

Then, I remember Siphon's powers.

"Pull up!" I shout. "Pull up!"

But it's too late. Just as Grace 2 changes course a black void opens in front of us, swallowing us whole!

Suddenly, we're flying through a pitch-black tunnel. The space around us is narrowing, closing in quickly. There's a powerful headwind pushing against us like we're going the wrong way through a vacuum cleaner hose! And then, with a loud POP, we tumble headfirst out the other side.

My mouth fills with sand. I try scrambling to my feet but lose my footing, landing on top of something hard. Lifting my head, I'm face-to-face with an unconscious Wind Walker! Thankfully, he's breathing. Then it dawns on me what happened. Siphon must have used Wind Walker's powers to yank us clear out of the sky! Aries is lying beside us, knocked out but clearly breathing too.

I check on Grace 2, who's bent over by the base of the pyramid, tossing her cookies.

I'm the only one in fighting shape.

Fan-freaking-tastic.

I move to stand up when the area around me darkens in a large shadow.

"Sorry about your friends," Siphon says. "They took out Overlord, so they didn't do too badly. But unfortunately for them, I'm on a completely different level."

I don't think truer words have been spoken. The last time we met, my negation powers didn't work at all on him. But this time, I'm not alone. I've got the Orb of Oblivion.

I look into Siphon's eyes, but surprisingly, his expression isn't threatening. Something tells me to hold back.

"The Building Block is inside the pyramid," Siphon says matter-of-factly. "There's a secret door on the outside leading to a maze of passages. Once you reach the main chamber, the Building Block is inside the pharaoh's sarcophagus. It seems kind of fitting, doesn't it?"

I stare at him, baffled. "If you know all of this, why didn't you grab it? You'd win the contest. You'd have your own planet to rule?"

"Oh, believe me," he says, "I considered it. But when I learned you were one of my opponents, I couldn't believe my luck. From that moment, game, or no game, destroying you became my number one priority. I decided that even if I found the Building Block before finding you, I'd wait to win the game. That way, I wouldn't miss my chance for revenge before we were transported off this crazy world."

Seriously? This guy is nuts! "I told you," I say, rising cautiously. "I didn't kill your father. It was the Skelton."

"Yeah, you did say that," Siphon says. "But the High Commander tells a different story."

The High Commander? I forgot! Siphon and the High Commander have been partners on Chaos' team for days! I need to think fast.

"And you believed him?" I ask, making it to my feet, shocked he let me stand at all without taking my head off.

And then I realize something.

If he wanted to kill me so badly, why hasn't he done it by now? My Mom's words echo in my brain: *Never judge a book by its cover.* Just because he looks like Meta-Taker, doesn't mean he acts like Meta-Taker. Then, I get an idea.

"You know, villains like the High Commander are

notorious for lying. And so was your father."

"What?" Siphon says angrily.

Okay, tread carefully. Think this through.

"When we first met, you said your father isolated you," I continue. "Which got me thinking—was he really protecting you from others like he told you? Or was he keeping you from finding out the truth about who he really was?"

"What are you talking about?" Siphon asks.

"Did you know your father wasn't just a villain, but he was the worst kind of villain—a cold-blooded murderer?"

"Liar!" Siphon yells. "My father did what needed to be done! To make a life for both of us! If someone needed to be destroyed, there was a reason for it!"

"No, Siphon," I say. "He murdered innocents—and he murdered often. You might not know this, but he murdered five members of the original Freedom Force— good people—heroes. You may be his son, but I don't think you're like him. In fact, I don't think you're like him at all. If you were, wouldn't you have killed me by now?"

Siphon is frozen. I can see the wheels spinning in his brain. It's working!

"Use me!" the Orb says inside my mind. *"Use me now!"*

"Shut up!" I command. *"Not now!"*

Suddenly, Siphon's eyes ignite with swirling, red energy. "What's this?" he says, astonished. "What's all of this power I feel coming off of you. You're trying to trick me. You're setting me up!"

"*Go dark!*" I yell to the Orb in my mind. "*Now!*"

"My father was right," Siphon says, "I can't trust anybody!"

"No," I say. "That's not true."

Siphon's red energy kicks into overdrive. Suddenly, I feel drained. Like all of my energy is leaving me.

Siphon's body starts to swell, growing larger and larger as he draws more and more power away from me... and into him!

"*Orb?*" I call into my mind.

But there's no answer.

"*Are you there, Orb? Talk to me!*"

Nothing.

I look back at Siphon who has ballooned in size. He's like a cartoon of himself, bloated and deformed. "The power," he mutters. "Such unbelievable power..."

I need to get away from Siphon—to draw the Orb's power away from him! But then—

BOOM!

There's a deafening sound from above.

I look up to find a silver, sleek-looking ship with a long, cylindrical body hovering in the sky.

The Ghost Ship! But how?

KABOOM!

Suddenly, there's an even more thunderous noise overhead, knocking me to my knees, and sending my ears ringing.

Looking up, I find the Ghost Ship surrounded by a fleet of ships. Skelton warships.

The Emperor has found me.

Meta Profile

Name: Ms. Understood (2)
Role: Villain Status: Active

VITALS:

Race: Human
Real Name: Kate Harkness
Height: 5'6"
Weight: 130 lbs
Eye Color: Brown
Hair Color: Blond

META POWERS:

Class: Psychic
Power Level: ▉ ▉ ▉ ▉

- **Extreme Telepathy**
- **Extreme Telekinesis**
- **Group Mind-Linking**
- **Long-Range Capability**

CHARACTERISTICS:

Combat	80	▉▉▉▉▉
Durability	42	▉▉▉
Leadership	88	▉▉▉▉▉▉
Strategy	85	▉▉▉▉▉
Willpower	95	▉▉▉▉▉▉

FOURTEEN

I LEARN WHY OPPOSITES ATTRACT

It's just another day at the office for your friendly neighborhood super-zero.

I'm fighting for my life in the middle of a desert, Grace 2 is still recovering from our psychedelic roller-coaster ride, Aries and Wind Walker are comatose, Siphon seems to have sucked the Orb of Oblivion's power into his body, and the Zodiac are being chased by an armada of Skelton warships.

Oh, and I almost forgot to mention the Building Block—the whole reason we're stuck on this crazy planet in the first place—which is sitting inside the tomb of an ancient pharaoh, just waiting for someone to grab it.

I seriously should consider a different line of work. One where my life isn't at stake every second—like dentistry.

But that'll have to wait because right now I've got to get my act together.

At the moment, Siphon is distracted by the aerial fireworks happening overhead. I could make a run for the Building Block, but there's no way I'd get two feet before he creamed me. I need a game plan, but at this point I'm flat out of ideas.

Just then, the Ghost Ship slams to the ground, skidding hundreds of feet in the sand before coming to a stop. The hatch pops open and out jumps a host of friendly faces: Gemini, Taurus, Pisces, Scorpio, and Sagittarius! And, of course, my old pal, Leo.

They see me and start running towards us!

"Stop!" I yell. "Stay back!"

The Zodiac freeze in their tracks. Thank goodness! I couldn't imagine adding even more powers to Siphon's growing arsenal.

Suddenly, dozens of Skelton warships touch down around us. But before we can organize, ramps deploy and hundreds of Blood Bringers swarm out. Within seconds, we're surrounded!

The Blood Bringers are as big as I remember— sumo-sized warriors clad in armor and carrying deadly spear-like weapons. Just then, a group parts in the center, creating a pathway for a Skelton wearing a gold cape and crown.

The Emperor!

He looks down at me with his neon-green eyes, grinning from pointy ear to pointy ear. "So, Orb Master, we meet again. You seem to have forgotten you are my prisoner."

I have to admit, he's even more intimidating in person. He's tall, broad-shouldered, and has a sinister quality to his face that makes you think someone's about to stick a dagger in your back. Which probably isn't too far from the truth.

"Sorry about that," I say. "Something came up."

I realize that standing before me is the most feared man in the universe, responsible for orchestrating countless acts of death and destruction. He ordered the murders of K'ami and her father. He endorsed what happened to all the villains who lost their lives at Lockdown—including Siphon's father.

I turn to catch Siphon's eye, but he's gone!

Where'd he go?

Instinctively, I look towards the pyramid, only to find Siphon stepping out of one of Wind Walker's rifts! He feels delicately along the pyramid's stone exterior and then pushes through a secret door. He's going for the Building Block!

I've got to stop him. But first I need to solve my present conundrum.

The Emperor looks me squarely in the eyes. "Grab the boy," he orders to his minions. "Dispose of the rest."

The Skelton charge forward!

Suddenly, they're on me, pulling my arms behind my back and lifting me off the ground! The next thing I know, I'm dropped in front of the Emperor!

"No more games, Orb Master," the Emperor says. "Now you will pay for running away by watching your friends die."

The Zodiac spring into action, but the Blood Bringers use their shapeshifting powers to transform into a horde of horrific creatures. Scorpio and Sagittarius fend off multi-headed beasts and tentacled monsters. Gemini and Taurus scatter an army of scampering scorpion creatures. Pisces is being chased by a flock of winged, frog-like things. And I have no clue where Leo is. It's only a matter of time before they're overrun.

But I need to catch Siphon!

Scorpio disappears under a pile of muscled rodents.

I need to act now before it's too late! I may not have the Orb's power, but I still have mine. I think back to my mission with the Destruction Crew—the one that got me kicked off the Freedom Force.

If I can use my powers to stop the Blood Bringers, it should be easy for the Zodiac to do the rest. But what if I mistakenly wipe out everyone's powers again? They'd be doomed! But if I don't try, they're doomed anyway!

For some reason, I hear Grace 2's words in my head: *you can't always shield the ones you love.*

Maybe, just maybe...

I close my eyes and focus harder than I've ever

focused before. I push my negation powers as far and as wide as I can. But this time, I picture all of the heroes in my mind: Scorpio, Sagittarius, Gemini, Pisces, Taurus, Grace 2, Wind Walker, Aries—even Leo—and I wrap them in a mental shield—protecting them from the effects of my powers. And then I pray. Please work, please work, please—

"What is happening?" the Emperor cries.

I open my eyes and do a double take! All of the terrifying creatures are gone! And in their places stand hundreds of confused Blood Bringers.

I... did it?

"Zodiac!" Scorpio yells. "Attack!"

And then Scorpio's tail turns bright orange, and he fires a laser blast straight through the heart of the Blood Bringer army!

Yes! The Zodiac still have their powers! I did it!

The Emperor turns to me, fuming with anger, "Take him to the ship!"

But before they can move, I feel two hands grab me beneath my armpits and lift me high into the air.

"Grace!" I yell.

"I figure I owed you one," she says, winking.

"Quick," I say, "drop me by the near side of the pyramid. Siphon's inside. I've got to stop him."

"Signed, sealed, and delivered," she says, picking up speed and depositing me at the exact spot. "Go get him!"

But I don't have time to respond. I've got to get to

the Building Block! I start pushing the area of the wall I saw Siphon touching. There's a secret door around here somewhere. Finally, I hear a CLICK, and a door swings inwards. I jump inside.

It's dark. So dark, that when my eyes adjust I can only see a few feet in front of my face. I don't have the luxury to go back out and find a flashlight. So, I take off, spreading my arms and using the sides of the walls to guide me as I move forward. I'm running blind, but that's the best I can do.

The passageway ends abruptly and I smack into a stone wall. Decision time. I can either go left or right. I follow my instincts and turn right. This happens over and over again. Hit a dead end, pick a side, and just keep going.

This whole process is taking too long. I feel like a rat in a maze with no clue how to find the cheese—which, in this case, is the pharaoh's tomb. Siphon told me he already found his way to the main chamber once, so I've got to assume he's reached the Building Block by now.

So, why hasn't the game ended already?

I smash face-first into yet another wall and then turn left. I hustle ten feet or so when, suddenly, everything opens up. Smooth, granite walls meet symmetrically overhead. Light streams through a small hole in the middle of the ceiling. Within the center of the chamber lies an open, granite sarcophagus.

I've found it! But where's—

"I couldn't do it," comes a voice to my left.

I spin to find Siphon sitting in the corner of the room. He looks sad.

"A voice in my head kept telling me to grab it," he says. "Just grab the Building Block, and then I'd be the ruler of my own world. But then I thought about what you said, and you were right. Deep down I knew exactly who my father was. And I'm not like him. I'm not a murderer. I could never kill billions of innocent people just to get what I want."

I can't believe my ears. He actually listened to me!

"I'm sorry," I say. "Look, I know that was hard, but I'm glad you made the decision you did. You did the right thing. You know, that kind of makes you a hero now."

Siphon looks at me strangely and laughs. "Me? A hero? Who would've thought? Anyway, the Building Block is in there. You take it. Let's go home already."

I smile and head over to the sarcophagus. I look inside, expecting to find a decrepit mummy, but instead there's just a silver cube—the Building Block!

Finally, this is all going to end.

"I wouldn't touch that if I were you," comes a high-pitched voice.

I turn to see a tall man with purple skin floating down from above. His hair is white and wild, like a raging inferno. He's wearing a black, leather jacket, and faded blue jeans riddled with holes. He lowers his sunglasses, looking at me with contempt. There's no need for introductions. I know him immediately—it's Chaos!

"Your side cheated," he says. "So, I win." Then, he reaches inside and takes the Building Block.

"Hey," I exclaim. "You can't do that!"

Cheated? What's he talking about. What's going on?

Suddenly, Order appears on the other side of the sarcophagus. "You lost fair and square, brother, and as usual, you are having a difficult time accepting the fact."

"Enough of your drama," Chaos says. "You brought in that spaceship filled with Meta teenagers. So that means you violated the rules by bringing participants into the contest who were not selected—which is also known as cheating."

Watching them argue is like watching two gods bicker over a game of chess. Except we're the pawns!

"I did no such thing," Order says. "These so-called 'participants' you are referring to happened upon Arena World by chance. I had nothing to do with it."

"Blah, blah, blah," Chaos says, rolling his eyes. "You never have anything to do with it, do you? You have forfeited the match. The world is now rightfully mine to destroy. And destroy it I shall!"

"Enough, Chaos!" Order thunders. "The only thing that will be destroyed is you!" He points at his brother, and suddenly, the Building Block in Chaos' hands starts glowing!

"What are you doing?" Chaos exclaims.

"You are so predictable, brother," Order says. "By

grabbing the Building Block, you are now locked to this place. Or have you forgotten?"

Chaos' expression changes to one of surprise. He looks down at the Building Block. "Release me at once!"

"No, brother," Order says. "You and I are the highest of all cosmic beings. And as it is written in the stars, we are unable to harm one another. But that does not mean we cannot be harmed."

"Are you mad, brother!" Chaos says.

"Perhaps," Order says. "But if I am, it is you who made me so. Just like the Orb of Oblivion, the Building Block is a cosmic entity—a parasite—that feeds off the desires of its host. But while the Orb of Oblivion brings out the darkness, the Building Block brings out the light. And resting in your vile hands, it is reversing your powers even as we speak. So, tell me, brother, do you feel your power slipping away? Do you feel yourself growing weaker and weaker by the second?"

Wait? Order said the Building Block was a living entity, but he never said it was the opposite of the Orb— that it's a cosmic force for good!

Suddenly, Chaos starts shrinking! "S-Stop! P-Please!"

"Like you and I," Order says, "the Building Block and Orb of Oblivion are opposite sides of the same coin. But while our purpose is to provide harmony, their purpose is to provide dissonance. And when they connect, the results can be rather... explosive."

O! M! G! This is what he meant when he said: *When*

the appropriate moment arises, you will act. He's going to use the Orb to blow Chaos sky high!

"Now that you are sufficiently weakened, brother," Order says, "it is time to rid ourselves of the burden of Chaos! Come forth, Orb Master!" Order says looking at me, an evil grin spreading across his face. "Come forth and claim your prize!"

Order snaps. But instead of me, it's Siphon who lifts off the ground!

"Hey!" Siphon exclaims.

"What is this?" Order asks, confused.

What's going on?

Then, it hits me! When Siphon absorbed my powers, he didn't just take the Orb's power from me—he took the Orb of Oblivion itself! No wonder it wasn't talking to me!

Siphon flies towards Chaos, but Chaos uses whatever power he has left to push Siphon back, keeping him away.

Siphon is now hovering between the cosmic brothers.

"Epic Zero, run!" Siphon yells.

"No!" I yell. "I'll help you!"

"Remember what you said," Siphon says. "Remember me as a hero."

"Do not do this, fool," Chaos says. "You need me!"

"Do I?" Order chuckles. "I am Order, and Order needs no one!"

"Want to know what I think?" Siphon interjects. "I

think you guys deserve each other!"

Suddenly, Siphon reaches out and grabs Order's arm.

"What are you doing?" Order yells.

They both start glowing.

"Since I've got this Orb thing," Siphon says. "I guess now you're frozen too!"

"Unhand me!" Order yells.

Then, Siphon reaches out for Chaos' arm.

Order's eyes grow wide. "Stop! What are you—"

"NO!" Chaos yells.

But before he clutches Chaos' wrist, Siphon looks at me and raises his eyebrows.

And I'm swallowed up in a black rift.

***

I fall out the other side into the desert sand.

The explosion is other-worldly.

A wave of pure white energy eclipses the sky.

And then everything goes dark.

When my eyes readjust, there's no trace of the pyramid. Order, Chaos, and Siphon are gone—all in the blink of an eye.

Siphon ported me out of there with one of Wind Walker's rifts. Siphon sacrificed himself to save... me?

Suddenly, the ground starts shaking violently.

Then, it CRACKS open, sending a plume of hot lava shooting into the air.

Arena World is falling apart!

I lock eyes with the Emperor, who's being helped to his feet by his henchmen. He stares at me, and then shouts, "Retreat!"

I nod my thanks and watch as he leads his men back to their ships.

"To the Ghost Ship!" Gemini yells. "Hurry!"

Taurus heaves Aries over her shoulder, while Scorpio lifts Wind Walker onto Sagittarius' backside. Grace 2 swoops down and grabs me, right as another crack opens beneath my feet.

"Thanks," I say.

"No problem," she says. "It's what heroes do."

We all tumble into the Ghost Ship, taking off just before the ground disintegrates beneath it. I know we need to get as far away from here as possible, but there's one thing we need to take care of first.

I push my way to the cockpit and find Scorpio.

"We need to make a stop," I say.

Within seconds, we're there.

The ground is shaking like mad, and buildings are collapsing around us, but we need to do this.

The hatch lowers and Grace 2 flies out. Moments later, she returns with her unconscious mom in her arms.

Then, we blast off into outer space as Arena World bursts into a ball of fire and rubble.

Meta Profile

Name: The Emperor
Role: Villain   Status: Active

VITALS:

Race: Skelton
Real Name: Unknown
Height: 6'6"
Weight: 275 lbs
Eye Color: Green
Hair Color: Bald

META POWERS:

Class: Meta-morph
Power Level: ▮▮▮▮

- Assumed Extreme Shape-Shifting—can morph into endless forms
- Assumed Extreme Flight, Strength, and Speed depending upon form taken

CHARACTERISTICS:

Combat	100	
Durability	100	
Leadership	100	
Strategy	100	
Willpower	100	

FIFTEEN

I PUT MY TRUST IN A MONKEY

We're all in our heads.

Other than Pisces and Scorpio, who are navigating the Ghost Ship, no one's talking. I know I'm still trying to process everything that happened, and I've got more questions than answers.

Like, why did Siphon sacrifice himself for me? Believe me, I'm grateful, but I can't help feeling partly responsible. I mean, I told him the truth about his father, but I suspect deep down he already knew. He had no family—no one to go back home to. I think he wanted to make up for his father's mistakes, and this was his chance to rewrite his family's legacy. So, he made the ultimate sacrifice, and for that, he'll always be a hero in my book.

And then, there's the question of what happens now

without Order and Chaos? When I met Order, he told me that he and his brother were the fabric of the universe. So, what happens when that fabric is shredded to pieces? If Order managed structure, and Chaos managed randomness, what's going to happen to the universe now that they're gone—all of the universes?

And then I get a more horrifying thought.

Who's going to control Ravager?

Without Order and Chaos, there's no longer a contest. And without a contest, there aren't any restrictions as to what that planet-eating pest can do. So, does that mean the Earth we nearly died saving may be at risk again tomorrow?

Suddenly, I feel nauseous.

And then there's the Orb of Oblivion. I keep trying to reach out to it, but there's just no response. Did it truly die with Siphon? Or is it somehow still inside of me, gathering its strength? Even though I can't sense its presence, can I ever be entirely sure it's gone?

I rest my throbbing head against the hull of the ship.

Grace 2 enters from the medi-wing. "Thanks again, Elliott. Saving my mom's life was an honorable thing to do."

"No problem," I say. "You would have done the same for me. How's she doing?"

"She's still unconscious," Grace 2 says. "But Leo says she's stable. He thinks she's going to make a full recovery. Wind Walker and Aries are back on their feet."

"Yeah, I heard the cheers when Aries realized he was back on the Ghost Ship. Do you think you're gonna be okay? You know, with your mom? I imagine that will be a tough thing to get over."

She looks at her feet. "I don't know. She's still my mom, you know. I hope she realizes how far gone she is and can make her way back. I know I won't ever forget, but maybe, one day, I'll be able to forgive. How about you?"

"I don't know how I feel," I say. "Everything that happened back there was so crazy. I just really want to get home, you know?"

She reaches out and rubs my shoulder, a sharp pain shoots down my left arm. "Ow!" I cry.

"You're hurt," she says. "Sorry, I didn't know."

"Honestly, neither did I," I say, my arm still smarting. "It must have happened when everything blew up. I was running on so much adrenaline I didn't even notice."

"Leo's still in the medi-wing," Grace 2 says. "Maybe he should look at it."

"Yeah, that's probably a good idea," I say, struggling to pull myself up. I hope nothing is broken.

When I enter the medi-wing, Mom 2 is lying on a table hooked up to a bunch of machines monitoring her vital signs. My favorite monkey is scrolling through a computer screen, a clipboard tucked under his hairy arm.

"Hey, Leo," I say. "Can you take a look at me? It's

my left arm."

The chimp turns, hesitating for a moment, like he's surprised to see me. Then, he grins and pats the empty examination table. "Sure, I'd be happy to."

I hop up, careful not to bump my left arm on anything. Leo's behind me, making a racket as he collects some equipment. That's when I remember something I've been meaning to ask him.

"Hey, I know we didn't get off on the right foot, but something is bothering me that I haven't been able to piece together."

"Sure, what is it?" he asks, clanging behind me.

"Scorpio told me the Zodiac only found me because of you. But I have no idea how you did it. I mean, how did you even know about the Orb?"

"Ah," Leo says. "I see. Perhaps an explanation is in order. But first, I need to do this."

THWIP!

Ouch! There's a sharp pain in my left shoulder! I turn to find Leo standing beside me, holding a small gun.

What the—? He tranquilized me!

"You'll soon be quite groggy," Leo says, swinging around the table to the door. "But I'm sure you're familiar with the feeling." He turns the latch, locking it shut!

What's going on? Everything starts getting blurry. I'm trapped inside with a psychotic primate who's trying to kill me!

Suddenly, he's standing in front of me. "Perhaps this will help to explain things." And then, before my eyes, he transforms from a chimpanzee into a boy—an alien boy with pale-yellow skin, and large, pointy ears. And then he reaches up and pinches his pupils, removing brown contact lenses to reveal a pair of neon-green eyes.

He's… he's…

"I can tell from your astonished expression that you realize I am a Skelton. My name is K'van Sollarr, younger brother of K'ami Sollarr. I think you knew her well before leading her to her death."

What? K'ami has a brother? She never mentioned a brother. By now, I'm struggling to stay conscious. I want to call for help, but I'm having trouble even holding myself upright. He must have drugged me twice as heavily as before.

"Perhaps she never told you about me, but I am not surprised. We never did get along. You see, I am the last of the Sollarr line, and the only one loyal to our Lord Emperor. As for how I found you…"

Now he's loading a syringe with some kind of serum.

"You may be aware that Skelton of the same bloodlines share a psychic bond—a mind-link if you will. Once my sister touched the Orb of Oblivion, I was, by association, directly connected with you. As soon as I realized this wonderful development, I informed the Emperor. You can probably imagine that after the treasonous acts of my father and sister, it took quite a bit of convincing for the Emperor to believe me. But after I held true through all of his torture sessions, he was finally convinced."

Suddenly, my left arm is on fire! He's rubbing something on it!

"He sent me alone to Earth to track you down. Given how you destroyed an entire Blood Bringer squadron, he was reluctant to risk more resources until you were found. I admit it took me longer than I expected. Your satellite was not obvious, and I spent weeks fruitlessly searching your planet's surface."

Leo grabs my left arm! The pain!

"Unfortunately, my ship was out of fuel, and I needed a way back into space to reach you. Fortunately, Canada had a secret space launch planned. They were sending a chimpanzee into orbit. The night before the launch, I infiltrated their building and took the place of their animal astronaut. After liftoff, I charted my own course, but your rockets are so primitive I quickly ran out of fuel. Fortunately, the Zodiac heeded my distress call. They are a ragtag band of misfits, so it was child's play to convince them the Orb was the answer to their prayers to defeat the mighty Ravager and avenge their worlds. Once aboard, I used the Ghost Ship's capabilities to track you down and land undetected on your satellite. The rest, they say, is history."

Then, everything clicks. That's why he didn't want to turn me over to the Overlord!

"You... called the Skelton Emperor... on Watcher World," I mutter.

"Yes, I did," he says. "And I thought that would be the end of it. I'd deliver you into the hands of the Emperor, clear my family's name, and my people would rule the universe—with me, of course, in a dangerously close position to the Emperor. But now the Orb is gone, so I need a new plan. And at this point, there is no need for you to blow my cover. I do enjoy manipulating these kids, and I have a few more tricks up my sleeve. So, I guess you just came down with a serious case of heart attack."

I feel a sharp pinch on my arm. He's putting the syringe in! He's going to kill me!

"Drop the needle!" comes a familiar voice.

I manage to open my eyes to find a woman's dark, gloved hand wrapped around Leo's wrist. Then, Mom socks the villain square across the jaw!

But what is Mom doing here?

And then I'm out.

***

"Elliott?"

When I come to, I'm surrounded by concerned faces. The Zodiac are here, and so is Grace 2, and Wind Walker. Gemini is squeezing my hand tightly.

"He's okay," she says. "Thank the stars."

I'm still woozy. I try to sit up, but there's something in the way. My left arm is in a cast!

"Leo!" I say, "Leo's—"

"No longer a problem," Grace 2 says. "Thanks to my mom."

Her mom?

Then, I remember everything. At first, I thought just Leo and I were in the medi-wing. But Mom 2 was also there! She was on that table. She saved my life.

Grace 2 steps aside and her mom is standing there, smiling. "I'm glad you're okay, Elliott," she says. "Despite everything I've done, you came back—you all came back—to rescue me. You reminded me of what it means to be a hero. And for that, I'll never be able to thank you enough." I watch as she reaches out for Grace 2's hand.

Grace 2 hesitates and then takes it.

"What about Leo?" I ask.

"We tranquilized him, and locked him in the storage closet," Scorpio says. "We're going to swing by Paladin Planet, the intergalactic prison planet, and drop him off there. We had no idea he wasn't who he said he was. I'm so sorry."

"It's not your fault," I say, "I guess it's been an adventure filled with surprises."

"Indeed," Gemini says. And then she plants a kiss on my cheek.

I turn beet red.

"And they just keep on coming," Grace 2 says.

And we all laugh.

Meta Profile

Name: Chaos
Role: Cosmic Entity   Status: Deceased?

VITALS:

Race: Inapplicable
Real Name: Chaos
Height: appears 7'0"
Weight: Unknown
Eye Color: Inapplicable
Hair Color: White

META POWERS:

Class: Inapplicable
Power Level: Incalculable

- Balances his brother, Order, to cause stress, disorder, and randomness throughout the universe
- Cannot harm other Cosmic Entities

CHARACTERISTICS:

Combat	Inapplicable
Durability	Inapplicable
Leadership	Inapplicable
Strategy	Inapplicable
Willpower	Inapplicable

EPILOGUE

THE END OF THE ROAD...

Going home is bittersweet.

For days it was all I could think about, but now that it's finally here it's hard to say goodbye.

Grace 2 and Mom 2 leave first. Grace 2 and I hug for a long time, both of us with tears in our eyes. Even though our relationship started rocky, it's amazing to think of how far we've come. I'm really going to miss her.

Then, Mom 2 gives me a big hug. I thank her for saving my life, and she thanks me for saving hers—twice. I sure hope she lives up to her promise and becomes a hero again. She has lots of damage to undo on her world—especially with her daughter.

I wave goodbye as they each take Wind Walker's hand, and then disappear into his mystical vortex.

Meeting these mirror versions made me realize how lucky I am to have parents who love me. As for my own Grace, I guess she's not so bad. We love each other, even if we have a funny way of showing it.

When Wind Walker returns, I know I'm next. The Zodiac surround me to say their goodbyes.

"Epic Zero," Scorpio says. "We couldn't have done it without you. And we couldn't imagine moving forward without making you an official member of our team."

"What?" I say. "Really?"

"From this day forward, within our circle, you will be known as Serpentarius—the thirteenth sign of the Zodiac—unifier and healer of worlds."

And then Pisces steps forward and hands me something. It's a badge—a symbol of a serpent!

"That's an official Zodiac communications link," she says, hugging me. "If you ever need us, just push the button and we'll be there."

I turn to the rest of the Zodiac. Taurus wraps me in a giant bear hug, and Sagittarius high-hoofs me. Then, Aries shakes my hand.

"You know," he says, "I really didn't think you'd find the Building Block before me. But you sure proved me wrong."

"What can I say?" I answer. "Good things come in small packages."

He pats me on the shoulder and grins.

And then I meet eyes with Gemini.

She looks really sad. I don't know what it is, but every time I'm around her I get a funny feeling in my stomach. "I'd love for you to visit my world sometime," I say. "I know it's not your home, but you might like it."

"I'd like that," she says. "But first, I need to finish what I've started. But I'll keep in touch. I promise." Then, she gives me a peck on the cheek, and whispers, "See you soon, Elliott."

I feel my cheeks go flush as I join Wind Walker. He takes my hand and summons one of his mystical voids. I scan the sad faces of the Zodiac one last time, and say, "Goodbye... team."

And then, they're gone.

Wind Walker leads me through his crazy, dark tunnel, and seconds later, we pop out the other side.

We're in my bedroom—on the Waystation!

Wind Walker puts his hands on my shoulders, and says, "I am glad we are friends and not foes. Be well, Epic Zero. If you ever need me, you only need to call." And then he conjures up another void, steps inside, and is gone.

I'm finally home and it feels really weird. The last time I was here, Leo shot me, and that started this whole crazy adventure. I wonder if anyone's around?

I enter the hallway, and everything seems back to normal—there aren't any alarms blaring or barricades in the way. As I head up the stairway my mind wanders to everything I've been through. There's no more Orb. No more Order and Chaos. Who knows what the future holds?

I enter the Galley where I find Mom, Grace, and Dog-Gone. Dog-Gone sees me first and charges me at full speed, bowling me over. I wrap my one good arm around his fuzzy neck and pull him close.

"Elliott?" Mom says, running over. "Where have you been? We've been worried sick."

But I can't answer under the barrage of face-licking.

"The entire team is out looking for you," Mom continues. "And what's wrong with your arm? You're wearing a cast." Mom grabs me and pulls me close. It feels so good to hug her again.

As soon as she releases me, I'm wrapped up again— this time by Grace, who has a tear in her eye. "I'm glad you're back, squirt," she says. "Just don't crease the cape."

"Elliott, what happened to you?" Mom asks.

But all I can do is stare at them with tears streaming down my face. Normally, I'd be embarrassed, but right now I just don't care. That's my Mom with her brown hair and my sister with her blond hair.

I'm home.

Grace hands me the end of her cape. "Fine," she sighs, "wipe away."

I dab my eyes. "Boy, do I have a story for you guys. You're never going to believe what happened."

"Can't wait," Grace says. "But do us a favor."

"What's that?" I ask.

"This time, try not to leave out any of the critically important details," she says with a wink.

Mom calls the rest of the Freedom Force back to the Waystation, and it's amazing to see them all again—especially Dad, who hugged me and wouldn't let go.

And then, over jelly doughnuts, I tell them everything.

Well, everything except for Gemini, of course.

I mean, I have to keep some things to myself.

Meta Profile
The Zodiac

♏ Scorpio

Class: Energy Manipulator
Meta: ■■ ■■

♓ Pisces

Class: Energy Manipulator
Meta: ■■ ■■

♊ Gemini

Class: Meta-Morph
Meta: ■■ ■■

⛎ Serpentarius

Class: Meta Manipulator
Meta: ■■ ■■ ■■

♈ Aries

Class: Super-Strength
Meta: ■■ ■■ ■

♐ Sagittarius

Class: Super-Speed
Meta: ■■ ■

♉ Taurus

Class: Super-Strength
Meta: ■■ ■■ ■

Epic Zero 3: Tales of a Super Lame Last Hope

ONE

I SCREW UP BIG TIME

I've totally got this creep in the bag!

The only thing standing between us is a lousy manhole cover, and once I crack this puppy open he's all mine! I stick my fingers in the holes and yank, but the only cracking I hear comes from my back! I let go and stretch my spine. Wow, that thing is heavier than Dog-Gone after a buffet lunch.

I'm going to need leverage to lift this sucker up. Well, I guess the only good thing about standing in a disaster zone is there's plenty of options. I grab a severed pipe and shove it into the pick hole. Pushing down with all my might, the manhole pops open like a bottle cap. I drop the pipe, snatch the metal disc with both hands, and roll it to the side.

A rotten stench floods out of the opening straight into my nostrils. As tempting as it is to turn away, I can't—not when there's justice to be served! Pinching my nose, I crouch down at the edge, ready to drop into the dark abyss otherwise known as the Keystone City sewer system.

All I need to do is jump.

But... I can't.

And what's worse, I know why.

Maybe I should rewind. The trouble started an hour ago. I was hanging with my family on the Waystation, watching reruns of old sitcoms when the Meta Monitor started blaring: "Alert! Alert! Alert! Meta 3 disturbance. Repeat: Meta 3 disturbance. Power signature identified as Alligazer! Meta 3 disturbance. Power signature identified as Alligazer!"

Popcorn flew everywhere as we leaped into action. I can still hear Dad's voice as we boarded the Freedom Flyer. "Remember, Freedom Force," he warned. "Alligazer is big trouble."

Look, I'm not saying Dad's wrong. I mean, I'd never faced Alligazer myself but I knew all about him. After all, his ugly mug was posted at the top of our Meta Most Wanted List. With big, yellow eyes, and teeth sharper than Ginsu knives, he had a face only a mother could love.

But I'd probably go a step further than Dad. I'd say Alligazer is more than big trouble. I'd say he's downright lethal.

You see, once we reached the scene of the crime the only part of Keystone Savings Bank left standing was the vault. The rest of the building was gone, as in, completely obliterated. Alligazer had blown it to bits. But that wasn't the worst part.

Not by a long shot.

Despite the massive damage, all these civilians were still hanging around. I couldn't imagine why they didn't run for their lives. So, I went up to one guy to see what his problem was.

And realized he was a statue.

And it wasn't just him. There were dozens more.

All solid, stone statues.

Petrified by Alligazer.

There were police officers, bank tellers, customers. All innocent bystanders who got petrified—forever frozen in fright—never to move again!

I was horrified. Immediately, I turned to TechnocRat. "We've got to save these people! We have to change them back to normal!"

But he just shook his little head and said, "It's not possible. Once they've turned to stone, their blood hardens and stops flowing. I'm afraid they're gone."

I was so outraged—we all were—that I knew we had to catch Alligazer before he could do this to anyone else. But he was nowhere to be found.

Dad suggested we split into search teams to cover more ground. I partnered with Makeshift, but we couldn't find Alligazer anywhere. I suggested Makeshift port to the top of a building to get a more panoramic view. I figured I'd be okay for a few seconds alone.

And that's when I spotted him—two yellow eyes, darting back and forth from beneath a truck. Then, he emerged, big, green, and muscular, dragging a long tail behind him. He was carrying a sack and scampered like lightning to the manhole. He lifted the cover like it was nothing, hopped inside, and closed it behind him.

If I hadn't seen him, he would have gotten away with it. But that wasn't going to happen on my watch.

I briefly considered calling the rest of the Freedom Force, but I figured I could handle it. I mean, I'm part of the team now, and here was my chance to show them how much I've grown. If I could get close enough, I could simply negate his powers. Then, he wouldn't be so dangerous. It all seemed pretty straightforward.

So, why haven't I jumped in to save the day?

Images of those statues flash through my mind: a woman talking on a cell phone, a man looking up from his paper, a police officer heroically drawing her weapon. The only thing they had in common was being in the wrong place at the wrong time. That, and the sheer look of terror on their faces.

I wonder if they felt their skin hardening? Their blood slowing? Their hearts stopping?

Sweat trickles into my eyes and I wipe it away. I'm totally freaked out. But if I don't shake this now, Alligazer will escape. And then he'll do it again.

I've got a job to do—and thanks to Shadow Hawk and TechnocRat—now I've got the tools to do it. After my last adventure, I realized I needed more help in case I got in over my head—which seems to happen with more regularity than I care to admit.

So, they designed a utility belt just for me.

Opening the front, left-side compartment, I pull out a mini-flashlight and clench it in my teeth. Then, I grab the rusty rails of the sewer ladder and begin my descent. Within seconds, I'm swallowed by darkness. Reaching the bottom, I jump off the last rung into ankle-deep, ice-cold sewer water.

Just. Freaking. Wonderful.

The funky smell hits me hard, making my eyes water. I flick on the flashlight and shine it around. The sewer tunnel is damp and gray, with patches of dark moss growing all over. Large, cobweb-covered pipes run along the walls in each direction. The water rushing over my feet is brown and sludgy.

Well, this gets my vote as the creepiest place ever.

Unfortunately, there's no sign of Alligazer. I'm kicking myself for waiting too long! I've got to catch him, but which way should I go?

Just then, I hear squeaky noises to my right. Flashing my light, I catch a pair of gigantic rats running along a pipe attached to the wall. I'm guessing TechnocRat isn't throwing a dinner party. But then I notice they're carrying something in their mouths.

It's money!

From the bank!

Alligazer must have headed that way!

I sprint ahead, but my sloshing feet echo noisily down the tunnel. Well, if he didn't know I'm here, he certainly does now. I shine my flashlight around, hoping to catch a glimpse of the villain before he catches me.

As I get sucked deeper and deeper into the bowels of the sewer, I start second-guessing myself. I mean, maybe I shouldn't be down here on my own. Maybe I should have called the rest of the Freedom Force. Maybe I'm—

"Welcome," comes a deep, slithery voice.

—in serious trouble!

That sounded like it came from in front of me! I aim my flashlight forward, but Alligazer isn't there.

"You're either really brave or really stupid," he says, this time from behind me. "These sewers are my home. You don't stand a chance."

I spin around, but he's not there either. He's too fast!

Suddenly, there's a splash, and my flashlight is ripped clean out of my hand!

"Now you're really in the dark," Alligazer says from yet another direction, his evil laugh reverberating through the sewer.

It's pitch black and I can't see a thing. He's probably standing right in front of me, watching me spin around like a blindfolded fool trying to bash a piñata. I know he can take me out if he wants to, but he's not, which means he's toying with me. He thinks I'm helpless.

The thing is, I'm not.

I dig into my utility belt and pull out a flare. I remove the cap and rub it against the rough surface of the stick. Suddenly, the sewer lights up like the Fourth of July. Now I know why Shadow Hawk never leaves home without one.

I hold the burning flare away from my body and look around. Time to render him powerless. Now, where'd he go?

Just then, I hear a scratching noise over my head.

Uh oh.

He lands on me hard—the force of his body pushing me underwater. My nose scrapes the cement floor, and my mouth fills with sewage. I try getting up, but the floor is so slick I lose my footing and re-submerge. Then, the current grabs me and I feel myself being pulled away.

I reach out for something to stop my momentum, but the pressure is so strong I'm carried away! I find myself going under again and again. It's hard to breathe! I flail my arms out, trying to hook onto something— anything. Finally, I grab a pipe dangling from the wall. My body slams hard into the cement surface and I dig in my heels, catching them on a ridge. Steadying myself, I swing my leg over the pipe, hugging it with everything I've got.

I'm gasping for air, lucky to be alive. Clearly, I'm miles from where I started. And there's no sign of

Alligazer. Then, I realize the only reason I can see at all is because there's another manhole right above my head—and it's open—streaming in sunlight.

Alligazer must have crawled along the ceiling and escaped! I didn't know he could walk on walls. Time to update his Meta Profile. But I'll have to do that later. Right now, I've got to get out of here.

I reach into my utility belt and pull out a grappling gun. Then, I aim at the manhole and fire. The claw-shaped projectile latches onto the rim, stretching the cable taut. I release the trigger, and the cable retracts, pulling my sorry self out of the sewer and towards freedom.

Reaching the surface, I roll back into civilization. I'm lying flat on my back—cold, wet, and reeking like a Porta-Potty. I close my eyes and take in the fresh air.

Well, that was an epic failure.

"Ewww, gross!" a woman cries.

Opening my eyes, I'm surrounded by video cameras. News cameras.

Fabulous.

"Is that a hero or villain?" some guy asks.

"You know any heroes that smell like that?" another man answers.

"Shut up and keep rolling," a woman says. "Hey, kid, you responsible for all of this?"

Wait. What?

"Did you blow up the bank?"

Are you kidding me?

Suddenly, I'm bombarded with questions. I've got to get out of here, but I'm so wiped I can't move.

"Back off!" comes a familiar voice.

Suddenly, the news reporters part, and Captain Justice strides through the crowd, his golden scales of justice a sight for sore eyes.

"Please, back away," he orders. "Give him space."

He kneels beside me and whispers, "Are you okay?"

"I think so," I whisper back.

"Where the blazes were you?" Dad asks.

"In the sewers. I-I chased Alligazer down there. But he got away."

"You chased Alligazer?" Dad says surprised. "You found Alligazer?"

"Yeah," I answer, my head still woozy. "We had a big fight in the sewer. Hey, did you know there are rats like five times the size of TechnocRat down there?"

"Forget that," Dad says. "Why didn't you call us?"

"I... I don't know," I answer. "I didn't want to lose him. And I wanted to make a difference."

Dad rubs his face with his hands. "Oh, you made a difference alright. But not in the way you were hoping for."

"What are you talking about?" I ask.

"I'm guessing Alligazer popped out of that manhole two minutes before you did," he says.

"Yeah, I figured," I say. "But how'd you know that?"

"It's pretty obvious," Dad says, turning away from me, "because only he could leave behind something like that."

Like what?

I sit up and look over to see what Dad's all worked up about, when I notice another statue.

But it's not just any statue.

It's Makeshift!

Meta Profile
The Freedom Force

Captain Justice

Class: Super-Strength
Meta: ■■■■

Ms. Understood

Class: Psychic
Meta: ■■ ■■

Glory Girl

Class: Flight
Meta: ■■■

Shadow Hawk

Class: None
Meta:

Epic Zero

Class: Meta Manipulator
Meta: ■■■ ■

TechnocRat

Class: Super-Intellect
Meta: ■■■■

Blue Bolt

Class: Super-Speed
Meta: ■■■■

Master Mime

Class: Magic
Meta: ■■ ■■

Makeshift

Class: Energy Manipulator
Meta: ■

TWO

I HANG UP MY TIGHTS

I totally messed up.

So, while the rest of the team loads Makeshift into the cargo hold, I climb into the Freedom Flyer and slump into my chair. I know I should have helped, but I couldn't bear to look at Makeshift's petrified face.

Not after what I've done.

When the team finally boards the jet, no one even looks my way. Instead, they take their places and we rocket home. My eyes are glued to Makeshift's seat. It's empty now, and it's all my fault.

The ride back is awkwardly silent. The team is probably thinking of ways to console me. They'll probably tell me everything is okay—that it was an accident—that these are the risks you take in this line of work.

But I know better.

Makeshift is gone because of me.

Deep down, I'm sure they're wondering if they can trust me. And how can I blame them? I seem to screw up royally over and over again. Who knows who I'll hurt next?

I can already guess what Mom and Dad will say. Despite saving the world twice, they'll tell me I'm still too green for this. They'll tell me I'll be taking a break for a while—a long, long while.

But I won't give them the chance.

As soon as we dock on the Waystation and deboard the Freedom Flyer, I make an announcement. "Ladies and gentlemen, effective immediately I'm retiring from the Freedom Force—for good."

Then, I hand Dad my utility belt and head straight for my room.

"Elliott, wait!" Mom calls after me but I pretend not to hear her.

Dog-Gone pads softly behind me, whimpering the whole way. Don't get me wrong, I appreciate what he's trying to do, but when we reach my room I tell him I need to be alone and shut the door. Then, I peel off my sewer-infested bodysuit, hop into the shower, and ball my eyes out.

I still can't believe what happened. I never thought Alligazer would get away. I never thought Makeshift would be turned to stone. I thought I was doing the right thing—the heroic thing.

But I'm clearly not hero material.

Instead, I'm a hazard—a moving violation—a risk to society. So, I have no choice but to give up caped crusading. For everyone's sake.

Tomorrow, I'll ask Mom to re-enroll me at Keystone Middle School and go back to the ordinary life of a run-of-the-mill 6th grader. No more hunting supervillains. No more putting lives in jeopardy. No more bonehead mistakes.

I towel off and stare at myself in the mirror. My hair is wet and soggy, my eyes red from crying. Yep, starting tomorrow, I'll be your typical anonymous tween-ager.

Instead of heroically responding to Meta alerts, I'll be plowing through homework. Instead of squaring off against supervillains, I'll be dodging bullies. Yep, doesn't that sound just awesome?

Or should I say awful?

I throw on some sweats and flop onto my bed. Awful is right. But this is my new life, so I'd better get used to it. I start counting ceiling tiles when—

BANG, BANG!

There's a knock at my door.

"No one's home!" I shout.

"Hey!" Grace yells. "Open up."

Grace? What's she doing here?

"C'mon, Elliott," she says, knocking again. "Let me

in or I'll get Master Mime to bust it open."

"Fine!" I answer, rolling off my bed. "What do you want?" But I suspect I already know the answer. Whenever I screw up I can always count on Grace to rub my nose in it.

I swing the door open to find her standing there with her arms crossed. Her mask is off, and her blond hair is pulled back in a ponytail. "To talk," she says, striding in and sitting on the end of my bed.

"Well, then," I say, slamming the door shut. "Talk."

"Listen, squirt," she says, "I know you feel horrible about what happened to Makeshift but you can't just give up. You're a superhero—a member of the Freedom Force, for Pete's sake. It's not your fault. Bad stuff like that is just gonna happen."

Hang on. Is she trying to console me?

"Look, you didn't do that to Makeshift," she continues. "That Alligazer creep did."

"But it's *my* fault," I say. "I mean, I didn't call you guys for help when I should have. I thought I could do it on my own. And… I couldn't. I just keep thinking 'what if?' What if I did call for help?"

"Elliott," Grace says. "You could 'what if' yourself to death. Okay, what if you did call us? Maybe this whole thing wouldn't have happened. Or maybe *you'd* be turned to stone right now."

"That'd be fine with me," I mutter. "I deserve it."

"Look," she says, standing up, "there's no how-to

manual on being a hero. In this business, anything can happen. You just have to do what you think is right, and most of the time, it turns out okay. But there's one thing you can't do, and that's give up—especially on yourself."

She lifts my chin with her finger and forces me to look into her blue eyes. "Okay?"

I fake a smile and say, "I'll think about it."

"Great," she says. "But do yourself a favor."

"What's that?"

"Don't watch TV." Then she winks and lets herself out, closing the door behind her.

I start pacing. Look, I appreciate what she's saying, but I really don't think I can do this anymore. I mean, I don't want anyone else to get hurt because of me. And what did she mean by don't watch TV?

Oh, no!

I throw open the door and bolt down the hall to the Lounge. Blue Bolt and Master Mime are relaxing on the sofa with their feet propped up on a leather ottoman.

They're watching the news.

A square-jawed reporter looks straight to camera with a smug expression and says, "And if you've been living under a rock, and haven't seen these images from today's Keystone Savings Bank fiasco, you may want to sit down for this one."

Then, it cuts to an image of Makeshift. He's petrified, his arms blocking his face. A field reporter begins to narrate, "Today, a villain known as Alligazer destroyed Keystone Savings Bank, and turned twenty-five people at the scene into statues—including this superhero who has been identified as Makeshift, an apprentice of the Freedom Force."

Suddenly, the camera pans down to a brown, gloppy mess clinging to Makeshift's stone leg.

"While the Freedom Force were on the scene, they were unable to apprehend Alligazer. However, they did manage to capture his accomplice who emerged from the sewer system."

His accomplice? Who's that?

The camera pans in on the mystery accomplice's dirty face.

Wait a minute! That's me!

"At this time, the identity of the criminal has not been disclosed," the reporter continues. "But those of us in the media are referring to him as 'Stink Bug' because—well, we'll let you draw your own conclusions. It's assumed the Freedom Force have transferred him to Lockdown where—"

"Turn it off!" I yell, startling Blue Bolt and Master Mime.

"Hey there, Stink Bug," Blue Bolt says with a smile.

"Not funny," I snap.

"Whoa, sorry," Blue Bolt says. "I was just teasing."

Master Mime flicks his wrist and a giant, purple peace sign magically appears.

"Elliott," Blue Bolt says. "You know it's not your

fault, right?"

"Why does everyone keep saying that? Of course it's my fault. It's all my fault!"

But before they can respond, I'm off. I just want to be alone. My stomach rumbles and I realize I haven't eaten in hours. All the food is in the Galley, and I hope no one's around so I can grab a snack and head back to my Fortress of Solitude, otherwise known as my room.

But no such luck.

Shadow Hawk is sitting at the table, polishing off one of his trademark peanut butter and banana sandwiches. "Hey, kid," he says. "Want one?"

"No," I say, salivating. "Well, maybe."

"My pleasure," he says, popping the last bite into his mouth. He rises and heads over to the counter. "How are you holding up?"

"Honestly," I say, leaning against the counter. "Not so hot." Here we go again. The last thing I want right now is more sympathy.

"I understand," Shadow Hawk says, unpeeling a banana. He reaches into his utility belt, flicks open a Hawk-knife, and dices the banana like a master chef. "After all, what happened to Makeshift was your fault."

Wait, what? Did he just say it was *my* fault?

"You were irresponsible," he says, spreading peanut butter onto the bread. "And I expected more from you."

What? I'm taken aback! I'm speechless! Flabbergasted! How dare he! What happened to the sympathy? Doesn't he care how I feel right now?

"What's wrong?" he says, reading my expression. He washes off the Hawk-knife, closes it, and puts it back into his utility belt. Then, he hands me my sandwich. "Being a superhero is a big responsibility. Innocent lives are at stake. Heroes' lives are at stake. I'm not going to sugarcoat it for you, if you don't think you're up for the job, giving up the suit is the right decision."

I swallow hard. I-I don't know what to say.

Then, he puts his gloved hand on my shoulder. "But I've seen you in action. I know you've got what it takes. Listen, real superheroes don't run away from their mistakes. They own up to them so they don't do them again next time. Take some time to think about what you could have done differently. Then, pick yourself up and put on the cape again. But don't wait too long. Got it?"

"Yeah," I say. "I got it."

"Great," he grins.

Suddenly, the Meta Monitor's alarm goes wild, "Alert! Alert! Alert! Meta 2 disturbance. Power signature identified as Blood Sport! Alert! Alert! Alert!"

"Maybe you sit this one out," Shadow Hawk says with a wink.

"Thanks," I say. "And thanks for the sandwich."

"Enjoy it," he says, and then he exits.

I meander through the halls, chewing on both the sandwich and what Shadow Hawk said. It was like a slap in the face, but one I needed. Of course, he's right—he's always right. I mean, all I've ever wanted is to be a superhero. If I'm going to get out there again, I'll need to get over this.

Which means there's something I need to do, no matter how painful it's going to be.

I'm already in the West Wing, so I hang a left and slowly make my way over to an area I'd rather not be—TechnocRat's laboratory.

The white doors slide open, revealing a large, sunken chamber, and my senses immediately kick into overload. Every square inch of the wall is lined with beakers, test tubes, and vials of various sizes and colors. Large, cylindrical chambers run from floor to ceiling, bubbling with strange gaseous substances. Black tables fill the center, covered with microscopes, computer monitors, circuits, and assorted machinery. It's a nerd's paradise.

Needless to say, the disaster that is TechnocRat's laboratory drives Dad batty. TechnocRat loves bringing him in here to help with his experiments and watch him twitch. I know Dad just wants to get a garbage bag and clean everything up, but he can't risk spoiling one of TechnocRat's inventions. It's a funny little game they play. I guess they're like the odd couple of superheroes.

I move past a cart of electromagnetic, worm-like thingies, and head towards the back—to the reason why I'm here in the first place. I find him in the corner hooked up to a network of monitoring equipment.

Makeshift.

I reach out and touch his cold, solid arm. I hate myself for not having the guts to face him before.

Or to apologize.

"Hi, buddy," I say. "Can you hear me?"

I look up at the overhead monitor, but all his vitals are flat-lined. I wonder if he's still in there. If he can hear me somehow, but just can't respond.

"I-I'm sorry," I say, as tears stream down my cheeks. "I didn't know this was going to happen to you. I hope you can forgive me."

But there's no response.

"If you're still in there. If you can hear me, just give me a sign."

WHOOSH!

Instinctively, I duck, as a warm sensation crosses my body. What the heck was that?

I step back and look at Makeshift, but he hasn't budged. Then, I notice something glaring bright outside the porthole.

It's a trail.

A fiery trail!

I follow its path. It looks like it came from deep space—and it's heading straight for Earth!

Then, I realize I've seen a trail like that before, and my heart sinks to my toes.

I know exactly who it belongs to.

The Herald!

Meta Profile

Name: Alligazer
Role: Villain   Status: Active

VITALS:

Race: Human
Real Name: Anton Bing
Height: 6'3"
Weight: 225 lbs
Eye Color: Yellow
Hair Color: Bald

META POWERS:
Class: Energy Manipulator
Power Level:
- Extreme petrification
- Limited super-strength
- Limited super-speed
- Can cling to surfaces

CHARACTERISTICS:

Combat	85	
Durability	90	
Leadership	55	
Strategy	69	
Willpower	87	

THREE

I CAUSE AN INTERNATIONAL INCIDENT

I scribble down a note for my parents, grab a fresh costume out of the Equipment Room, tiptoe around a snoozing Dog-Gone in the hallway, and hit the Hangar.

Within seconds, I'm piloting a Freedom Ferry through space, hot on the Herald's trail. So many things are flying through my brain I don't know where to begin. I mean, the last time I saw the Herald, he descended upon a planet named Protaraan, and marked it for destruction by a globe-eating creature called Ravager— the Annihilator of Worlds!

I've been afraid something like this might happen ever since Siphon destroyed Order and Chaos back on Arena World. Once those two cosmic brothers were gone, no one was left to control that planet-gobbling monster. It was only a matter of time before Ravager showed up to destroy someone's world. I just never thought it would be mine!

I mean, recently I learned there are all of these other universes out there! Mirror universes, like the one Grace 2 lives in. And somehow, out of all of those, Ravager has chosen mine.

Why do I have all the luck?

Fortunately, the Herald may be the worst hide-and-seek player of all time. His trail is brighter than the sun. But being easy to track is one thing, catching up to him is quite another. I mean, the guy can really motor!

According to the Freedom Ferry's monitor, I enter Earth's atmosphere somewhere over Asia. I pick up the Herald's path weaving through mountains and then jetting across the ocean. It looks like he's now somewhere over Japan.

As far as I'm concerned, my job is simple. First, catch him. Second, get him off the planet. Seems pretty straightforward. I only see one little hiccup.

I've got no clue how to do that.

Not too long ago I was kidnapped by the Zodiac, a band of alien, teenage vigilantes because they thought I had the Orb of Oblivion—the only object capable of destroying Ravager. Even though I didn't know it at the time, they were right. I did have the Orb. It was buried inside of me. But Siphon pulled it out when he absorbed my powers, and then used it to destroy Order and Chaos. Now the Orb is gone.

And I'm on my own.

So much for early retirement.

I follow the Herald's trail through a cluster of thick clouds, and when I come out the other side, it's clear I won't be chasing him much farther.

Because he's waiting for me.

The heat blast comes fast and furious. I try to pull up, but it catches my left wing full-on, bursting it into flames. I activate the exterior cooling jets to extinguish it, but when the foamy liquid clears, my wing is still burning! Whatever he's hit me with isn't standard-issue fire! And the flames are creeping towards the cockpit!

My sensors are going nuts, so I check the radar to find even more bad news.

He's on my tail!

I spin the Freedom Ferry as another heat blast shoots over my right wing. I've got to lose this creep and fast! But how? I'm a sitting duck in the open sky.

Looking below, I see a giant expanse of water—wonderful fire-extinguishing water.

I push the yoke forward and nose drive straight for the ocean, switching the Freedom Ferry to amphibious mode. Then, I brace myself for impact.

SPLASH!

The Freedom Flyer knifes through the water, diving deep so he can't spot me from the air. I check the radar again and this time there's no sign of the Herald. I've lost him! Whew!

Then, I check my wing, fully expecting the fire to be snuffed out, but it's not! Giant flames are still crackling away! But how's that possible?

Suddenly, I'm blinded by an intense burst of light. Instinctively, I hit the brakes. What's going on? For a few seconds, all I see are spots, but when my vision clears I'm faced with something I'm not expecting.

Floating five feet in front of my ship is the Herald! He's breathing underwater and still very much on fire.

If I don't beg for mercy I'm cooked! I scan the control panel and flip on the external communications system. But before I can speak, I hear—

"I know you, little one."

I look up to find him staring at me—studying me— his arms folded across his chest. Then, I realize I'm only seeing him because he's lowered his intensity. He's big and broad-shouldered, but his facial features are impossible to see through the dancing flames. All I can make out are pointy-ears and a crooked nose.

"Y-You do?" I reply nervously.

"Yes," he says, his voice crackling like a campfire. "You battled on Arena World. You were there for the final battle before everything disintegrated. You were one of the so-called heroes. A little hero."

All this 'little' talk is making my blood boil.

"And you're a minion," I shoot back. "For Ravager!"

The fire man laughs. "So, you know of Ravager. And soon, Ravager will know of you. And your world."

Wait? Did he just say *soon*? Does that mean Ravager doesn't know about us yet? I've still got a chance!

"Why don't you get lost," I say. "While you still can."

"Is humor your superpower?" he says. "I suppose in the end, it does not matter. Your fate is sealed." He looks upwards. "My job is to find fertile planets for Ravager to consume. But I fear this has become more difficult. Without Order and Chaos, the multiverse is collapsing. Whole galaxies are vanishing in the blink of an eye, taking all of their planets with them. But I could tell from deep space that your galaxy is not yet affected. Yours is one of the stable ones. Yours is free of the Blur. At least, for now."

"Blur? What are you talking about?"

"I have wasted enough time with you," the Herald says. "Ravager must feed."

He's going to take off! I've got to stop him! I can't let him get away and lead Ravager here!

I'm not sure the Freedom Ferry's weapons are powerful enough to affect him. But I've got something better. I've got Meta powers!

I only hope it's enough.

I concentrate hard and wash my negation powers all over him. Suddenly, his bright, orange flames flicker and then blow out like a candle.

It worked? It worked!

"What is happening?" he says.

Now I've got to reel him in. I reach down to operate the pincers when I notice something strange on the radar. Something coming in fast—heading straight for us!

That can't be right? It looks like a—

BOOM!

The Freedom Ferry lurches backward. Luckily, my seatbelt keeps me from flying out of my chair, but as the ship rights itself my cheek slams down on the console.

That's gonna leave a mark.

I don't know what happened, but I can't worry about it now, I need to catch the Herald! But I can't spot him anywhere. Where'd he go?

Just then, the Freedom Ferry is lifted completely out of the water! I'm rising hundreds of feet into the air at ridiculous speed! And then, everything stops. I brace myself for a big fall, but nothing happens. Looking down, I see that, incredibly, the ship is balancing on a giant plume of water!

"You do not have clearance to fly over Japanese air space," comes a man's voice. "Identify yourself."

That's when I see a dude wearing red goggles and a blue wetsuit riding a wave like a surfboard. He makes a cutting motion with his arm, and my stomach drops as the Freedom Ferry free-falls toward the ocean! Then, with an upward sweep of his hand, I'm buoyed by another wave!

He was that blip on the radar!

He can control water!

"H-Hold on!" I yell, feeling queasy. "I'm Epic Zero! Who are you?"

"I am Tsunami," he says. "And you have five seconds to tell me whose government you work for, otherwise I will drown you in my sea." He lifts both hands, and I go flying back in the air.

"Wait!" I scream. "It's not what you think!"

I land with a thud on top of another wave! I'm totally seasick!

"Speak," he says. "Quickly."

"Look, I'm sorry if I broke some sort of international treaty, but I'm a member of the Freedom Force, and I'm trying to stop that fire guy before he escapes Earth and brings back something so big and nasty it'll knock your flippers off."

"What fire guy?" Tsunami asks.

Suddenly, a bright, orange streak breaks through the surface of the water and launches into the sky, leaving a blazing trail behind him.

"That fire guy," I say, watching the Herald disappear into the stratosphere. He got away. I had him and he got away. "Well, I guess we're all belly up now."

"You are a member of the Freedom Force?" Tsunami asks.

"Yeah," I say.

"But you are just a boy?"

"Yep," I say. "Can't deny that one."

"You are coming with us," Tsunami says.

"Us?" I say. "Who's 'us?'"

"*We* are the greatest heroes of the East," comes a booming voice to my left. "*We* are the Rising Suns."

I turn to find four other costumed characters hovering next to the Freedom Flyer. Where'd they come from? There's a big guy with a green cape and a dragon emblem on his chest, another guy dressed like a samurai warrior holding a glowing sword, a long-haired woman in a karate uniform, and a girl wearing a white mask, with a teardrop painted below her right eye.

Well, this doesn't look good.

Now that the Herald's gone, there's no reason for me to stick around. These guys are clearly Metas, and I suspect if I don't make a quick exit, I'll be in major trouble. The problem is, my wing is still on fire.

"Zen," Tsunami says. "Neutralize him."

What? But before I can react, I feel something enter my mind. And then, I hear a gentle voice.

Sleep.

The masked girl is a psychic!

Suddenly, my eyes feel droopy.

I need to use my powers!

I...

need...

to...

get...

out...

Meta Profile

Name: The Herald
Role: Cosmic Entity Status: Active

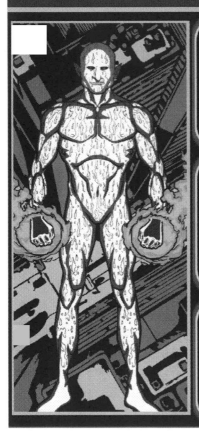

VITALS:

Race: Unknown
Real Name: Unknown
Height: 6'7"
Weight: 325 lbs
Eye Color: Yellow
Hair Color: Bald

META POWERS:

Class: Inapplicable
Power Level: Incalculable

- A being of extreme power that can generate and manipulate solar power
- Scouts and marks planets for Ravager to consume

CHARACTERISTICS:

Combat	100	
Durability	100	
Leadership	75	
Strategy	86	
Willpower	100	

FOUR

I GET TAKEN HOSTAGE

"**W**ake up!"

The girl's voice rings in my brain. My eyes jolt open, then close quickly from the bright spotlight glaring in my face. Squinting, I take in my surroundings.

I'm sitting at a table in a small room. Across the way are five figures shrouded in darkness. But I don't need to see them to know who they are.

I try standing up, but I can't move. I feel cold metal scrape against my wrists. Shackles?

Great. I'm trapped.

The figure seated across from me shifts in his chair, his muscled silhouette growing larger as he leans forward. I'm pretty sure he's the big one, the one with the dragon insignia on his chest. "Who was the red, flying man?" he demands.

"Santa Claus," I answer hoarsely. My throat is dry, like I haven't had water in days. How long have I been here?

"I will ask you again," he says, more sternly this time. "Who was the man of fire?"

I stare at my inquisitor—his face still hidden in shadows. I could lie, but at this point I've got nothing to lose. I'm clearly not talking my way out of this one.

"He's called the Herald," I say. "He's a scout for the cosmic monstrosity called Ravager, the Annihilator of Worlds. I had him captured, but thanks to your fishy friend over there, he got away. Now he'll come back with that planet-eating terror and destroy us all."

My captors exchange words in Japanese. Unfortunately, I'm not very multi-lingual. I barely remember a handful of middle-grade Spanish, like 'me aprietan mucho los zapatos.' So, I can't understand a darn thing they're saying.

"How did you come to our land?" the man continues.

"Um, by jet," I say. Why are they asking me that? I mean, I was in the Freedom Ferry when they captured me.

There's more back and forth in Japanese.

The man turns back and faces me. "Let me rephrase my question to be more precise. This jet, from which planet does it originate?"

What? Which planet? Is this a trick question? I look at him like he's got two heads and say, "Um, Earth."

"Really?" he says. "Then how do you explain this?" He looks back at his armored colleague and calls, "Silent Samurai."

Suddenly, the guy dressed in samurai gear steps forward and draws his sword. It's long and sharp and could probably slice me into a million pieces. Then, he raises it over his head!

"Whoa, big fella!" I say. "Watch where you're pointing that thing!"

But when he swings downward, the sword misses me and produces some kind of energy field in its wake. Then, the vibrating energy forms into a holographic image. That looks like me! And the Rising Suns! Wait a minute, it's a re-creation of our fight!

There's the Freedom Ferry—with me inside! I watch Zen wave her arm, putting me to sleep. And then, the Silent Samurai guy and the karate woman board the Freedom Ferry and pull my unconscious body out.

Watching myself get captured is weird. But then, things get weirder.

Suddenly, the Freedom Flyer goes transparent! And then it comes back again! It does this several times like it's popping in and out of the scene. And then, to my astonishment, it's gone! Like, completely vanished!

What's happening? I mean, I could have been inside that thing!

"Now," the man continues. "Where did you send your ship? Back to your planet?"

"What?" I say. "No, I-I don't know what happened."

"Not true!" he bellows, slamming his fist onto the table which promptly splits in two. "Do I need to be more persuasive?"

"Stop, Green Dragon," the karate-clad woman says. "Look at his eyes. It is clear the child does not know."

"I will judge what the child does and does not know, Fight Master," the Green Dragon says. "Look me in the eyes, boy."

Suddenly, they kill the spotlight and I can see everyone clearly. Behind the Green Dragon stand the rest of the Rising Suns. Fight Master must be the woman. And there's Zen, and Tsunami, and Silent Samurai.

"Look," I say. "This is all a big misunderstanding. I'm not from another planet, I'm a superhero from America. I was simply trying to save the planet from extermination, that's all. Maybe if you call the Freedom Force we can straighten this whole thing out and I can go home?"

"You are going nowhere," Green Dragon says. "Perhaps you are a spy, capturing unlawful surveillance of our country. Did you transport your findings back to your government in that ship?"

"No, I'm just a kid."

"Then listen closely, kid," Green Dragon says. "Only when you return the jet can we begin to discuss the remote possibility of your freedom."

"But I didn't make it disappear."

"Perhaps an evening in solitary confinement will help revive your memory," he says.

"Now hang on—"

"Zen."

Oh no.

"Sleep," she says, inside my head.

And I'm out.

***

When I wake up, it takes about a nanosecond to realize I'm in serious trouble. I'm a prisoner inside the tiniest cell in existence. But what it lacks in square footage it more than makes up for in efficiency, because there's only me, a cot, and a toilet. Yep, that's pretty much everything you need in life.

I run my hand along the surface of the wall. It's tungsten steel, the strongest metal on Earth. There's no way I'm getting out of here. Even the door looks triple-reinforced.

I feel super groggy, so I try shaking out the cobwebs. That Zen girl may be a more dangerous psychic than Mom. I mean, I never even felt her enter my mind. The next time I see her, I'm going on the offensive.

I stand up and stretch my legs. There's not much room to walk around. And because there's no window, I can't tell if it's day or night.

How did I get myself into this mess? I'm sure my parents found my note and are flipping out by now. If I could just get in contact with them they'd bust me out of here. Then we'd show the Rising Suns what real good guys look like.

My mind drifts to Ravager. While I'm rotting in this cell, the Herald is probably leading that monster straight to Earth by now. The only way to stop him is with the Orb of Oblivion, but that's gone. And who knows if it would have worked anyway? Especially in my hands.

I've got to get out of here! I push hard against the door, not that I expect anything to happen. I'm absolutely kicking myself for leaving my utility belt on the Waystation. Not that it would have mattered because I'm guessing the Rising Suns would have taken it from me anyway.

I'm about to pound on the wall and yell for help when I lose my balance. I guess I'm not as steady as I thought. And my vision is still sort of blurry.

Wait a minute?

Blurry!

The Freedom Ferry was blurry!

It was out of focus—fading in and out before it disappeared. What did the Herald say about the Blur? Something about whole galaxies collapsing, vanishing in the blink of an eye.

O.M.G.

Was the Freedom Ferry a sign? Is our galaxy next to disappear?

I feel myself hyperventilating. I've got to get out of here! I've got to tell the Freedom Force! Maybe TechnocRat will know what to do!

But I'm trapped. And soon, the Rising Suns are going to come back for me, and who knows what they'll do when I don't tell them what they want to hear. If I only had the power to get out of this joint. To bust out like Dad. Or teleport like Makeshift. Or jump into a wormhole like... like...

Wind Walker!

That's it!

The last time I saw him, he transported me home from another universe. What did he say before he took off? Call him if I ever needed help? But he didn't give me a communications device or anything. And how's he going to find me here? I don't even know where I am.

I close my eyes.

Wind Walker! I call out with my mind.

Then, I open my eyes and wait, but there's nothing.

Okay, that's not going to work.

I put my ear to the door—there's no noise on the other side. I scan the room for security cameras or monitoring equipment. Nothing. Well, what have I got to lose? Here goes nothing.

I take a deep breath, and yell as loud as I can, "WIND WALKER!"

Suddenly, a blue-skinned man with long, dark hair materializes before my eyes.

It's him! He's here!

But something is wrong. He's holding his right arm, and there's a large slash across his face. And his eyes. They look... defeated?

"Epic Zero," Wind Walker says feebly. "I came as soon as I heard your call. I am sorry for the delay."

"There wasn't any delay. What happened to you? What's wrong?"

"I-I will be fine, my friend," he replies. "But soon, my world—all of our worlds, will not be."

"Does this have to do with the Blur?" I ask.

"The Blur?" he says surprised. "Then you are aware of the great cosmic upheaval. Yes, I suppose we could call it that. For at this very moment, the multiverse is collapsing—blurring into one. And when it is complete, every mirror universe except for one will be destroyed, taking countless lives with it."

"What can we do?" I ask. "There's got to be a way to stop it?"

Wind Walker brushes a strand of hair off his face and looks me straight in the eyes. "I do not know," he says. "My powers only allow me to walk across dimensions. I have tried to intervene in every way possible. But all I can do is watch helplessly as whole universes die."

"The Herald said this is happening because Order

and Chaos were destroyed," I say.

"The Herald was here?" Wind Walker says, his eyes widening.

"Yes, and now Ravager is loose—coming here to destroy my planet."

Wind Walker looks at me solemnly. "I am sorry, my friend. I am afraid there is nothing we can do."

"Nothing?" I shout. "I won't accept nothing. Look, I don't know how to stop this 'Blur thing' either. But, I'm not going to sit around and watch Ravager eat my home."

"Of course," Wind Walker says. "I am sorry. You are right. We are heroes and need to act as such. Even in the face of impossible odds. Let me assist you. I assume you contacted me to free you from this prison?"

That's a good start. But then I've got to figure out a way to destroy Ravager. And the only way to do that is with the Orb of Oblivion.

But my Orb is gone.

My Orb.

The words strike me funny. I mean, the Orb was never mine. It chose me. I never chose it.

My Orb.

And then a lightbulb goes off. Wait a minute. Wind Walker can cross universes, which means...

He can take me to another universe!

A mirror universe!

Where there might be a mirror Orb of Oblivion!

"Big guy," I say. "I know exactly what I need you to

do."

Just then, we hear angry voices outside.

The Rising Suns!

I leap into Wind Walker's arms and shout, "Get us out of here!"

"Who is that?" Wind Walker asks.

"Later!" I yell. "Right now, I need less talking, more worm-holing!"

Suddenly, the door swings open and Green Dragon bursts in.

But he's too late.

Because we're gone!

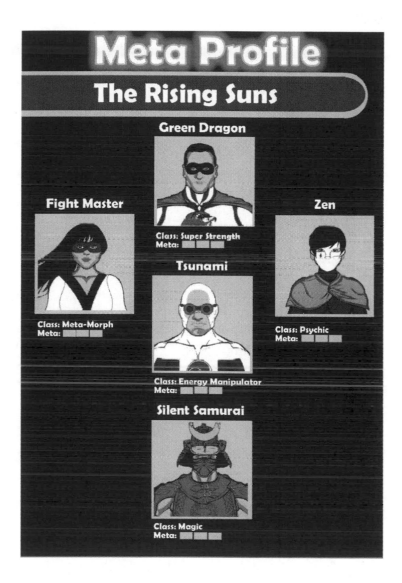

FIVE

I GO WHERE NO KID HAS GONE BEFORE

We hit the ground hard.

Wind Walker touches down smoothly, but I'm wobblier than a newborn deer. Everything is spinning like crazy, so I reach out for something—anything—to keep from toppling over. Then, I feel Wind Walker grab my arms, steadying me.

"Are you okay?" he asks.

Wow! I completely forgot what a roller coaster ride it is traveling through Wind Walker's inter-dimensional wormholes. "I-I think so," I say. "You know, I'm not sure I meet the height requirements to ride that thing."

After a few seconds, I get my bearings, but something is off. I mean, why are birds the only things at eye level?

That's when I realize we're up high, standing on top of some green structure with giant spikes flaring out in all directions. I clutch Wind Walker's arm and peer over the edge. There's like, all these tiny people milling around below.

Hang on, those aren't tiny people—they're real-sized people! Which means we must be hundreds of feet in the air!

I look back at Wind Walker and see a gigantic hand holding a torch behind him.

No way!

"We're on top of the freaking Statue of Liberty!"

"Yes," Wind Walker says. "You desired freedom. This is the first place that came to mind."

"Strangely," I say, "that kind of makes sense."

"Shall I take you home now?"

Home? Now there's a great question.

Honestly, going home never crossed my mind. While it would be great to have the Freedom Force by my side, there's so many of them it would ruin any possibility of surprise. Besides, if I told them what I was planning to do they would try to stop me. So, that pretty much seals the deal.

No home. No family.

I'm going solo.

"No thanks," I say. "But, I need you to drop me somewhere else. And you've got to promise not to tell anybody. Deal?"

Wind Walker gives me a suspicious look. "Deal."

***

Okay, I'm clearly nuts for doing this again.

Wind Walker's got me by the arm, dragging me through yet another wormhole of doom. It's like we're swimming inside a pitch-black washing machine. I feel the space narrowing around us, closing in, while an unrelenting wind blows against our faces.

I'm wiped. This is the longest wormhole I've ever been through. It feels like we've been traveling forever. Then, without warning, we POP out the other side. Wind Walker lands with the grace of a cat. I hit the ground like a hippopotamus.

"Are you hurt?" Wind Walker asks.

"Just my pride," I mutter, lying face down. "Don't worry, I'll be fine."

"Are you certain about this?" he asks.

I scramble to my feet, my stomach still doing flips. Wind Walker studies my face for signs of weakness, but I'm not breaking. No matter how terrified I am—and believe me, I'm terrified—I've got a job to do.

"Very well," he says. "Remember, you are no longer on your world. Places may appear identical, people may look familiar, but nothing is as it seems. For as long as you remain here, your greatest enemy is yourself. If you lower your guard, even for a second, it could cost you your life."

I take a deep breath and force a smile. "Okay, okay," I say. "I've got it. I can handle this."

"I hope so," Wind Walker says. "Now, I must try to solve the riddle of the Blur before it is too late. Good luck, Epic Zero. If you need me, call my name. Hopefully, I will be able to return for you."

"Good luck," I say, as we shake hands.

"Do not forget what I told you," he says. Then, he steps into a black void and disappears.

I'm alone.

In Keystone City.

On another Earth.

Earth 2.

When I battled on Arena World, I learned that I lived on just one version of Earth. That my reality was only one version of reality and there were possibly billions of other realities out there. Wind Walker called them mirror universes. So, while I exist in my world, other versions of me likely exist in other worlds.

At first, it was hard to get my head around that idea—until I met Grace 2 and Mom 2. Then, I realized it was real. There really are mirror universes out there.

And while I may not have the Orb of Oblivion to stop Ravager from destroying my world, I'm pretty sure there's one person in this world who has another Orb of Oblivion.

Elliott 2.

From what Grace 2 told me about him, he's not like me at all. He's evil and supposedly rules his Earth with an iron fist. Plus, he's blond while my hair is brown which is kind of strange to imagine.

So, my three-part plan is simple. First, get to Earth 2. Check—thanks to Wind Walker's dimension-crossing ability. Second, find Elliott 2 and steal the second Orb of Oblivion. Third, get back to my world in time to prevent Ravager from destroying it.

It seems simple enough. Right?

Wrong, and I know it, but I can't look back now. Not if I have a shot at saving my Earth.

So, where would I be hanging out if I were an evil version of myself?

Suddenly, I hear the unmistakable rumbling of an oncoming car, so I dive behind the nearest hedge. Peeking through the shrubbery, I watch as a camouflaged jeep drives past carrying three costumed goons. That's weird, those guys looked like the Terror Triplets, a trio of Meta 1 villains on my world. What are they doing casually driving around a nice suburban neighborhood?

But as I look around from my hiding spot, I realize the neighborhood isn't nearly as nice as I thought it was. Every house looks abandoned and in need of massive repairs. Windows are smashed. Front doors are kicked in. Roofs have gaping holes. It's like a war was waged here, and no one bothered cleaning up the mess!

Then, I remember my talks with Grace 2 on Arena World. She told me that with all of the heroes out of the picture, criminal Meta gangs had taken over everything and battled over turf. At the time, I thought that sounded bad, but I never imagined it would be this bad. I mean, there aren't any regular people around. And where did all the heroes go?

This is completely depressing. And to top it off, I have no idea what to do next. But one thing I do know is that I can't sit here.

I wait for the jeep to speed past, and then race across the street as fast as I can. Ducking behind a tree, I catch a street sign dangling loosely from its pole. Wait a minute! I'm on High Street. So, that means I'm only a few blocks away from...

The Prop House!

Suddenly, things are looking up! In my world, the Prop House was the fake house we used to travel from the Waystation to Earth and back again. If it's the same thing here, then maybe I can use the Transporter to find Grace 2 and the Freedom Force and pull this thing off!

I feel strangely giddy booking down the street towards my old home. I reach the end of the road and hang a left. Just a few more blocks to go. This is going to be so much easier than I thought!

Then, I hear footsteps behind me.

Somebody is running after me.

Closing in on me.

I spin around, ready for a fight, but to my surprise, there's no one there. That's weird, I could have sworn I heard something. I shake my head. I mean, it wouldn't be the first time my mind has played tricks on me.

Suddenly, out of the corner of my eye, I catch movement from high above. I throw myself beneath a burnt-out truck and look up. Six Metas are soaring high up above. I can't tell who they are, but it looks like they're flying in a 'V' formation—like they're on patrol!

I scoot as far beneath the truck as I can, my heart pounding a mile a minute. Hopefully, they didn't see me. But how could they miss me? I was running down the middle of the street like a bonehead! If I get captured before I can even get inside the Prop House, it's over.

I wait a few minutes before I risk poking my head out. When I finally do, the patrol is gone. And even better, I spot the Prop House straight ahead. Seeing it again takes my breath away, but not for the reasons I'd hoped.

The house is leaning hard to the left. The roof is sagging, the door and windows are boarded up, and the posts flanking the front porch are piles of rubble scattered over the patch-work front lawn.

It's a teardown.

All the air escapes from my happiness balloon.

There's not going to be any reunion with Grace 2 and the Freedom Force. I'm on my own.

Seeing the Prop House like this is utterly

heartbreaking. I think of all the good times we had there. Like when Grace and I hid TechnocRat's electromagnetic power rods and accidentally shorted out the Waystation. Or when we tracked Dog-Gone's gravy-stained footprints here after he stole the Thanksgiving turkey. Or when our neighbor called the cops when Dad forgot to take off his mask before mowing the lawn.

Of course, there was also plenty of drama. Like the countless times I took the Transporter to school while Grace was off fighting with the Freedom Force. Or when the Worm's goons broke in and discovered the Waystation. After that, we removed the Transporter and sold the Prop House, but I miss it. Strangely, it was the only 'normal' home I ever had.

Even though it's hopeless, I'm still itching to look inside. I'm sure the Transporter is long gone, but I'm curious to see if anything else was left behind. I mean, we decorated the Prop House with family pictures and other sentimental stuff. Maybe there's some clue in there I can use to track down Grace 2.

I make sure I'm in the clear, and then break for it. Stepping onto the Prop House's dilapidated porch, I press my ear against the boarded door. Just as I thought, there's no noise coming from inside. So, I push hard against the wood, opening a space just large enough to slip inside.

It's dark.

Instinctively, I reach for the light switch and flick it

on. Surprisingly, it works!

And then I get the shock of my life.

The blue sofas, the coffee table, the TV, the pictures. They're all here. In perfect condition.

But... how can that be?

I walk through the room stunned. It's an exact replica of the Prop House on my world. Then, I remember...

The full-length mirror! The miniature Statue of Liberty! They're here!

Is it possible?

I walk over and wrap my hand around the mini figurine when...

"Let go," commands a deep, voice.

What the—?

I turn to find the silhouette of a large, broad-shouldered man filling the doorframe. A dead rabbit swings freely by its ears in his left hand.

I'm not sure what to do. There's nowhere to run. And if I pull the Statue of Liberty, there may not be a Transporter to escape into.

I'm trapped.

Then, he steps into the light. He looks like a mountain man—with dark, scraggly hair and a bushy mustache and beard. He's wearing a long trench coat that covers his body from his shoulders to his legs.

There's something oddly familiar about him.

Then, I notice his blue eyes staring me down.

And that's when I realize I know him.

O! M! G!

"D-Dad?" I stammer.

"I don't know why you came back, Elliott," he says. "But I'll tell you this, one of us isn't leaving here alive!"

Meta Profile

Name: Captain Justice 2
Role: Hero   Status: Inactive

VITALS:

Race: Human
Real Name: Tom Harkness
Height: 6'3"
Weight: 220 lbs
Eye Color: Blue
Hair Color: Black

META POWERS:

Class: Super-Strength
Power Level: ▮▮▮▯▯

- **Extreme Strength**
- **Invulnerability**
- **Enhanced Jumping**
- **Shockwave-Clap**

CHARACTERISTICS:

Combat	95	
Durability	96	
Leadership	100	
Strategy	94	
Willpower	91	

SIX

I LEARN TO TRUST NO ONE

Dad 2 is about to ground me, but I mean like, bury me six feet under.

"Sorry, son," he says, tossing the dead rabbit to the floor. "But you've had this coming for a long, long time."

I watch his giant muscles ripple as he removes his trench coat. He thinks I'm his kid, the evil ruler of his world! Somehow, I've got to convince him I'm not. Otherwise, I'll be worse off than that rabbit!

"Listen, Dad—I mean, Captain Justice, I know this will be surprising to hear, but I'm not your son." I've got to think fast. I could wipe his powers, but he'd easily crush me anyway. Plus, that would only convince him I'm exactly who he thinks I am. I need a different approach. Pronto!

"No more games, Elliott," he says, wiping his long, dark hair out of his face. "I'm tired of your games."

That's it! Hair!

"Wait!" I say, pointing to my head. "Look! I've got dark hair, just like you."

"So?" he says. "It won't stop me from doing what I need to do."

"No," I say. "Don't you get it? *Your* son has blond hair. I'm not who you think I am. I'm Elliott but from a different universe."

This isn't working! He's still coming at me! I need another approach!

"I'm friends with your daughter, Grace. And I saved your wife's life."

That part stops him cold. I keep going. "The last time I saw her she was a villain. But then I saved her from death and she promised to become a hero again."

"She promised what?" he says. "Who are you?"

"I'm a hero from a mirror universe. I'm here to stop your son, just like you! So please don't clobber me!"

Dad 2 looks at me, confused. "A mirror universe? TechnocRat talked about it once, but I never thought it was possible."

"Oh, it's possible," I say. "In fact, it's real. Your world is exactly like mine, but all mixed up. In my world, I'm a hero—a member of the Freedom Force—just like you."

Suddenly, his face falls. "I'm no hero. Not anymore."

Then, I remember what Grace 2 told me. That her version of Dad gave up the superhero business after my double took over his planet, outlawed all superheroes, and turned his wife into a supervillain.

"So, you just hide in here?" I ask. "While all that bad stuff is happening outside?"

He strolls over to the sofa and sits down, his head in his hands. "What else can I do?"

"You can fight!" I say strongly. I can't believe my ears. Captain Justice 2 is a… coward?

"For what?" he says. "There are hundreds of Meta villains out there, all of whom would love to make a name for themselves by hauling me in. You think I want to get captured and have you—or my kid, rather—cancel my powers permanently and feed me to the wolves? They'll lock me up and make an example out of me. Just like they did to Master Mime and Blue Bolt."

Cancel his powers? What's he talking about?

"It's safer in here," he continues. "Thankfully, I managed to steal TechnocRat's Distorter before our headquarters was overrun. The Distorter makes the house look like a disaster on the outside, but inside it's fine. No one ever thinks to look in here. To survive, all I need to do is hunt for food and stay out of trouble."

Did he say headquarters? If I can get to the Freedom Force's headquarters, then I may be able to find Grace 2.

"You said your headquarters was overrun," I say. "Can you take me there? Can you take me to the

Waystation?"

"Waystation," he says. "What's a Waystation?"

"Hang on," I say shocked. "Do you mean there's no—" Suddenly, I notice the Statue of Liberty figurine is fading in and out!

"What are you doing?" he asks.

"Nothing," I say. Is that the Blur?

He stands up and races over to it. One second the mini statue is there, the next, it's gone. He reaches for it.

"Wait!" I warn. "Don't touch it. It's going to vanish. For good."

Then, as if on cue, it disappears.

"Bring it back!" he cries.

"Relax," I say. "It's just a statue. On my world, it took my whole Freedom Ferry."

"Get out of my way," he says, bumping me aside. His eyes look crazed, like something is seriously wrong. He leans over and lifts the mirror. It must weigh hundreds of pounds, but for him it's nothing.

"No!" he says, frantically looking inside the empty space behind the mirror. "It's gone!"

I peek inside. There's no Transporter. Great. Now I've got zero chance of finding Grace 2.

"The Distorter," he says. "I hid the Distorter in here, behind the mirror. And now it's gone!"

"Sorry about that," I say. "But look, I've got bigger problems. See, there's this cosmic alien mist coming to swallow my Earth, so I really need to find your son and get something from him. You wouldn't happen to know where to find him, would you?"

But he can't hear me. His face is flush with anger. "It's your fault the Distorter is gone! It's your fault I'm going to get caught! You're going to pay for this!"

I get the sense this is going downhill fast.

He turns, about to drop the mirror and grab me, when—out of nowhere—his trench coat comes flying across the room and drapes over his head.

"Hey!" he yells.

How did that happen?

Then, he's shoved back into the empty space behind the mirror. The giant mirror SLAMS down to the floor, trapping him inside. I don't know what's happening, but I know I've got seconds to get out of here before he busts through that mirror.

But before I can move, a German Shepherd appears before my eyes.

"Dog-Gone!"

His tail wags from side to side, and then he takes off, heading out of the Prop House through a large opening he made in the boarded door. I hear Dad 2 yelling something from behind the mirror, but I'm not sticking around to find out what.

I squeeze through the hole and bolt into the front yard. Dog-Gone is way ahead, and I'm huffing to keep up. I'll tell you one thing, humans may have opposable thumbs, but when it comes to running for your life I'd take four legs any day of the week.

I glance back at the Prop House, and to my surprise, it no longer looks like a dump. The cherry red door is back. As are the windows, posts, roof, and landscaping. Dad 2 was right, that Distorter really worked.

I try making sense of what just happened. I can't believe Dad 2 has given up. I mean, he's not my dad but he's still Captain Justice, the leader of the freaking Freedom Force! Suddenly, Wind Walker's words ring truer than ever: *nothing is as it seems.*

Dog-Gone races down the block and peels off between two abandoned houses. I'm probably a block behind him, so I dig deep and try to pick up speed. I don't know how he tracked me down, but boy I'm glad he did. Right now, a friendly face is exactly what I need.

I hit the spot where he turned off, but Dog-Gone is nowhere to be found.

"Dog-Gone?" I whisper. What happened to that mutt? Did he take off or did something bad happen to him? I look around for clues, like footprints, doggie doo—anything—when something plows into me, taking out my legs!

I land hard on my rear with a thud. But before I can react, I feel hot breath, accompanied by a low, threatening growl.

"Dog-Gone?" I say. "What are you doing?" Dog-Gone's head appears inches from my face and I'm staring at his razor-sharp teeth. Clearly, he's not so happy to see me.

"Whoa, boy," I say. "It's me, Elliott, your mas... ter."

And then it hits me. This isn't my Dog-Gone. It's Dog-Gone 2! And based on his incredible sense of smell, he knows I'm not his Elliott!

He growls again—a menacing, throaty growl.

"Hang on," I plead. "I never tricked you. You saved me, remember?"

Another growl.

"Look, we both know I'm not your Elliott. But that doesn't mean I'm a bad person. I'm just looking for your master. Do you know where he is?"

Suddenly, he lets out a high-pitched whimper.

What's going on? Why is he reacting that way? Hold on. I would never, *ever* let my Dog-Gone roam the streets alone unsupervised. He could get hurt. And this world is way more dangerous than mine.

So, maybe that means...

"Is your Elliott missing?"

Dog-Gone 2 bows his head and lets out another whimper.

He *is* missing!

"Look, boy," I say. "That's why I'm here. I'm trying to find your Elliott too. Maybe we can work together and figure out where he is? What do you say?"

The German Shepherd studies me with his big, brown eyes. I try to look trustworthy. After all, I'm not going to tell him I'm only here to steal the Orb of Oblivion.

I feel wet slobber on my chin.

I guess that's a yes!

Dog-Gone 2 backs up and I get to my feet. "Okay, maybe we should start with where you saw him last."

The mutt nods and takes off again. Great, a dog that's even more impulsive than mine! I don't know where we're heading, but my thoughts are completely scattered.

I mean, what could have happened to Elliott 2?

Maybe somebody took him out? But if he has the Orb of Oblivion, then whoever did that must be pretty powerful.

Or maybe the Orb took over his mind? I know how powerful the Orb can be, and my greatest fear was always losing control. It's possible Elliott 2 lost the battle and the Orb is using him as its host.

The very thought makes me shudder.

I catch up with Dog-Gone 2 who's waiting for me behind a tall hedge. He's panting lightly, meanwhile, my lungs are burning. You'd think after all the times I've run from danger, I'd have more endurance by now.

"Is this where… you saw him last?" I wheeze.

Dog-Gone nods his head 'yes,' and walks to the other side. I round the corner and find him standing stock-still, staring straight ahead. As I see what he's pointing at, my stomach sinks and I realize this mission is going to be a lot harder than I imagined.

Because rising before us is a monstrous structure resembling a steel octopus.

Lockdown.

Meta Profile

Name: Dog-Gone 2
Role: Villain   Status: Active

VITALS:

Breed: German Shepherd
Real Name: Dog-Gone
Height: 2'1" (at shoulder)
Weight: 85 lbs
Eye Color: Dark Brown
Hair Color: Brown/Black

META POWERS:

Class: Meta-morph
Power Level: ▮▮
- **Considerable Invisibility**
- **Can turn all or part of body invisible**

CHARACTERISTICS:

Combat	45	
Durability	16	
Leadership	10	
Strategy	12	
Willpower	56	

SEVEN

I CAN'T BELIEVE MY BAD LUCK

Well, this is the last place I thought I'd ever be.

On my Earth, Lockdown is the Meta-Maximum Federal Penitentiary designed to keep the world's most dangerous super-powered villains under lock and key. Essentially, it's where the good guys put away the bad guys—for good. So, to say I'm shocked by what I'm seeing is a gross understatement.

The inmates have taken over the asylum.

Lockdown looks like an ant farm for costumed criminals. They're manning guard towers, patrolling the walls—even guarding the front gates! There isn't a superhero or law enforcement officer in sight.

I glance over at Dog-Gone 2 who's busy relieving himself on a nearby tree. I had asked that fleabag to take me to the last place he saw Elliott 2, but I never thought it would be here. Maybe he misheard me?

I mean, if he's like my Dog-Gone, he has what I'd call 'selective hearing.' If you're miles away and open a bag of potato chips he's by your side in a flash, but if you ask him to get his snout out of the trash can it's like his ears are suddenly stuffed with cotton. Go figure.

"Dog-Gone," I whisper. "Are you sure about this? Remember, I asked you to take me to where you saw your master last."

Dog-Gone nods and turns back to Lockdown.

Just. Freaking. Wonderful.

Not only do we need to break into an impenetrable prison controlled by super-powered villains, but we also need to get Elliott 2 out before we're caught, killed, or all of the above. Sounds like a suicide run.

"We need a plan," I say, looking to the heavens for inspiration. "And since I've got the bigger brain, I guess it's up to me. Let's figure this out. We need to get inside without being seen, which should be easy for you. Unfortunately, we just can't march up to the front gates and—"

I hear a rustling noise. The next thing I know, Dog-Gone 2 is wading through the underbrush heading straight for Lockdown's front gates! And he's not invisible!

I duck behind the hedges. "Dog-Gone!" I whisper firmly. "Dog-Gone, come! Get back here! Bad dog!"

But it's too late, he's halfway to the gates by now. I hear shouting when the watchtower guards finally see him. That's fine, he can get caught if he wants to, but not me. No siree Bob! I'm getting out of here while I still c—

Wait a minute! What's he doing? Why is he turning around and facing me? He's just standing there, using his nose like a pointer.

That mongrel! He's selling me out! I've got to split!

But it's too late.

The Super-Speedsters reach me first. I recognize them from their Meta-profiles: Speed Demon, Whirlwind, Break-Neck. Then, the Flyers drop in: Atmo-Spear, Dark Storm, Bicyclone, Terrible Tempest. Then come all the rest—waves of them.

I'm surrounded.

"Hey, it's great to see you guys," I say. "How's the family?"

Just then, a pack of villains split apart, and a masked figure wearing a long, dark robe approaches. He looks me up and down through the white slits in his black mask. "Your Excellency," he says, with a grisly voice. Then, he bends in a slight bow. "We are thankful for your safe return."

Your Excellency? Is he talking to me?

Wait a minute! That voice. I know that voice!

"Shadow Hawk? What are you doing at Lockdown?"

"Of course, your Excellency," he says, looking surprised. "Where else would I be? I see Dog-Gone found you. Fortunately, that saves us from paying a large bounty, although now I'm sure I need to find a lifetime supply of dog biscuits. So, where did you wander off to? And if you don't mind me asking, what happened to your hair?"

My hair? I reach up and touch my head. Wait a minute, my hair! They think I'm Elliott 2—the ruler of this world! So, that means Shadow Hawk 2 must be evil too. This is so weird, but I've got to play along!

"I went for a stroll," I say.

"Three weeks is quite a long stroll, your Excellency," Shadow Hawk 2 says, his eyes narrowing. "And your hair?"

Okay, think fast. I need an excuse for why I'm not blond. "Oh, I ran into some weird Meta 1 hero named Color Clash. He turned my hair brown, so I made sure he saw black and blue."

"I see," he says, looking at the villains around us. "Perhaps we should discuss this at a more appropriate time. Why don't we head back to Lockdown? You seem tired and I'm sure you're hungry. Besides, in your absence we found something I'm sure will pique your interest. Shall we?"

I nod, and he leads us towards the prison. The villains fall in line, as does Dog-Gone 2 who pads next to me with his head held high.

"Okay," I whisper. "Maybe you have the bigger brain. But next time, warn me first."

Dog-Gone 2 lets out an "I-told-you-so" growl as we march straight through the front gates. I peer up at the main building and think back to the last time I was here—with K'ami.

This is where the Worm brainwashed and freed an army of Meta 3 prisoners. This is where we fought the Blood Bringers over the Orb of Oblivion. This is where K'ami died.

It's strange how often I dream about that day, but no matter how many times I relive it, it always ends in the same nightmare—with me holding K'ami's lifeless body. K'ami sacrificed her life for me—for all of us. I wonder if I could ever do the same?

As we enter the main building, I hear her voice, calmly saying: *Never show weakness.*

And she's right. On the outside, I keep a poker face, but inside I'm a mess. I mean, I'm being escorted inside a flipping prison by a bunch of Meta prisoners! This wasn't exactly the plan I had in mind. But it's not like I've got better options.

We walk through several dimly lit hallways until we reach a security checkpoint. Shadow Hawk 2 swipes a card and the doors open into another hallway lined with dozens of cell doors. A sign above reads: *Former Hero Wing 5: Official Access Only.*

Former Hero wing? What does that mean?

Shadow Hawk 2 continues down the hall. As we pass by each cell, I read the signs:

Cell#27: Magnet Man — ex-Meta 2: Former member of the Hero Hive. Used to control magnetic objects. Is permitted to use silverware at mealtimes.

Cell#28: Electric Defender — ex-Meta 3: Former member of the Strike Force. Once able to fire electricity from his body. Is permitted to shower daily.

Cell#29: Blue Bolt — ex-Meta 3: Former member of the Freedom Force. Once able to move at super speed. Is allowed outdoor exercise once per day.

Blue Bolt? Or rather, Blue Bolt 2?

I stop and look inside the window. Blue Bolt is sitting cross-legged on the floor, her head hung low. She looks weak—almost broken.

Suddenly, Shadow Hawk 2 is by my side. "Pathetic, isn't she?"

Anger wells up inside me, but I can't blow my cover.

"She's powerless?" I ask.

"Completely," Shadow Hawk 2 says. "You saw to that, remember?"

Me? That's right! Back on Arena World, Grace 2 told me my evil double used his powers to render heroes powerless. Now what Captain Justice 2 said about having his powers canceled makes perfect sense! I can't look surprised.

"Of course," I say. "Um, I forgot. How long has she been in there again?"

"I don't know," he says. "Three months, maybe four. But don't worry, we're not feeding her much. We're only keeping her around until her friends inevitably try to rescue her. Once we capture them, we'll dispose of her like all the rest. Thank goodness heroes are so predictable."

"Y-You mean you're using her as… bait?"

"Yes, of course," he says, throwing me a suspicious look. "Those were your orders."

"Right," I say quickly. "Sorry, it's been a long week."

"Three weeks," Shadow Hawk 2 reminds me. "But your strategy has been very effective. Since you went on your little stroll, we've captured every member of the Do-Gooders, the Great Samaritans, the Honor Roll, and sixteen out of twenty members of the Liberty Legion."

I know those teams! In my world, they're all superhero teams. Mostly Meta 1's and 2's, but still, they're good guys. This is completely nuts!

"But we're still working on the grand prize," he continues. "Come, I have more to show you."

I take one last look at Blue Bolt 2. This is worse than I thought. But even I have to admit it's a brilliant strategy. I mean, no respectable hero could sit back and watch their colleagues suffer like this.

Unless, of course, you're Captain Justice 2.

We pass the cells of other fallen heroes. But right before the exit, something catches my eye. There's a flash of movement, and then a face presses against the glass window.

Yellow eyes follow me as I move down the hallway. I

swear I've seen those eyes before. But where?

And then it hits me—Alligazer!

I flinch, fearing I'll be turned to stone. But then I realize if he's in here, he's powerless!

We reach the final set of double doors and I get an incredible sense of déjà vu. The last time I walked through here, I fought the battle to end all battles. Who knows what's waiting for me this time?

Shadow Hawk 2 swipes again, and the doors open.

A familiar courtyard stretches out before us. It's massive in size and open to the night sky. This time, there are rows and rows of chairs set out, all facing a giant, golden chair situated on a platform.

Shadow Hawk 2 steps to the side and motions. "Your throne, your Excellency."

My throne? Well, okay then. I smile and make my way over to the platform.

Just then, doors open on all sides of the courtyard, and hundreds of costumed creeps come spilling out. I've never seen so many bad guys in one place before. They line up in front of the chairs, their right hands across their hearts.

Um, okay. What's going on?

Shadow Hawk 2 approaches quickly and whispers in my ear. "Your Excellency, they will not sit until you do."

"Oh, yes, of course," I say. Then, I step up onto the platform and sit in the chair.

The villains follow suit.

Dog-Gone lies in front of me, forming a furry barrier between me and the crooks.

Hundreds of evil eyes are fixed on me. I feel really, really uncomfortable. I mean, what am I supposed to do now?

The next thing I know, Shadow Hawk 2 appears by my side and starts speaking. "My vile friends, thank you for putting aside your differences to join us for a most historic occasion. I am aware that many, if not all of you have attempted to further your positions during the temporary absence of our liege. But, as you can see, he has returned and is stronger than ever."

I sit up and try to look dangerous.

"Now," Shadow Hawk 2 continues. "Let's waste no more time. Let's get to the main event, the reason you are all gathered here today."

The criminals start buzzing. Something big is about to happen.

"Henchman!" Shadow Hawk 2 calls. "Bring forth the cage!"

Suddenly, a door opens and two strongmen enter the courtyard carrying a large, square-shaped object covered by a cloth. All eyes are on it as they place it in front of the platform.

"Watch and be warned!" Shadow Hawk 2 says. "For if you fail to comply with the commands of our King, what happens next may happen to you!"

Um, okay.

"Now," Shadow Hawk 2 says. "Bear witness to the superiority of our King as he renders another Meta hero powerless!"

Wait! What?

"Unveil the captive!"

Everyone rises as the cover is ripped off the box and my jaw drops in surprise.

"Now, Your Excellency," Shadow Hawk 2 shouts. "Destroy the girl!"

The villains erupt in a deafening cheer.

But to my horror, trapped inside the metal cage is a frightened, brown-haired girl wearing a blue costume with white stars.

It's Grace 2!

Meta Profile

Name: Shadow Hawk 2
Role: Villain   Status: Active

VITALS:

Race: Human
Real Name: Unknown
Height: 6'2"
Weight: 215 lbs
Eye Color: Unknown
Hair Color: Unknown

META POWERS:

Class: None
Powers Level:
- Meta 0
- Master detective, expert marksman, and highly-skilled martial artist.

CHARACTERISTICS:

Combat	92	
Durability	56	
Leadership	93	
Strategy	100	
Willpower	100	

EIGHT

I BECOME KING FOR A DAY

I think this is called 'irony.'

I mean, I've been looking for Grace 2 everywhere, and now, she's delivered to me on a silver platter! Of course, she's locked in a cage surrounded by hundreds of Meta villains who are cheering me on to remove her powers. So, it's not exactly the warm and fuzzy reunion I was hoping for.

"Zero her out!" comes a cry from the crowd.

"Filet that Flyer!" comes another.

Grace 2 looks at me, her blue eyes wide with fear.

Somehow, I've got to let her know I'm me, and not her brother, without giving myself away. Then, I've got to figure out how to get us out of this mess. Otherwise, they'll lock me up with her. Or worse.

"Your Excellency?" Shadow Hawk 2 says, the urgency in his voice signaling me to get on with it.

"Right," I say. I guess it's showtime.

As soon as I stand up, the villains go silent. I look at them, sitting at full attention like schoolchildren, waiting to see what I'm going to do next.

Boy, I only wish I knew.

I feel totally awkward standing here.

"I hate you!" Grace 2 shouts, breaking the silence.

The villains boo.

"I'll teach her to show respect!" someone yells.

Okay, I'd better do something before this gets out of hand. Time to turn on the acting chops.

"I'm guessing you're not feeling so glorious now, are you *Glory Girl*," I say mockingly, ensuring I can be heard throughout the courtyard. "You may be a member of the Freedom Force, but soon you'll find freedom hard to come by."

The villains roar with approval.

Okay, not bad. Got to keep going.

"See, you live in my world," I continue, "and in my world, heroes are a distraction, and distractions must be dealt with."

There's another cheer and I feel a strange boost of confidence. Who knew I'd be so good at this evil monologue stuff? Just keep talking. Keep stalling.

"Take her powers!" someone cries.

"Take 'em for good!"

Oh, geez, that's what they're all here to see, isn't it? Okay, think!

I know I can't remove her powers permanently, but I *can* take them away temporarily. That should fool them, at least for now. But before I do that, I need to clue her in as to who I really am. So, how am I going to do that?

Wait, did I just say clue? That's it! I can drop in some clues!

"Now is the time!" I shout. "Now, I will remove the powers of this... this... jelly doughnut-eating girl."

Shadow Hawk 2 shoots me a funny look.

Okay, I'm probably blowing my cover, but I need Grace 2 to be sure, so I press on. "This terrible fate will befall her despite... having brown hair whereas, she may have been blond if she were born elsewhere. In addition, this punishment will be meted out despite her heroic achievements on Arena World where—"

"What are you doing?" Shadow Hawk 2 whispers sharply. "Get on with it!"

I look into the crowd. The villains are getting restless.

Did she get it?

I glance down at Grace 2, who's staring back at me with her arms crossed and a giant smirk across her face.

I'm taking that as a yes.

Okay, time to finish the job.

Pointing down at her, I declare, "Glory Girl, you've been a thorn in my side since the day I was born! Now, you will suffer the agony of being a Zero—for the rest of your life!"

I concentrate and then wash my powers over her.

Now for the big finale—the proof.

"Release her!" I command.

The villains rise to their feet as the two henchmen rip the cage apart.

To her surprise, Grace 2 is free.

"If it's freedom you want," I offer, "then go ahead and fly away. If you can."

Grace 2 raises her arms to lift off, but she can't.

"My powers," she says. "They're… gone."

The villains erupt in a victorious cheer.

It worked! It's over. Thank the stars it's over.

"Kill her!" someone yells.

Or not.

"No!" I react. "She's valuable to us. With her as our captive, we can lure the remaining members of the Freedom Force—like Ms. Understood and Captain Justice—to their deaths. Now, take her to a cell. Make sure she's as… uncomfortable as possible."

Grace 2 looks back at me, eyebrows raised, as the henchmen grab her arms roughly and drag her back inside Lockdown. Hopefully, she'll forgive me. But I had to look convincing. Now, I've got all these bad guys to deal with.

"This demonstration is over," I command. "Go back to your territories. All of you."

"Bow before your liege!" Shadow Hawk 2 orders.

All this pageantry is wonderful, but I'm not planning to stick around for tea and biscuits. Instead, I whisper to Dog-Gone 2, "Get me out of here."

Dog-Gone 2 scratches behind his ear, and then hops off the podium. I follow him to a large door on the far side of the courtyard. It's different than all the others, made from steel and surrounded by cameras. Dog-Gone 2 presses his nose against a touch screen that scans his schnoz. As the door slides open, I try to make sense of what I'm seeing.

Instead of a dull, dreary prison, I'm looking into a brightly lit, marble-tiled foyer.

"Is this where your master lives?" I ask.

Dog-Gone 2 nods and we go inside, the door sliding shut behind us.

He leads me down a hallway and past several prison cells which have been converted into living spaces of various functions. There's a game room filled with arcade machines, a recreation room with trampoline floors, a snack room packed with candy boxes and soda machines, and a reading room loaded with comic books and bean bag chairs.

It's like walking through heaven.

I follow the mutt into a large room at the end of the hallway, where I'm stopped in my tracks. I can't believe it.

It's my bedroom!

Or rather, it's exactly like my bedroom back on the

Waystation. It has the same blue-and-white bedspread, the same Batman posters on the wall, the same desk, the same cabinets, the same everything! There's just one difference. His walls are covered in black marker scribblings.

But stepping inside, I realize they aren't scribbles at all—they're equations! Hundreds of them, all over. So, here's another mirror-universe difference between Elliott 2 and me: he's a math whiz and I'm allergic to algebra.

What's with all the formulas? It's obvious he was trying to solve for something, but what? The only thing I know is there's not a snowball's chance in Hades I'm gonna figure it out.

Then, something catches my eye. It's an illustration of a bunch of tiny, irregular circles packed tightly together around a much larger circle. The little circles form a barrier of sorts. It looks strangely familiar.

It looks like... an asteroid belt?

"Feeling better?"

I jump out of my skin.

Shadow Hawk 2 is standing in the doorway with his arms folded across his chest. He steps inside. "Nice performance out there. Despite whatever you were doing to spoil the occasion."

Uh-oh, I need to be careful here. Shadow Hawk is no dummy. He knows something is up.

"So," he says, "did you make it?"

Make it? Make what?

"After all, you didn't think I'd ignore the fact that one of our Freedom Flyers went missing? Or did you?"

Oh, geez! This is worse than I thought.

"Based on the maps decorating your walls, I assumed you took the Freedom Flyer to reach that planet you were so desperately searching for."

Planet? My eyes dart back to the asteroid belt and the circle inside of it.

O! M! G!

I know exactly where Elliott 2 went!

"Well?" he asks. "Anything you'd like to share?"

My heart is racing but I try to stay cool. "Not really." The longer I stay in Lockdown, the faster he's going to find out I'm a phony. I stretch into a fake yawn. "You mind if we pick this up later? I'm wiped."

"Certainly, your Excellency," he says with a bow. "Let's do that. When we regroup, I'd love to hear the story of how you returned to Earth... *without* the Freedom Flyer you departed in." And then, he leaves.

He knows! Time to make my exit. But first I need to collect something.

"Dog-Gone, take me to Glory Girl's cell."

He looks at me funny and then cocks an ear.

I guess some things never change, even in a mirror universe. "Fine, I'll give you five doggie treats. Now do it!"

Dog-Gone takes off like a rocket. I chase him outside, back through the courtyard, and into the prison wing Grace 2 was dragged through. I get plenty of odd stares along the way, but I just smile, point to Dog-Gone, and say, "He loves a brisk walk."

He leads me into a small corridor that's empty save one prison cell and two large goons guarding it. I notice there's no window in the cell door which is good news for what I'm planning. So, here goes nothing.

"Open the door," I command.

The goons bow, and then swing the door open. Dog-Gone 2 and I step inside, and I instruct them to close it behind us, shutting us in.

The cell is dark and cramped. Slivers of daylight stream through a barred window up high. Grace 2 is lying motionless in the corner, bundled beneath a blanket.

I hope she's not dead.

"Grace," I whisper.

"E-Elliott?" she says meekly, raising her head. Her face is bruised.

"Are you okay?" I say, kneeling beside her. "I'm sorry they were rough with you, but I had to act the part."

"It's okay," she says. "I can take it. I knew it was you. Although I still can't believe it. What are you doing here?"

"I'll tell you later," I say. "Right now, we've got to get out of here."

"But you took my powers," she says. "I-I can't fly."

"That's temporary," I say. "Your powers will come back. But that's not going to help us now. We've got to get out of here. I have an idea. Hang on to your blanket."

I look over to the German Shepherd. "Dog-Gone, vanish."

He cocks another ear.

"Fine, I'll give you a bag of treats! Whatever!"

As soon as he disappears, I put my plan into action.

"Help!" I yell.

The door opens and the henchman burst in.

"My Lord?" says one.

"Are you okay?" says the other.

"I'm fine," I say. "But you're not." I concentrate hard and take away their super-strength. "Dog-Gone!"

Suddenly, both thugs are knocked to the ground. I grab Grace 2's hand and pull her out of the cell. As soon as Dog-Gone materializes next to us, I slam the door shut, locking the guards inside.

"Let's go," I say.

"But where?" Grace 2 asks.

"I know where your brother is," I say. "But we've got to get off this Earth. I need a ship."

Dog-Gone barks and nods his head.

"What's he saying?" Grace 2 asks.

"I think he wants us to follow him. Is that right?"

Dog-Gone 2 barks and then takes off.

Here we go again.

"We can't let anyone see you," I say to Grace 2. "Cover yourself in your blanket and follow that furball!"

We attract more strange looks, but I simply smile as Dog-Gone 2 leads us through a series of corridors, and out a side door.

Within minutes, we're in the woods, and Grace 2 and I collapse in a heap. We're out of breath, but we're safe, at least for the moment. Once Shadow Hawk 2 finds out what I've done, he'll be hot on my trail.

Dog-Gone 2 marches over to a thicket of tall bushes and barks again.

"What's he saying now?" Grace 2 asks.

The mutt paws at the thicket.

"I don't know," I say. "I think there's something behind there."

He barks again.

"Okay, okay," I say, walking over and sticking my gloved hands into the underbrush. As I push the thorny branches aside, I gasp out loud.

"What is it?" Grace 2 asks.

But, I don't have any words.

I wouldn't even know how to explain it.

It's my Freedom Ferry.

The one that vanished from my Earth.

Meta Profile

Name: Glory Girl 2
Role: Hero   Status: Active

VITALS:

Race: Human
Real Name: Grace Harkness
Height: 5'3"
Weight: 101 lbs
Eye Color: Blue
Hair Color: Brown

META POWERS:

Class: Flight
Power Level:
- **Considerable Flight**
- **Limited Super-Speed in combination with Earth's gravitational force.**

CHARACTERISTICS:

Combat	29	
Durability	26	
Leadership	40	
Strategy	28	
Willpower	57	

NINE

I LOOK INTO A DARK MIRROR

We hop aboard the Freedom Ferry and blast off before Shadow Hawk 2 shows his beak.

I'm manning the controls, with Grace 2 and Dog-Gone 2 stuffed into the passenger seat. As we enter outer space, I relay everything I know about the Blur, which quite honestly isn't very much. But I'm guessing the appearance of my Freedom Ferry on Grace 2's world can only mean one thing—our two worlds are merging into one.

"So, why is this happening?" Grace 2 asks.

"Great question," I reply. "According to some intel I picked up back home, this whole thing started with the destruction of Order and Chaos on Arena World. Without those two bozos managing the rules of the multiverse, everything has gone whacko."

"Wonderful," Grace 2 says. "So, it's like survival of the fittest, galactic style."

"Seems that way," I say.

"Well, that stinks," she says. "By the way, are you ever planning on telling me where we're going?"

"Oh, sorry," I say. "I may be way off here, but based on the graffiti covering your brother's walls, I think he went to see the Watcher."

"The Watcher? Who's the Watcher?"

Another great question. I mean, who *is* the Watcher anyway? The last time I saw that weirdo was when the Zodiac took me to his planet to find out what happened to Aries. But the Watcher had no interest in answering that question. Instead, he tormented me about the location of the Orb of Oblivion—which he knew was inside my body!

But there's no need to get into that now. So, I give her the straight answer. "The Watcher is a cosmic entity who's fated to watch the events of the universe in exchange for immortality. He's also blind and several fries short of a Happy Meal."

"Wait," Grace 2 says. "The Watcher is blind? Isn't that like a total oxymoron."

"What did you call me?"

"Not you," she says. "An oxymoron is a figure of speech that's self-contradictory. Like a 'cruel kindness' or a 'living death.' I mean, how could anyone be called 'the

Watcher' and be blind?"

"Oh, I get it," I say. "Yeah, it's strange. He said he lost his sight because of something he did, we just never found out what. And something tells me I don't want to know."

"Okay," she says, "my creeper alert is now on high. Why would my brother want to see this Watcher dude anyway?"

"Well, *they* say—and please don't ask me who 'they' are—that the Watcher knows everything. So, I'm guessing your brother had questions and needed some answers."

Suddenly, the Freedom Flyer BEEPS and says, "You will arrive at Watcher World in 1000 meters."

"What kinds of questions?" she asks.

"How am I supposed to know? Maybe he wanted to know if Bigfoot is real, or why round pizza comes in a square box. You know," I say, looking up, "meaningful things... like... that..."

Something is wrong.

By now we should have visual confirmation of Watcher World. Yet, when I look out the window, there's nothing but black space and bright stars. I recheck the navigator.

"What's the matter?" Grace 2 asks.

"Um, I think we've lost a planet," I say. "And it's not a small planet."

"Could it be the Blur?" Grace asks.

I didn't think of that. I guess it could have been

wiped off the map by the Blur. But if that were the case, why would the navigator tell us we're almost there. According to TechnocRat, there's only one thing to do when your electronics go funky. So, I turn off the navigator and then turn it back on. When it reboots, I re-enter the coordinates.

"You will arrive at Watcher World in 700 meters," it says.

The navigator seems to be working fine. But when I look up I still don't see anything. Is this some sort of trick?

And then it hits me.

It's a test.

The last time I was here with the Zodiac, we had to pass through an imaginary asteroid belt. I guess after we cracked that illusion, he created a new one. This time he's pretending his planet is missing. Nice try.

"It's there," I say. "We just can't see it."

"Elliott," Grace 2 says nervously. "You sure about that?"

"Yep," I say, lowering the landing gear.

"400 meters," the navigator says.

"You're really, really sure?" Grace 2 says. "I mean, there's nothing down there. You can see that, right?"

"300 meters," the navigator says.

"Uh-huh," I say.

"200 meters."

"So, shouldn't you be pulling up now?" Grace asks.

"Uh-uh," I say.

Dog-Gone 2 howls.

"100 meters."

"Elliott!" Grace 2 screams.

"Brace yourself," I say, touching the Freedom Ferry down onto a patch of pure space. We THUMP hard and I step on the brakes. The Freedom Ferry bumps along before coming to a relatively smooth stop. "Told ya," I say, turning to my companions who are holding onto each other for dear life.

Suddenly, the area beneath us transforms from starry blackness into purplish, rocky terrain. Towering mountains appear all around, their peaks climbing high into the red sky and disappearing into thick, black clouds.

I'm back, and it's just as bleak as before.

Lightning flashes and Dog-Gone 2 whimpers.

"Well, this place looks like a party," Grace 2 says. "So, where are we supposed to go?"

Based on experience, we could easily spend days walking around lost. So, it's time for a shortcut. I punch a few commands into the navigator and within seconds it comes back with a direct hit.

"Stay seated," I warn, taking the Freedom Ferry airborne again. We break through the cloud cover and travel north for several miles. Then, I find what I'm looking for—a white structure sitting high atop a mountain.

The Watcher's sanctuary.

Nothing has changed from my last visit. There are still four marble columns supporting the marble roof, marble stairs leading up to the platform, and a giant, robed figure sitting in his oversized chair.

"That's him?" Grace 2 asks. "He's humongous!"

"Yeah, that's him," I say. "Look, I'm not sure how this is going to go down, so let me lead."

I set us down twenty yards away. As we exit, I start rehearsing what I'm going to say. I know we need to be super careful. I mean, anything can set this looney tune off. We need to be organized. We need to be commanding. We need to look like we mean business.

Then, I hear a trickling noise from behind me.

Turning around, I find Dog-Gone 2 with his hind leg in the air, soaking the Freedom Ferry's front tire.

"Seriously?"

"Give him a break," Grace 2 says. "It's been a long ride."

"Need anything else?" I ask. "Belly rub? Scratch under the chin? Flea removal?"

Dog-Gone 2 cocks an ear.

Freaking furball.

Time to lower my blood pressure. I take a deep breath, think calm thoughts, and then march up the staircase. When I reach the top, I'm face to face with a being I had hoped to never see again.

At first glance, the Watcher looks exactly like I remembered—tall, pale, and ugly. But then I realize something is off, I just can't figure out what.

"Watcher," I say, mustering all my confidence, "I've returned and we need your help. No games."

But the Watcher doesn't move a muscle. Instead, he just stares at me with his white eyes. It's like he's looking past me—through me.

I lower my voice and try again. "Watcher, I need your help."

But he doesn't respond. What's wrong with him? It's like he can't hear me, like he doesn't even know we're standing here.

Then, I realize what's different. The last time I was here he had this white, celestial glow around his body. And now, it's gone!

"Um, is everything okay?" Grace whispers.

"I'm not sure," I say, waving my arms. "Watcher? Are you okay? Can you hear me?"

"Oh, he can hear you," comes a kid's voice. "He's just not capable of answering you."

Looking up, I see a blond-haired, skinny kid sitting cross-legged on top of a boulder. He's wearing a red-and-blue costume with a 'no-symbol' across his chest.

I can't believe it! I've found him!

It's Elliott 2!

Dog-Gone 2 starts running in circles, his tail wagging with excitement.

"I see you, boy," Elliott 2 says, and then more coldly, "and you too, sister."

"What are you doing here, Elliott?" Grace 2 asks, unconsciously taking a step backward.

"I could ask the same of you," he says. "After all, few people know who the Watcher is, and fewer still know how to find him."

"I've been here before," I say. "Although the last time it was against my will. But you're here because you want to be. Why?"

"Why am I here?" Elliott 2 says with an unnerving smile. "Because I'm seeking knowledge. I want to know once and for all where *this* came from."

And then, he raises his right hand, and what's resting in his palm sends a chill down my spine.

It's the Orb of Oblivion!

I was right! There is a second one!

"What's that?" Grace 2 asks.

"Precisely, dear sister," he says. "The object has a name, but not an identity. At least, not one I can get it to tell me. And oh, have I tried. Isn't that right, Orb?"

The Orb gives off a weak glow.

My stomach sinks as I watch him shift the Orb from hand to hand. All of my fantasies about Elliott 2 being a victim of the Orb go completely out the window. The Orb hasn't exerted its will over him, he's exerted his will over the Orb! He's in absolute and total control. And that means all of his actions were done of his own free will.

He's pure evil.

"At first, the only thing I could squeeze out of the

all-mighty Orb of Oblivion was an image of this guy," he says, nodding to the Watcher. "So, let's just say I had to dig a little harder. Finally, the Orb gave up the Watcher's name and location. It took me a few months to plot out how to get here—and the journey took far longer than I imagined—but we arrived just in time because my Freedom Ferry is out of fuel. And then, after all of that travel, we get here and the bald guy won't answer any of my questions. So, I put him on a time out."

"A time out?" I blurt. "You put a cosmic entity on a time out?"

"Yep," he says. "I don't like to be bored, and you'd be surprised at how easily you get bored when you can do anything."

Suddenly, he leaps down from the boulder and lands between the Watcher and me. For a moment, I'm taken aback. His face, his body, his posture—everything looks like me! Except, of course, for his hair color. It's like I'm staring into a mirror. But unfortunately, I'm not.

He looks me up and down. "You're quite boring, aren't you?"

"Excuse me?" I say.

"You live a pathetic life, don't you?" he continues. "On the outside, you pretend to be a great hero. But on the inside, you're shaking like a leaf. You're a coward. A poser. Am I right?"

"No!"

"Are you sure?" he continues, holding the Orb in

front of his face. "Because I know I'm right. I can feel it."

I gaze deeply into the white, pulsating Orb. I'm mesmerized by it—lost in it, when...

"Save me," comes a tiny cry inside my head.

The voice is feeble, yet familiar. Who?

"Save me. Save us all."

It's the Orb! It's talking to me!

But how? I thought Elliott 2 mastered it?

"So," Elliott 2 says, snapping me back to reality, "What's a brave hero like you doing in a dead-end place like this?"

"I was looking for something," I say. "But now I've found it."

At first, he looks confused, but then he glances down at the Orb and the smirk disappears from his face. "This? You were looking for this? Really? I can't imagine what for, but if you think I'm just going to give it to you, you're more delusional than I thought."

This is it. If I don't get the Orb of Oblivion away from him now, I've got zero chance of stopping Ravager from eating my world.

I look him dead in the eyes.

"Oh, I never expected you to give it to me," I say coolly. "That's why I'm going to take it from you."

Meta Profile

Name: Epic Zero 2
Role: Villain   Status: Active

VITALS:

Race: Human
Real Name: Elliott Harkness
Height: 4'8"
Weight: 89 lbs
Eye Color: Brown
Hair Color: Blond

META POWERS:

Class: Meta Manipulation
Powers Level:

- **Extreme Power Negation and Manipulation**
- **Vulnerable to non-Meta attack**

CHARACTERISTICS:

Combat   25
Durability 12
Leadership 55
Strategy   65
Willpower   77

TEN

I FIGHT MY OWN SHADOW

Somehow, I always knew it would come down to this.

I mean, how else was I going to walk away with the Orb of Oblivion? I guess deep down I kind of wished a second Orb didn't exist. That way, I'd never have to face what I'm about to face now.

Which is probably the end of my life.

So, let's get realistic and break down my chances for success. One, we're both scrawny kids, so we're even there. Two, we both have Meta Manipulation powers—even again. Three, he's got the Orb of Oblivion, the most powerful weapon in the universe, while I've got a serious case of anxiety.

Major advantage to him.

Looks like I'm doomed.

I mean, how can I possibly win? He just put the Watcher down for the count—a freaking cosmic being! I'm no oddsmaker, but I'd say I've got a better chance of finding a unicorn than beating him.

Well, at least Grace 2 is here to help.

Suddenly, Elliott 2 extends his right hand and commands, "Sleep!"

Grace 2 crumples to the ground like a rag doll.

Okay, now I've got a better chance of finding a whole herd of unicorns.

Dog-Gone 2 bares his teeth and growls at me.

"Down, boy, he's mine," Elliott 2 says, the Orb pulsating in his hands. "You know, I always suspected there was some goody-two-shoes version of me out there who never realized his own power. And now here you are."

"Lucky me," I say. Great, now I'm being insulted by my own double. Honestly, I'm having a hard time matching what I'm hearing with what I'm seeing. I mean, he looks exactly like me, yet our personalities are like night and day. My only chance is to distract him until I can figure out what to do.

"So, Dr. Sunshine," I say sarcastically. "What made you so happy-go-lucky? I know a bit about the Orb of Oblivion and how it feeds on your innermost desires, but even a boring, goody-two-shoes like me managed to resist it."

"You want a medal or something?" he says with a

laugh. "I can tell we aren't so different. Before I discovered the Orb, my life pretty much stunk like yours. No one paid any attention to me. I was considered a nuisance—a pest. But when opportunity knocked, I didn't close the door. I opened it—embraced it. And look at me now."

Yeah, I'm looking at him, and he's rotten to the core. My eyes dart around for something—anything—to help me. But all I see are purple rocks, orange plants—and the Freedom Ferry! If I can get to the ship, then maybe I can blast out of here. But then again, I can't just leave Grace 2 here. Plus, I really need that orb.

I'm stuck!

"I'd feel terrible if you came all this way and left empty-handed," he says, flashing a menacing smile. "Since you want the power of the Orb so badly, let me give it to you."

Oh, n—

Suddenly, there's a sharp, stabbing pain in my head.

He's entered my mind!

My brain feels like it's being stepped on! Squashed!

I drop to my knees.

He's trying to overpower me! If he breaks through he'll control my mind, then there's no telling what he'll do. I can't let him in. I muster every ounce of negation power and push back.

"Maybe you resisted the Orb on your world," he says, through gritted teeth, "but you won't be able to resist me."

The pressure is overwhelming. It feels like my head is going to explode! I've got to get him out. I push back harder.

"You're strong," he says, with a hint of surprise. "Stronger than anyone I've taken over before. But don't worry, I'll break you down soon enough."

Suddenly, I'm flat on the ground. With all of my energy focused on defending myself, I have no control over the rest of my body. I'm holding him at bay, but for how long? He's way too strong!

"*Use me,*" comes a feeble voice inside my head.

What? Who's that?

"*Use me,*" it repeats, a little louder.

The Orb? But how's it talking to me? Can't Elliott 2 hear it?

"*No,*" it says. "*I barely managed to shield my innermost conscious from him. But if you want to live, you must use me now.*"

"*H-How?*"

"*All you need to do is stop pushing back,*" it says. "*Just open your mind, let me inside, and I'll do the rest.*"

"*Let you inside? Are you bonkers? As soon as I do that he'll take over and I'll be eating baby food for the rest of my life!*"

"*If you don't use me,*" it says. "*You're as good as dead.*"

"You're weakening," Elliott 2 says. "I'm almost through."

And he's right! My head feels like it's being drilled in half by a jackhammer.

"Use me!" the Orb pleads again.

I'm getting loopy. Dizzy. Images of Mom, Dad, and Grace flash before my eyes. If I can't find a way to defeat him, they're as good as dead.

The pain is so intense!

I-I've got no other choice!

I close my eyes... and then I let go.

Instantly, the pressure releases.

An intense wave of energy rushes through my body. I open my eyes, and it's like every fiber of my being is on hyper-alert. I can see the tiny pores in Elliott 2's skin. I can hear Dog-Gone 2's neck hair blowing in the breeze. I can feel thousands of invisible molecules bouncing off my skin.

I've never felt so alive. So... powerful. It's like I've gone from Zero to... to... Meta 4?

"Hey!" Elliott 2 cries, looking at the orb in his hand. "What happened? It's not working?"

Despite the energy coursing through my veins, it feels like I'm moving in slow motion. Like I'm stuck in molasses. Like I'm having an out-of-body experience.

Elliott 2's brown eyes widen as he realizes the Orb of Oblivion has left the round object in his hands—and entered my body.

"Now," the Orb says. *"Strike now."*

While I'd love nothing more than to go off on some epic monologue about good triumphing over evil, my body is being compelled to do something else. My eyes shut and one overriding thought fills my mind.

NO. MORE.

Then, my eyes pop open and a wave of strange, orange energy comes pouring out, washing over Elliott 2.

Huh? Where'd that come from?

But before I can figure that out, the energy dissipates, and Elliott 2 is on his hands and knees, mumbling, "N-no. My… powers."

And then I realize what happened.

The Orb negated his powers.

Permanently.

He's a Zero.

"Y-You did this to me," he says, rising to his feet. He throws the useless orb to the ground. "You took the Orb of Oblivion's power from me. Give it back. Give it back to me, or I'll kill you."

"Now," the Orb says. *"Finish him."*

"What? No!"

"Do not block me," the Orb urges. *"Open up to me."*

I watch as Elliott 2 picks up a sharp rock. "The Orb is mine. Not yours. Mine!"

Dog-Gone 2 joins his side and barks threateningly.

My arm extends magically and I hear my self saying, "STAY!"

Dog-Gone 2 freezes like a statue.

Elliott 2 springs towards me, the rock held menacingly over his head, when suddenly, a streaking blue fist connects squarely with his jaw.

Elliott 2 flies backward into a rock, and then face plants to the ground.

"Enough, little brother," Grace 2 says, rubbing her knuckles. "We've all had enough."

Dog-Gone 2 whimpers and I release him from my hold. He scampers to his master's side and starts licking his face, but Elliott 2 doesn't move. He's out cold.

"You should have finished him," the Orb says. *"You still can, while he's defenseless. You need to open everything to me."*

"Quiet," I command, trying to shut the Orb down, but I can tell things are going to be different this time around. This Orb is much stronger than the one I had before.

I pick the sphere up off the ground. The Orb of Oblivion is mine again. Heaven help us all.

"You okay?" Grace 2 asks.

"I'm... not sure," I say. "You know, we never found out why he came here in the first place. But I've got this funny feeling we're running out of—"

"—time?" rumbles a deep voice behind me.

I spin around to find the Watcher fully conscious in his chair. Man, I can't catch a break around here.

"Time, Elliott Harkness, is your greatest enemy."

Great. Just what I need right now.

"I've got no clue what you're saying, but I know we've got no time to figure out your crazy riddles. So, be a pal and just tell me what you know."

"What I know," the Watcher says, tilting his head

towards the stars, "is that everything is about to end. And it is all my fault."

"Your fault?" I say. "What are you talking about?"

"In exchange for immortality, I have sat here for countless millennia witnessing the events of the multiverse. Over that expanse of time, I have watched billions of creatures become parents, and in turn, their children became parents, and so on. I sat, and I watched, and I wondered. What was the purpose of my bargain? What would I have to show for it? Who would I ever share it with?"

"Um, okay," I say. Where is this going?

"By nature, I was not born a cosmic being, but I was granted a measure of cosmic power. And though it was forbidden for me to exercise this power, century by century, decade by decade, my will became weaker and weaker. And then, one day... it broke, and I violated my solemn oath to be an impartial observer."

I glance at Grace 2 who's eyes are bugged out of her head. Whatever's coming next is gonna be a doozy.

"So," the Watcher continues, "I created a child."

"You what?" I blurt out.

"At first, I was able to mask its existence. But as it grew larger, so did its appetite. I tried to satiate it, but it soon became impossible. In time, it wandered away, looking to alleviate its hunger pains."

Hunger pains?

Wait a minute? No way...

"Y-You mean your child is… is…," I stutter.

"Ravager," the Watcher says. "My child is Ravager."

I feel my jaw hit my toes. I immediately think of all those innocent people, all of those helpless creatures—billions of them—destroyed by Ravager, simply because he was hungry.

"After a while," the Watcher continues, "it grew too large for even my powers to conceal. It was destructive, and soon its presence became known to the cosmic regulators, Order and Chaos. They reprimanded me, and as a consequence of interfering in the affairs of the multiverse, they took away my sight, but not my immortality. Thus, I have been punished to sit here in darkness until the end of eternity."

"You should be punished!" I yell. "You're responsible for all of this death and destruction! All because you wanted a stupid kid?"

"Yes," the Watcher says, lowering his head. "As its father, I swore I would protect it at all costs. I begged Order and Chaos to spare it, to use it in any manner they pleased, but to let it live. And use it they did—in their twisted games. That is, until they were destroyed on Arena World and Ravager was set free once again."

"Yeah," I say. "Free to eat more worlds like mine."

"This is my greatest regret," the Watcher says. "I became a father to realize the joys of parenthood, but instead I have unleashed an evil so dark it robs the multiverse of the same light. Ravager may be my child, but I know it must be destroyed."

"And how are you going to do that?" I ask.

"I may be the one who created it," the Watcher says, "but I am not destined to destroy it."

Great. Well if it's not him then who...

Oh, no.

"Elliott Harkness, once again you are the Orb Master. You possess the final Orb of Oblivion, the most powerful weapon in the multiverse."

"Annnnd, what exactly am I supposed to do with it?" I ask, dreading the answer.

"Is it not obvious?" the Watcher says, peering through me with his dead, white pupils. "You must take the Orb of Oblivion to Ravager's brain and blow it up."

Meta Profile

Name: Watcher
Role: Cosmic Entity   Status: Active

VITALS:

Race: Inapplicable
Real Name: Watcher
Height: 10'0"
Weight: Unknown
Eye Color: White
Hair Color: Bald

META POWERS:

Class: Inapplicable
Power Level: Incalculable

- Observes all events in the universe
- Cannot interfere in any way, or will suffer dire consequences

CHARACTERISTICS:

Combat	Inapplicable
Durability	Inapplicable
Leadership	Inapplicable
Strategy	Inapplicable
Willpower	Inapplicable

ELEVEN

I ENTER BIZARRO WORLD

"**E**lliott? Are you okay?"

I hear my name, and I know I should respond, but I can't. I'm completely numb.

Everything spins as Grace 2 guides the Freedom Ferry into a barrel roll. I feel weightless for a moment, the seat belt digging into my chest, but then we're right-side-up and gravity takes hold again. Grace 2 is pushing the Freedom Ferry to the max, and rightly so because after the Watcher's shocking revelation we're running out of time—time to stop Ravager.

We didn't have a holding cell for Elliott 2, so we left him on Watcher World for now. And quite frankly, I couldn't think of a more fitting punishment than being trapped listening to the Watcher blow hot air. At least

Dog-Gone 2 stayed behind to keep them company.

What I can't understand is why all this bad stuff keeps happening to me? It's like there's some giant "kick me" sign on my back. Look, I knew I needed the Orb to stop Ravager—that's why I came here in the first place— but I always pictured using it from a distance, not up close and personal. I mean, even if I somehow manage to blow up Ravager's brain, won't I blow up with it?

It's like a suicide mission.

Fabulous.

"There is another way," the Orb says.

Speaking of fabulous…

"Quiet," I say. *"I'm not taking advice from you."*

"You would listen to that blind fool over me?" it says. *"His path leads to your demise. My path leads to your ascension. Your crowning as king of the multiverse!"*

"No dice," I say. *"And shut your trap."*

I try silencing it. Pushing it down. But it's not moving.

"You can't control me," it says. *"I'm not like the other one. Just wait, you'll see."*

Great. Can't wait.

The Orb. The Blur. Ravager. It's way too much. And, of course, it's all up to me.

And that's what worries me the most.

I take a deep breath and exhale.

I think back to Elliott 2's words. I can put on a brave face and pretend to be a great hero. But I know the truth.

I'm not superhero enough for this.

I mean, if I couldn't even jump into a sewer to face Alligazer, how am I ever going to do this? Poor Makeshift paid the ultimate price for my mistake. Now I'm supposed to take on a nebulous, globe-eating monstrosity with billions of lives at stake? Who's kidding who?

I just want to crawl into a hole and hide. Maybe Captain Justice 2 had it right. Maybe some people aren't cut out to be heroes.

"Prepare to submerge," Grace 2 says.

"What?" I say. I was so lost in thought I didn't notice we'd already made it back into Earth 2's atmosphere. Looking down, I realize we're making a beeline for a large body of water. "Um, what's that?"

"The Atlantic Ocean," she says.

"And why are we aimed at it?"

"To get reinforcements," she says. Then, she flicks a few switches and the Freedom Ferry converts to amphibious mode. "Hang on."

I brace myself as we jackknife through the water, and thousands of tiny bubbles blanket the windshield. I wait for her to level off, but she's not straightening up. I check the navigator and realize we're 2,000 feet deep and still diving! I'm not sure the ship can hold up under this kind of pressure. "We're too deep!"

"Relax," Grace 2 says calmly. "We do this all the time."

All the time? I've got no idea what she's talking

about, when suddenly, the bubbles clear, and I'm staring at something humungous sitting on the ocean floor.

It's an underwater fortress!

It's big, and gray, and divided into three sections connected by airlocks. It looks thick—like it's forged from alloyed steel. On top are several rotating radar dishes and the largest antenna I've ever seen. Rows of portholes line each compartment, indicating there are multiple levels inside. The entire structure stands proudly on four giant, metal legs burrowed deep into the ground.

"What's that?" I ask.

"The Hydrostation," Grace 2 says. "Hydro means water, but phonetically it's Hide-ro, as in hidden. Get it? Not a bad name for the secret headquarters of the Freedom Force."

That's the secret headquarters of the Freedom Force 2? Now I realize why no one has heard of the Waystation around here. Because there is no Waystation. It's a Hydrostation!

We cruise around the building's perimeter, stopping in front of a giant hatch door that slides welcomingly open. Grace 2 maneuvers us inside and the door shuts behind us. Large, rotating wheels lock us in tight.

We're inside, but still hovering in seawater, making me wonder how we're actually going to get out of the ship. But that's quickly answered when large pumps in the hangar floor kick on, expelling the water and gently lowering us to the floor. Then, giant fans hanging from the ceiling take care of any remaining moisture.

The hangar is bone dry. Pretty impressive.

"Are you ready to meet the rest of the team?" she asks, popping open the Freedom Ferry door.

"As ready as I'll ever be," I say.

Grace 2 exits first and is greeted by a motley crew of costumed heroes. Ms. Understood 2 leads the pack, running up and giving Grace 2 a big hug. "Grace, what happened? We thought you were captured. We were about to come rescue you."

"I was," Grace 2 says. "But Elliott rescued me first."

"Elliott?" Ms. Understood 2 says.

Before my foot hits the ground she wraps me up in a big hug. "I never thought I'd see you again," she says. "But I'm so glad you're here. Thank you for saving her. I guess we owe you twice now."

"My pleasure," I say. It's still weird seeing a version of my mom with blond hair instead of brown, but that's why I think of her as Mom 2. Then, I notice a small gray rat sitting on her shoulder that could only be this world's version of TechnocRat.

"That seals it," he says, staring at the Freedom Ferry with his beady little eyes and pulling on a long whisker. "My theory is confirmed."

I've got no clue what he's talking about. But what interests me more is the skinny, spikey-haired man standing behind them. He's wearing a green costume with gold electric volts that meet in the center of his chest.

Taser? He's a good guy?

Then, to his right, comes a small, thick-set man with an orange costume and a mohawk. Could it be? Without thinking, I run over and throw my arms around him.

"Makeshift! I'm so happy to see you alive!"

He looks down at me funny and says, "Um, do I know you?"

Suddenly, I realize this isn't the Makeshift from my world. It's Makeshift 2! I back up, my cheeks flush with embarrassment. "Sorry, I thought you were someone else. It's a long story."

"I bet," he says.

I take in the ragtag group of heroes standing before me. This is all that's left of the Freedom Force 2? If so, I don't know how we're going to defeat Ravager. We need more help. Major help.

"Mind if I lend a hand?" comes a deep voice.

I turn to find a dark-haired man in a red, white, and blue uniform stepping out of the airlock—the scales of justice insignia stretched across his chest. It's Captain Justice 2! His beard is trimmed and his hair is cut short.

"Dad?" Grace 2 says. "What are you doing here?"

Dad 2 puts his hand on my shoulder. "Someone reminded me of what it means to be a hero. It doesn't matter what powers you have, or how good you are at using them, being a hero is about never giving up, no matter the odds."

"So, you're back?" Grace 2 asks.

He looks at Mom 2 and smiles. "Yes, I've rejoined the Freedom Force."

Grace 2 gives him a big hug. "That's the best news ever."

"So, where exactly have you guys been?" Mom 2 asks.

Grace 2 and I look at each other.

"Speaking of long stories," she says. "How about we give you the quick version over some jelly doughnuts? I'm starving!"

***

After recapping our crazy adventures in the Galley, we take a much-needed bathroom break and then reconvene in the Mission Room. As I enter, I marvel at how eerily identical the Hydrostation is to the Waystation. Some of the rooms are on different levels, but both headquarters have a Combat Room, a Monitor Room, a Lounge, a Galley, a Vault, a Lab, and, of course, living quarters.

The Freedom Force 2 take their seats around the large, circular conference table. There are twelve seats in all, so I hop into one of the empty ones.

"So, Elliott," Mom 2 starts, "from what I understand, the entire multiverse is collapsing into one, there's a giant mist coming to swallow your Earth, you're carrying the most powerful weapon in the universe, and my son and his dog are stranded on a distant planet being watched by a cosmic, blind babysitter. Did I miss anything?"

"Nope, that pretty much sums it up," I say.

"So, what's our next move?" Dad 2 asks.

"I need to get back home," I say. "As quickly as possible."

"And how are you going to do that?" he asks.

"Well, my friend Wind Walker got me here, and he told me to call him when I want to go back. So, I guess I should give him a shout. I suggest you cover your ears."

The heroes look at one another and then comply. I stand up, inhale deeply, and yell, "WIND WALKER!"

But there's nothing.

From the stares I'm getting, I've clearly identified myself as a crazy person. "Sorry," I say. "That's how I got him last time."

Before Wind Walker took off, he told me he was trying to figure out the Blur. He said that hopefully he could come back for me. So, if he's not here, something must have gone terribly wrong. And now there's no way for me to get back home.

My legs feel wobbly and I slump back into my chair. I can't believe I got this far, and now I'm stuck. My family, my friends, they're all doomed.

"I... I failed my mission," I say.

"Perhaps," TechnocRat 2 says, scampering to the center of the table, "but perhaps not. Follow me." Then, he leaps onto the floor and runs into the hallway.

We follow him through the Hydrostation until he bolts into a familiar-looking sunken chamber—his laboratory.

Apparently, this TechnocRat isn't any neater than mine. He's got all the beakers, vials, Bunsen burners, microscopes, and other assorted equipment my rat does, but there's one noticeable difference. Smack-dab in the center of the room is a giant sphere.

"What's with the hamster ball?" Taser 2 asks.

"Very funny," TechnocRat 2 says, climbing up a mini-ramp and parking himself in front of a computer. "I call it the Jump Ship."

"Also known as big trouble," Grace 2 whispers.

"You see," TechnocRat 2 continues, punching computer keys with his paws, "I've been picking up some odd readings in our atmosphere." Then, he points at me with his tail. "The fact that he's standing here is astonishing in its own right—although I presume this Wind Walker character transported him here through a wormhole. But what's more astonishing is the vehicle they arrived in. That Freedom Ferry is from his universe, and it entered our universe on its own."

"So?" Taser 2 says. "Get to the point, cheese head."

"So, according to my analytical models, at this very moment, his universe and our universe are literally sitting on top of one another."

"What?" Makeshift 2 says.

It's the Blur. It's happening to us. Like, right now!

"Our two universes are in a state of pre-merger," TechnocRat 2 says. "At any time, the molecules could shift and one of our universes will be completely and totally wiped out."

"Well, that's comforting," Taser 2 says.

"If I could have everyone step inside the Jump Ship. Except you, Captain, you'll need to wait here."

We scramble up the ramp and inside the strange sphere. It's not as roomy as it looks from the outside, but at least it's translucent, so it feels larger than it is.

"Okay, TechnocRat," Dad 2 says. "What's going on here?"

"The Jump Ship is constructed entirely from unstable molecules that don't conform to the traditional rules of our universe. So, if my calculations are correct, when propelled with the right amount of force we may be able to exit our universe and enter Elliott's universe. All we need is for our resident strongman to pick us up, and pitch the fastest fastball ever recorded."

"And if your calculations are wrong?" Mom 2 asks.

"Captain Justice will have a lot of cleaning up to do."

"Lovely," I say.

"Is there any way I can join you after?" Dad 2 asks.

"I'm afraid not, Captain," TechnocRat 2 says. "This may be the last time we see each other."

"Dad, no!" Grace 2 cries.

"Sorry, darling," Dad 2 says, lifting the enormous sphere with one hand. "But as I've come to realize, being a hero is about sacrifice, no matter how painful the consequences may be."

And then, with tremendous strength, he stretches back and hurls us towards the far wall.

Meta Profile

The Freedom Force 2

Taser 2

Class: Energy Manipulator
Meta: ■

Glory Girl 2

Class: Flight
Meta: ■ ■

Captain Justice 2

Class: Super-Strength
Meta: ■ ■ ■ ■

Ms. Understood 2

Class: Psychic
Meta: ■ ■ ■

TechnocRat 2

Class: Super-Intellect
Meta: ■ ■ ■ ■

Makeshift 2

Class: Energy Manipulator
Meta: ■

TWELVE

I ATTEND A FAMILY REUNION GONE WRONG

Ripping through the fabric of the universe is deafening stuff.

It sort of sounds like splitting your pants— not that it's ever happened to me—but magnified a million times. Inside the Jump Ship, we're smashing into each other like kernels in a popcorn machine, and I'm pretty sure at one point a rat tail went up my nose!

This whole experiment is a crazy gamble. Our only hope is that TechnocRat 2's unstable molecules do their job. In hindsight, I probably should have asked a few more questions before putting my life at risk. Like, what's the probability this will actually work? But it's too late now.

Looking through the exterior of the Jump Ship is like looking through frosted glass. I can tell it's dark outside—like we're spinning through nothingness—but that's about it. Who knows, maybe we're already dead? Boy, wouldn't that solve all my problems, at least in the short run?

I think I'm gonna be sick.

"Are you enjoying yourself?"

"Not now," I answer in my mind. *"Please."*

"You can still rule," the Orb says. *"Just say the word."*

"Here are two words," I say, *"shut it."*

"Suit yourself," it says. *"Hope you don't barf."*

CRACK! comes a sharp, bone-rattling noise, and suddenly, we're bathed in light.

"Yes!" TechnocRat 2 cries. "We're through!"

The Jump Ship skips along with reckless abandon. Every time we bump the ground it feels like a sucker punch to the gut. Arms and legs are flailing about everywhere. Finally, we break into a smooth roll, cruising along for what seems like miles before SMACKING into something solid that stops our momentum cold.

I'm lying face down, my nose pressed into the bottom of the sphere. Propping myself on my elbows, I take in the scene around me. The Jump Ship looks like a hospital ward: Grace 2 has a bloody nose, Taser 2 is nursing his left arm, Mom 2 has a bruised eye, and Makeshift 2 is hugging TechnocRat 2 like he's a teddy bear.

"Is everyone okay?" TechnocRat 2 squeaks out.

He's answered with moans and groans.

My neck is so sore it feels like I've got whiplash, but I don't have time for pain. Right now, I just need to know if we made it back to my universe. There's only one way to find out. I look around hopelessly for the door before I realize it's spun to the top of the Jump Ship.

"We need to make a plan," I hear TechnocRat 2 say.

A plan. Right, sounds good. I get up on my feet, and step on Makeshift 2's back. "Hey!" he shouts, but I ignore him, and reach up for the latch.

"Elliott, wait!" I hear Mom 2 say.

The latch is outside my reach. I just need to stretch a little further... a little more...

Got it!

I pull down, and the door opens inwards. With considerable effort I swing up, grabbing the side of the opening, and haul myself up. When I'm halfway out of the Jump Ship, I balance myself and take a look around.

Hey, I know those buildings!

That's Main Street! There's the ice cream shop! The police station! I'm back in Keystone City!

My Keystone City!

We did it! We really did—

"Duck!" cries the Orb.

Without thinking, I drop into the Jump Ship, just as something large WHOOSHES overhead!

Luckily, the heroes catch me before I break my legs.

"Elliott?" Grace 2 says. "You look as white as a ghost? What was it?"

I'm not really sure.

I need to get back up there.

"Elliott?" she says.

"Lift me up," I say.

This time, Makeshift 2 kneels and I climb up onto his shoulders. He pushes me up and I wiggle my way out of the Jump Ship. I look into the sky.

It's filled with objects.

Floating objects.

They're not clouds. Or airplanes. Or birds.

They're warships.

Skelton warships.

Hundreds of them.

"Get out here now!" I order. "We're under attack!"

Grace 2 flies up and pulls me out of the Jump Ship. The other heroes scramble out and join us on the ground.

"Holy guacamole!" TechnocRat 2 says.

"Is that what I think it is?" Grace 2 says.

"There's too many of them!" Taser 2 says.

"We don't have much time," Mom 2 says. "We need to get every civilian to safety. Quick, let's assign roles."

The heroes converge, but I can't concentrate on anything they're saying. My mind is completely somewhere else. I mean, what are all these Skelton warships doing here? The last time I saw the Skelton Emperor, Arena World was breaking into a billion pieces and I thought we had an understanding. I wanted nothing to do with him, and since I didn't have the Orb of Oblivion, he had no use for me.

He wouldn't know I had another Orb, would he? It's not possible. So, what's his fleet doing here?

"Elliott?" comes a female voice in my brain. *"Is that you?"*

Spinning around, I find a colorful group of heroes heading our way. It's the Freedom Force!

My Freedom Force!

They stop a few feet short of us and stare at the strange crew around me.

"Epic Zero," Dad says, his fists clenched, "are you in danger?"

"No, sir," I say. "These are my friends. They're the Freedom Force, but from a different universe."

"Say what?" Grace says. "What are you talking about?"

"Look," I say, "I know this is gonna sound weird, but our two universes are like, right on top of each other. In fact, they're merging together and only one of them is going to survive because of a cosmic crisis called the Blur. But trust me, that's not even our biggest problem right now. See, there's this galactic monster on its way to eat our planet. And now, for some reason, we're about to be invaded by Skelton. Are you guys following me?"

"You mean, like, to the insane asylum?" Grace asks.

"Absolutely fascinating," TechnocRat says, rocketing

over us in his jetpack to get a closer look at the Jump Ship. He turns to his gray double. "Unstable molecules?"

"Yes," TechnocRat 2 says excitedly. "I've been working with them for over a decade, but only in a laboratory setting. You wouldn't believe how difficult it is to get unidentified—"

"—atomic nuclei to cooperate?" TechnocRat finishes.

"Great," Grace says. "Now we've got techno-babble in stereo. Anyway, are these weirdos you're with for real? And who in their right mind thought I'd look good as a brunette?"

"Hey!" Grace 2 says. "You're right, Elliott, she is rude!"

"Rude?" Grace says. "I'll show you rude!"

"Isn't that Taser?" Blue Bolt asks. "Isn't he a villain?"

"If you're looking for villains," Taser 2 says, pointing to Shadow Hawk, "Just look at him."

"You got a problem?" Shadow Hawk says menacingly.

"Yeah," Makeshift 2 says, stepping forward. "How'd you like a one-way ticket to Exile?"

"Makeshift?" Dad says. "You're alive!"

"Yeah," Makeshift 2 says, powering up. "Which is more than I can say for you."

"Whoa! Whoa! Time out!" I say, stepping in between the teams. This isn't exactly the reunion I was hoping for.

They're at each other's throats! "Look, we're all heroes here."

"Ell—I mean, Epic Zero," Mom says firmly, "I'm sure your new friends are lovely people, but can you please tell me exactly where you've been? Clearly, disappearing for days on end without communication isn't an issue for you, but for those of us responsible for your well-being it's been a little nerve-wracking."

Oh, boy. I know that tone. "Didn't you see my note?" I ask.

"What note?" she asks, her arms crossed and foot tapping.

"The note I left for you in… TechnoRat's incredibly messy laboratory. Right, sorry."

"We'll finish this discussion later," Dad says. "Now, about these friends of yours…"

Okay, I'm in big trouble, but we're all toast if I can't stop them from being so distracted by each other that we fail to focus on what matters most.

Distracted? Hang on. That's it!

O. M. G.

I know what the Skelton arc doing here!

"You finally figured it out, huh, genius?" says the Orb.

"Don't start," I respond.

"We can take them," it says. *"You have all the power you need. It's standing all around you."*

"What? What does that mean?"

Suddenly, there's an intense blast of light,

temporarily blinding us. Shielding my eyes, I look up.

Hovering above us is the Herald!

"Good day, heroes," he says.

"Um, is that the galactic monster you were telling us about?" Grace asks.

"No," I say.

"Then, who is he?"

"I vote for bad news," Taser 2 says.

"I am called the Herald," he says. "So, we meet again, little hero."

Of course, more insults.

"Wait," Grace says. "You know this guy?"

"Yep," I say.

"Is he a good guy?" she asks.

"Nope," I say.

"Fabulous," she says.

"I told you I would return," the Herald says.

"And I see you brought friends," I say.

"Ah, yes," he says, looking around. "When I required assistance to destroy Earth it did not take the Skelton long to sign up. In fact, they were quite motivated. I knew they would be."

"Why are they here?" I ask. "You didn't need them when you helped Ravager destroy Protaraan."

"Protaraan did not have heroes," he says. "I have found that heroes tend to interfere where they do not belong."

"I thought so," I say. "So, the Skelton are here to

distract us while you do your dirty work, huh? I guess you're scared we'll stop you."

"Oh, you will not stop me," the Herald says. "I just prefer not to be slowed down."

I look him dead in the eyes. "We'll do a lot more than slow you down."

"You amuse me, little hero," he says. "But you cannot slow, what you cannot catch."

Then, he takes off in a flash, leaving a fiery trail behind him.

"I'll get him!" both Grace's say simultaneously.

But before they can move, there's a THUNDERING noise from above.

The Skelton warships are heading right for us!

It's begun.

Meta Profile

Name: Orb of Oblivion 2
Role: Cosmic Entity   Status: Active

VITALS:

Race: Inapplicable
Real Name: Inapplicable
Height: 4.0 inches
Weight: 7.0 oz
Eye Color: Inapplicable
Hair Color: Inapplicable

META POWERS:

Class: Inapplicable
Power Level: Inapplicable

- A parasite that seeks out unfulfilled desires and feeds off of them
- Limitless power—can do whatever its host imagines

CHARACTERISTICS:

Combat	Inapplicable
Durability	Inapplicable
Leadership	Inapplicable
Strategy	Inapplicable
Willpower	Inapplicable

THIRTEEN

I TRY TO CATCH FIRE

"Freedom Force—it's Fight Time!"

I watch Dad rally the troops as hundreds of Skelton warships race towards us. I wish I could stay and help, but I've got to stop the Herald. The only problem is how?

He's fast and already has a big head start. There's no Freedom Ferry to jump into, and I certainly can't fly.

"Are you sure about that?" the Orb says.

"I think I'd know if I could fly?" I answer.

"That's the old you talking," it says. *"Not the new you."*

"What are you babbling about?"

But there's no time to figure that out because the Skelton are on top of us. Master Mime encases us in a bubble of purple energy, blocking the barrage of laser fire, but his shield is taking a pounding. I can see Master Mime struggling to keep it intact. I'm not sure how long he'll hold up. In fact, I'm not sure how we're going to survive this!

"We need to draw them away from the city!" Mom says. "Captain Justice, Master Mime, Blue Bolt, you provide cover. Everyone else follow me."

Suddenly, the two Graces grab my arms and lift me into the air. "Let's go, Bro," my sister says.

"Wait!" I yell, "Put me down!" But they're not listening. They're carrying me away—in the opposite direction of the Herald!

"Stop squirming and relax," Grace 2 says. "We've got to get you safe, then we'll deal with that fireball."

But they don't understand. The Skelton aren't the real danger here—it's the Herald!

I watch as Dad, Master Mime, and Blue Bolt stand their ground against the advancing armada. Dad is grabbing anything he can get his hands on—abandoned cars, street poles, trash cans—and launching them into the heart of the Skelton formation. Blue Bolt is running in circles, kicking up tornadoes that catch Skelton warships and spin them back into space. Master Mime created a giant purple tennis racket and is backhanding warships left and right.

But there's just too many of them.

Dozens are slipping through the cracks.

They'll be on us soon.

"Now!" the Orb says.

"Now what?"

"Open your mind," it says. *"Use me."*

"No!"

"Last time you gave in to me," it says. *"But then you pulled back. Let me in. Let me in completely. It's the only way."*

Despite my objections, I feel myself being drawn to its power—it's like an itch I need to scratch deep inside my brain. I feel it pulling me. Luring me in.

I try to resist, but it's so hard. Then, I realize the Orb has simply been biding its time, patiently waiting for the moment where I need it so desperately that I have no choice but to let it completely occupy every nook and cranny of my mind.

I can't let that happen.

"You are strong," it says. *"Far stronger than your duplicate. But your time is running out."*

The ships are closing in fast.

"The Herald is already at work. This may be your final chance," it says. *"Open your mind. Let me in."*

But I can't.

"Then you have lost," it says. *"You have lost everything."*

The lead Skelton warship fires a blast near Makeshift 2. His scream pierces the air as he falls. He's hurt, clutching his leg!

Images of my Makeshift cross my mind. He's dead now— a petrified statue—because of me. Because I failed to act when I needed to. I swore I wouldn't let anyone get hurt because of me again.

Dad 2's words echo in my mind: *being a hero is about sacrifice, no matter how painful the consequences may be.*

I know what I've got to do.

I close my eyes.

"Give me the power," I say. *"All of it. Now."*

"Yes!" the Orb exclaims.

I relax my mind and feel a strange sensation running through my body. It's like my cells are opening up—unlocking—filling with incredible energy. Suddenly, I feel super-charged. Electric. Dominant.

The only other time I felt like this was when I was inside the mind of... of... Meta-Taker!

"Am... am I a Meta 4?"

"You are all-powerful," the Orb says. *"You can call it whatever you wish."*

So, if I'm like Meta-Taker, then that means I can duplicate the powers of other Metas! Is that why he told me I could...

Holy. Freaking. Cow!

"How do I do it?" I ask quickly.

"It's simple. You just reach out and take it," the Orb says.

I close my eyes and push out with my mind. But instead of negating Grace 2's powers, this time I copy it, reproduce it, and pull it back into my body.

"Elliott, what are you doing?" Grace 2 says. "Stop twisting, you're going to—Elliott!"

I break loose from their grip and start freefalling.

For a second, I'm terrified. Visions of splattering on

the ground fill my brain. But then, I extend my arms and think 'FLY.'

And suddenly, I stop my descent.

I'm… floating?

I… I did it!

"Hey," Grace says. "How'd you do that?"

"Tell you later," I say. Suddenly, I remember Meta-Taker's profile. There was a part about him being able to duplicate the powers of more than one Meta of the same power type. "But right now, I'm going to need your power too." I reach out and copy Grace's flying ability as well. I can feel their powers multiplying inside of me. "Look, I've got to stop the Herald. Do your best to get rid of these Skelton. And please, don't get killed."

"Elliott," Grace says, "wait a—"

But before she can finish, I'm gone.

The wind snaps against my face as I fly through the sky under my own power. It kind of feels like swimming, where the water you displace weighs more than you do, keeping you afloat. But instead of water, I'm being buoyed by air molecules, and there's no chlorine stinging my eyes.

A few Skelton warships break formation and get on my tail, but with the flight powers of both Glory Girls, I'm way too fast for them. After a few seconds, they fall behind and give up. I'm guessing I've dropped completely off their radars.

I make my way back to Keystone City where there's

not a Skelton in sight. The combined powers of the Freedom Force did a great job pulling the shapeshifters away from the city, but there's tons of damage. Unfortunately, I can't clean it up now, because I'm here to pick up something else—the Herald's fiery trail.

Fortunately, it's still blazing strong.

I take off, following its path.

"Wait, there are no Meta's here," the Orb says. *"The city is vulnerable."*

"So?"

"So, now is a good time to begin your reign," it says. *"To take command of your lowly subjects and rule."*

"Yes, good point."

Wait a minute! What did I just say?

Why would I think that? The Orb is messing with me. And besides, that's crazy talk. I don't want to rule anything! Right?

"Stop it! Get out of my head!"

"Remarkably, you are still holding back," it says. *"Trust me and let go."*

I feel the Orb burrowing into my brain. Somehow, I've got to keep it in line. I can't let it take me over. I've got a job to do.

I'm over the west coast when I notice something disturbing—there's a second blazing pathway. That can only mean one thing, the Herald's made two rotations around Earth already!

I vividly recall what I saw him do to Protaraan,

circling the doomed planet over and over again until he left a signal in the form of a bright, fiery atom which was visible from any point in the universe.

A signal for Ravager to come and feed.

I switch to the new trail and kick into overdrive.

I'm really motoring now when I notice a strangely familiar set of islands dotting the ocean below.

And that's when I see him, a bright fireball cruising through the sky.

"Halt!" I yell.

The Herald peers over his shoulder and smirks. Then, he stops on a dime mid-flight, and I go shooting past. Not exactly the heroic entrance I was hoping for.

"Little hero," he says. "You have come for more punishment."

I manage to put on the brakes and head back towards the villain. During our last encounter I didn't have nearly enough power to take him down. But this time it's going to be different. "This ends now," I say.

Just then, I notice something is wrong. I'm sinking. Lowering in the sky.

"Are you sure about that?" the Herald says amused.

"What's happening?"

"You did not store enough power. And you have drifted too far from your power source," the Orb says. *"You have lost your ability to—"*

Oh. No.

Suddenly, I drop like an anchor.

"Take his power!" the Orb yells.

But I can't focus. I'm plunging towards the ocean from thousands of feet in the air! From this height I'm gonna hit the water and scatter into a million pieces! I can't breathe! I feel like I'm passing out!

Then, my momentum stops.

How?

Drops of water pitter onto my face and my entire backside feels wet. I look down and realize I'm being held up by a giant plume of water.

Not again.

Suddenly, I'm lifted into the air by a green-caped man with a dragon emblem on his chest. "So, we meet again," Green Dragon says.

The Rising Suns!

"Listen," I say. "Thanks for the lift, but I really don't have time to fight you right now."

"We are not here to fight," Zen says, suddenly appearing beside us. "From our last encounter, I was able to share everything I discovered inside your mind. We apologize for before, isn't that right, Green Dragon?"

"Yes," Green Dragon says begrudgingly. "I... apologize. We now know that you are who you claim to be. And this man of fire is our joint enemy. We are here to help you."

I turn to see the Herald holding off Tsunami, Silent Samurai, and Fight Master. And then I realize with the Rising Suns here, I have more powers I can borrow.

"A lot has changed since the last time we met," I say. "And the best way you can help me is by sticking around for a while."

I close my eyes and pull in Zen's Meta 3 psychic abilities, Green Dragon's Meta 3 super-strength, and Tsunami's Meta 3 energy manipulation. Then, I grab their powers of flight.

Now, it's showtime.

I pull away from Green Dragon and fly over to the Herald.

"Little hero," the Herald says. "You have returned. Have you sorted out your problem?"

"Nope," I say coldly, "you're still here."

He smiles. "Still with the sharp tongue, I see. I think it is high time I rip it out." Then, he extends his arms and sends a blast of fire my way.

I use Tsunami's powers and block it with a wave of water, then I push it back towards him using Green Dragon's strength, dousing him in ocean water. The Herald flickers out for a moment, and then flames back on.

"You are stronger," he says. "But not strong enough." Suddenly, he erupts into a bright ball of fire, blinding me. The heat is so intense it feels like my skin is melting! He's trying to vaporize me!

"Now," the Orb says, *"negate his power permanently!"*

I want to do it, but something tells me it's not the right move. Instead, I tap into Zen's psychic power and reach into the Herald's mind.

A series of images flash before me: A green world with yellow, puffy clouds. An image of a pointy-eared woman. Children playing.

"What are you doing?" the Herald cries. "Stop!"

This is incredible! I'm seeing things exactly as the Herald saw them! He's inside a space shuttle drifting into a nebulous, green mist. He's pushing commands on a bomb. But then, his ship is pulled apart around him. He's trapped inside a... a cocoon? Then, he's bathed in fire...

No freaking way! I pull out of his head.

"You tried to destroy Ravager," I say.

He looks at me angrily. "Yes," he says, powering down. "Once upon a time."

"But I don't understand. If you wanted him dead, then why are you helping him destroy other planets?"

"It is... complicated," he says, putting his head in his hands.

"Try me," I say.

"Once I was a scientist," he begins, "an astrologer, who made a remarkable, yet fateful discovery. There were holes in the universe where my ancestors had mapped planets. It seemed as if entire worlds on the far side of the galaxy had disappeared. I did not understand how this could be possible, so I brought my discovery to the Federation, but they did not care. With the ongoing wars, they said they had higher concerns than my lost worlds. But I knew something was wrong."

The Rising Suns surround the Herald, but I raise my hand, stopping them from attacking. "Go on," I say.

"I knew what was happening could not be natural. Something was causing it to happen. I studied the phenomenon for years, until one day, my equipment caught the perpetrator in the act. It was a strange, undefined mist that was swallowing planets whole, and then destroying them. I knew if this cosmic predator was not dealt with, one day it would come for my world, my family, my children."

A fiery tear streams down his face.

"I built a nuclear warhead and said goodbye to my loved ones. I knew I would never see them again. Years passed before I finally came upon the monster, descending upon a small planet in the Oberon system. As I watched it in its ephemeral form, I realized my weapon was useless to destroy it. At least, until it solidified. So, I flew into its center and waited. But, as you saw, I did not destroy it, it destroyed me."

"What happened?" I ask.

"It transformed me," he says, "into this. A servant to hunt habitable worlds for it to consume."

"But why?" I ask. "Why are you doing this?"

"Because, it made me a bargain I could not refuse. In exchange for my service, it offered to spare my world—to save my family."

"But you helped it murder billions."

"Yes," he says, looking down. "I have not thought of

my family for a long time. I saved them, but in the process destroyed many, many others. I... I have lost sight of what matters most. Life. All life."

"Destroy him!" the Orb says.

My fingers twitch and I feel the urge to take all his powers away. To punish him for what he's done, but I can't.

I need him.

"Look, I know what it's like when you're willing to do anything to save your family," I say, "but with the decisions you've made, you've only let them down. You've let yourself down. This is your chance, maybe your only chance to redeem yourself and do what's right. You've got to help me destroy Ravager before he comes to Earth. You have to help me save billions of lives. Do you understand?"

He hesitates for a moment, and then says, "Yes, I understand."

Suddenly, the sky darkens, like someone threw a blanket over the sun.

"But I am afraid it is too late."

Meta Profile

Name: Ravager
Role: Cosmic Entity   Status: Active

VITALS:

Race: Inapplicable
Real Name: Inapplicable
Height: Unlimited
Weight: Incalculable
Eye Color: Inapplicable
Hair Color: Inapplicable

META POWERS:

Class: Inapplicable
Power Level: Inapplicable

- A cosmic predator that consumes habitable planets to satiate its endless hunger

- Crosses the multiverse as a shapeless mist

CHARACTERISTICS:

Combat	Inapplicable
Durability	Inapplicable
Leadership	Inapplicable
Strategy	Inapplicable
Willpower	Inapplicable

FOURTEEN

I FACE THE ULTIMATE EVIL

Under a blackened sky, the first tendrils of a menacing green fog descend slowly towards Earth.

My nightmare has come true.

Ravager is here.

"What is happening?" Tsunami asks.

"Just the end of the world," I answer cryptically, hypnotized by what's unfolding before my eyes.

The green cloud rolls in thick and fluffy, almost inviting. But that couldn't be further from the truth.

While I've had nightmares about Ravager attacking Earth before, the sheer terror I'm feeling at this moment is more intense than I ever imagined. As Ravager fills the sky, it dawns on me we're only occupying one tiny section of the globe. If it can swallow entire planets, it must be absolutely huge!

How am I ever going to find its brain? It's going to be impossible—like finding a needle in a haystack. I mean, it could take years! Clearly, I don't have that luxury. And besides, how does a creature made of mist even have a brain?

Suddenly, warning bells go off in my head, and a million reasons why I shouldn't trust the Watcher's advice come to mind. First off, he's batty. Second, Ravager is his child. I mean, does he really want to off his own kid? Third, he hates me. After all, I have the Orb of Oblivion, the only weapon rumored to be capable of taking down his precious Ravager.

Maybe he's sending me to dig my own grave.

Something tells me he'll get his wish.

Hazy, green waves drift past my face and I gag. Yuck, this stuff smells like rotten eggs. Then, I notice something strange. The wispy green particles are covered with small, shiny flecks. At first, they look like they're falling alongside it, like snowflakes from the sky. But then I realize the flecks are somehow attached to the green mist, riding down with it.

That's weird.

"Little h—," the Herald starts but then stops himself. "Epic Zero, I hope you understand the impossible odds before us. I have seen countless others attempt to stop Ravager. Scientists. Soldiers. Superheroes. All have tried, and all have perished. What makes you think we are capable of succeeding where others have failed?"

"Because I have this."

I watch the Herald's eyes widen as I hold out the Orb of Oblivion. "So, it is real," he whispers.

"Yes," I say, "and if we're going to use it, I need you to take me to Ravager's brain. That is, if it actually has a brain."

"It does," he says. "I can take you there. But I fear the journey will be treacherous. We will need to intercept the beast in the harshness of space. You will not survive."

"That's not a problem," I say. And then I concentrate hard, tapping into the Herald's power, copying every iota possible. As I draw in his abilities, I can feel my cells expanding, crackling with energy.

And then I burst into flames.

"Tsunami, put him out!" Fight Master cries.

"No, it's okay," I say quickly. "I'm not hurt. I've simply duplicated the Herald's power. Now I must go and slay the dragon."

Green Dragon raises an eyebrow.

"Sorry," I say. "It's just an expression. What I mean is it's time for me to destroy Ravager before he destroys us."

"Epic Zero," Zen says, "the fate of mankind is in your hands. Good luck."

"Thanks," I say, swallowing hard. Talk about pressure! This is it. There's no turning back now. I take a deep breath and say, "Let's do this."

Without a word, the Herald takes off. He's fast, but this time I'm right there with him.

The Herald cuts through the fog like a flaming knife, leaving a blazing trail in his wake. Suddenly, I realize we're flying straight through Ravager's body. It's like he's a ghost, like he's not really there. I only wish that were true.

One thing that is there though, are those shiny flecks. They're everywhere, pelting lightly against my face. What are they?

"I was wondering the same thing," the Orb says. *"I sense a cosmic energy about them. Something familiar."*

"For such a know-it-all, you sure don't know much," I say.

"Don't worry, I'll figure it out," it says. *"Speaking of 'knowing,' you do know what to do once we reach Ravager's brain, right?"*

"Yes, I'm going to blow you up."

"Wrong," it says. *"When we reach Ravager's brain, we will take control of Ravager. After we master the beast, the entire multiverse will bow before us. Imagine the power you'll have. Imagine the respect you will earn."*

Yes, that would be something, wouldn't it? I'd be unstoppable! I can just see Grace's face when I swing by the Waystation with Ravager on a leash. Boy, will she be sur—

"Hey!" I shout, "Get lost!"

The Herald stops. "Excuse me?"

"Sorry," I say, embarrassed. "Just having a private

conversation." Suddenly, I realize we've left Earth's atmosphere altogether. We're floating in space! I'm floating in space! But my excitement is short-lived when I catch full sight of Ravager.

It's like there's no end in sight. The creature extends from deep space all the way to Earth! And he's covered half the globe already! We're running out of time!

"Where's the brain?" I say, panicked. I'm looking around for something, anything, but there's nothing. "We need to get there! Now!"

"But we are here," the Herald says. "Look."

I follow his outstretched hand, which is pointing to a cloudy area that is subtlety darker than the rest. It's the size of a football field, expanding and contracting.

"That's the brain?" I ask.

"Yes," he says. "But it is in transient form. If you try to destroy it now, its molecules will simply scatter and reform again. If you want to ensure its demise, you must wait until it solidifies."

"Okay," I say. "So, when will that happen?"

"When it fully swallows your planet."

"Whoa," I say. "So, you're saying I need to wait for it to start pulverizing Earth before I can destroy it? I can't let that happen. It'll kill billions!"

"That," the Herald says, "is the only way."

Suddenly, there's a THUNDEROUS BOOM.

"What's that?" I ask.

"Master!" the Herald screams.

The brain shakes violently and out comes something that is not so much a voice, but a rumble.

"YOU BETRAYED ME."

"No, Master," the Herald says. "I was just... bringing this boy here... to witness your mighty power."

"DO YOU TAKE ME FOR A FOOL? THIS IS NO ORDINARY BOY. HE IS THE ORB MASTER. AND YOU BROUGHT HIM HERE TO DESTROY ME."

"Now!" the Herald screams. "Destroy it now!"

I reach into my mind to activate the Orb's power, when—

"Wait!" the Orb says. *"It's not solid. It won't work."*

I hesitate. The Orb is right. Based on what the Herald told me, using the Orb's power now wouldn't do any good.

"FOR OVER A CENTURY YOU HAVE ACTED AS MY LOYAL SUBJECT. BUT NOW YOU HAVE CONSPIRED AGAINST ME. OUR BARGAIN IS TERMINATED. YOUR WORLD WILL BE RAVAGED AND NOW YOU WILL BE PUNISHED!"

"No!" the Herald cries, dropping into a begging position. "I'm sorry, Master! Please, let me make it up to—"

Just then, the Herald's fire is extinguished.

For the first time, I see the man beneath the flames—his skin is white, his eyes are gold. He stares at me desperately and then clutches his throat.

He can't breathe! Without his powers he can't breathe in space!

"Herald!" I cry, moving towards him, but the green mist between us thickens, forming a barrier. I try pushing through it, but the fog has solidified! I can't break through! I've lost sight of him.

Just then, the fog dissipates, and as it creeps away I see the Herald's body floating before me. Limp. Lifeless.

He's gone.

Suddenly, I panic. My power source is gone!

"Don't worry," the Orb says, *"this time you've stored enough juice to last a while. But don't dilly-dally."*

That's a relief. But as the Herald hovers there, all I'm thinking is here's another senseless death. Another life I'm responsible for. My blood is boiling. All I want is to destroy Ravager—to end this nightmare. But how?

"I REQUIRE A NEW HERALD."

"You're going to need more than that," I say, "after I blow you into a gazillion pieces."

"HOW ABOUT YOU?"

"What?"

"YOU ARE STRONG. DETERMINED. I WILL TAKE YOU AS MY HERALD, AND IN EXCHANGE I WILL SPARE YOUR WORLD."

"Um, is that a joke?"

"SERVE AS MY HERALD. SCOUT THE MULTIVERSE TO FIND HABITABLE PLANETS

TO SATIATE MY HUNGER. HELP ME, AND YOUR WORLD, AND ALL OF THOSE YOU LOVE, WILL LIVE. THE OFFER HAS BEEN MADE, THE FINAL DECISION IS YOURS."

FIFTEEN

I DETERMINE THE FATE OF EVERYTHING

My head is spinning.

Ravager just offered Earth a get-out-of-jail-free card. There's just one catch. To cash it in, I need to become his new Herald.

My gut tells me to say, 'thanks but no thanks.'

But my head tells me it may be an offer I can't refuse.

I mean, everything I've done up to this point has been for the sole purpose of preventing Ravager from eating Earth. All of my adventures flash through my mind: getting captured by the Rising Suns, traveling through wormholes to another universe, wrestling Elliott 2 on Watcher World, fighting with the second Orb of

Oblivion. It's been an insane whirlwind.

Now, if I just say 'yes' the whole threat is neutralized. My family will be spared. My friends on the Freedom Force will survive. My planet will be left alone. It's an amazing deal.

But not for everyone.

I think about my old friends on the Zodiac: Gemini, Taurus, Aries, Sagittarius, Pisces, and Scorpio. They're all orphans, the last of their kind, all because of Ravager's hunger pains.

Then, my mind turns to Grace 2 and her family. Their world won't be safe either. One day, Ravager will come for them too.

I remember how sad the Herald looked when I confronted him about his actions. Even though he thought he was doing the right thing, he knew he was as guilty as Ravager in the slaughtering of billions.

I can't do that.

I could never do that.

"*Are you nuts?*" the Orb says. "*This is the chance of a lifetime.*"

"*No, I don't think—*"

"*Listen, dummy,*" it interjects. "*This is your one chance to save everyone you care about. I know you think you can use me to blow that monster up, but what if it doesn't work? You'll be responsible for what happens next. Don't doom everyone you love because of some silly moral code. Step up and show them you're the hero you were meant to be.*"

Maybe the Orb is right. If I screw it up, Earth is lost. Maybe this is my one shot to save my planet. Plus, who knows what's going to happen with the multiverse collapsing.

But if I become the new Herald, I'll be responsible for hurting so many innocent people. I... I don't know what to do. How come I'm always stuck making these decisions? I'm sure Dad or Mom would know what to do. I bet even Dog-Gone could make the call better than me.

"DECIDE, EARTHLING!" Ravager rumbles.

"Do it!" the Orb says. *"Before it's too late!"*

I rub my thumb along the smooth surface of the Orb. Great, so here I've got the most powerful weapon in the universe, but no clue how to use it. The Watcher said to take the Orb to the brain of Ravager, and then blow it up. He didn't provide any instructions after that.

But Ravager is a trail of gas fumes right now. According to the Herald, it needs to be in solid form for me to do any real damage. The last time I saw it turn solid was when it cracked Protaraan like a walnut, extracting all of its life energy for nourishment. If I wait for it to do the same to Earth, it could destroy it.

So, how am I going to blow it up?

Hang on.

Blow. It. Up?

Maybe I'm looking at this the wrong way.

Okay, so I've got the Orb of Oblivion—the cosmic parasite that specializes in one thing other than rudeness—mind control. And for all his gaseous grossness, Ravager clearly has a brain—a mind of its own.

I know what to do.

"Orb," I command, *"make Ravager retreat."*

"What?" the Orb says. *"I'll do no such thing."*

"Oh, yes you—"

"EARTHLING," Ravager bellows, regaining my attention. "WHAT IS YOUR DECISION?"

Really? Like it couldn't have waited another second. I could try stalling for more time, but I've got a feeling that isn't gonna work. I've got no choice. Here goes nothing. "Thanks for the generous offer," I answer. "But I'd rather die an epic failure than ever be a herald for you!"

"THEN THE FATE OF YOUR WORLD IS SEALED."

Suddenly, Ravager shifts towards Earth in double time! A feeling of dread washes over me, but there's no time to second guess myself. I've made my decision and now I've got to get down to business!

"Orb!" I command. *"Make Ravager retreat!"*

"No w—"

"Enough!" I demand. *"You are the Orb and I am the Orb Master! You will do as I say! NOW!"*

I recall the Orb telling me it hid part of itself from Elliott 2. That's how it was able to transfer to me. Somehow, it never allowed the other Elliott to take it over completely. But for this job I'm going to need the Orb—the whole Orb.

I drive deep into the Orb's conscious.

The Orb screams. It pushes back.

But I'm too strong.

I dig deeper.

It squirms, trying to avoid my pressure.

But I won't be denied.

I surround it. Trap it. Seize it.

And then, I break its will.

I feel the Orb yield. Open itself up.

And I take it all.

The Orb is mine. Fully mine.

Then, I focus my energy on one thought.

BRING BACK RAVAGER.

A massive wave of orange energy explodes out of the Orb and grabs hold of the beast, wrapping around its vaporous middle, cinching tight. Ravager lurches forward, pulling me with it. But I yank back hard, dragging the monster backward.

Ravager SCREAMS—an other-worldly primal scream—like a cranky child pulled from his highchair before finishing his meal. The cosmic monster loses its grip on Earth, its tendrils flailing. But it's not going down without a fight. It fires a shockwave back through the Orb, stunning me.

But I hold firm.

I pull harder, reeling it in like a fish. When I finally get it clear of Earth's atmosphere, I begin part two of my plan. I remember Dad 2's Distorter. How it made people think something was there, even when it wasn't. And I know what I need to do.

"*Orb,*" I command. "*Trick Ravager into thinking he's consuming a habitable planet.*"

"*Yes, master,*" the Orb responds.

Suddenly, Ravager's wispy molecules blow up and out, forming a gigantic balloon shape, larger than Earth. Ravager has wrapped itself around the imaginary planet.

Now, it's time to end this once and for all.

"*D-Don't... do it,*" the Orb begs. "*Please...*"

What? How is the Orb still resisting me?

"*No dice,*" I say.

Suddenly, Ravager turns solid. It thinks it's going to crush the imaginary planet.

This is my chance.

"*You'll destroy Earth, you fool,*" the Orb says. "*You're too close. It'll be wiped out in the explosion.*"

Oh, jeez! I didn't think of that.

And then—

"Do not listen to it," comes a familiar voice. "It is manipulating you. Act now."

"But what about Earth?" I say.

"We will protect it," comes another voice. "All of it."

"*No!*" the Orb says. "*That's not possible! You're dead! You're both dead!*"

"Act now!" urges the first voice.

"*Orb,*" I command, "*get into the sphere. All of you.*"

I feel a rush as the Orb of Oblivion leaves my body

and enters the sphere in my hand.

Then, I grip the sphere tight and hurl it as hard as I can at Ravager.

With incredible velocity, the Orb flies through the vacuum of space, straight and true.

But as it reaches Ravager, something amazing happens. Millions of those strange, tiny flecks leave Ravager's body, forming a barrier in front of Earth.

"Now," comes the second voice, bringing me back to reality. "Do it now!"

I reach out and connect to the Orb of Oblivion. And then I make one final command.

DETONATE!

As the massive explosion begins, I'm covered by tiny flecks of light.

And then everything goes black.

***

It's dark. At first, I think someone's turned out the lights, but then I realize my eyes are closed. My whole body is sore. It feels like I've been hit by a Mack truck. How long have I been lying here? Am I dead?

I open my eyes, expecting to see either angels or devils. What I find instead is pretty darn close, because standing on opposite sides of the bed are two familiar faces.

Order and Chaos.

I shoot up. "B-But you're dead?" I say. "I saw you both killed on Arena World."

Order smiles, his teeth still perfectly straight. "One cannot kill the very fabric of the universe. Instead, let us say we were temporarily displaced."

I try to make a sense of what he's saying when suddenly it all clicks. Those tiny flecks attached to Ravager. Those voices I heard in my head. All of those shiny particles that protected Earth.

"So, wait a minute," I say. "Those tiny flecks on Ravager? That was you guys?"

Chaos brushes some lint off his leather jacket. "Yes. And I can assure you having a simple thought when you are scattered across the galaxy is nearly impossible. So, we were glad you finally arrived when you did. You followed our plan to a tee."

"Plan?" I say. "What plan?"

"Our plan to restore our power," Order says. "After your colleague surprised us on Arena World we were dispersed into millions of atoms. Together, we gravitated to the strongest source of cosmic energy we could find— Ravager. We clung to the monster, but being so weak, we did not have the power to reassemble ourselves. To do so, we required a large influx of cosmic energy."

"As you surely noticed," Chaos continues, "without my brother and I to manage the rules of the multiverse, things started to go awry. We knew we had to act quickly, otherwise, everything we had built over an eternity would be undone in the blink of an eye. And while I like disorder, I like it on my terms. So, we merged what little strength we had, and focused our combined power to redirect Ravager away from his diversions, and towards your planet."

"What?" I say. "You mean Ravager coming to Earth was your fault?"

"Yes," Order says. "Because we needed you, Orb Master. With the threat of Ravager looming, we hoped you would realize the need for an Orb of Oblivion. And given your exposure to the duplicate heroes of Earth 2, it would only be natural for you to find your way to their world. If you successfully recovered the second Orb, we knew you had a chance to destroy Ravager, which would release enough cosmic energy for us to restore ourselves to our proper forms."

"So, good job, kid," Chaos says.

"And the Orb?" I ask, bracing myself for the answer. The Orb has been stuck to me like Velcro. Every time I think I'm done with it, it comes back with a vengeance.

"It is gone," Order says. "You have nothing to fear. The Orb of Oblivion, all Orbs of Oblivion, are no more."

I feel a tremendous sense of relief. Finally!

But then I feel angry. I mean, this whole time I was just a puppet in their plan. Earth was just a chip in their game. This whole thing was a scheme to get me to free them. I feel like I'm going to explode.

"Do not be upset with us," Order says, reading my

expression. "Your actions have saved what is left of the multiverse. The 'Blur,' as you call it, has ended. Structure and discipline have returned."

"For the moment," Chaos says with a sneer in his voice.

"Indeed," Order says. "And your world is safe. We thought it a fitting reward for all you have accomplished. And we have also agreed to bestow upon you a gift."

"Reluctantly," Chaos adds.

"Gift? What gift?"

"You will receive it when the appropriate time comes," Order says. "Farewell, Elliott Harkness, you have done well. You are truly a hero. Perhaps the best of your kind."

"Wait!" I say. "What's this g—"

But then, everything vanishes.

EPILOGUE

IT'S HARD TO BELIEVE...

I never thought I'd live to see two genius rats debate over the stability of unstable molecules. But I guess it's better than the alternative.

Since Order and Chaos dumped me back on the Waystation, I've been trying to sort through everything that's happened. I can't believe they played me like the thimble in their galactic game of monopoly. They were using me the whole time, I just didn't know it.

The odds of me beating Ravager must have been a quad-trillion-billion to one. Yet somehow, I got it done. Now that I saved Earth and stopped the Blur, I hope I never see those two cosmic clowns again.

So, sitting in the lab watching both TechnocRat's go back and forth over the technical fitness of the Jump Ship is a welcome distraction. And speaking of distractions, the combined Freedom Force successfully turned back the Skelton invaders, but Keystone City looks like a war zone. Fortunately, no civilians were seriously hurt. I don't think the Skelton can say the same.

According to TechnocRat 2's readings, Earth 2 is still there, which I'm thankful for. After all, Grace 2 just got her dad back and I'd hate for her to lose him again. Plus, they get a chance to rebuild their world without the threat of Elliott 2.

I wonder what he and the Watcher have been up to. I can just see them sitting around a campfire exchanging ghost stories over s'mores. Of course, Dog-Gone 2 probably stole all the marshmallows.

My Dog-Gone is lying by my side. I think he's forgiven me for sneaking off without him to chase after the Herald. When I materialized in the Galley, he pounced on me, licking my face until I nearly drowned in slobber. Then, he demanded ten doggie treats which I was more than happy to pay up.

I catch Grace 2's gaze and she smiles back nervously. I can tell she's anxious about making it home. While all the threats have been neutralized, there's still the risk the Jump Ship won't work. Traveling by wormhole was crazier, but more reliable with Wind Walker doing the driving.

You know, I never did hear back from Wind Walker. The worry on his face as he left was haunting. I hope he's okay, but I've got a funny feeling he's in trouble.

Suddenly, TechnocRat 2 puts down a wrench and declares, "The Jump Ship is officially operational."

Mom 2 turns to my mom and says, "Well, I guess this is it."

They hug and Mom says, "It was a pleasure working with you. We'll have to do this again sometime."

Mom 2 smiles and says, "Yes, but next time why don't you visit us. Hopefully, under less dire circumstances."

"Deal," Mom says.

The rest of the heroes all say their goodbyes.

"You know," Grace says to Grace 2, "I've got to admit, I look pretty good as a brunette."

"And I'm thinking of going blond," Grace 2 says, hugging my sister. "Take care of that brother of yours."

"I'll keep an eye on him," Grace says, putting her hand on my shoulder. "But I think he's proven he can take care of himself."

Grace 2 gives me a big hug. "The next time you're in town, give me advance notice so I can warn everyone else. See you soon?"

"You can count on it," I say. "Thanks for all of your help. And say hi to your dad for me. Let him know he ended up helping me out in a big way."

She smiles. "Will do."

The Freedom Force 2 step into the Jump Ship.

"Captain?" TechnocRat 2 says.

"Ready," Dad says, lifting the Jump Ship into the air.

TechnocRat scrambles up onto Dad's shoulder. "Are you certain you've properly factored the difference in atmospheric pressure of—"

"—being inside a cabin in outer space?" TechnocRat 2 finishes. "The answer for the five hundredth time is 'yes!' Now, my dear Captain, if you will do the honors."

The heroes inside the Jump Ship grab on to the newly installed safety rails—a welcome addition added by my TechnocRat.

Grace 2 waves at me.

"Here comes the heater," Dad says. And then he rears back and launches the Jump Ship.

I cover my eyes. This better work!

Fortunately, the bubble vanishes before it hits the far wall. Hooray for unstable molecules!

"I hope he got those calculations right," TechnocRat mutters. "Why, I've never met such a stubborn rat in all my life!"

We all laugh.

"I say we celebrate with some jelly doughnuts in the Galley," Blue Bolt suggests.

"And peanut butter and banana sandwiches," Shadow Hawk adds.

"I'm in!" Grace says.

The heroes begin to exit, but I can't move! For some reason, I can't lift my feet. It's like I'm stuck to the ground. What's going on?

"Elliott," Dad says. "Aren't you coming?"

Something tells me not to mention what's happening. I have this strange urge to stay here. "No, you guys go ahead," I say. "I'll be there in a minute. Promise."

"Okay," Mom says. "We'll see you in a bit."

After they leave, I'm suddenly able to move again. But instead of heading for the door, I find myself walking to the back of the lab.

To the back corner.

To Makeshift.

Through all of this craziness, he's been stuck here hooked up to all of those wires and monitors, like a permanent monument of my failure.

"I'm so sorry, old buddy," I say. "But if you knew what I did, maybe you'd be proud of me."

I lay my hand on his cold, solid arm when all of a sudden a strange orange energy flows out of my fingertips.

What's going on?

It runs up Makeshift's body and down the other side.

And then, before my eyes, he transforms from a cold, petrified statue, back to warm flesh-and-blood!

I catch him as he collapses to his knees.

"Makeshift? You're alive!"

"What h-happened?" he asks. "Elliott?"

I don't have a ready answer. And then I remember.

The gift!

I'm suddenly overwhelmed with emotion. Tears

stream down my cheeks.

"Hey, buddy," Makeshift says. "Are you okay?"

"Never been better," I say, wiping my eyes.

"Man, I'm starving," he says. "Got anything to eat?"

Good old Makeshift.

"Plenty," I say, helping him to his feet. "Let's head down to the Galley. There are some old friends and a furry food partner who are dying to see you."

As we walk out, I look through the nearest porthole, into the starry expanse of space and whisper, "Thanks."

And a million stars twinkle at once.

DON'T MISS THE EPIC ADVENTURE!

Elliott realizes a time-trotting troublemaker has gone into the past and changed everything! To fix the present, Elliott must follow him back in time. Can Elliott make things right without destroying the future?

Get the Epic Zero Series Collection: Books 4-6 today!

YOU CAN MAKE A BIG DIFFERENCE

Calling all heroes! I need your help to get Epic Zero in front of more readers.

Reviews are extremely helpful in getting attention for my books. I wish I had the marketing muscle of the major publishers, but instead, I have something far more valuable, loyal readers, just like you! Your generosity in providing an honest review will help bring this book to the attention of more readers.

So, if you've enjoyed this book, I would be very grateful if you could spare a minute to leave a review on the book's Amazon page.

Thanks for your support!

R.L. Ullman

META POWERS GLOSSARY

FROM THE META MONITOR:

There are nine known Meta power classifications. These classifications have been established to simplify Meta identification and provide a quick framework to understand a Meta's potential powers and capabilities. **Note:** Metas can possess powers in more than one classification. In addition, Metas can evolve over time in both the powers they express, as well as the effectiveness of their powers.

Due to the wide range of Meta abilities, superpowers have been further segmented into power levels. Power levels differ across Meta power classifications. In general, the following power levels have been established:

- Meta 0: Displays no Meta power.
- Meta 1: Displays limited Meta power.
- Meta 2: Displays considerable Meta power.
- Meta 3: Displays extreme Meta power.

The following is a brief overview of the nine Meta power classifications.

ENERGY MANIPULATION:

Energy Manipulation is the ability to generate, shape, or act as a conduit, for various forms of energy. Energy

Manipulators can control energy by focusing or redirecting energy towards a specific target or shaping/reshaping energy for a specific task. Energy Manipulators are often impervious to the forms of energy they can manipulate.

Examples of the types of energies utilized by Energy Manipulators include, but are not limited to:

- Atomic
- Chemical
- Cosmic
- Electricity
- Gravity
- Heat
- Light
- Magnetic
- Sound
- Space
- Time

Note: the fundamental difference between an Energy Manipulator and a Meta-morph with Energy Manipulation capability is that an Energy Manipulator does not change their physical or molecular state to either generate or transfer energy (see META-MORPH).

FLIGHT:

Flight is the ability to fly, glide, or levitate above the Earth's surface without the use of an external source (e.g. jetpack). Flight can be accomplished through a variety of methods, these include, but are not limited to:

- Reversing the force of gravity
- Riding air currents
- Using planetary magnetic fields
- Wings

Metas exhibiting Flight can range from barely sustaining flight a few feet off the ground to reaching the far limits of outer space.

Often, Metas with Flight ability also display the complementary ability of Super-Speed. However, it can be difficult to decipher if Super-Speed is a Meta power in its own right or is simply a function of combining the Meta's Flight ability with the Earth's natural gravitational force.

MAGIC:

Magic is the ability to display a wide variety of Meta abilities by channeling the powers of a secondary magical or mystical source. Known secondary sources of Magic powers include, but are not limited to:

- Alien lifeforms
- Dark arts
- Demonic forces
- Departed souls
- Mystical spirits

Typically, the forces of Magic are channeled through an enchanted object. Known magical, enchanted objects include:

- Amulets
- Books
- Cloaks
- Gemstones
- Wands
- Weapons

Some Magicians can transport themselves into the mystical realm of their magical source. They may also have the ability to transport others into and out of these realms as well.

Note: the fundamental difference between a Magician and an Energy Manipulator is that a Magician typically channels their powers from a mystical source that likely requires the use of an enchanted object to express these powers (see ENERGY MANIPULATOR).

META MANIPULATION:

Meta Manipulation is the ability to duplicate or negate the Meta powers of others. Meta Manipulation is a rare Meta power and can be extremely dangerous if the Meta Manipulator is capable of manipulating the powers of multiple Metas at one time. Meta Manipulators who can manipulate the powers of several Metas at once have been observed to reach Meta 4 power levels.

Based on the unique powers of the Meta Manipulator, it is hypothesized that other abilities could include altering or controlling the powers of others. Despite their tremendous abilities, Meta Manipulators are often unable to generate powers of their own and are limited to manipulating the powers of others. When not utilizing their abilities, Meta Manipulators may be vulnerable to attack.

Note: It has been observed that a Meta Manipulator requires close physical proximity to a Meta target to fully manipulate their power. When fighting a Meta Manipulator, it is advised to stay at a reasonable distance and to attack from long range. Meta Manipulators have been observed manipulating the powers of others over great distances.

META-MORPH:

Meta-morph is the ability to display a wide variety of Meta abilities by "morphing" all, or part, of one's physical form from one state into another. There are two sub-types of Meta-morphs:

- Physical
- Molecular

Physical morphing occurs when a Meta-morph transforms their physical state to express their powers. Physical Meta-morphs typically maintain their human physiology while exhibiting their powers (with the exception of Shapeshifters). Types of Physical morphing include, but are not limited to:

- Invisibility
- Malleability (elasticity/plasticity)
- Physical by-products (silk, toxins, etc...)
- Shapeshifting
- Size changes (larger or smaller)

Molecular morphing occurs when a Meta-morph transforms their molecular state from a normal physical state to a non-physical state to express their powers. Types of Molecular morphing include, but are not limited to:

- Fire
- Ice
- Rock
- Sand
- Steel
- Water

Note: Because Meta-morphs can display abilities that mimic all other Meta power classifications, it can be difficult to properly identify a Meta-morph upon the first encounter. However, it is critical to carefully observe how their powers manifest, and, if it is through Physical or Molecular morphing, you can be certain you are dealing with a Meta-morph.

PSYCHIC:

Psychic is the ability to use one's mind as a weapon. There are two sub-types of Psychics:

- Telepaths
- Telekinetics

Telepathy is the ability to read and influence the thoughts of others. While Telepaths often do not appear to be physically intimidating, their power to penetrate minds can often result in more devastating damage than a physical assault.

Telekinesis is the ability to manipulate physical objects with one's mind. Telekinetics can often move objects with their mind that are much heavier than they could move physically. Many Telekinetics can also make objects move at very high speeds.

Note: Psychics are known to strike from long distances, and in a fight it is advised to incapacitate them as quickly as possible. Psychics often become physically drained from the extended use of their powers.

SUPER-INTELLIGENCE:

Super-Intelligence is the ability to display levels of intelligence above standard genius intellect. Super-Intelligence can manifest in many forms, including, but not limited to:

- Superior analytical ability
- Superior information synthesizing
- Superior learning capacity
- Superior reasoning skills

Note: Super-Intellects continuously push the envelope in the fields of technology, engineering, and weapons development. Super-Intellects are known to invent new approaches to accomplish previously impossible tasks. When dealing with a Super-Intellect, you should be mentally prepared to face challenges that have never been encountered before. In addition, Super-Intellects can come in all shapes and sizes. The most advanced Super-Intellects have originated from non-human creatures.

SUPER-SPEED:

Super-Speed is the ability to display movement at remarkable physical speeds above standard levels of speed. Metas with Super-Speed often exhibit complementary abilities to movement that include, but are not limited to:

- Enhanced endurance
- Phasing through solid objects
- Super-fast reflexes
- Time travel

Note: Metas with Super-Speed often have an equally super metabolism, burning thousands of calories per minute, and requiring them to eat many extra meals a day to maintain consistent energy levels. It has been observed that Metas exhibiting Super-Speed are quick thinkers, making it difficult to keep up with their thought process.

SUPER-STRENGTH:

Super-Strength is the ability to utilize muscles to display remarkable levels of physical strength above expected levels of strength. Metas with Super-Strength can lift or push objects that are well beyond the capability of an average member of their species. Metas exhibiting Super-Strength can range from lifting objects twice their weight to incalculable levels of strength allowing for the movement of planets.

Metas with Super-Strength often exhibit complementary abilities to strength that include, but are not limited to:

- Earthquake generation through stomping
- Enhanced jumping
- Invulnerability
- Shockwave generation through clapping

Note: Metas with Super-Strength may not always possess this strength evenly. Metas with Super-Strength have been observed to demonstrate powers in only one arm or leg.

META PROFILE CHARACTERISTICS

FROM THE META MONITOR:

In addition to having a strong working knowledge of a Meta's powers and capabilities, it is also imperative to understand the key characteristics that form the core of their character. When facing or teaming up with Metas, understanding their key characteristics will help you gain deeper insight into their mentality and strategic potential.

What follows is a brief explanation of the five key characteristics you should become familiar with. **Note**: the data that appears in each Meta profile has been compiled from live field activity.

COMBAT:
The ability to defeat a foe in hand-to-hand combat.

DURABILITY:
The ability to withstand significant wear, pressure, or damage.

LEADERSHIP:
The ability to lead a team of disparate personalities and powers to victory.

STRATEGY:
The ability to find, and successfully exploit, a foe's weakness.

WILLPOWER:
The ability to persevere, despite seemingly insurmountable odds.

GET MORE EPIC FREE!

Don't miss any of the Epic action!

Get a **FREE** copy of
Epic Zero Extra: Tales of a Superhero Screw Up
only at rlullman.com.

DO YOU HAVE MONSTER PROBLEMS?

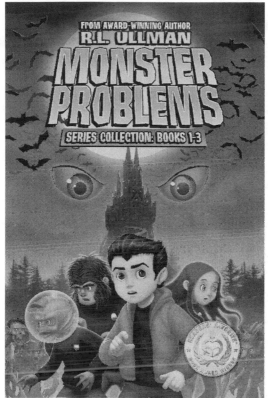

Half boy. Half vampire. All hero…
Readers' Favorite Book Awards Winner

It turns out monsters are real—and only a half-vampire kid hero can save us all! You'll sink your teeth into this fun, award-winning series.

Get the Monster Problems Series Collection Books 1-3 today!

ABOUT THE AUTHOR

R.L. Ullman is the bestselling author of the award-winning EPIC ZERO series and the award-winning MONSTER PROBLEMS series. He creates fun, engaging page-turners that captivate the imaginations of kids and adults alike. His original, relatable characters face adventure and adversity that bring out their inner strengths. He's frequently distracted thinking up new stories, and once got lost in his own neighborhood. You can learn more about what R.L. is up to at rlullman.com, and if you see him wandering around your street please point him in the right direction home.

For news, updates, and free stuff, please sign up for the Epic Newsflash at rlullman.com.

ACKNOWLEDGMENTS

Without the support of these brave heroes, I would have been trampled by supervillains before I could bring this series to print. I would like to thank my wife, Lynn (a.k.a. Mrs. Marvelous); my daughter Olivia (a.k.a. Ms. Positivity); and my son Matthew (a.k.a. Captain Creativity). I would also like to thank all of the readers out there who have connected with Elliott and his amazing family. Stay Epic!